D0979192

CHOKEHOLD

RECEIVED

FEB == 2020

NO LONGER PROPERTY OF
SEATTLE PUBLIC LIBRARY

ALSO BY DAVID MOODY

All Roads End Here

One of Us Will Be Dead by Morning

Them or Us

Dog Blood

Hater

Autumn: Aftermath

Autumn: Disintegration

Autumn: Purification

Autumn: The City

Autumn

CHOKEHOLD

DAVID MOODY

ST. MARTIN'S GRIFFIN NEW YORK

This is a work of fiction. All of the characters, organizations, and events portrayed in this novel are either products of the author's imagination or are used fictitiously.

First published in the United States by St. Martin's Griffin, an imprint of St. Martin's Publishing Group

CHOKEHOLD. Copyright © 2019 by David Moody. All rights reserved. Printed in the United States of America. For information, address St. Martin's Publishing Group, 120 Broadway, New York, NY 10271.

www.stmartins.com

The Library of Congress Cataloging-in-Publication Data is available upon request.

ISBN 978-1-250-22951-9 (trade paperback)
ISBN 978-1-250-10846-3 (ebook)

Our books may be purchased in bulk for promotional, educational, or business use. Please contact your local bookseller or the Macmillan Corporate and Premium Sales Department at 1-800-221-7945, extension 5442, or by email at MacmillanSpecialMarkets@macmillan.com.

First Edition: November 2019

10 9 8 7 6 5 4 3 2 1

CHOKEHOLD

1

Fifteen Miles East of Cambridge

The first few enemy figures appear on the horizon, and the fighters lying in wait for them are desperate to engage, starved of conflict. It's been too long. These fuckers have had it coming. These fuckers will be shown no mercy.

It's taken weeks to get to this point. Every meter of mud has been fought for; every reclaimed centimeter of concrete and tarmac has been won at a cost. They're not going to give it up now, not after all those sacrifices, all those lives lost. There's no going back. It's them or us.

Word of the approaching attackers spreads quickly along the front line, accompanied by a nervous tension that borders on excitement. Some of these men and women dare to dream that the bulk of the bloodshed is behind them now, that this is the last push of the final war. There's an unspoken belief that each new bloom of violence will bring them closer to restoring some semblance of normality to what's left of their lives.

The service station is accessed by a single road that splinters off what used to be one of the major routes into Cambridge. The main road had been midway through a massive, years-long rebuild-and-regeneration program when the war began, and here, alongside the services, lies the abandoned remains of a construction base the size of a small town. The fighters used the roadworks equipment to strengthen and fortify their position while secreting their armored vehicles and heavy weapons among the highway maintenance vans and flatbeds. Diggers were used to carve deep trenches at a distance from the main buildings, and the ballast, soil, and scree they excavated now protects the service station itself—great drifts of the stuff used to block access, strengthen walls, and camouflage metal and glass from view. Inside the building, the familiar plastic façades of long-gone restaurant chains and fast-food outlets remain, reminding people of what they've lost. But the rawness of their pain is eased knowing that what they have here is more than almost everyone else.

It's October, but it doesn't feel like it. Since the bombs dropped, the climate has gone haywire. The sun has been hidden for weeks behind a layer of dirty, stodgy cloud that looks so heavy it feels like it's about to drop from the sky and smother everything. Gray, muck-filled rain hammers down constantly, leaching color from the landscape. This part of the country was notoriously prone to flooding, and the unprecedented rainfall has had a dramatic effect. Much of the land around here is now submerged. There are stagnant, filthy lakes where towns and villages used to be. Rivers run along once-busy roads.

The cold is bone-deep. Day before yesterday, there was sleet. Sleet just after the end of summer! And people are saying things will get worse before they get any better.

Another squad emerges from the service station to bolster the numbers on the front line. Ali Varn climbs down into the trench and works his way along to take up his position. "Gents," he says as he pushes past, and the two fighters he nestles himself between acknowledge him with the most cursory of grunts. Varn wipes his face and spits to clear his throat. They used to worry about the toxicity of the rain, but not anymore. They've all spent days and weeks soaked to the core, and anyway, there are bigger things to worry about. No point worrying about your long-term health when getting through each day is an achievement in itself. A little bit more radiation's not worth writing home about in the grand scheme of things, Varn thinks. *Home.* Now there's a concept he's struggling with. What's home these days? This trench? The service station? The derailed train carriage he sheltered in for days on his way to get here? The car trunk he hid in immediately after the bomb? No one belongs anywhere anymore. It feels like the entire population of the country has become nomadic. Feral.

Varn's glad he has a military background. There are plenty here who don't. He pities the civvies who've come into this without any real experience of fighting, though it's getting harder to tell the difference. None of them look like soldiers anymore. They've all lost weight, skin hanging off their bones like baggy suits. The woman next to him looks sick as a dog. Her hair's patchy. Bomb-style, he calls it. Big, raw-looking bald spots on her scalp. He knows he doesn't look any better himself, but that's the price you pay for picking a fight in the middle of a nuclear winter.

Up ahead, a spotter is flat on his belly with his mud-smeared face peering over the top of an artificial dune that was built here for the purpose of keeping watch. Only the whites of his eyes are visible from up ahead. He turns back and gives a signal to the troops and the bosses watching from the service station. He holds up seven fingers for seven incoming attackers, then gestures with his fist, indicating they appear to be unarmed.

Sometimes Varn thinks the anticipation is worse than the fight. No matter who you are or which side you're on, it's nerve-racking waiting to kill when you've only got a club and a rusty blade for company, but that's the way it goes these days. He knows it'll only be seconds before the battle begins, a minute at most, but that's plenty long enough to think and rethink and overthink what's about to happen. Will I survive, or will this be the day my luck runs out? Are any of the attackers any good? Are they here because they know we're here, or are they just randomers who've stumbled across the outpost by chance? He thinks that's likely the case, because Chappell's done a good job of keeping this place well hidden. Word in the ranks is that Chappell was a pen pusher before all this, that he put the *office* into *officer,* but credit where credit's due, he picked up the rules of engagement pretty quickly.

The massively reduced population numbers mean there's more room to hide out here, more space to disappear, but everyone knows that counts for nothing because it only takes one brief encounter to fuck it all up. Meet one of the opposition coming down the track toward you, and you can bet the little you still own that this will be the day only one of you gets where they were going. Varn knows he has to fight and keep fighting, that there are no second chances. He tries to visualize himself bludgeoning the enemy till there's nothing left of them but blood and broken bones.

This looks like something from the Somme, the troops on the front line armed with rudimentary weapons. There are guns and munitions held in the stores, but Chappell's saving those for the big one, whenever that might be. Until then, they're relying on aggression and physicality to see them through.

The spidery figures continue to creep forward. Jittery. Uneasy. The spotter signals again, letting the troops know that contact is imminent, and Varn knows he has to strike first, kill before he's killed. He blinks with nerves and shuffles from foot to foot, toying with the weight of the metal club in his hands and shifting his grip, imagining caving in someone's skull, battering their face to a pulp and not stopping until they've breathed their last.

There's an expectant, apprehensive hush. Vacuum-like.

Then footsteps.

Wild. Skittering. Frantic.

The first of them tries to pull up fast when he reaches the edge of the unseen trench and realizes he's about to go over, but his speed and the rain and the greasy mud combine, and he skids and slides and drops into the deep dugout. Varn swings wildly and clubs the man hard around the head and face. *They're not human . . . ignore the screams . . . ignore the blood . . .* It makes him feel sick to the stomach, but he does it just the same.

More of them spill into the trench ahead and behind. There's a mass of chaotic movement right along the narrow space now, everyone fighting for their lives. Varn lifts his club to take out the next of them, but in focusing on one, he loses sight of another. Despite just being slashed across the back of her legs with a machete, this woman still has enough energy and hate to thump her stubby blade down between Varn's shoulder blades. They collapse on top of each other, both dead in seconds.

The trench is filled with violence. There are more attackers than the spotter first saw, and this next one's all arms and legs. He drops to the ground with a wet thud, then spins around so fast he loses his footing. Initially appearing weak and spindly, the reality is he's anything but. There's wild fury in his eyes as he faces one of the troops, both of them knowing that whatever happens in the next few seconds, one of them won't survive. The kid—because he is just a kid—digs his fingers into the muddy walls on either side to get a grip, then throws himself forward and is impaled on a fearsome-looking metal spike the soldier holds out in front at the last second. The kid whimpers and looks down at the weapon sticking out of his chest and sounds almost disappointed that the fight's over before it's really begun. He tries to pull it out, but there's so much blood pouring out he can't get a grip. His hands slip and slide as the soldier pushes the spike deeper.

The line between attack and defense is blurred more than ever. At times like this, it's impossible to tell who's a Hater and who's Unchanged.

The pissing black rain makes it even more difficult to see who's who and what's what, but enough remains visible for the soldiers in the trench to know that the sudden burst of fighting is over. For now. Another short-lived, small-scale attack has been successfully repelled, and the service station base has been defended for a while longer.

The soldiers traipse back toward the outpost buildings, swapping places with the next watch. The troops are based in a dilapidated-looking hotel alongside the main building. There's relative comfort inside with individual rooms and real beds and space to think and breathe, because it's important our fighting boys and girls stay strong, isn't it? The civvies, on the other hand, bed down wherever they can find a space in the concourse of the service station next door. A group of them is ordered outside to clear the bodies from the trenches.

There's little talk among the civilians; nothing much to say. Everyone's got a job to do, and that's all there is to it. Dealing with the dead is as straightforward as it sounds. Grab a corpse by the wrists or by its ankles, wait for someone to take the other end, then carry the body over to the pit and chuck it in. A body is a body once they've breathed their last—doesn't matter who or what they were before. We come in the same way, and we all go out the same way in the end.

The pit is an enormous hole in the ground that was originally for the footings of a new bridge spanning the A14. It's almost certainly the largest mass grave ever dug on British soil, and that's a record that'll likely stand, too. Bigger pits may well be dug, but finding enough corpses to fill them will be another matter altogether.

Two of the men—Parker and Dean—go everywhere together. They're a tag team, they tell people. Dean's struggling with the weight of the Hater corpse they're shifting. He loses his balance, then loses his footing, then almost loses his grip altogether. "I think you need a holiday, Dean," Parker says, sarcastic.

"Wouldn't say no. A couple of weeks by the sea would do me a world of good."

They reach the pit where another civilian is directing operations. "Quit talking," he tells them. "Minimal noise out here, remember."

"Jesus, Joseph," Parker sighs, "give us a break."

Joseph Mallon's not impressed. "You need to take this seriously. Give those Hater bastards an inch and they'll destroy everything."

Parker and Dean swing the corpse between them, then hurl it into the pit. Parker shakes his head. "These ones are dead, remember? You need to take it easy, Joe. You'll give yourself a heart attack at this rate."

Joseph ignores him.

Another man delivers the next corpse by himself. He's odd-looking, this one, with thick-lensed glasses and bad comb-over hair. The dead Hater is draped causally over one shoulder. "Wait," Joseph says before he can dispose of the body. "Drop that one."

The other man does as he's told and lowers the corpse to the ground. Joseph quickly pushes him out of the way, unsheathes a blade, then plunges it into the Hater's temple. He then rolls the body into the pit and watches it drop heavily into the mass of tangled limbs below.

"Can't afford to take any chances," he says. "Thought I saw his eyes move."

The other man seems taken aback. "I'm pretty sure he was dead anyway."

"*Pretty sure's* not good enough anymore," Joseph tells him. "Haters think in black and white, and we have to do the same. I got caught out before. Won't let it happen again."

The two men walk back toward base. "What do you mean?" the other man asks.

"I fucked up. I made a mistake and gave some of them a way in. I thought I was doing the right thing, thought I was helping

7

all of us stay alive, but I got it wrong and people died. Thousands of people. I tried to tame them, but they're too far gone. They're anything but human now."

They reach the service station entrance. The glass outer doors are permanently wedged open, no longer automatic, and the heavy revolving door beyond can now only be rotated with brute force and much effort. The space between is like an airlock; a shelter from the wind and rain and noise.

"It's Joseph, isn't it?" he says, catching up.

"That's right."

"I'm Peter, Peter Sutton."

"Good for you."

"What you were saying out there just now . . . I'm sure you weren't completely responsible."

"No, maybe not, but I contributed, and I'm damn sure I'm not going to let it happen again."

"We're all going to have to work bloody hard to get through this in one piece," Peter says, taking off his glasses and wiping them, "but it's not impossible. We're well organized here, and the chiefs have a plan."

Joseph shakes his head. "If you think this place is going to be your salvation, friend, then I'd think again. The only person you can rely on these days is yourself. You'd do well to remember that."

"I will."

"Keep your head down and your mouth shut, Peter, and you might just get through this."

2

Cambridge University

"Face it, boss, they're not coming back."

Johannson looks at Nicholas Pinch, one of her inner circle, and nods. She's been leading this ever-growing Hater pack unopposed since the bombs fell, and he's been fighting with her—*for* her—since before then. She trusts him (as much as anyone trusts anyone these days). He looks the part, with all his tattoos and scars and implants. He ran a tattoo shop before all this. Fucker's even got horns—lumps of metal bolted to implants on either side of his forehead. Gold-capped teeth. More ink than bare flesh. He looks like something out of *Mad Max*. He's adapted to the post-apocalyptic lifestyle better than most. He was halfway there before they pushed the button.

The two of them stand either side of the arched entrance to the cathedral-like college building from which Johannson bases her army. She picked the university intentionally. For the first few weeks after the collapse of the city-camps, it was just about staying alive and wiping up what was left of the Unchanged, but that's changing now. Johansson's graduated from the warehouses and barns where she originally hid with her people to this impos-ing, rock-solid, gothic-looking construction. This place is a status symbol, a dramatic *fuck you* to the old world. The university was viewed as a place of privilege before—an exclusive, high-class haven for the chosen few. The entry criteria are wholly different today—you fight for admission. Today, they burn books and art for fuel and have turned playing fields and gardens into parking lots and stockpiles.

The various college buildings still standing are surrounded by collected ruin: a fleet of beaten-up, but still just about roadworthy vehicles, scavenged supplies, discarded junk. The classic architecture makes the structures look like gems in the center of a landfill site, but what matters most of all is that Johannson has a half-full fuel tanker parked in an enclosed and well-guarded courtyard and a fuck-load of looted food held in cold storage in a crypt-like building across the way. These things alone are enough to keep her people sweet. There are plenty of empty houses near here where folks can still find a crumb of comfort between battles, but many of them prefer to sleep close to the boss. They're afraid of missing anything. Afraid of being left out and dropping down the pecking order. Herd mentality. *Pack mentality.*

"So did we lose anyone of note, Pinchy?"

"Just grunts. Ten a penny."

"And what do you think's happening to them? Are they jumping ship?"

"They'd have to be pretty fucking dumb to turn their backs on you, boss. I reckon they're either dead or you're right and they've found someone they think can outfight you, me, and the rest of us here."

"It's a possibility."

"A remote one. Now I'm not just saying this to keep you happy, boss, but you're the nastiest bitch I've come across in a long time. You get what you want, and you don't take no prisoners."

"I was like that in business before all this."

"I don't doubt you were."

"Same principle, different approach."

"I get that. We follow you because none of us want to be the poor bastards you're hunting down. Speaking as a friend, I don't want to do anything that's going to piss you off."

"Glad to hear it."

"But the fact remains, we've lost more than twenty people in the last ten days."

"There's another explanation, isn't there?"

Pinchy pauses before speaking. "Yeah. Unlikely, though."

"It's Unchanged. I can feel it in my gut. We thought we'd got rid of all of them who'd gone back toward the city. Looks like some of them might have given us the slip."

"So how do you want to play this?"

Johannson's brow furrows. Her face hardens. "First thing, I don't want word of this getting out, not yet. I want this contained until I know what exactly we're dealing with. Cut off any potential information flows. Plant a few false flags."

"Such as?"

"Do I have to do all your thinking for you, Pinchy? Get creative. Start talking to people and spread a few rumors. Paul Scobey."

"What about him?"

"We lost him a couple of days back, didn't we?"

"Yep."

"He was the little Manc kid, wasn't he? The one with the whiny voice."

"That's him."

"Most of the people we have here are faceless and nameless. If I've remembered Scobey, you can bet other people have, too. Make a big deal about the fact he's gone. Tell them he was bad-mouthing me, so you had him killed. Don't give them space to start looking for other explanations. Understand?"

"I get it."

"We need to put a positive spin on this. When I was in sales, I used to go on about turning negatives into positives. Sounds like a cliché, but it happens to be true. You follow?"

"Yes, boss."

"I'm going to talk to the masses, stop any rumors before they start. Get everyone gathered in the big room after dark. If these people think they're not being told the full story, they'll start inventing the bits they don't know. I'm going to tell them what they need to believe."

Even in this poisoned ruin of a world, this gothic, Georgian hall remains an awe-inspiring location. But history means nothing to Johannson; all that matters is today. She doesn't care who any of the faces looking down from the few remaining paintings on the wall belong to. For hundreds of years, scholars and dignitaries and royals have dined here, but she doesn't give a shit. She calls it the big room because it's the biggest room they've got, and this evening, it's packed with fighters. *Her* fighters. There's standing room only. People bunch forward to hear what their leader has to say. Gatherings like this are rare, so there's no questioning the importance of what Johannson might be about to announce. The acoustics in this high-ceilinged, cavernous space are church-like, and whether it's intentional or not, while they're waiting for her to appear, Johannson's flock talk in hushed, subdued tones. Ceremonial candles have been burned down to stubs, and illumination now comes from a couple of braziers full of embers and the occasional lamp.

She's in an anteroom, pacing up and down, readying her pitch. She ordered Pinchy and Marc Myndham, another of her generals, to get everyone assembled for just after eight, and now she's deliberately keeping them waiting. It's a power thing. It reminds them who's in charge.

Johannson was never a fan of the establishment. Places like this used to make her feel uneasy, but now it's home turf. She hated the superiority of the upper classes and how they made her feel inadequate and judged. The fear of being looked down upon because she didn't have the right qualifications or connections. Now Johannson *is* the fear, and it feels good. She's fought her way up from nothing.

Johannson's a tough bitch who's always been able to hide her emotions in even the most pressured of situations, but even she can't help feeling some nervousness when she walks out and looks down over a sea of faces. There are cheers when she appears, followed by a reverent hush the moment she signals for quiet. All talk stops. The only noises now are the crackle of bonfires and the drumming of the incessant black rain on the windows. There's got to be at least three hundred people crammed in here, maybe more.

"How many of you have been with me from the start?" she asks, and the room fills with noise. "Remember what it was like back then? We were a pack, remember? Like a pack of bloody animals. We found whatever shelter we could, but in the first days after the bomb, half the battle was just staying alive."

She pauses for a moment, just long enough to let them remember how hard those times were.

"Now look at us. Hundreds strong. Organized. *Safe*. Times back, we'd have turned our noses up at being in a situation like this, but after the war and the bombs and the radiation, this is better than we could have hoped.

"It's all about perspective. Remember the people who tried to take from us? The Unchanged first of all, then people like us who wanted what we had. We beat them all, and we showed them who's in charge, didn't we?"

More noise. Sections of the crowd are going wild, unnaturally loud. It's a self-defense mechanism; if Johannson or one of her generals doesn't think you're as keen and grateful to be here as you should be, there's every chance you'll be thrown out on your ass. Or worse.

Johannson is having to shout to make herself heard now, her bellowing voice echoing off the walls. "Everything changed when we found this place. It's more than just a base of operations for us now; it's a home. A fortress. It's strong, defendable, impenetrable. We've built something truly remarkable here out of the ashes of the shitty old world we've left behind, and now it's time for us to take the next step. That's why I've gathered you all here tonight.

"Starting tomorrow, we're going to be spreading our wings. We've not seen hide nor hair of any Unchanged for weeks, but we're going to keep hunting until we know for sure that there's none of them left alive."

At the mention of the Unchanged, the crowd has become increasingly vociferous. People shout abuse. Others spit and curse, offended by the thought of the foul enemy they fought so long and so hard to destroy. Good. That's exactly the kind of response Johannson hoped to provoke.

"Even when the Unchanged have all been dealt with, our job won't be done. We need to defend what's ours and keep growing our numbers. We're not going to allow anyone to take what we've worked so hard to build here. I'm not going to allow it to happen, and neither are you. We're going on the offensive to prevent it."

This vast crowd's clearly in a fighting mood, though there's barely any other kind of mood left these days. In a world that's been stripped of warmth and emotion and purpose, killing is perhaps the only positive action that remains. And that's the message Johannson's now doing her best to get across.

"It doesn't matter who you were or what you did or what you had; the Hate has stripped all that back to nothing. All that matters now is fighting hard and staying alive.

"First light tomorrow, I'm sending you out into the wilds.

We're going to take the initiative and search mile by mile from this central point. Find who you can. Recruit those who'll listen, get rid of those who won't. Understand?"

She pauses for the particularly raucous response. There's nothing like inciting violence to fire this crowd up.

"Get yourselves organized into groups tonight and go see Pinchy, Ullah, or Myndham. They'll give you an area to cover. We take no prisoners, got it? It's our way, or no way."

The room is filled with more noise than ever.

Johannson's words are designed to provoke maximum response, and in the bulk of the crowd, they do just that. Elsewhere on the fringes, though, the reactions are more muted. Most people make sure they're deep in the scrum so their enthusiasm for chaos can be noted, but others do the opposite. Some of the Haters—the weaker, the less aggressive—cling to the shadows and do what they can to disappear. They'll do what they have to do to prove they're up for the fight if challenged, but all many of them want is to be left alone. Some are sick and unable to survive without the protection of the pack. Others just can't match the kind of fury and aggression that gets you noticed by Johannson's best.

Some of the non-fighters edge farther back into the darkness until they're no longer there. Some are elderly; others are sick. Shivering with cold, a stick man leans against an oak-paneled wall and pulls his legs up. The burns on his back from the bomb still sting, and his chest rattles like it's filled with grit. He sounds empty inside. That thought almost elicits a smirk, because that's exactly what he has become. He's a hollow man. All he has left is the breath in his lungs. Everything else—his family, his home, his health, his daughter—is long gone.

He does what he can not to be noticed, but some of the nastier bastards are already looking for volunteers to join their hunting groups, and Karl Bryce is heading his way. Bryce sweeps the floor with a bright flashlight, looking for stragglers. He grabs the hollow man's wrist and hauls him to his feet like he's picking up an empty bag.

"You'll do," Bryce says. "You're coming with me."

"I won't be any use. My leg's busted. I'll just slow you down."

"Not interested."

"But I'm sick."

"We're all sick. Did you not hear boss lady?"

"Yeah, but I'll just slow you down."

Bryce tightens his grip, making the other man wince. "I'm not asking, I'm telling. Everyone has their uses. I'll tie you to a frigging post and use you as bait if I have to. What's your name, you useless piece of shit?"

"McCoyne. Danny McCoyne."

3

Underground

The skies have been filled with dense, oily clouds ever since the bombs. A double strike on what was left of London opened the floodgates. After that, whoever had their finger on the button got trigger-happy: Manchester, Leeds, Birmingham, Edinburgh, and Glasgow . . . all reduced to smoldering mounds of toxic ash. None of the people who survived the blasts will ever know who fired the missiles, but that's not important now. The end result has affected everyone the same, Hater and Unchanged alike. Each individual strike generated massive amounts of damage and pollution, enough to choke the life out of vast swaths of the country. The cumulative effect of all the nukes has been devastating.

This place was on the outermost fringe of the blast wave. North of here, most buildings, trees, lampposts, and electricity pylons were flattened. A housing estate on a hillside is now nothing but rubble. A once-forested incline is carpeted with fallen trees, the base of the valley piled high with detritus. Nothing is as it was. The colors of autumn should have been well established now, but not this year. The lush greens of spring and summer were burned away, and where there should now be traces of russet reds and golden browns, there's nothing but dirty black and muted grays. Color has been drained from everything, leaving behind a monochrome hell. It's hard to tell where the land ends and the cloud cover begins. What's left of the natural world feels like it's giving up.

Out here, it doesn't even sound right anymore.

There are no animals, no birds, barely any people, and yet the constant wind and rain mean it's never silent. Shells of buildings groan, shudder, and sigh with the effort of staying upright. Anything that hasn't already fallen is at risk of crashing down.

The monsoon-like rain weakens the roots of trees and the foundations of buildings. On the exposed high ground, the endless downpours have eroded the topsoil, which now slips away like sloughing skin. Countless trickles of polluted water combine to become torrents that, in turn, become a single powerful deluge of muck. An avalanche of waste-filled slurry races downhill, obliterating everything in its path. It keeps spilling ever forward, a noxious and unstoppable tsunami that seems almost to be racing with itself, trying to see how far it can get and how much it can destroy. A group of seven fighters camped out inside a ruined school are overcome with barely any warning. Though they try to get away, there's no point running because the flood is on them in seconds. There's barely the blink of an eye between the first distant rumbling noises and the total, all-consuming carnage that follows. The quickest of the group, a girl in her midtwenties, glances back over her shoulder as she sprints across the playground for cover, but no matter how fast she runs, she'll never beat the horror that's coming after her. She sees several of the others swept off their feet and submerged, and she knows she's next. She'll run out of energy long before the wave does, that much is certain, but the thought of drowning—lungs filling with the filthy, soup-like mire—is a terrifying enough prospect to keep her moving. She's halfway along a rubble-strewn road when the wave crashes over her. It sweeps her up and hurls her against the wall of a partially collapsed building with impossible force: dead before she can drown.

For a moment, it looks like the remains of the building might act as a dam and stem the flow, but the corrupted tide shows no sign of abating. The building is an empty shell, three sides intact. The walls hold firm for a second or two longer, but as the water pressure builds, it begins to give. And once the first few cracks appear, it's barely any time at all before the whole thing comes crashing down, allowing an unprecedented amount of sludge and debris to spill out across the land beyond. It rages through what's left of an industrial estate, bringing numerous other already weakened buildings tumbling down as if they were made of cardboard and paper, not concrete and steel.

For a time, the world is filled with noise. It sounds like the end of everything, like the last death throes of a planet in terminal decline. But eventually it passes.

The racing wave disappears, petering out to nothing many miles after it began, leaving behind it an immense gray lake that seems to stretch out forever in every conceivable direction. The contrast is stark. Thirty seconds ago, mayhem. Now, a bizarre sense of calm.

Some of the group feel it before they hear it. Conversation and activity are sparse down here at the best of times, and many people initially dismiss the low rumbles and distant groans as figments of their already overstretched imaginations. Aftershocks? More bombs? Another attack? They've been down here too long. You can see and hear all kinds of things that aren't there in this never-ending darkness. You can hear people talking when there's no one around, convince yourself you've seen faces you know are long gone.

Cheryl Bashford's lying on her back on the camp bed where she's spent most of her time since they've been sealed in this tomb-like place. She sleeps in the far corner of this overfull room, as far from the entrance to the bunker as she can get. Suddenly uneasy, she holds her breath to try to cancel out her own noise, convinced she can hear something. She has no idea what it could be. It's different from the bombs (she still hears that noise in her sleep—*feels* it, even), but she knows in her gut that whatever she's now hearing is also bad. Very bad.

She sits up quickly and swings her feet around, disturbing the kid camped out next to her. She switches on her flashlight and shines it around, illuminating his face. His eyes are as wide as hers. "You hear that?" she asks him.

"Yeah. What is it?"

More lights and more movement. Other people are starting to get scared. Fear's never far off the radar down here, but this is different, and panic spreads like a bushfire through dry scrub. "Get Darren," Cheryl says, but Darren's already on his way. He's made it as far as the foot of Cheryl's bed when the volume of the noise overhead becomes so loud it's all he can hear. It's like a train racing through a tunnel. He reaches out for the wall to steady himself and feels it shaking. It's at times like this he wishes he was just one of the masses, not the leader of the group. Suddenly, there are nervous questions being fired at him from all directions, the volume inside the bunker competing with the noise elsewhere. "Shut up!" Darren yells, and they all immediately do as they're told.

The shelter's shaking now, the noise and vibrations like the approaching footsteps and roar of some immense monster. Equipment and belongings clatter down from shelves, and dust spills from cracks in the ceiling. The chaos reaches a tumult, then it stops.

As quickly as it began, it's over.

But Jesus Christ, this sudden silence is even more terrifying. Darren looks for Jason, keen to find someone else whose opinion he trusts.

"More bombs?" Jason asks, voice low.

"That was no bomb. It went on too long. There's nothing left up there to destroy."

"What, then?"

He pulls Jason close and whispers, "Sounded like a landslide."

"Fuck. We could be trapped."

"We *are* trapped, remember? We can't go out there anyway."

"That it, d'you think?" Cheryl asks.

Another man calls Darren over, and he threads his way through more bodies to get to where Wayne Heath is standing. Wayne shines his flashlight and shows Darren dirty water running down the back wall.

"Shit," Darren says. "Where's it getting in?"

Wayne points out an area to the top left that is dark with damp. There's water dripping through the mortar between concrete blocks as if the wall itself is perspiring, sweating under the pressure. He illuminates another wet patch. And another. Then another. The fifth leak is a trickle. The sixth is oozing mud being forced through a crack, like toothpaste from a tube. "We can block it up, right?" Wayne says, half telling, half asking.

"Yeah, 'course we can," Darren quickly replies, and he starts looking around for inspiration. He gestures for people to shift their beds and belongings and for others to help. It's barely organized chaos. This part of the shelter is already a mass of people and possessions, and it's hard making progress. Those trying to get nearer are held up by others trying to get out of the way.

A woman wearing a headlamp is trying to plug up the worst leak with an old T-shirt.

"Any good?" Darren asks.

"Seems to be working," she tells him, though the silt-filled water's still coming, trickling through her fingers and down her arms.

"I don't think it's going to hold," a voice says from deeper in the shelter.

No one reacts. He clears his throat and speaks again.

"The noise that filled this place just now . . . that water must be under a hell of a lot of pressure to be forced through the brickwork like that."

"We're fine," Darren tells him. "It's under control."

"You might want to start thinking about getting essential supplies away from this part of the building. Move yourselves up toward the entrance. There are no leaks up there yet. We need to consider the possibility that we might have to evacuate and—"

Darren snaps. He turns and marches over to Matthew Dunne, then backs him up against a recently emptied storage rack. "You're going to freak people out with that kind of talk. Keep it to yourself, and let me get on with making the shelter safe."

Matt doesn't react. Doesn't fight. Doesn't have the energy.

"I'm just trying to help."

"Yeah, well, you're not. You're doing the exact opposite. Scaring the shit out of people . . . how's that supposed to be helping?"

Matt lowers his voice. "I get that, but telling people everything's gonna be all right when it isn't won't help anyone, either. By that logic, if you'd shut your eyes and put your fingers in your ears when they dropped the bomb, you'd have been okay."

Jason pulls Darren away from him. "It's not worth it, Darren," he says. "Come on, mate, we need your help."

Darren goes back to help those working on the leaks. They've moved empty racks across the width of the area where the water's getting through and are now building a protective wall with whatever they can lay their hands on. Darren coordinates the work, piling up sacks of garbage and nonessentials: redundant electrical equipment and the like. A human chain has been formed to move the improvised building blocks from one end of the bunker to the other.

"Will this work?" Jason asks, watching by yellow flashlight.

"It has to," Darren tells him.

The bunker is formed of two distinct spaces with a single connecting door. Despite the leaks, the group still congregates in the larger second room, putting as much distance as possible between themselves and what's left of the outside world. The smaller room tends only to have one regular occupant. He's back there again now, sitting cocooned in a sleeping bag at the bottom of the steps leading out, back against the wall with a pile of surreptitiously scavenged supplies close to hand. His heart sinks when the door opens and someone invades his space. He's become adept at seeing without using his eyes. He listens more than looks and uses his knowledge of human nature to fill in the blanks. He knows who this is before she sits down. But then again, it doesn't take a genius. She's just about the only one who still gives him the time of day.

"It's me, Kara," she says, whispering though there's no need.

"I know."

"You okay?"

"Fine and dandy."

"Did Darren hurt you?"

"Nope."

"Good. Just wanted to see how you're doing."

Much as he'd like to be alone, Matt knows he can be himself with Kara. She's the only person he's close to down here. The only one who shares his frustration with the way Darren and Jason run things.

"He's taking a hell of a risk. I reckon it's fifty-fifty as to whether that wall holds."

"So what are we going to do?"

"You'll need to talk to the boss about that."

"Come on, Matt . . ."

"No, seriously, every time I try to help, he shuts me down. He doesn't want to know. None of them do."

"They don't trust you."

"We've been buried down here together for months."

"In group, out group, remember? You're still a stranger. He sees you as a threat. None of us had clapped eyes on you until you turned up with the truck and shipped us out."

"Yeah, you'd have thought I'd get a little gratitude for saving your necks and risking mine."

"You went back out again, though, didn't you?"

"I had to. I needed to."

"Look, you don't need to persuade me; I get it. You needed to try to get back to Jen. Thing is, though, all this lot remember is you dumping them, then heading back out and leaving them vulnerable when the bomb dropped and the shit really hit the fan."

Matt has nothing to say. They've had this conversation too many times before. He wishes he could redirect it into safer waters, but he can't; it's too painful to talk about the past, too confined and unpredictable in here to try to make sense of the present, and there's no point talking about the future because it's doubtful any of them have one.

Kara's not going anywhere, though.

"It's not going to hold, is it? And for the record, I already tried talking to Darren about it."

"And what did he say?"

"He said everything'll be fine."

"There you go, then. Panic over. If the boss tells you you're safe, you're safe."

"He's full of shit."

"You don't say."

"That's why I came to talk to you. It's why I always talk to you. What do you think's going to happen?"

Matt wishes he could give her a little hope to cling to, but he can't, and he knows she'd see straight through any bullshit. "You need to take the emotion out of the situation and look at the facts, focus on the physics. Even if the water that's getting in is slowed up, there's no reason to think it won't keep coming. It might be a slow flood, but it'll be a flood all the same. So we can wait patiently to drown or be poisoned by whatever shit's going to be brought in with that stuff, or we can cut our losses and leave here now and take our chances with whatever's left aboveground. The end result will probably be the same. So yeah, it's looking pretty grim whichever way you look at it."

She pauses. Gets up. "Thank you, Matt. Just wanted to hear you say it. You're the only one who's ever honest with me."

4

Matt wakes up with a start when the connecting door flies open. He thinks, *This is it, this is the big one,* but it's immediately clear that it isn't. Not yet. He pulls his feet up to his chest and gathers his belongings close as this anteroom rapidly begins to fill up. Lamps are used to illuminate the space, and another chain of people start shifting supplies, stacking them up against the wall opposite. "Just a precaution," Jason tells Matt when he catches his eye.

"You've not stopped the leaks yet, then?"

"We've got it under control."

"Good," Matt says, and he half shuts his eyes and feigns sleep.

On the whole, from what Matt can currently see, the group appears to be reasonably calm. There's plenty of emotion in their muted voices, and some people are cooperating and others aren't, and some are sitting watching while others get overly involved . . . and it's no different from usual. But Matt's uneasy. The stale air down here has a different taste to it since the leaks were discovered. The ventilation in this place is rudimentary—it was never designed to be used for this purpose—so fresh air is a distant memory, but there's a muddy dampness to each lungful that wasn't there before. And he can feel a background pressure building, too, like before a storm. Maybe that's it. Who knows what's going on with the atmospherics up there? He remembers watching Cold War–era movies about nuclear attacks when he was a kid. Most of the focus was on the blast and the radiation, but the medium- to long-term prospects they portrayed were equally terrifying. All that toxic crap being thrown up into the air, blocking out the sun and causing the temperature to plummet . . . Matt can't even begin to imagine what the outside world will be like if they ever leave here. When he thinks about those movies he watched, which traumatized him at the time, they seem quaint and rose-tinted.

There's no privacy down here in the bunker. Toilets are improvised and shared. Discretion and confidentiality are long-lost luxuries. Matt's used to catching sleep when and where he can, and though he watches the essential supplies being stockpiled for a while longer, it's not long before he drifts off again.

When he next wakes up, the anteroom is well lit and is rapidly filling with people. He's on his feet in seconds, and he looks down at his boots, expecting to see water rising. He's relieved they're still dry.

Even though this part of the bunker is now overfull, a quick count of heads reveals this is only part of the group. He looks for Darren or Jason, the self-appointed chiefs, but the only face he sees worth talking to is Kara. She's right alongside him. "Trouble?" he asks.

"A precaution," she whispers. "More leaks. They're moving the kids up here, trying to get people into the dry areas."

"They do realize there won't be any dry areas soon?"

"It might not get that bad."

He just looks at her.

"Where's the big man?"

"What, Darren? I don't know. Somewhere in there."

Matt wishes he could go back to sleep and keep his mouth shut, but this time he can't. He makes sure his stuff is safe at the top of the steps up to the exit, then pushes his way through the tightly packed bodies. Kara's hanging on to his jacket. "What?"

"I'm coming with you."

"Stay here. There's no point."

"What are you going to say to him?"

"Nothing."

There's a lot of work going on at the far end of the bunker; many men and women, all pulling in the same direction. All the spare lamps are lit, and Matt can already see that an area around a third of the total bunker length has been cordoned off. The remaining two-thirds are chaotic, with people, beds, metal racking, and other less easily identifiable shapes all competing for the rapidly reducing floor space. Matt steps over and around things and bodies to get to the business end of the room.

He seems to be moving in the opposite direction of everyone else. When he reaches the cordon, he uses his flashlight to scan the wall up ahead. More water. No longer trickling. Hissing in places. More worryingly, it's also dripping through the ceiling.

Matt's seen enough.

He retraces his steps and walks straight into Darren coming the other way. Darren goes to speak, but Matt gets in first. He keeps his voice low. No need to cause panic. Yet. "We can't stay here, Darren. You need to evacuate."

"Don't be so fucking stupid. We can't leave, you know that."

"Lesser of two evils. You might die outside; you definitely *will* die in here. I'm taking my chances."

"You do that. You must be crazy."

"Quite the opposite."

This is a pointless conversation Matt can't afford to prolong. He goes to walk away, but Darren grabs his arm and pulls him back. "If you go out there, you need to understand two things. One, you go alone. Two, there's no way you're coming back in when you realize you've fucked up. Got it?"

Matt doesn't answer. He pulls his arm away and keeps walking. He forces his way back out into the anteroom and picks up his belongings from the top of the steps.

"Don't be fucking stupid!" he hears Darren shouting at him. "It's suicide!"

There are a thousand things he could say in reply, but instead he says nothing. He knows there must be some safe space out there, because the bottom of the door to the outside world is dry, and right now anything is better than waiting in here for the inevitable.

"Matt, wait!"

He looks around for her, but Kara's separated from him by everyone else, and now Jason and a couple of others are moving closer, intent on helping him make his decision quickly and with the minimum of disruption.

"It's okay!" he shouts back to her, and he genuinely believes it will be. It *has* to be.

The key has been left in the padlock in case of emergencies. As Matt turns it, he becomes aware of everyone else moving back, terrified what he might let in when the door that has kept them secure since the day the world ended is finally opened. The click of the padlock is at once both liberating and terrifying, but Matt knows he has no choice. He opens it and takes a step out into the unknown.

No building. The walls and roof are gone. The inside is outside now.

Fading daylight.

Black skies overhead; clouds so low he could touch them.

The slam and lock of the door behind him are the loudest noises he's ever heard. Louder even than the bomb.

5

The rain never stops. Not even for a second.

It's two days later when the wall in the corner and a section of the ceiling at the far end of the bunker finally give way. Though the water has kept coming all this time, until now its flow has largely been stemmed, and as each hour has passed, so the mole-like refugees have become accustomed to their further degraded confines. They've spent months making do in the darkness, resigned to the fact that what they've got is the best they'll get, and the loss of almost half their remaining space has been met with a collective shrug of inevitability. It's either misplaced optimism or the fact they've lost so much already that's resulted in them continuing as they were until now, business as usual, but there's utter pandemonium when part of the roof caves in, sheer terror, because they know that no amount of shifting, bracing, and packing is going to preserve the integrity of their precious shelter now.

The main room begins to fill, gallons of turgid water pouring in with remarkable speed. The makeshift dams the group spent hours constructing are swept aside in seconds. The surge of water has an almost awe-inspiring power behind it, picking up bulky metal furniture that took many people to maneuver and casting it aside as if it were made from twigs.

The entire floor of the bunker is awash. The only thing moving faster than the water is the wave of panicked people now surging toward the anteroom. Darren pauses to try to help a man who's been pinned against a wall by a mass of equipment that's been picked up by the flood. He's yelling in pain, one of his legs broken, and even though he and Darren are just meters apart, the roar of the deluge completely drowns out his noise. Darren knows there's nothing he can do, and he hates himself for it. In the few seconds he's delayed, the water level has risen to above his knees. If he doesn't leave now, they'll both die. He keeps moving, glad the rush of water is loud enough to drown out the terrified screams.

He gets through into the anteroom, then turns back to look for the others, only about half of them having escaped the main room so far. He can see many people still weaving through the flooded chaos, illuminated by their own flashlights and lamps. But then there's an almighty cracking noise, and another massive section of ceiling caves in. Some are crushed by falling masonry, others swept away by an unprecedented amount of water that drops like a vertical tidal wave. From knee-deep to chest-deep in a heartbeat. The force of the sudden inundation catches the door between the two rooms and slams it shut in Darren's face. There's no way they'll be able to open it again from the other side, but the way the water's now hissing through the gaps between the door and the frame leaves no one in any doubt that it's not going to hold for long. In the anteroom itself, the water level is already such that many of the supplies they'd moved into this space for safety are floating at waist height. The few kids who've made it out, those who aren't already in other people's arms, are up to their chins.

"Get us out of here!" someone pleads.

Kara's at the front of the line, and though she's doing every-thing she can, the pressure of the floodwaters on this side means she can't get the outer door open. Jason pushes his way through along with another man who's found a hand ax from some-where. He starts chopping at the latch, the lock, the hinges, the frame . . . anything that might help them get out. Someone else has a crowbar, and they start working on the opposite side.

Between them all, they work hard and fast, exerting more ef-fort in the space of a couple of minutes than anyone's needed to in the entire time they've been incarcerated. The man with the ax is breathless, arms like lead, but he keeps on chopping. He's desper-ate to get out but is petrified at the thought of what might be out there. The fear of the unknown is almost enough to make him stop, but the fear of drowning keeps him moving.

Under pressure from the crowbar, the top hinge gives way. At the other end of the water- and body-filled room, Darren is be-ing pushed back by the weight of the crowds. Jesus, he can feel the door bulging behind him under the pressure of the flood, water continuing to hiss at high pressure through the narrow gaps around the parts of the frame that are above the fill. He thinks about the others who didn't get out and convinces himself they're still trying to escape—banging against the door he's praying will hold firm. His mind is filled with nightmare images of it finally giving way and this rapidly disappearing space filling to the ceil-ing with polluted water in a heartbeat.

The outer door latch is submerged now. The guy with the crowbar exerts as much pressure on the padlock as he can until it finally gives, but the water level is preventing them from getting out, keeping the door shut. Jason now has the ax and is work-ing frantically to chip away the top corner of the hardwood tim-ber door, trying to do enough damage. It begins to splinter. A few more ax blows and it starts to split. Now there are grabbing hands everywhere, ripping, yanking, and pulling at the damaged wood.

Gray daylight starts trickling in from outside.

They work on the door with increased speed until there's a big enough gap up top. Jason's immediately given a leg up so he can scramble through. No one gives any thought as to what he's scrambling through into, because all that any of them care about now is escaping the toxic water.

Children next, then the remaining adults. Next one through. And the next and the next. And a few sodden bags and boxes, for what it's worth. Then more people, and now those who are left are competing with each other to be the next in line. Darren's bringing up the rear, barking out orders. He convinces himself he's trying to help everyone else and get them up, but the reality is he doesn't want to be the one who doesn't make it. The water's up to his chin now, so cold he's numb. He knows you're supposed to stay calm in cold water and not thrash around, but he thinks if he stays calm now, he'll die in here. The flood is pouring over the top of the broken door. He reaches for the top edge to haul himself up and over but loses his grip and is sucked below the surface. He's kicking and fighting, swallowing more and more of the foul-tasting mire. His eyes are open, but he sees nothing but black, and he's only vaguely aware when a couple of hands manage to grab hold of his flailing limbs and pull him out.

Darren's dumped on the ground in a layer of mud several inches thick. He bucks and flaps like a fish on dry land, eyes screwed shut in the brightness after months of almost complete dark. When he finally opens them, he sees there's nothing left of the printing house and the industrial estate. Thirty-two soaked survivors stand bunched up together on a vast, featureless plateau of gray-brown mud, just a few piles of salvaged gear between them. The occasional heaps and mounds in the oily muck are the only indications there was ever anything here. Otherwise, there's nothing. Absolutely nothing.

Right now, the state of the dead world into which they've emerged is more frightening than the prospect of imminent enemy attack. Jason realizes the danger and scans their surroundings, looking for signs of *them*. He's sure they must be here. Fuckers are everywhere, so how could they not be? His eyes are stinging through a combination of dirt and the sudden brightness, running with bitter tears. He freezes when he hears someone whistle from way over to their left. He spins around and slips, almost losing his footing, ready for the inevitable Hater attack. He struggles to focus. Wait . . . that's no Hater.

Kara pushes past him, sliding in the mire, shivering with cold. "It's Matt," she says.

They might have tried to keep their distance from him in the bunker, but right now there's not a single man or woman who's not delighted to see Matthew Dunne standing a hundred or so meters away, beckoning them over.

At first, it looks like he's found a building to shelter in, but as Kara approaches, she realizes it's what's left of the truck he'd used to drive them to the printing house all those weeks ago. It's been picked up and thrown around like everything else and has landed at an awkward angle in a furrow, wheels sticking up. Were it not for the open roller shutter, they'd probably have never seen it. It's completely covered in the same ash- and mud-covered gloop as everything else.

There's a piercing wind whipping across this alien-looking tundra, colder than the water that drenched them. They trudge over to where Matt's waiting, and he helps them into the back of the truck. "How did you know we were out?" Kara asks, teeth chattering. He reaches down and pulls her inside.

"Jesus, you were making enough noise to wake the dead."

Thirty-three of them in total. They wonder if they're all that's left of the human race.

It's dark again now, and colder than ever, but they've wedged the roller door at the back of the truck shut, and inside it's relatively dry. They've some salvaged supplies, and they know this is as good as it's going to get tonight. Tracy Barnish, an ex-GP, is checking people over by flashlight, assessing cuts and bruises as best she can and trying to prevent them dying of hypothermia.

Matt managed to piece together what happened here. He explained that the landslide they'd heard a couple of days back must have brought down the remnants of the already partially collapsed distribution center next door to the printing house and that its exposed foundations had filled with water. The constant rain had swollen the artificial lake until it broke its banks and flooded the remains of the building adjacent. He'd seen it coming, he tells them.

"And you didn't think to warn us?" someone yells back at him from the darkness.

"Would you have let me back in if I'd tried? Would you have even opened the door?"

"Then why did you bother staying? Why not just disappear?"

"I told Darren I thought you'd all end up out here sooner or later."

"And you thought you'd wait here to come to the rescue?" Jason says, sarcastic.

"Yes. Look, if it weren't for me, you'd probably still be walking through the mud, looking for somewhere to hide."

"So what now?" Kara asks. "We've got hardly any food and no way of cooking it or even getting the tins open. We're soaked, but there's no water fit to drink, and we've got nothing to burn and no way of lighting a fire."

"We'll survive," Darren says, loud enough for everyone to hear. "There's got to be somewhere. We'll start looking in the morning."

Hollow words fall on deaf ears.

"You're not even convincing yourself, mate," Kara says, but Darren ignores her and continues.

"There can't have been many people who've survived like we have. Who else is going to be in such good shape?"

"Good shape?" Kara says. "Get a grip, Darren. We're freezing cold and starving. I don't reckon I'm ever going to dry out." There's plenty more she could say, but she stops herself because she knows it won't help anyone, and in the gaps where her words would be, all they can hear instead is more driving rain. There's a growl of thunder in the distance, loud enough to make the sides of the upturned truck rattle and shake. Ominous. Seems to go on forever.

Darren changes tack. "Remember all the things we talked about while we were waiting to leave the city and all the stuff we've talked about since? We don't have any choice; we *have* to keep going. We have to survive because we might be all that's left now. We're the future of the human race."

It takes all his self-control, but Matt manages to keep his mouth shut. He thinks Darren's full of shit, but right now his vague words and empty promises are all any of them have left to cling to.

6

The Hunt

Johannson's fighters have been on the road for several days now. In twos and threes, others in packs, some alone, some on foot, others behind the wheel, they've spread out from Cambridge across the flooded countryside in a semi-coordinated wave, armed with the arrogance that comes from knowing they're completely fucking untouchable. Even the weakest of them believe they'll be stronger and better equipped than anyone else they find alive out here.

A supermarket delivery van has been repurposed as a makeshift troop transporter. Jordan Keller is leading this particularly shabby group, and this truck is his lucky ride. There's something about the way it looks that disarms people, he's discovered. The colorful supermarket livery and the once-familiar logos and slogans are distracting. Folks see the innocuous-looking vehicle coming toward them and feel a fuzzy nostalgia, not the sheer terror they should. Back in the early days, Keller used to play dumb. He'd just park and sit in the back, wait for no-good Unchanged stragglers to turn up and start sniffing around for scraps of food. They'd find the truck and open it up, and the last thing they'd expect was for him to come flying out at them with his blades and his clubs. The deception could only have been any more perfect if Keller had been driving an ice cream van.

He has another six fighters with him today. There's a trio—two women and a man who had a vague association before the war and who've, more through chance than design, stuck together so far. They're good. They work hard and fight hard, and Keller couldn't ask for more right now. There's also an impossibly tall Asian guy, and two more blokes who are decent enough, run-of-the-mill fighters and who, most importantly, do what he tells them.

The group is working its way on foot along a desolate residential street at one end of a ghost village when another vehicle arrives, making a hell of a noise. It's the kind of car that used to be a boy racer's dream: a bright red Subaru Impreza. The driver parks nose to nose with the supermarket truck and gets out.

"Looking for something, Bryce?" Keller asks.

"Ullah sent me this way."

"Then you can go back and tell Ullah we've got this place covered."

"Tell him yourself."

Another man gets out of the Subaru and starts mooching through a pile of debris at the side of the road. "Can't you just get on and work together?" he asks, sounding tired and hopelessly naïve. Annoyed, Keller goes for him, but Bryce gets there first. He shoves McCoyne backward into the waste he was just inspecting.

"You should learn to keep your damn mouth shut."

McCoyne stands up and brushes himself down. He takes a couple of steps back to make sure he's out of range, then clears his throat. "There's no one here. This place isn't worth arguing about."

"And how would you know?" Keller demands.

He shrugs. "I can just tell."

"Who is this prick?" Keller asks Bryce.

"He's nobody. Just here to make up the numbers."

McCoyne ignores them both and keeps talking. "You're not going to find anyone around here. We've hardly seen any Unchanged in weeks. And when we do find them, they're never in places like this, are they? It's places like this where they know we'll be looking."

Bryce and Keller both just stare at him. He has a point.

"So why are we here?" McCoyne asks. Now he's the one asking the questions.

"Because this is where Johannson told us to be," Keller immediately answers.

"Yes, but why *here?*"

"Because this was the next point on the map that the boss and her generals wanted checking out."

"You still don't get it, do you? Look around you. You can see this place has been turned over time and time again. There's nothing and no one left here, but you've both been sent in again regardless. The boss may be many things, but she's not stupid. There has to be a reason."

Bryce is also flummoxed. Is he missing something? "You heard Johannson the other night. She's expanding her empire. Pushing out from the center. Taking more ground."

"Yeah, you're right, I suppose," McCoyne says, though he doesn't sound convinced.

"You don't believe her?" Keller asks.

"I didn't say that."

"So what are you thinking?"

"Nothing."

Bryce corners McCoyne against the side of the supermarket truck. "Tell us what you're thinking or I'll snap your scrawny neck."

He probably could, too.

"Look, all I'm saying is there are better ways to build an empire, and I think Johannson knows that. I don't think we're out here spreading the word, I think she's using us to suss out who else is left."

"Same thing, ain't it?" Keller says, confused.

"No, I don't think so. She's not interested in who we bring back; I think the only thing she's watching is who comes back at all."

7

Exposed

They can tell from the grubby light seeping in under the door of the truck that it's morning. There's been little rest since the panicked exodus from the flooded shelter. Adrenaline and fear kept the group awake long into the night, but exhaustion eventually overtook all of them. Kara shuffles down toward the door, concerned because it wasn't open before. "Who's missing?" she asks.

"Matthew Dunne," someone answers. "Who d'you think?"

Kara opens the roller a little farther and sticks her head out. "Get back inside," Darren orders. "We're a group, remember? We need to work together. Stick together."

"Whatever," she says, and with that, she lowers herself down into the mud.

Matt's a short distance away from the truck, standing up to his ankles in sludge at the foot of a low, slime-covered hill. He hears her squelching footsteps approaching. "You could never creep up on anyone in this shit," he says, glancing back to see who it is.

"What are you doing?"

He stands with his hands on his hips and takes his time answering, scanning their alien-like surroundings. There's a brief intermission in the rain, and the sun is just about visible through a layer of insipid, almost ghostly clouds.

"I'm thinking we need to move. It's relatively safe at the moment, but it won't last. That landslide or whatever it was did us a favor and got rid of anyone near, but it's only going to be temporary. Others will come."

"I agree. But where do we go? You're probably the only one who knows this area."

"Hardly. I drove here a couple of times, that's all. And besides, it looks nothing like it used to. We could be anywhere."

He starts to climb the hill, every step taking ten times the effort it should. He feels like he's halfway up the incline, but when he looks back he's barely moved. He sees Kara looking up at him and, beyond her, a few more brave souls have ventured outside. The only other distinguishing feature is the sinkhole that marks the entrance to their abandoned underground shelter, little more than a dimple on the surface of the mud flats now.

Because some of the group has moved, the rest follow like sheep. Carrying the few supplies they've managed to keep hold of, they trudge toward Matt. He watches Darren, who looks around their unearthly surroundings like a wide-eyed child, hopelessly out of his depth. And behind him is a motley collection of thirty or so equally unprepared individuals. "This is going to be interesting," he says under his breath.

"What is?" Kara asks.

"This lot," he replies, gesturing at the approaching bunch.

"Ease up on them, will you?"

"I'm just concerned, that's all. You were all sheltered from the worst of everything that's happened since the war began. You had weeks in the camp followed by weeks underground. I just don't know how some of these people are going to cope."

"What are you thinking?" Darren asks when he reaches him, struggling to keep his balance.

"We have to move. Can't stay here," Matt tells him, and for once, Darren doesn't argue.

"So where do we go?"

"Back toward the city."

"Seriously?"

"Think about it. You'd have to be insane to head back toward the center of the bomb blast. Everyone will have spent weeks trying to go the other way. We don't need to get that close. Maybe just as far as the suburbs."

"You sound like you've got it all thought out."

"Maybe I have. You should have planned for it, too. We all knew something like this was probably going to happen sooner or later. Shit always happens."

Matt decides there's no point prolonging the conversation and continues up the hill.

"I think he's right," Kara says to the others. "It makes sense. The city's a dead place. There's no reason anyone would try to go back there."

"But what about radioactivity?" Jason asks.

Tracy Barnish is listening closely. "I don't think it's going to make much difference now."

"What, you suddenly a nuclear physicist, Trace?"

"No, but I was GP, remember? I got involved in occasional civil defense exercises as it happens. This is just common sense."

"Go on," Darren says.

"We're, what, about twenty miles from the city?" She gestures as the vast, empty space around them. "Fallout is carried by the wind and rain, and there's no shelter whatever direction we go in. We're exposed whatever we do. Besides, from what I remember, the radiation is at its worst in the first few weeks. We've been underground for months. It'll likely be down to relatively safe levels by now."

"Relatively safe?"

"Yes, and that's the best we can hope for right now. I agree with Kara. Matt's got the right idea. We don't know how many bombs there were or where they hit. Might have just been the one, might have been a hundred, but there's nothing we can do about it. Seriously, I'm more concerned about being caught out here in the open by Haters."

"We'll see them coming."

"And they'll see us. They might already be watching. When we first got out of the bunker, I thought it might be an advantage being surrounded by all this space, but it's not. It leaves us exposed."

It takes an age for them to reach the top of the hill. Matt feels the ground beneath his feet beginning to level out at long last. It's a hell of a walk back to the city from here, but it'll be a hell of a walk anywhere today. He glances back at the rest of the group. They're still following, though the line is stretching. Some are struggling to keep up. Others are slowed down looking after the handful of children to have made it this far.

"You okay, Matt?" Kara asks.

"Yep. You?"

She just nods, panting hard with effort.

"See anything?"

"Unfortunately, yes."

When Kara reaches the top, she stops, too. There are no words to fully describe what lies ahead of them. The dead world stretches away into the mist in all its hopeless glory. Even after everything they've already seen, the scale of the devastation is hard to comprehend. It's endless, absolutely endless. There's not a sign of life anywhere, not a single bird in the sky. The only movement is the low cloud that races overhead at a furious pace, driven by an icy wind. There are no leaves on the trees. No grass.

"Fuck me," Kara says, numb with shock.

The longer Matt's staring, the more he's gradually able to make out. He can see what looks like the remains of the battle through which he'd driven to get to the printing house: a freeze-frame convoy of heat-charred vehicle shells. He thought he'd seen it all, but this . . . this is beyond compare.

What's left of the city itself is hardest of all to look at. Despite the poor visibility, from here he can see all the way into the heart of the place he used to call home. He's immediately struck by how textbook it looks—just like the black-and-white photographs of Hiroshima and Nagasaki he remembers from history lessons. And it's so damn quiet . . . But the thing that hurts most, the thing that causes an involuntary sob, is the realization that he actually feels nostalgic for the squalid, overcrowded city-camp that was vaporized in the bomb blast. He remembers his house and Jen and the Walker family and working on the garbage trucks and queuing for food and . . . and he wishes he were back there again. The realization of just how much he's lost, how much he'll never get back, hits him like a sucker punch.

"What are you thinking?" Kara asks.

"I'm thinking that I should have gotten Jen out of there. I failed her."

"You didn't."

"And how would you know?"

"Jason told me."

"What exactly did he tell you? How he screwed me over and got my girlfriend killed? How he let me think she was safe when all the time he'd left her behind so he could save his own skin?"

"Actually, no. He told me how gutted he was, how sorry. He told me he tried to make her leave with him, but she wouldn't go anywhere without you."

The others have caught up. "Jesus. You got us away from all that," Tracy says. "Good job."

Darren's as shell-shocked as Matt. "Fuck," is all he can say for several overlong seconds. "They did it. Can't believe the crazy bastards actually did it . . ."

Distances are deceptive. It looks close, but the dead city is still miles away. "We're never going to cover that distance in one go," Kara says, and Matt knows she's right.

"Then we should get as close as we can for now. Find somewhere to shelter. Take it step by step."

8

They don't seem to be getting any closer, no matter how long they're walking. They walk alongside the road, not on it, doing what they can to keep out of sight and merge into the background, and every time they pause to regroup, it seems like they're no farther forward at all. Matt tries to pace himself, but it's not easy being out in the open like this—his instinct is to run, but he can't risk expending energy or making noise. There are bodies everywhere, the remains of running battles fought on the day of the apocalypse. He consoles himself with the fact that, caked in mud, he and all the others are as indistinguishable as everything else: gray specks moving slowly through a similarly gray landscape. A zigzag line of barely discernible figures, their arms loaded with the few supplies they've managed to cling to from their basement hideout.

"Feels like we don't belong here anymore," Kara says, whispering instinctively.

"That's because we don't," Matt tells her. "This isn't our world. It belongs to them."

"Bit overdramatic, don't you think?" Jason pipes up from close behind.

"I think Matt's right," Kara tells him. "It's like we were buried in one place, then dug up in another."

"Exhumed," Matt says under his breath.

Jason sounds nervous. "I hate how fast you get used to it. All these dead people . . ."

His comment makes Matt feel slightly better. He'd thought it was just him. Trudging through all this death and destruction, he just feels numb. He's incapable of emotion. Dead himself.

Here lies the tangled wreck of a helicopter on its side. It looks dried out and mummified, like the husk of an insect baked in the sun, its rotor blades buckled like spindly shriveled legs. It looks like it's been here forever. Matt recalls a near miss with a helicopter when he was driving the truck away from the city that night. Is this the same one, or is he miles off course? Are they close to the airport he saw being overrun and evacuated as all hell broke loose? He shakes his head and tries to focus on the here and now again, not get bogged down in the past. If he lets himself get distracted, then—

A piercing scream truncates his train of thought. Matt spins around and pushes past Jason, Kara, and several others to get a better view, though he already knows what he's going to see. It was only a matter of time. He curses his shell-shocked naïvety. What the hell were they thinking being out here like this?

A woman at the tail end of the straggly line is under attack from a lone Hater. There's a telltale blur of movement as the Hater strikes, then another as everyone else immediately moves the other way, trying to put maximum distance between themselves and the inevitable.

It's the noise that bothers Matt more than anything, the effect the woman's screams will have on any other Haters nearby. Without thinking, he pushes through the crowd, filled with a sudden nervous energy, desperate to quell the god-awful din. He's conditioned from those torturous weeks he spent alone trying to get home. He knows too well how a situation like this can rapidly spiral out of control.

He can see two Haters now. One young, one older, both skeletal and scrawny. Animallike. Unnaturally pallid. All wiry limbs, shaggy hair, and uncontrolled fury. It's too late to do anything to help the woman the monsters are attacking—she has blood spurting from a savage neck wound—so Matt doesn't bother trying. Instead, he snatches up a hefty fallen branch and moves for the nearest of the Haters.

What he does next he does on autopilot.

There's no thought, no consideration of the consequences, no hesitation—just an innate, guttural need to end the attack.

He clubs one of them around the back of the head, knocking it out cold. And the jolting force of the impact with the creature's skull makes him focus and makes him think, *What the hell am I doing?* He's always done everything he can to avoid confrontation and has used other people's battles as a shield to hide behind. He's rarely been the one to attack.

The second Hater pushes itself—*herself*, he realizes when her flaps of ragged clothes fall open—away from her victim and charges directly at Matt. Christ, this evil monster is a fearsome sight. What she lacks in physical bulk she more than makes up for in aggression and intent. She runs straight at him, wide eyes filled with rage and utter hate.

He swings the heavy branch around and clubs the woman with enough force to knock her clean off her feet. Then he panics, scared she's going to get up and fight back. Even in this pitiful state, he knows she could do some serious damage, and so, before she can move, he unloads on her. He brings the branch down across her face with such force that the wood splinters and snaps. He's left with a makeshift stake, which he drives down into her belly. He turns it around in his hands, grinding her guts and tying them in knots.

Matt's aware of the other creature stirring nearby, and quick as a flash, he cracks the Hater across the back of the skull again. The vile fucker tries to get up, but Matt's having none of it. He jabs it twice in the face, pushing it farther and farther back, then swings wildly at its head and almost decapitates it.

Matt shakes a lump of gristle from the end of his stick and holds it ready like a bō. He looks up and around, checking for other attackers, and realizes he's now the sole focus of attention. "What?" he grunts.

The rest of the group just look at him. Stare at him. Some move away from him.

"What?" he asks again.

The silence is all consuming. He's conscious he's still holding the stick like a martial arts weapon, but he doesn't want to let it go. He's shaking with nerves, but he won't let them see.

"Cover the bodies," Kara says as she starts to drag one of the dead Haters off the road they've been following. Others help while Matt kicks the leaf litter, then mixes spilled blood into the mud. To leave those nasty bastards out in the open, brutally hacked down, will leave any even nastier bastards nearby in no doubt that a potential enemy could be close.

"We have to keep moving," Matt says once he's satisfied their tracks have been sufficiently disguised. "There will be more of them. There always are."

He marches away. Kara goes to follow, but Jason blocks her way forward. "Do you think he's killed like that before?"

"I don't know. We've got to get used to it. If Matt hadn't done what he did, more of us would have died. We have to think like them if we want to stay alive. Act like them."

"And you believe that, do you? It makes us as bad as they are."

"No, it doesn't."

"Do you think any of us are safe when he's capable of killing in cold blood like that?"

"I think the more we're capable of doing that, the safer we'll be."

Kara stops talking and sidesteps Jason, not wanting him to see that she's as concerned as he is. She doesn't think there's any turning back from what just happened.

9

More of them. Another three, at least.

It's like something out of a horror movie as they emerge from the chaos—spindly shadow creatures that move like monsters, creeping, then pouncing.

This time, Matt's rooted to the spot. It's somehow harder the second time around. Knowing he's already killed is one thing, but the thought of having to do it again is altogether different. His arms are heavy with nerves, and the thing in his hands feels like a branch again, not a weapon. He looks around and sees that he's on his own, the rest of the group having all stepped back, volunteering him by default.

The first Hater is lame and covered with grime. He scrambles over a mound of ash-covered masonry, his instinctive desire to kill forcing him to try to move faster than his malnourished limbs allow. He trips and falls, but Matt still holds back, nervousness increasing. He alters his grip on the branch and shifts his weight, trying to work out how best to attack, knowing that he's overthinking the process, that he should just go with his gut and lash out like they do. The Hater picks himself up and stands fully upright, towering over Matt. His face is badly burned, scar tissue covering the entire right side of his skull. There's a shriveled mass where his ear used to be. He throws himself at Matt, and Matt trips over his own feet trying to get away. He's quicker than the Hater, in much better physical shape, and he boots the creature in the crotch. The Hater yells with pain and rolls away, and Matt gets up and kicks him in the side of the head. And again. And again. And again, this time hard enough to boot a ball from one end of a football pitch to the other. The first Hater stops moving just in time for the second to reach him. Kara grabs the Hater from behind, giving Matt time to reclaim his bō and inflict enough damage to prevent this bastard from ever killing again.

Other members of the shell-shocked group are fighting at last, growing in confidence now they're aware of the physical gulf between them and their poisoned, bomb-scarred enemy. The third Hater is tackled by Darren, then finished off by Jason, who drops a lump of concrete onto its head. It's almost comical watching the foul creature's limbs thrashing for those final few seconds before its crushed brain loses all control and its life is ended.

Dr. Tracy is carrying a knife. She makes short work of the last of them, driving the blade up into its gut, then yanking it out and stabbing again.

The panic is over as quickly as it began. "Makes you wonder why the hell we were hiding away for so long," Darren says, fired up by the violence and the victory.

"Don't you get it?" Tracy answers, breathless. "It's precisely because we've been hiding away that we can do this. Look at these poor bastards. These are the sick, the injured, the poisoned, the dying . . . we wouldn't have stood a chance if any of them had been at full strength."

"And there's likely to still be thousands more of them out here," Kara warns.

"Yeah, and it won't be long before we're in the same state if we don't find shelter and food and water. We're living on borrowed time here."

"Where's he gone?" Jason asks, concerned.

"Who?"

"Matt."

They look around, but he's not there.

Darren starts to get the rest of the group ready to carry on down the road when Matt reappears, bursting through a gap in a stretch of brittle-looking hedgerow. "This way," he says, and he leads them along an overgrown garden toward the rear of a dilapidated house with a naked-looking, tile-stripped roof. "This was their nest," he explains. "It's clear inside now, I checked. That must have been all of them."

"We can shelter here, then," Darren suggests.

Matt agrees. "It'll do for tonight." He hands Darren a supermarket carrier bag containing a few tins and packets of food. "Found this. It's all they had."

Darren takes the bag from him. "Good," he says, doing his best to sound more authoritative than he feels. He hadn't even thought to work out where the Haters were coming from or check if there were others nearby.

Darren's still deciding whether or not to follow Matt's advice and hole up here for a while, but the group is voting with their feet and is already heading for the house.

"We should keep a couple of people on watch, just in case," Matt suggests.

"Okay."

"And there's something else."

"What?"

As the others enter the building, Matt beckons Darren to follow him along the side of a separate garage out front. Matt stops when they reach the edge of the road.

"I'd have expected the Haters to be more nomadic around here, wouldn't you? We're close to what's left of the city, but they've got the whole country to choose from."

"What are you saying?"

"I think they were here for a reason. I don't think we're the only recent visitors."

"What?"

"Look at your feet."

Nonplussed, Darren does as he's told. There are tire tracks in the mud. "Fuck."

"Exactly. This could be a problem. Doesn't matter if they're like us or like them; whoever's been here is clearly better equipped than we are, so we have to assume they're stronger than we are, too. There are more than two sets of tracks, so there are either a decent number of them or they've been using this route regularly. Think about what's happened here. There might have been other routes until recently, but the landslide's changed the landscape, maybe forced them to come this way. I say we stop here and catch our breath, then move on when we can."

"Do we tell the others?"

"Up to you. They're your responsibility, so you do what you think is best. Personally, now we're out of the bunker, I wouldn't share this. You want them to stay calm and collected, not freak them out. Be economical with the truth. Only tell them as much as you think you need to."

It gets dark earlier than it should. The sun occasionally peeks out when the clouds are thin enough, but most of the time its evening descent is hidden behind an opaque gray-black curtain. The group settles in the house, away from doors and windows, huddled together in the shadows. This is uncomfortable, hell on Earth, but there's no complaint. This is as good as it gets for now. Even the kids who've survived remain quiet.

The house feels overcrowded, and Matt decamps to the garage next door. It's a cold, cluttered space full of junk, but he finds himself a relatively comfortable spot, sinking into a bagful of rags and decorator's dust sheets. He sits diagonally opposite the side door, in a position where he also has a clear view of the up-and-over garage door. It's buckled, jammed in its frame, left six inches open at the bottom. It lets the biting wind in, but it also lets him see out.

He counts the concrete blocks that make up the wall, trying to work out how many it took to build the entire garage. It's a coping mechanism, distracting himself with pointless crap to avoid thinking about anything else. He's exhausted, but he doesn't want to sleep. When he sleeps, he dreams about Jen and their house and the mushroom cloud. When he's awake, he feels like the others are constantly looking to him for advice he doesn't feel qualified to give. Asleep or awake, he can't switch off.

"You staying out here all night?"

Kara catches him by surprise. He curses himself for dropping his guard. Again. "Don't know yet. Came out here to be by myself."

"'Course you did. I was looking for somewhere to bed down. Mind if I join you?"

"As long as it's just you," he says.

She shuffles herself into half a space next to him, almost on top of him. They both appreciate the warmth of each other.

"I'm not much company," he tells her.

"I know that. You're a miserable bugger."

"Then why do you want to stay with me?"

"Because you make me feel safe."

"I doubt that. I don't have the best track record for keeping people safe."

"It wasn't your fault what happened to your missus."

"It was. I let her down. I trusted someone else. Won't let it happen again. Anyway, I don't want to talk about it."

"Shut up, then."

"With pleasure."

The silence doesn't last long.

"You're not going to walk out on us, are you, Matt?"

"And go where?"

"I don't know. I just get the feeling you're not planning on sticking around. We need you. *I* need you."

"I'm not needed. You've got Darren and Jason. They'll see you're all right."

"Now say it like you mean it."

But he can't.

Kara shuffles around to get comfortable. She puts her head on his chest. He puts his arm around her. Awkward. Self-conscious. From where he's slumped, he can see through a window up into the house next door. The slates, he thinks, were ripped from the roof by the atomic blast. Matt closes his eyes, and he can almost feel the shock wave battering the building, can almost smell the carbonized stench as the curtains caught and the paper burned away from the walls, can hear the screams of any poor fuckers who were still out here . . .

"Tell you the truth," he says, "it doesn't matter who's in charge; the odds are stacked against us. We can't take any risks. All it'll take is for us to run into a pack of Haters who aren't half-dead, and we've had it."

"So work with Darren."

"Happily. It's him who has the problem with me, though, in case you hadn't noticed. He's the big *I am*."

"I get that. He was spinning his *future of the human race* bullshit from the moment the group got together. I think you're a threat to him. He needs to be the alpha male. He's worried everyone will realize what a useless dick he is and start looking to you for guidance. After all, you're the one who saved them."

"No, thanks. I don't want the responsibility."

"Well, I don't reckon you have much choice. I've watched you in action. You got out of the bunker before it was too late, and you didn't disappear—you stayed close. Deny it all you like, you were looking out for the rest of us."

"Some of you, maybe. Well, you."

"I don't think we'll get far without you, Matt. Even tonight, after the rest of them had all disappeared indoors, I saw you clearing up after them, getting rid of our footprints in the mud."

"I just don't think they realize how precarious our position is. Even the slightest trace might be enough to attract attention. We can't afford to leave any clues."

10

The Car Hypermarket

It's ice cold out here, even sitting around this fire. The flames seem to give out ten times more light than heat. Camp tonight for Keller, Bryce, and their combined pack is the office of a long-silent car dealership. The Car Hypermarket, no less (according to the signs). Parts of the dealership appear largely untouched, but one-quarter of the site is a total ruin. There was a fire here at some point. The flames must have jumped from vehicle to vehicle unchecked; upward of a hundred cars have been gutted.

This place offered shelter and a decent stash of fuel. That's why the enemy had once been here. McCoyne spotted the signs and led the pack to the remains of a couple of Unchanged hidden in the sales office with a reasonable supply of looted food to keep them going. They'd escaped the violence, it seemed, but not the radiation.

When daylight returns, Keller, Bryce, and the others are due to return to Cambridge and report back to Johannson. For now, though, they rest, stomachs full. One of Keller's men rigged a few basic traps to alert them if anyone comes near: precariously balanced piles of scrap that'll topple and fill the air with noise.

It's a good thing the others are sleeping soundly, though,

because they'd not be best pleased if they could see what's happening right under their noses. McCoyne waited until the rest of them had all clocked out to help himself to a few looted items from each of their backpacks—not enough for any of them to notice individually, but enough of a stash to keep him going for several days, maybe as long as a week. Plenty of time, he thinks, to put some distance between him and everyone else.

McCoyne wants out.

He's worked his way back through the traps and burned-out cars and is now on the other side of the dealership. With a gutful of nerves but no guilt at all, he's gone.

Sometimes you just can't compete with the big boys (and girls). Sometimes it's not even worth trying. McCoyne's not stupid, he used to tell people before all of this happened, he just sometimes finds it hard to give a shit. He's done with Johannson and her merry band of psychopaths. It's time to look for somewhere they won't find him, where he can wait for this all to blow over, because the longer this goes on, the harder he thinks it's going to get. Before long, staying alive in the company of killers will become impossible for someone like him.

He's leaving what's left of the human race behind for good.

11

The House by the Road

When Matt wakes up, the light levels are almost the same as when he went to sleep. He's confused—did he sleep for hours or just minutes? He's not even sure if he's slept at all. Kara's not here, and now he can't remember if she ever was. Christ's sake, he can't make sense of anything. Has the radiation gotten to his brain already?

A creak of the door and she reappears, holding on to the doorframe as she leans back into the garage. "Morning," she says with more energy and effervescence in her voice than he has in his entire body. "Lovely day out there."

"Is it?" he asks, momentarily wrong-footed.

"What do you think?"

Annoyed, he doesn't reply. He picks himself up, turns his back on her, and pisses in the corner.

"You're a real charmer, Matt."

She's doing nothing to help his mood. He pisses harder. Makes more noise.

He's not the only one who's needed to answer a call of nature. When he looks out through a dust-covered window, he sees a line of several figures squatting down behind the house. Despite the degradation, he still feels embarrassed watching this most necessary and personal of acts. He turns away, finishes what he's doing, then shakes himself dry.

"So what do you reckon?" Kara asks.

"About what?"

"What we do next."

"Let the boss decide," he answers, jabbing his thumb in the general direction of the house next door.

"No, Matt, I want to know what *you* think we should do."

"Did he put you up to this? I'm not babysitting. Think I might just stay here."

"You won't."

"Come on, then," he goads. "You're so smart, *you* tell *me* what we do."

She shuts the door behind her and clears her throat. "I think we got lucky yesterday. I think things could have been much worse when we were attacked. If they'd been any stronger or there'd been more of them, they'd have wiped us out." She tries to gauge his reaction, but his face remains impassive. "I know you're more worried about being attacked than you're letting on because you mentioned it several times last night. You're also worried about those tire tracks out front."

"Darren tell you about that?"

"No, I did a recce for myself after you went all Sleeping Beauty on me and passed out. Personally, I think whoever's still driving around here is almost certainly bad news and we should keep our distance."

"And what do you think *they* think?" Matt asks.

"What, our lot? I think they're on a high . . . they're still alive, and after yesterday, I reckon they're thinking they might be able to win this fight after all. Personally, I think that's a mistake."

"You might be right."

"You know I am. I think that having to spend all that time

hiding—first in the camp, then when we were in the chapel basement, then under the printing house—it left blokes like Darren and Jason feeling worthless . . . emasculated, even. Now they're looking for a chance to prove themselves. That's another reason why they're so shitty toward you."

"Hadn't thought about it that way," he admits.

"See. You're not the only one who likes sitting in the corner figuring everyone else out."

"Is that why you keep checking with me?"

"Maybe. Or maybe I just like being around you? Or I'm just trying to protect myself? You've seen more of this than anyone. I think following your lead might be a pretty smart thing to do."

"I don't want to be followed. I just want to be left alone."

"We don't have that luxury. Like I said, I think those tracks could mean bad news. If it's people like us, they'll shoot first, ask questions later. If it's Haters, they'll attack first and not bother asking any questions at all. We need to keep out of the way."

He nods approval. "Absolutely. And that's why these people are such a fucking liability. All that effort yesterday to keep them hidden, and now there's a bloody line of them crapping outside the back door. Might as well have written *We're here* in shit on the wall."

She laughs. He likes that noise. Wasn't expecting it. Had almost forgotten it.

"Right. So we pack them up, head out, and find somewhere more substantial that's way off the beaten track until we've fully worked out what's going on in what's left of the world."

He nods. "Sounds like a plan."

They're on the move within the hour, all of them tucked up tightly against the unruly hedgerow that marks the length of a vast furrowed field. They move in silence and in line. Some have arms loaded with the sparse food and belongings they've managed to cling to, others look after the five children left alive. How do you explain something like this to a kid? How do you make them stay quiet? How do you make them understand why it's suddenly okay to kill some people but not others? Matt brings up the rear and watches them with sadness and concern, thankful he never had children himself. Always wanted to, never going to.

The closer they get to the remains of the city-camp and the epicenter of the blast, the fewer signs of life they see. They're in the field, deliberately keeping off the road, and despite the rain, the frozen soil here is hard underfoot. It's obvious nothing's going to grow in this dead zone for a long time, if ever. The uniformly planted rows of wilted yellow shoots add insult to injury. The world's changed beyond all recognition since these crops were sown.

Darren has the lead with Jason close behind, but the Hater attack comes two-thirds down the line. The lone woman has been sleeping rough, and though she barely seems to have enough energy to move, her instinct and hatred are such that she's compelled to strike. They didn't even see her till she moved; she looked like a long-discarded bag of rag and bone until she was disturbed. She collides with one of the kids. Kara grabs the boy and pulls him clear, covering his mouth with her hand to stop him screaming. Spoiled for choice, the sickly Hater turns on the next available Unchanged. Bad move. It's Matt. Still carrying the stick from yesterday, he clubs her to the ground, and though she continues to fight and halfheartedly lifts her arms to try to defend herself from the beating, the end is inevitable. Matt's barely out of breath by the time he's killed her.

But where there's one Hater, there are almost always more.

They can see them on the other side of the hedge in the road they're walking parallel with, the most active of them reaching and stretching, trying to find a big enough gap to get through to the Unchanged in the field.

"What do we do?" Darren asks Matt.

"We can take them, right?" Jason says.

"Be my guest," Matt tells him. "We've been lucky so far. Won't last. All we need is to try taking on one of them that's in a half-decent state and we're in trouble. There are, what . . . six of them in the road. Double that number and we'd be screwed."

"Yeah, but look at them. Some of them can barely stay standing."

"Don't assume," Matt warns. "Sick or not, they're still vicious bastards. We're not."

"Says the man who's battered three of them to death with a fucking stick in the last twenty-four hours. Come on, we can do this," Jason says, fired up.

Darren agrees, but Matt grabs his arm and pulls him back. "Don't. They're stuck in the road. There's no need to fight."

"We need to kill them."

"You don't. That's Hater mentality. Try to take them on at their own game and they'll kill you eventually, no question."

The Haters are going wild on the other side of the hedge, but there's no way through. Matt keeps walking. Kara follows him, as do the others. Soon only Darren is left standing by the hedgerow, watching the rabid creatures still trying pointlessly to reach him from the other side.

Kara quickens her pace to catch up with Matt. He lowers his voice so that only she can hear him. "We can't afford to take chances. Idiots like Darren and Jason will get us all killed."

12

Freedom

McCoyne's relieved to finally be alone out here, not constantly looking over his shoulder. There's no weight of expectation when the only person you need to think about is yourself.

He's hungry and cold, though. Then again, he can't remember the last time he wasn't. Even when he was sitting around the fire with the others last night, he couldn't feel any heat. He threw up half of what he ate. Nervous about being caught by Bryce after going AWOL, probably. But that doesn't explain why he felt the same way yesterday morning, or the day before that, or the day before that. He thinks everybody's probably in the same boat. The bomb filled the air with so much toxic shit that it would have been just about impossible for anyone to avoid breathing it in. He hopes he'll start to feel better soon, but he doesn't think he will. That's why it's important he has some *me time* to rest and build up his strength.

Easier said than done.

Christ, even the basics feel like impossibilities now: the food he'd taken for granted, the flat he'd called home, the family he'd shared it all with, the warmth of lying alongside another person who wanted to hold him, not kill him . . .

He blocks it all out. Can't risk going down that route again. Can't think about any of it. It's a dead end. All gone now. Never coming back. None of it.

He's been walking for hours, and his twiglike legs are numb with cold. The skin on his burned back feels tight and rubs under the straps of his backpack. His lungs sound like they're filled with dirt. Tastes that way, too. When he spits, it's brown. *I'm a fucking wreck,* he thinks.

He gets off the road, worried that Bryce will track him down if he sticks to obvious routes. But he soon thinks he might have made a mistake, because the path he's following is getting wetter and wetter. He sinks ankle-deep but keeps going until he reaches the edge of a vast pool. It might have been a quarry once, might have always been here, it's impossible to tell. The semi-constant mist makes it difficult to see too far in any direction. He staggers on through the sucking mud until he reaches the point where low, murky waves lap up against the shore. If he had a boat, he thinks, and he knew how to sail, he'd maybe head out onto the water and look for an island. That'd be best. A little speck of dry land he could call his own where no one would find him or want anything from him.

There's something floating on the water, coming toward him. Driftwood? Something worth keeping hold of? He finds a branch nearby and uses it to hook the thing and drag it over. Just a corpse. He's seen enough dead people to last a hundred thousand lifetimes, and this one is nothing special.

Or is it?

Something about this particular stiff has piqued his interest. He flips it over onto its back and sees it's like him, not Unchanged. There's some bloat to the face, but it looks like a relatively recent kill. A single stab wound to the neck. It puts him on edge, because it strikes him as a quick, clean, and controlled way of dispatching someone.

He remembers reading something once about how bodies swell up like a balloon after death and float on water because of all the gases brewing in their rotting guts. He pushes the cadaver away, but it only drifts a few meters deeper into the mist before butting up against something else and stopping again. Intrigued, McCoyne wades a little deeper in.

Another body.

This place is obviously bad news, and he turns to head back to shore but catches his breath when he finds himself face-to-face with a third corpse. This one is bent over double, bobbing in the rippling waves with its feet weighed down. And now he can see two more. And another couple beyond them. All like him, none of them Unchanged. Several have had their throats cut, others have less obvious wounds, all have obviously been murdered. He doesn't want to know who did this, he just wants to get away fast before they find him. He's met some foul fuckers since the war began, but the butchery on display here is on another level.

13

Exposed

Late morning, and the rain's pelting down so hard it hurts, soaking everything and everyone. Jason spots a building in the near distance and points it out to Darren. "What do you think? Got to get under cover soon," he says, and Darren doesn't argue. They're desperate for shelter.

The building was a leisure center. There's a gym with lines of dust-covered exercise machines, and a long-empty swimming pool with a mound of bodies dumped at the deep end. The glass ceiling directly above the pool is damaged, and rainwater pours in, steadily refilling it. There are a couple of inches of standing water covering the tiles and lane markings. Even at this rate, it'll be weeks before the water reaches any depth. It's loud like a waterfall, though. An unstoppable, clattering torrent.

Matt finds a small café area. There's some food and drink in a stockroom, which he brings out and distributes. It's probably full of all kinds of radiation, but it tastes so good and has such a positive effect on the others that he decides it doesn't matter. The food probably only has a fraction of the toxicity of the rain.

The leisure center is relatively isolated and appears more substantial than the house where they'd spent last night. In comparison to the endless gloom they'd endured under the printing house, it feels positively luxurious with space to move around, high ceilings, and light-colored walls. Matt, Jason, Kara, and several of the others check the building from top to bottom, making sure it's clear and looking for anything that might be of use. There's clothing in the changing rooms—*dry* clothes, thermal layers, too—and equipment they can repurpose and use as weapons if need be. Matt spools a leather jump rope and hangs it from his belt like a cowboy's lasso.

Despite the space that's suddenly available to them, all the group gravitate around the café. There's safety in numbers.

Hours pass. Some of them are asleep now. Others are sitting staring into space. A woman and a man get up together and walk away from the group. Matt growls at them, "Where you going?"

"To the toilet," the woman says. "Back off. Jesus."

Matt thinks people are weird. This woman has spent weeks living in squalid confines with no choice but to do everything in full view of everyone else. He can't understand why she feels the need to show discretion now just because they've got a little more space. He also thinks it's strange how little he knows about any of the others, bar Darren, Jason, Kara, and a couple of others. Christ, he doesn't even know their names.

The woman and her chaperone tiptoe toward the entrance doors, which Darren secured earlier by threading a metal weight-lifting bar through the handles. She goes into the dried-up toilets, and he dutifully waits outside.

And he waits.

Matt's uneasy. Is something wrong? He sits upright to get a better view, then relaxes when she eventually reappears.

Bloody woman. What the hell was she doing in there?

The two of them walk idly back toward the group, chatting as if they don't have a damn care in the world. The noise of the non-stop rain drowns out their noise.

And then they stop.

Matt's guts flip, and he gets up and walks toward them. He can tell from the woman's face that something's not right. She walks over to the long floor-to-ceiling windows along one side of the corridor and presses her face against the glass. It's uniformly discolored: caked with dried-on mud and dust from the summer, then layered with all kinds of grime that's since been spat down in the rain. It's almost opaque.

"Get away from the window," Matt tells her.

"Thought I saw something," she says.

"What?"

"Don't know . . . Could have been anything."

"Exactly. Get back to the others."

"It was probably nothing," her companion says, but then something—*someone*—slams against the filthy window. Whoever it is, they're having as much trouble seeing in as the woman has seeing out. He or she adjusts their position constantly, trying to find a clear spot but failing. They wipe furiously at the window, but succeed only in smearing the grime, not shifting it.

"They didn't see me," the woman says to Matt. "They couldn't have. If it was one of them, then they'd—"

She's silenced by an ungodly commotion coming from the front of the building. Darren securing the doors has stopped whoever it is from getting in, but it's also let them know someone's in here. Either that or there's something here worth taking.

Matt sees more faces pressed against the other windows. Four of them, at least. No, wait . . . seven . . . ten. The noise at the front door has acted like an alarm bell. Darren and Jason are on their feet now, too. He gestures for them to hold back and not react.

Kara appears from a doorway opposite Darren. "Where've you been?" he whispers.

"Upstairs. Fire escape."

"And?"

"Haters. Has to be."

"How many?"

"Fucking loads."

"Shit."

"How many is fucking loads?" Matt asks. "Be specific."

"I didn't do a head count," she snaps at him, nervous.

"A rough idea, then. Five? Fifty?"

"Fifteen. Maybe twenty. Something like that."

"We can deal with that many," Darren announces, sounding more confident than he is.

Matt shakes his head. "We can't assume. Like she said, she didn't do a head count. This might just be the first wave. There could be hundreds of them watching us. Could be an army out there."

"Fight, hide, or run?" Kara says, narrowing down their options.

"Hide," Matt immediately answers. "Can't risk fighting, can't risk running. Soon as we're out in the open again, they'll pick us off. They'd be all over us before the last of us is out the door."

"There are rooms upstairs we can use. We can go out on the roof if we have to."

Matt's about to tell her to start getting everyone organized, but it's too late. A rock is thrown through one of the windows nearest the entrance, filling the building with noise. And rather than stick together, the group instead panics and scatters. Matt tries to herd people toward the staircase Kara just used, and though plenty of them do as he says, many more head in the opposite direction. He can see several of them lowering themselves into the corpse- and rainwater-filled swimming pool, intending to hide among the mass of decomposing bodies. The toilet woman runs the wrong way and is caught. Her screams are louder than anything else and fill the cavernous building as a pack of hate-filled animals attack her, practically tearing her limb from limb. "Move," Matt tells Darren, shoving him back. "There's nothing we can do for her. Take advantage of the distraction to get away."

He stands there, dumbstruck, but Matt's not hanging around. He races up another staircase, then takes a wrong turn and finds himself out on a viewing balcony overlooking the swimming pool. There are more Haters surging in through the broken window. He can only look down helplessly as the raggedy, evil-looking fuckers prowl around the edge of the pool. He sees familiar faces buried among the unfamiliar dead, and he knows there's absolutely nothing he can do to help them. There are already too many of the enemy inside the leisure center, and he knows more will inevitably come.

Matt doubles back on himself and this time takes a right through a door marked Staff Only. It's some kind of plant room: a mini-maze of pipes and machines, air-conditioning control panels. There's a metal ladder going straight up to the roof, an open hatch, and he climbs out into the hissing rain, figuring there might still be some slight advantage in claiming the higher ground. Maybe it just mean he'll have farther to fall?

Kara and Jason are already up here with one group. Darren bursts out onto the asphalt through another door, and Dr. Tracy's not far behind, following a group of three bedraggled kids she herds ahead of her. Matt leans over the edge of the building and looks down. The bastards are circling the leisure center, far more than Kara originally estimated. And their numbers are only going to increase.

"We'll have to fight our way out," Darren says.

"We'll never make it."

"We've got to try, though, right? The rest of our people are still down there."

"Do whatever you think you have to."

"What do you suggest? Stop up here and wait until it's all over?"

"That's his usual tactic," Jason says. "That's how he stays alive."

"You all found your way up here, and so did I," Matt says, ignoring him. "If the rest of them want to stay alive, they're going to have to show some initiative."

One of the Haters is clearly in charge down there. Kara watches him giving orders to another pack who pour in through the smashed window. "You called this wrong, Matt. We can't stay up here and leave the rest of them to die," she says, and before anyone can argue, she's on her way back down.

Matt watches her disappear. Jason was right—all he wants to do is find somewhere to shelter and sit this out, but he knows he can't. This isn't like it was when he was on his own out in the wastelands all those months ago, trying to get back to Jen. He follows Kara back down into the bowels of the building, horrified by the prospect of her facing the enemy on her own. She has a determination and drive about her that the others lack. He doesn't want her to get hurt.

Upward of thirty Haters are running roughshod around the ground floor of the leisure center now. One of the group who hid in the pool loses his nerve and makes a break for the smashed window, trying to get out as more vicious, scrawny fighters are clambering to get in. He doesn't have a hope in hell, but that doesn't stop Kara wanting to help him. She's about to run out into the open, but Matt grabs her shoulder and drags her back. "Get off me," she rages at him, but he doesn't.

"Don't be stupid. He's had it."

She knows he's right. She watches helplessly as two of the foul bastards beat the life out of him with baseball bats.

Most of the group are still stranded on the roof, many others playing dead in the pool. The enemy are temporarily distracted, picking through the meager supplies the group left around the café area.

"They think they've gotten rid of us all. They don't know how many of us are here," Kara says.

"You might be right."

"I *am* right. We need to move," she tells him, and this time Matt agrees. He gestures toward another door adjacent to the one they're hiding behind. They make the quick dash across several meters of open space, then find themselves in a damp-smelling sauna room. Jason's already found his way down here, along with several others.

"Thought you'd be long gone," he says when Matt appears.

"Sorry to disappoint."

There's a second door leading into a large changing room area, and another door after that, which emerges close to the main entrance Darren blocked off. Matt's about to lead them out, but he stops. "Wait. Listen. You hear that?"

The air outside is filled with new noises now. Through a cracked window, Kara sees several speeding vehicles come to a sudden halt outside the leisure center. Some of them are ramshackle and unremarkable, while others are ex-military. They're all dirt-streaked and paint-charred and appear to have been well used since the bomb. "That's us screwed."

"What do you see?"

"A fucking Hater army, that's what."

Can't go forward, can't go back. There's no option but to try to fight, but Matt knows none of them are natural fighters. Christ, the only weapon he's carrying is a damn jump rope.

No choice.

He takes a deep breath and steps out into the corridor, then immediately dives back the other way. A Hater woman sprints past, moving so fast that she doesn't even realize Matt's there. He's about to move again when a man wearing bike leathers runs past and tackles the woman to the ground. She's trying to get away, on all fours now, but he has a boot on her ankle. He stands over her and clubs her around the back of her head with a length of metal pipe that's already dripping with blood.

Change of plan.

"What going on?" Jason asks, frantic.

"Looks like we've found ourselves in the middle of a turf war. Go back the way we came. Quick!"

Matt tries to shepherd the others back, but it's too late. The door flies open, and the leather-clad man appears. He lunges for Matt, who covers his head, ready for the inevitable battering. When it doesn't immediately begin, he dares to look up. The man's holding the door open. "Poolside. Move!" he orders.

There's no hesitation and no dissention, because there's only one logical explanation for what's happening here—these people aren't Haters. Matt, Jason, Kara, and the others are marched through the leisure center, where they see Darren, Tracy, and the rest of the group lined up by the poolside, hands behind heads like police suspects. The fact that the last few Hater stragglers are being rounded up and executed is proof positive these people are human. Matt watches with an uneasy mix of horror and hope. Jesus, whoever these people are, they're fearsome bastards. They might prove to be worse than the enemy.

Farther down the line, someone's begging for mercy, but mercy's the absolute last thing on offer here today. A woman comes up behind the man who's wailing and grabs a fistful of his hair. She pulls his head back and holds the point of a savage-looking knife to his throat. "Keep the fucking noise down," she warns, and he immediately shuts up.

Other shell-shocked survivors are being plucked out of the pool, then shoved across the tiles to stand shaking with Darren and the others. There's an uncomfortable, muted silence now; everyone's too afraid to protest.

No faces.

Matt realizes that all these people have their faces covered, and the only reason he can think of for that is to throw Haters off the scent. He assumes his directed position alongside the others: legs apart, hands behind his head, looking dead ahead. A guy dressed in a mix of bike leathers and army camouflage gear walks along the line, looking at each of the group in turn, studying them from behind dark goggles. Matt thinks he should probably keep his mouth shut, but he knows he has to say something.

"We're like you," he says, and the man stops. He has an automatic rifle at his side, which he raises and shoves under Matt's chin.

"And how would you know what we are?"

"The fact you haven't fired that thing, for a start. You've killed a lot of people since you've been here, but you've done it quietly. Relatively quietly, anyway."

"And why shouldn't I kill you?"

"No reason. You can if you want. I think we're on the same side, though."

A figure behind Matt kicks the back of his legs, and before he realizes it, Matt's on his knees with the barrel of the rifle pressed against his forehead. Again Matt thinks he should stay quiet, but equally he knows he has to try to reason with these people.

"You made enough noise getting in, but you're keeping intentionally quiet now. You don't want to attract any more attention than is absolutely necessary. You've only killed Haters, from what I can see, and you know by now that we're not like them because we're doing what you tell us and not trying to fight back."

"Except you. You don't know when to shut up."

"Maybe. I just don't want to die pointlessly, that's all. We can help you. Help each other."

The man with the gun laughs. "You think?"

"It's all about numbers these days, isn't it? There are about thirty of us."

"Are you sure? You just lost a few, I think."

"Still more than double your number, from what I can see."

"Believe me, there's a lot you can't see from down on your knees. You're in no position to start bargaining, pal. Right now, all I want to know is who you are, what you're doing out here, and why we haven't seen you before."

"We were sheltering. Underground. Been there since the bomb."

"And you thought you'd come up top and see how things were working out?"

"Nope. Landslide. Shelter got flooded. We'd have drowned."

"And before then?"

"In the city. Planned evacuation when it all started to go to hell."

"You did well to get out alive," the man says. Matt looks up and detects a slight softening, a chink in his façade. He drags Matt back up to his feet, then nods at another similarly garbed figure standing nearby. "Check 'em."

There's a flurry of activity. More unspoken orders are issued by way of gestures and expressions. Matt thinks this—whatever *this* is—appears to be a well-rehearsed routine. He sees there are guards stationed at every exit, others acting as lookouts, patrolling the borders. Out of the corner of his eye, he sees a lone Hater burst into the building. Two guards cut him down fast. One covers the invader's mouth with his hand, then slits his throat. Silent. Brutally effective. Ninja-like. Matt's impressed. And apprehensive as hell.

Elsewhere, another one of the new arrivals walks along the side of the swimming pool with a dying Hater in tow, barely alive and with its head covered with a bag. It half walks and is half dragged, left leg buckling whenever it tries to put any weight on it. Soaked with blood from the waist down. Bleeding out from a savage-looking wound in its gut.

"Look at me," the leader with the rifle says, and Matt obediently obliges. The guy's removed his dark goggles and the scarf that covered his mouth. Matt thinks he looks in reasonably good shape. There's some scarring to his right cheek, but a little superficial damage is par for the course these days. He appears to be strong and physically fit—a far cry from the Haters they've so far seen. He knows appearances can be deceptive, but first impressions are that these people have been spared the worst of the fallout. Matt's mind is racing now, trying to join the dots . . . does this mean they've traveled here from a distance?

The woman with the Hater drags the pathetic-looking creature over, leaving a glistening snail trail of blood along the poolside.

Matt thinks he's figured out where this is going.

And he's right.

The dying Hater is hauled upright in front of him, and the bag covering its head is removed. It's a young woman, and as soon as she sees Matt, she reacts exactly as any Hater would: her injuries and the obvious danger she's in are immediately forgotten, and she launches a volley of spit and fury at him. He stands his ground as the filthy, scrawny creature thrashes and squirms, fighting to free her hands and wrap them around his throat.

"Believe me now?" Matt says, heart racing, but there's no answer until the same routine has been repeated up and down the entire line. Once everyone's been checked, the Hater-wrangler finishes the dying woman off by drawing a blade across her throat. There's blood everywhere, but she's still trying to fight.

"That settles it, then," the boss says as he rolls the Hater into the pool with his boot. "You can relax. Looks like we're all friends together."

"Where did you come from? Are there more of you?"

The boss reaches out and shakes hands with Matt. "Yeah, there are a few of us. We're based a fair distance away. Name's Aaron Rayner, by the way."

"Matthew Dunne."

"You're bloody lucky we found you."

"And how did you find us?" Matt asks.

"That landslide you were talking about . . . we were doing a recce of what's left of the airport and got diverted by the mud. Saw you trekking away from wherever it was you'd been holed up."

"And you've been watching us all this time?"

"Yep. Can't take any chances these days. Had to be sure what you were before we stepped in. Good job we did as well. This place would have been swarming before long. They attract each other like flies around shit, in case you hadn't noticed."

"So what now?"

"Unless you're planning on staying out here on your own, you're coming with us."

"You Civil Defense Force?"

"Yep. You got a problem with the CDF?"

"No problem."

"Good. We've been looking for stragglers, but you're the biggest group we've come across in an age. We could all benefit from this."

14

On the Road

Matt doesn't trust anybody, but being in the back of this van, being driven to god knows where by god knows who, is still preferable to how he's spent the rest of his time since they were forced back aboveground. Their saviors / captors / potential killers might prove to be as deadly as a pack of full-strength Haters, but at least he has half a chance of reasoning with someone who's Unchanged like he is. They're in the middle of three vehicles currently moving at speed through the otherwise eerily quiet countryside, heading away from the charred remains of the city-camp. There's another van behind and a powerful-looking CDF military truck in front. One thing's for sure—they were right about the enemy numbers in the area around the leisure center. As they drove away, the surrounding area was rife with movement. Matt saw hundreds of sickly, half-starved killers converging on what was likely the biggest disturbance the region had seen since the days immediately after the bomb.

He looks around the interior of this battered van at the faces of the people he was buried underground with, and he wishes they'd share some of his cynicism. They're all standing up, packed in like cattle, but they're smiling. Chatting. Relatively relaxed.

Temporarily filled with hope. "Must be me," he says to no one in particular.

"What is?" Kara asks.

"Nothing. Don't want to rain on anyone's parade."

"Miserable sod. Come on, tell me what you're thinking."

"Nothing's like it used to be anymore, you know? Just because someone hasn't killed you doesn't mean they're not still planning to shove a skewer up your ass and spit-roast you over the campfire."

"Does it matter?"

"Of course it matters."

"Yeah, but right now? At this moment? Just take that skewer out of your ass for a sec, Matt, and relax. Instead of thinking about what might happen, think about what *has* happened. We're safe. This time an hour ago, we thought we were dead and buried."

He leans against the side of the van and considers her words. "Yeah, you're right. But we don't know anything about these people."

"We know they're not Haters. We know they're in good shape, all things considered, and they're well equipped. They've obviously got a decent base somewhere. Biggest thing for me? They're smart. That stunt they pulled with the Hater woman, checking we weren't like her, that wasn't a spur-of-the-moment thing. They clearly know what they're doing, and even if they have us cleaning their toilets and shining their shoes, so what? Would that be such a bad thing compared to what we've been through?"

This group's story about doing a recce of the area near the airport seems to check out. As they evacuated, Matt saw that the back of the truck they're following is loaded up with equipment and ammo, supplemented by the supplies his group had managed to hold on to at the leisure center. He presses his face against the window as the convoy follows a lazy arc in the road, and he watches with equal parts disgust and satisfaction as a sickly-looking Hater is mown down with arrogant disdain. It feels good to be on the side of the aggressor for once, but he's conscious their unexpected saviors have been less than forthcoming with information. He has no idea where they're going other than east; no idea what they might have signed themselves up for here.

The first part of the answer is revealed after another half hour's drive. While moving through a more heavily built-up area, the convoy takes a sudden diversion through a once-green and leafy suburb. "Nice place," he hears someone say as they drive along the front of a succession of large detached executive houses. "Better than last night's digs, anyway."

They swing around onto the sweeping drive of one of the houses, and Kara notices there's a spotter in a downstairs window who disappears as the vehicles appear. A few seconds later, a large wooden gate around the side of the main building swings open, letting the convoy through and into a hangar-sized garage with room enough for all the vehicles and several more besides.

"Not a lot of bomb damage round here," Matt says to no one in particular, stating the obvious.

"That's a good thing, isn't it?" Kara says.

"Guess so. Trouble is, if the buildings aren't bomb damaged, then the Haters won't be, either."

They disembark, and more than fifty people group together at one end of the garage. Aaron Rayner climbs up onto a workbench to address them. His voice is loud enough to be heard, not so loud as to be overheard. "Right, we're almost home. We're about an hour's walk away."

"This isn't it?" Darren asks.

"Nope."

"So why have we stopped?"

"First things first. Keep your voice down. You're safe with us, but you need to do exactly what we say. Got it?"

"We get it," Matt answers for him, not wanting any trouble.

Aaron continues, "I understand how you must be feeling, I really do. If I were in your shoes, I'd be thinking all kinds of stuff. You have to forget all that and understand that we all want the same thing here; we want to stay alive. Now in order to do that, we have to keep our distance from those nasty bastards out there, and the best way we've found of doing that is to lead them on a bit of a merry dance. That's what this place is all about. We'll stay here a while longer—long enough to make sure we haven't been followed or tracked, usually a couple of hours max—then we leave. It's several miles back to base, and we cover those miles on foot in absolute, complete, total fucking silence. Everyone understand that?"

There are a few mumbled responses, and a couple of subdued conversations spring up in different parts of the group. Aaron looks less than impressed.

"Well, you clearly don't get it, because if you did, you'd keep your fucking mouths shut."

Now there's silence. Pin-drop time.

"That's better. Look, I'm not pissing around here, people; we're talking life or death. *Your* life or death. There are a couple more things you need to get your heads around. First, once we're out in the open, we stick together, but you're on your own. Anyone falls behind or goes ahead and ends up getting attacked, that's just too bad. Doesn't matter who it is. You get yourself in trouble and no one's going to come to your rescue. You lot used your only get-out-of-jail-free card when we found you back at that leisure center. Got it?"

Nods this time. No words.

"Good. So there's no heroics, no risk-taking, no jumping in and trying to save the day. We're all of us only responsible for two things—getting ourselves to the base in one piece, and not giving the game away for everyone else. Again, same goes for everyone.

I get caught, I'm dead. *You* get caught, *you're* dead. And that's another thing—you do anything that gives a Hater even the slightest clue where we are, and I'll kill you myself."

Aaron waits for his words to sink in, then speaks again.

"We'll answer all your questions when we get home. We'll feed you, make you comfortable, and keep you safe."

Matt's still not sure he's buying any of this, but right now, food and safety are all he wants.

"From now until I tell you otherwise," Aaron continues, "no one makes a sound."

The wait feels endless, but it's nothing compared to what this group has already endured. Down in the shelter, the hanging on was interminable. Here, they know it's only temporary. Matt finds himself near a cobweb-covered window overlooking the forgotten lawns at the back of this grand house. Kara's sitting on a workbench next to him, her knees drawn up to her chest.

She spots something outside. Nudges him with the toe of her boot, then nods.

There's a single Hater in the garden. It's like a ghost; a twisted apparition from the pages of an old horror comic. The strangely shapeless figure moves slowly along one edge of the yellowed lawn, limping and lurching, halfheartedly trying to keep out of sight. Its disheveled appearance makes it difficult to make out, and Matt loses sight of it as it merges with the background, only its movements bringing it back into focus. It's getting closer to the house, and with each step forward it takes, so his concern mounts. Has anyone else seen it? Is anyone going to do anything about it? Is it all down to him as usual?

The creature is dealt with before it gets anywhere near. Two of Aaron's people cut off its approach and attack in a pincer movement.

It's another well-rehearsed routine: a swift and silent assassination with one of them acting as bait while the other goes in for the kill. Both the body and the CDF killers are out of view in seconds, and it's like no one was ever there. The clinical brutality of the execution is startling; impressive and unnerving in equal measure, proof positive of this CDF faction's survival credentials. Christ, Matt thinks, his group barely managed to stay alive, and all they had to do was remain buried underground.

The light fades earlier than it should, the sun choked out of existence by swaths of impenetrable clouds. Matt's beginning to wonder if there's been a change of plan and they're staying here for the night, but his question is answered before he can even ask.

The CDF chaperones use flashlights to communicate, flashing lights at each other to signal their intent. In no time at all, everyone is standing together at the back of the house, ready to leave. They've formed a single column, which snakes through the kitchen and down the hallway. There's a bizarre atmosphere—subdued and excited at the same time, terrified yet hopeful, keen to move yet feeling hopelessly underprepared. Matt's keeping his options open. He deliberately positions himself toward the back of the line. If he doesn't like how things are going, he'll slip away and work his way back to this place.

Aaron has a final warning for the group. He speaks in hushed tones, but the stillness of this building allows everyone to hear. "Like I said earlier, not a damn sound while we're out there. Be under no illusions, we're all expendable. If we think you're going to jeopardize our collective safety, we'll kill you before the Haters can get a sniff. The louder you try to argue your case, the quicker we'll do it. My people will be spaced along the line to make sure we all comply. Just remember, we're all as keen as each other to stay alive and get to base in one piece."

Matt believes this bloke. He's in no doubt that if anyone fails to comply with his clear and unambiguous instructions, they won't live to see the morning, but he doesn't get the impression Aaron and his crew are trigger (blade) happy. If they didn't want numbers, they wouldn't have risked the rescue. This base of theirs—wherever it is and however many people are there—is clearly all that matters.

Whether his instincts prove to be right or not, Matt will find out soon enough. They're finally on the move.

15

The walk through the encroaching darkness is slow and hard and tense. They follow a path through a heavily forested area. You don't realize how much noise you unconsciously make until you're forced to very consciously stay silent, Matt thinks. He soon sees there's good reason for the silence, though the gloom makes it difficult to discern details. That's probably for the best. From what he can tell, two Haters traveling one way meet this line of Unchanged traveling the other, and the results are predictably bloody. The noise of the Hater attack is expected, the ominous silence of the swift CDF response is not. The enemy is quickly dealt with, but there are casualties. Though Matt can't be completely certain, he's sure he sees one of the CDF smothering an injured member of their own crew to prevent them from screaming, then putting them out of their misery with a stab of a blade to the temple. *I know they'd do that to any of us in a heartbeat,* he thinks.

He hears more movement around the area where the attack took place. The bodies are being trussed up and carried back to base. The person at the far end of the line quietly kicks over the leaf litter, covering their tracks.

There's another incident a short while later, this one far more satisfying than the last. An injured Hater man, sheltering in the forest, lying shivering in the leaf litter, is swallowed up by CDF fighters and killed. There's a brief, muted struggle, then the bedraggled figure is slashed and bound and hauled over the shoulder of a huge militiaman before he's finished bleeding out.

The last hour has felt like ten, but they're approaching the end of the journey. Initially, there are no obvious signs, but Matt can tell. He detects the slightest quickening of pace as the finish line nears. The trees thin out, and after a period of time spent walking along the side of a towering hedge, blocky building shapes become visible in the near distance. Fairly low to the ground with a large footprint, miles away from anywhere and anything—ideal.

They reach a wire perimeter fence, then follow it around until they reach a concealed access point where the heavy-duty wire mesh has been cut open and folded back temporarily to let them through. Clever. When the mesh is replaced, Matt notes, the fence appears completely intact. Again and again, he's impressed by what he's seeing (rather, what he's *not* seeing) here. These people have survived by thinking as much as they have by fighting.

The group pauses again a little way inside the barrier so the bodies they've been carrying can be disposed of. Matt and Darren are conscripted by a couple of the CDF fighters to help, and between them, they lug the corpses in another direction for a couple of hundred meters to a lake of some description. Judging from the stench, the water's stagnant, but that's no surprise given the state of what's left of the world. There's a layer of glistening, oily muck on the surface, coating flotsam and jetsam and bodies. The corpses they've brought down here with them are weighed down with rocks, then carried out into the murk and dumped. It's a well-hidden, partially submerged graveyard.

They return to the others and begin the long walk from the perimeter to the first of the low buildings Matt glimpsed through the trees. Whatever this place used to be, it's vast and well protected.

At the end of a stretch of track up ahead, there's a full-sized fighter plane mounted on a stand at an angle designed to make it look like it's taking off. Was this an RAF base? Matt has a vague recollection of there being a number of them scattered across this part of the Midlands and into East Anglia. Up ahead, there are hangars and other buildings arranged in formation. A long-silent runway cuts diagonally across the middle of the site, the remains of a burned-out plane crashed at one end with its nose scraping the ground and what's left of its blackened tail sticking up into the air.

There are no signs of life whatsoever. No light. No noise. The longer this goes on, the more concerned Matt becomes, again convincing himself there might be a more sinister ulterior motive behind this CDF faction's hospitality and helpfulness. He's followed this train of thought too many times before . . . what if these people intend using Matt's group for target practice or as decoys or to feed to Haters to keep the enemy placated and at a distance? What if they're cannibals? Nothing seems beyond the realms of possibility anymore. Just when you think this world can't get any worse, it usually does.

They use a door Matt didn't even see to enter a featureless building he thought they were walking past, and once they're inside, everything changes. There's movement in here where there was empty stillness before, dull light where everything else was dark. But even now, they're still not done walking. The group is led deep to the center of the complex, which is squirreled away along many interconnected corridors, hidden from outsiders by turn after turn, wall after wall, room after room. Despite the openness of this location, the people based here clearly confine themselves to this central section of the base, far from the fence and any obvious entrances. There are battery- and gas-powered lamps on the walls as well as candles and several burning torches, which give the place an almost medieval appearance.

Their long journey is finally over when they reach a large assembly room. All the windows have been boarded up. No light gets in, no light gets out. Aaron Rayner breathes an audible sigh of relief. "And relax. Made it. Got most of you here in one piece."

"And where exactly are we?" Darren asks, finding the confidence to speak again after hours of enforced silence. Aaron shines a flashlight across the room and illuminates a painted wooden sign over the door through which they've just entered.

"RAF Thornhill."

"Why are we here?" Kara asks.

"I'll answer that," a woman's voice replies from nearby, and she pushes through the crowd. She's average height, remarkably prim and proper, dressed in impeccably kept fatigues.

"Bloody hell," Matt says.

Jason turns around and glares at him. "What's up with you? You look like you've seen a ghost."

"I think I have."

The woman climbs up onto a chair, Aaron instinctively offering a hand to steady her. She clears her throat. "It's lovely to see you all. Welcome to RAF Thornhill, to our little sanctuary. My name's Estelle Bisseker. I'm the commanding officer here."

Matt's numb with surprise. He's sure she'll have long forgotten him, but he's thought about Estelle a lot since his encounters with the CDF in the city-camp. His interactions with her were brief, yet their ramifications have in one way or another defined virtually everything he's done since. His head fills with memories of their first encounter after he'd tracked Franklin through the camp, then he remembers the Hater hunts with Franklin and Jayce and how they led him to the group he helped escape. Then he recalls Franklin's death and the frantic escape from the city to the printing house. Jayce had told him Estelle had disappeared, and he'd put two and two together and come up with a murder or suicide or some other kind of grisly demise. Seems he was way off the mark. She'd been one step ahead of the game all along and had beat a hasty retreat before the shit had hit the fan. Matt had harbored concerns about Estelle from the outset, but seeing her today leaves him in no doubt she knows exactly what she's doing. It looks like it might make sense to stick with the CDF after all.

16

RAF Thornhill

His chance to speak to Estelle comes a short time later. The group has been fed and watered and billeted in another connected part of the base, and after being left for a couple of hours to rest and recuperate, they're gathered together in the mess hall to be briefed. He intercepts her as she walks past. "Remember me?"

She has a look on her face that is part confusion and part concern. Eventually, it gives way to surprise. "Good grief, yes, I remember. It's Matthew, isn't it?"

"That's right."

"You were the chap my Mr. Franklin was having so much trouble trying to get rid of."

"The one and the same."

"Where is he? Is he here? I owe him an explanation." She sounds hopeful and stands on tiptoes to look over his shoulder at the faces in the crowd.

"He didn't make it."

"Damn shame," she says, deflated. "And you . . . weren't you the hopeless romantic trying to get back to your sweetheart?"

"She didn't make it, either."

"I'm sorry to hear that. Genuinely I am."

He tries to steer the conversation into safer waters. "How long have you been here?"

"Probably since a little after you last saw me. The CDF already had a presence at this place, so when things started to turn nasty in the camp, we evacuated."

"We noticed."

"It was necessary. The city was lost the moment we built a wall around it. I tried to tell the higher-ups it was a tactical mistake that played into the hands of the enemy, but when the higher-ups turn out to *be* the enemy, what can you do? They had a hand in all of this, you know."

"I know."

She stares at Matt for longer than is comfortable. "So you did it again."

"Did what again?"

"Managed to stay alive against the odds. You're very resilient, aren't you? No matter what the world throws at you, you seem to always come up smelling of roses."

"Smelling of something."

"Quite. You did it, though. The city was destroyed by a nuclear strike, and yet here you are."

"Just about."

"Well, you look in much better shape than most."

"Appearances can be deceptive . . ."

Another soldier in fatigues taps Estelle on the shoulder and says something Matt can't quite make out about. Estelle nods. "Thank you, Jessica," she says. "Right, everyone's here. Take a seat, Matthew, and let me bring you up to speed."

There must be more than a hundred people in the mess hall, but all eyes are on Estelle, who's front and center. Lighting in here is sparse by necessity, because if even the faintest chink of brightness is seen from outside by one of *them*, everything could be compromised. The fragility of this place is not lost on anyone. People talk in hushed whispers all the time, making as little noise as they can. Even now, the silence in the room means there's no need for Estelle to raise her voice. Everyone can hear her.

"Let me start by saying how pleased we are to have so many new faces here today. We'd all but given up on finding survivors anywhere near the city. We'd almost stopped looking. It must be the best part of a month since we went back out that way. You're very fortunate we chose this week for Aaron and his team to make one last scavenging trip to the airport.

"I understand from Darren that you've been out of the loop since the camp fell, so allow me to bring you up to date on the current state of the nation." She pauses as if it's an effort to recall and repeat. "London was the first to fall. It was inevitable. Only to be expected when you've about a tenth of the population of the country crammed into a relatively small space, all doing their best to try to kill each other. Two bombs, apparently, about a week before the rest. Then, as well as your home, we also lost Leeds or Manchester—possibly both, Cardiff, Portsmouth, Edinburgh and Glasgow, Liverpool, we think . . . those are the strikes we're reasonably certain about, but it's all academic, really. Half that number of nukes would probably have been enough to cause catastrophic environmental damage."

It's hard to comprehend the scale. The enormity of the devastation is humbling. "So who pushed the button?" someone in the crowd asks.

"Another excellent but equally academic question. Ultimately, it doesn't really matter. There have been conflicting reports. Best guess is that they were all fired from the same sub somewhere in the North Sea, but we have no way of knowing who actually had their finger on the trigger."

"You get reports?" Darren says. "There are other groups left like this?"

"We had some radio contact for a while, but we've heard nothing from anyone else since a couple of weeks after the bombs."

She waits a moment for the news to sink in. It's a lot for the new arrivals to absorb.

"The upshot of all of this," she continues, "is that we're operating on the assumption we're no longer a faction of the CDF but that we are the CDF in its entirety. We're operating out of two locations—RAF Thornhill, which is where we are currently, and a farther outpost some twenty miles east of here, just outside what's left of Cambridge. We're in the process of transferring our entire operations over there. We'll be leaving here in the next few weeks. There are somewhere in the region of two hundred soldiers based at the outpost, well armed and well equipped and supported by civilians."

"Supporting them?" Matt asks. "Supporting them doing what?"

"What do you think?" a lone voice answers from across the room. "More fucking fighting."

Estelle shakes her head. "It's more than that, much more. Think about what I just told you and how much of the country has been destroyed. In my office, there's a map with the potential blast zones marked out if you'd care to look, but it doesn't take a genius to understand the implications of what's happened here. We're in a hell of a tight spot. We're not in good shape, none of us. Even those of you who've just arrived and who've been fortunate to spend much of the last couple of months underground—and yes, I do consider you fortunate—will already have seen enough to realize that we're just about dead on our feet.

"Darren and I had a brief conversation earlier, and I think it's fair to say we're of a similar mind-set. We're all about the long game. What's left of the enemy will inevitably burn itself out before long, and we'll be there to pick up the pieces when the infighting's over."

Darren turns around and addresses familiar faces in the crowd. "Remember what we talked about when we were waiting in the hideout? About waiting for the war to be over so we can pick up the pieces and start again? I believe we're in a place to be able to do that, and to do it with the support of the CDF."

Matt gets up and goes to leave.

"Where are you going, Matthew?" Estelle asks.

"To get some sleep. I've heard enough for one day."

Darren's appalled. "You can't just turn your back on all of this. This is important."

"No offense, Darren, but it isn't, and I can."

He tries to get through, but the room is packed, and picking his way between the bodies takes longer than he'd like. Time enough for Estelle to start on him again.

"Don't walk away just yet, Matthew. There's a lot you still haven't heard."

"That's what I'm worried about."

"Give me a few more minutes of your time, please."

His way through is blocked, and the decision's made for him. He turns around and leans against the wall, its solidity and coolness oddly comforting. "Go on."

"Back to the map of the country I was alluding to," Estelle continues. "All those cities I reeled off a minute ago, they're all uninhabitable. More than that, the contamination from fallout has most likely rendered much of the rest of our little island uninhabitable. Anyone with even the most basic grasp of geography can work out the potential scale of the damage and the implications for what's left of us. We could stay here, but our feeling is that we're too close to the center of the country and, therefore, the effects of the bombs that hit to the north, south, and west. Given what's happened, we believe our best option, probably our only option, is to head east."

"Won't the other side come to the same conclusion?" Kara asks.

"Almost certainly," Estelle agrees. "That's why we're taking our time and carefully coordinating our next move. You see, the Haters are by their very nature an uncoordinated mob, and the bombs have increased that lack of coordination. We're exploiting that."

"How?"

"By working as a single cohesive unit and strengthening the Cambridge outpost. Work had already begun to fortify the site long before the bombs were dropped."

Aaron clears his throat, then speaks. "Honestly, you've seen nothing like this place. It's so well hidden and well defended, the enemy don't even realize when they've strayed onto our turf until it's too late. It's like a black hole, sucking them in. We've killed loads of them."

"But there are thousands more out there," Matt says. "Tens of thousands, probably."

"And we'll hold our ground until we've dealt with every last one of them," Estelle immediately replies.

"You have a habit of making very difficult things sound remarkably straightforward."

"Do I? Or is it just that the things I'm talking about actually are straightforward? That remains to be seen."

"And what happens when things get tough this time, Estelle? When we were back in the city, you just upped and left."

"I didn't just walk away," she replies, the authoritative tone suddenly stripped from her voice and replaced with more than a tinge of anger. "I should explain to those who aren't aware, Matthew and I have crossed paths previously. But don't you get it, Matthew? I didn't run away, I came here to get this place ready and to coordinate the Cambridge outpost. And if I hadn't done that, then when you were forced out of hiding and into trouble today, you'd have been killed."

"Sure. You're right. Thanks for everything," he says, and he tries again to leave.

The crowd is getting restless, the level of noise becoming uncomfortably loud. Darren gestures for them to simmer down. "Don't listen to him," he says, pointing at Matt, "listen to Estelle. Tell them what happens next, Estelle."

"As I said, we'll move everything to the outpost, then we'll push on from Cambridge. We'll create a new forward position, and the process will start again, then again and again until we've found ourselves somewhere safe and defendable. It's going to be hard, and not all of us will make it, but I believe we can do it. This will be our last battle, I'm sure of it, but if ever there was something worth fighting for, it's us."

"I've always had my concerns about him. He's disruptive. I worry about the effect he'll have on everyone else," Estelle says, talking to Darren, Jason, and Aaron later over mugs of coffee in the relatively civilized confines of her small private office. "We need people to work together. We can't afford for there to be divisions in the group. It's divisions that caused all of this in the first place, remember?"

"I'll keep him under control," Darren says. "He's stubborn, and he's a loner. I share your concerns, though. My worry is that people will start to listen. You're offering them a future here, but it's going to take a lot of effort and sacrifice. I don't want them seeing him and trying to take the easy way out."

"What about that girl? You said they're close. Can she help?" Aaron asks.

"Kara? Yeah. I don't know what she sees in him. She's pretty smart otherwise."

"We should have a word with her. See if we can't get her to talk some sense into him."

"What do you think?" Estelle asks Jason. He's not listening at first, distracted by the fact he's where he is, drinking coffee like the end of the world never happened, and also by the map on the wall showing the nukes. It brings everything into sharp focus, seeing how much of the country has been reduced to ash.

"Come on, Jason, keep up," Darren says, annoyed. "You've known Matt for longer than the rest of us. What do you think?"

"He's been through a lot."

"We all have."

"If you want my honest opinion, I think the guy is struggling. His missus was a bag of nerves, and with hindsight, I reckon much of that was down to him. He resents the rest of us. I think he's a liability."

17

The CDF Outpost Near Cambridge

It's just after dawn, and the countryside is alive with movement. This is the largest and most sustained Hater incursion in weeks. The numbers are relatively insignificant in the scheme of things, but every man and woman in the trenches, every spotter, every member of the support crew, everyone from the youngest civilian right up the chain of command to Chappell himself is concerned that this is something new. Before today, there's been no question that the enemy fighters who've ended up here have done so by chance; wrong place, wrong time. This feels different. These Haters arrived here in a pack. Seventeen of them at least. Their numbers are concerning.

The corpses are clogging up the trenches.

Now that the first of them have been dealt with, on the front line, they're getting ready for the next wave. The enemy didn't expect a fight here; that much is clear. The camouflage covering the outpost did its job. It was only when a couple of them reached the trench and were killed that the others realized there were Unchanged here. The noise of their deaths rang out like an alarm across the empty fields, and rather than eliciting concern for their fallen brethren, the sounds of Hater killings instead filled the others with excitement, all of them desperate to fight again.

The spotter can see them homing in on the area where the others disappeared and were dealt with, and from her elevated position, she can also see the soldiers in the trench trying to shift the dead Haters so they have room to fight. She signals for support.

Moira Kay, Chappell's second in command, is down at ground level, coordinating the troops. There's a backlog of bodies to be shifted. She grabs a Hater kid's feet and drags him away like he's a sack of coal. The back of his head cracks repeatedly as it bounces along the uneven ground, and he groans with pain. *Shit*. He's still alive. He stirs, but she knows he's too far gone to be any threat. His useless right arm, bones shattered, trails through the mud. Blood oozes from stab wounds. Detestable fucking thing. He'll soon be dead.

Dean and Parker are on pit duty. "Might have known it would be you two causing a backlog," Moira says as she dumps the Hater. "Get a move on, and get these bodies dealt with."

"Could do with some more hands; there's only us and Joseph working," Parker says.

"I'll see what I can do."

Moira goes to find more civilians she can volunteer, but stops and doubles back on herself first. She stamps her boot down on the almost-dead Hater's unprotected face to help speed up his demise.

"What did she want?" Joseph asks, appearing from behind a huge yellow-painted digger.

"Just letting us know we're not working hard enough," Parker tells him. "She wants to try doing this job."

"At least she gets her hands dirty," Dean says. "More than that Chappell bloke. He just stands up on his platform watching everyone else getting the shit kicked out of them."

A distinctive rain-soaked figure runs over to the pit. It's Peter Sutton. "Moira told me to—" he starts to say, then he slips in the mud and ends up on his backside next to the dead Hater. For a second, all he can do is look down into the mass of tangled limbs below him: hollowed-out faces, collapsed rib cages, punctured lungs, gashes and gouges in paper-thin flesh that allow the insides to spill out, and the stench . . . Jesus Christ, the stench of all that death and decay. He salivates, sure he's about to throw up . . . He almost goes over the edge, but Joseph yanks him back.

"Pull yourself together, man."

"Sorry," Peter says, picking himself up.

"We can't risk any weak links in the chain here."

"I know. I get it."

"You do appreciate the seriousness of what's happening here, don't you? If we give those monsters out there any room to maneuver, they'll be all over us. Show them the slightest sign of weakness and they'll kill the damn lot of us. You understand me?"

"I understand," Peter says.

Joseph strips anything of value from the Hater corpse. The boy had a little food in his pocket and an improvised blade—nothing much, but everything counts these days. He hands it all to Dean, who climbs up into the cab of the nearby digger and stashes it away.

Peter's watching all of this. He looks away as soon as he realizes Joseph's now watching him. "You stockpiling?" he asks. "Stashing stuff away for a rainy day?"

"There's nothing but rainy days now, in case you hadn't noticed," Parker says. "Keep your fucking nose out."

"I won't say a word."

"Good," Joseph tells him, leaning in close. "You do and you'll be next in the pit."

"Got it. I don't want any trouble."

Peter pushes the body closer to the edge. He pauses and looks into the dead kid's face. His eyes are filled with an intolerable mix of pain and hate. He has a boot mark across his cheek and a mouthful of broken teeth, courtesy of Moira. "Like the look of him, do you?" Parker goads. Peter shakes his head and shoves the body over. He stands up and wipes mud and blood from his hands. He turns around to go back to the trench for more, but Parker and Joseph are blocking his way.

"Don't give me any reason to have to report you to Chappell," Joseph warns.

"You're the ones siphoning off supplies."

"Be careful, friend."

"I won't say anything. Why would I? Look, I might be talking out of turn here, but if you're planning something, then—"

Parker squares up to him. "If we were planning something—which we're not—then it's none of your fucking business. Understand?"

"I get it. It's just that—"

"It's none of your fucking business," Parker says again.

"We're all too quick to jump to conclusions these days," Joseph tells him. "Whatever you're thinking, I guarantee you're wrong."

Peter puts his hands up in submission. "I won't say anything, I swear. I don't want any trouble." He goes to walk away, then stops. "Anything's got to be better than this. Way things are going, I think we're all going to end up fighting before long. There's got to be an alternative, and if you think you've found it, then you've got my support. I won't do anything to get in the way."

"Glad to hear it."

"In fact, I'd like to help. Things are never as black and white as they seem, and—"

"Black and white implies an option, Peter, a choice. None of us have any choices right now."

"I agree. Like I said, the chiefs are pushing us toward the edge of a cliff."

"That's right, and all we're trying to do is cushion the landing when we fall."

"I can help. Seriously."

"Right now, the only thing you need to do is keep your nose out and your mouth shut, okay?"

"Okay."

Parker pushes him away. "Good. Now piss off and help us get the rest of those bodies over here."

They watch him walk away, shoulders stooped.

"Do you think he'll talk?" Parker asks.

"Doubt it. What would he say? We'll move the stuff when we're done so they won't find any evidence. And even if he does talk, so what? The CDF isn't going to do anything about it. We're a valuable resource, don't forget. They can't afford to lose manpower."

"I just don't trust him."

"Who really trusts anyone these days?"

18

Approaching Fordham

A silver Audi races across the waterlogged Cambridgeshire countryside along otherwise silent roads, heading for what's left of a filling station near Fordham. The approaching engine noise alone is enough to strike fear into the hearts of the foot soldiers who've been stationed out here. This place is a prized asset—another precious fuel stockpile—and it's one that only a fool would risk trying to steal from. The immobilized, half-full tanker that straddles the forecourt, along with everything else here and for miles around in every direction, belongs to Johannson.

Pinchy spends a lot of time out here, coordinating looting trips and keeping an eye on the fighters keeping an eye on the fuel. He knows the area better than most. He'd spent a lot of time around these parts before the war began, and his knowledge is one of the reasons he's been able to find favor with Johannson. Now, while his men are trying to hide their nerves and look busy before Queen Bitch turns up, he's cool as a fucking cucumber, leaning against the side of the dirt-streaked tanker, chewing a strip of gum he found in a corpse's jacket.

The engine noise increases rapidly as the car comes into view. Johannson brings the Audi to a screeching halt, then marches up to Pinchy, looking absolutely fucking furious. "Well?" she demands. "You got anything for me, or have you just been standing there chewing gum all frigging day?"

Pinchy's unfazed. Or if he is fazed, he's doing a damn good job of hiding it. "I told you, boss, I found something."

"What?"

He gestures for her to follow him. The filling station is just off a traffic roundabout. There's a footbridge spanning the road on the opposite exit. Pinchy leads her up a grassy bank and up onto the bridge. The wind's bracing up here, and the dirty rain's like nails, but if it's bothering either of them, they're not letting it show.

"What am I looking at?"

"I've been keeping a track of people's movements like you asked," Pinchy explains.

"And?"

"And the last few times we sent people out, the ones we sent in that direction are the ones who've disappeared."

"How many?"

"Almost thirty have gone that way over the last couple of days."

"And how many have come back?"

"Eight, so far."

"Who's missing?"

"No one special. That girl with the skinhead and big tits."

Johannson looks at him. "That's the best description you can come up with?"

He shrugs. "What can I say? She has a skinhead and big tits. And now she's missing."

"Who else?"

"The university lecturer guy."

"Porterhouse?"

"I told you, boss, I don't know their names."

"Freaky blue eyes. Had a chunk missing from one of his ears."

"That's him. Yeah, he was here."

"He was a good fighter. Smart bloke. He's not come back?"

"Nope."

"Have I got a problem here, Pinchy?"

"I think we might have, but I don't want to go jumping the gun."

"Think they got a better offer?"

"Maybe. Who in their right mind's going to risk pissing you off, though? You're on the fucking ascendancy, boss. People know they can't risk walking away from you, 'cause before long, all this will be yours. Better to stay on your side, I reckon."

"True."

"Look, ultimately, it don't matter what happened to them. Don't matter if it's another boss, a trap, radiation, even a bunch of Unchanged that's got lucky; we can deal with them, can't we?"

"Damn right. I can't afford to take any chances, though. If there's a problem brewing, we need to deal with it. *I* need to deal with it."

"You're right, and that's why I wanted you to come here. And it's not just about this fight. It's the next one, too, and the one after that and the one after that. We need to show people who's boss, boss."

"Exactly."

"We need to go on the offensive. Get the upper hand."

"And you reckon trouble's down that road?"

"I'd put money on it. Given the timing and who we've lost, I'd say there's something worth checking out about ten or twenty miles in that direction."

"Good work. Get back to base and get things moving. Keep on top of this, Pinchy. Don't let me down."

"I wouldn't dare," he tells her.

She walks back from the bridge to the filling station, Pinchy following close behind. There's a pile of supplies gathered from today's looting trips. She inspects the stash—*her* stash—then helps herself to a bottle of beer. "This stuff okay?"

"As far as we can tell," one of her fighters tells her. She twists the cap off the bottle, sniffs, then drains it.

"Get it loaded into my car," she orders, and six men immediately get to work. She watches intently, arms folded. Then something catches her eye. "You," she barks, and all six of them freeze. They slowly turn to face her, each of them hoping they're not the poor bastard she's interested in.

One guy remains rooted to the spot, two trays of canned food in his arms. He looks around and double-checks, trying to hide his nerves. This time last year, he was working on a construction site, going home at night to his Unchanged wife and their kid (both of whom he killed, thank god). The advent of the Hate was a blessed relief, but all the confidence and fury he used to feel when he was slaughtering Unchanged back then has evaporated. Johannson's gaze makes him meek and mild and completely unremarkable again.

"Me?"

"Yes, you. Come here."

He does as he's told, not even stopping to put down what he's carrying.

"You think you can steal from me?"

"No, boss."

"What's your name?"

"Richard. Richard Morris."

"And are you fucking stupid, Richard?"

"No."

Other than the wind, the forecourt is silent. All eyes on Richard.

"You know how angry I get when people take stuff from me, don't you?" She waits. He nods. "All these goodies you've been collecting, they're like cash these days. You collect for me, I'll see you're looked after."

"I know. We all know."

"Good. Find much out there today?"

"Got most of this from a truck on the road. It had overturned. Found it in a ditch."

"Nice haul. You do understand the importance of what I'm saying, though, don't you? We need to keep safe and strong, all of us, and we can only do that if we play by my rules. Don't think that just because we've seen the last of the Unchanged, all our battles are done."

"No one thinks that," Pinchy says from just behind her. "We're all behind you here."

"Good to hear it. Right, get on and get yourselves back to base. That's enough for one day."

Richard slumps with relief. He continues with his work, arms heavy with the weight of the stuff he's still carrying. He stops when she calls out to him again.

"What's that in your jacket pocket, Richard?"

His legs turn to jelly for the second time in as many minutes. Then he slowly, reluctantly, turns around. Come clean and fess up? Act dumb? Neither option feels like the right one.

She moves closer and pulls a tin of cat food from his outer pocket. Richard curses himself. Should have buried it and come back for it later like last time.

"What's this?"

"Cat food, boss."

"I can see that. What's it doing in your pocket?"

He improvises, nods at the tray in his arms. "Dropped it. Was carrying it over with all the rest of this."

"And it fell into your pocket?"

"No . . . I mean . . ."

"Who does this belong to?"

"You," he answers without hesitation.

"You were going to steal it, weren't you?"

He tries to bluff his way out of trouble, but there's no point. Honesty is the best policy, his dad used to say. But his dad never had to deal with a bitch like Johannson. "I'm sorry. I'm just so fucking hungry."

"I get that," she says, taking Richard and all the others frozen watching by surprise. "Times are hard. I understand. We're all under pressure."

"I'm really sorry. Won't happen again."

"I'll let you have this one," she says.

"Thanks, boss."

She smashes the tin into his face with vicious force. He crumbles, out cold, but she's not done. She drops down and thumps the base of the tin into his face repeatedly, again and again until there's nothing but blood and gristle. Then she picks herself up, throws the can onto the pile, and wipes her bloodied hands on the back of her trousers. She looks around at the rest of them; they are silent, eyes wide. "Work with me and I'll see you're okay. Steal from me, I'll kill you."

With that, she's gone. She gets back behind the wheel of the Audi and waits for the rest of their scavenged supplies to be loaded up, then drives back toward Cambridge.

The silence when the sound of her car's exhaust finally fades is deafening.

"You heard the lady," Pinchy says.

"She ain't no lady," one of the other blokes jokes.

"She's more of a man than you," another one says.

"Stop pissing about and get yourselves back to base," Pinchy orders. "Don't make me have to report any of you pricks. You've seen how she deals with people who don't play ball."

There's no arguing. As the rest of his men get into their vehicles and head home, Pinchy crouches down and strips anything of use from dead Richard's pockets. He takes his jacket, belt, and boots also. No sense letting them going to waste.

He stands over the body and waits until the others are all out of view, then he waits longer still. When he's absolutely certain he's on his own and he's not going to be seen, he hides his truck around the back of the filling station. They sold secondhand cars from a lot next to this garage. Pinchy and his men have managed to get several of them started over time, but he'd told them this particular Citroën was a write-off, and they'd believed him. He takes the keys from his pocket, and after a couple of misfires, the engine spits into life.

Pinchy's reached a metaphorical crossroads. North of here in Cambridge is Johannson and the rest of her pack. To the south, a slow, creeping death in the radioactive ruins of the capital awaits anyone dumb enough to travel that road. To the west, more radiation and whatever (whoever) is killing (or co-opting) Johannson's fighters.

He puts his foot down and drives east.

19

RAF Thornhill

Matt jumps out of his skin when Kara touches him on the shoulder. "Fuck's sake," he hisses at her. "What the hell are you doing?"

"Calm down, Matt. You were asleep."

"I wasn't. I closed my eyes for half a second, that's all."

"Bullshit. You've been asleep for over an hour. I've been watching you."

"Why? What's wrong with you?"

"Nothing's wrong with me. It's you who's got the problem. You are allowed to go to sleep, you know. This is the first time in months we've not been buried underground or on the run. This is the first time we've been able to breathe."

"Yeah, and it doesn't feel right."

"It's going to take some getting used to, that's for sure."

Matt stands up and stretches his back as he looks around the mess hall. His body aches. He feels double his age, and he wonders how much of it is down to the fact he fell asleep facedown on a table, and how much is a combination of his exhaustion and exposure to the pollution outside. "Where's everyone else?" he asks. There are more than a few people missing.

"Sleeping in beds like normal people. Some of them are talking to Estelle and Aaron."

"Who?"

"Estelle, remember? You told me you knew her."

"No, who's talking to her?"

"Darren and Jason, I think. Does it matter? I'll leave the suckers like them to jostle for position. Anyway, you should see this place. There's so much here. It's a massive site. I heard someone say there's about half a kilometer of space all around the outside, so it looks empty from a distance. We're so well hidden here, and there's a decent amount of food and weapons . . ."

"Then why leave?"

"You heard what Estelle said earlier."

"Yeah, I heard."

"Apparently, there are hundreds more at the outpost."

"Like I said, I heard."

"You don't sound very enthusiastic."

"You're picking up on that, are you?"

"I'm just looking forward to having something to do. They've asked me to help out in the infirmary tomorrow."

"Cool."

"You should come and help."

"Maybe."

She knows he won't.

Kara's quiet for a couple of minutes, but it doesn't last.

"Don't you ever stop?" Matt asks when she pipes up again.

"It's the novelty of being about to talk out loud. Didn't realize how much I missed making a noise."

"Yeah, well, don't be too loud."

"Killjoy." She tries to bite her tongue again, but she's seen and heard so much since they arrived here. "I was talking to Aaron about their outpost. Jesus, Matt, it sounds incredible. They've got loads of gear."

"What kind of gear?"

"Military stuff. Tanks, trucks, ammo . . . couple of helicopters, apparently."

"Yes, but have they got any pilots?"

"That's not the point."

"It is if you want to fly anywhere."

"It's all hidden like this place," she continues, her enthusiasm not dampened in the slightest. "There was some massive roadworks scheme going on there. Loads of diggers and other machinery."

"That they won't be able to use unless they fit the exhausts with silencers."

She ignores him. "Aaron was telling me how they've been covering their tracks. There are false flags and dummy traps all the way from here."

"How many Hater attacks have you actually seen up close, Kara?"

"Why?"

"Just answer the question."

She hesitates. "Plenty since we left the bunker."

"They don't count. They were weak. Sick. I'm talking about before the bunker. Before the camp."

"Both my dad and my boyfriend tried to kill me," she says, remembering things she's since done her best to try to forget. "I ran away from the house and got picked up by the army. They took me to the camp."

"That's what I'm getting at. See, I think a lot of you have been sheltered. Most of you are underestimating what those nasty bastards out there are truly capable of because you've been spared the worst of it. I spent weeks on foot trying to get home, then I ended up working outside the camp again after I'd got back. I've seen a lot, more than most. I know there's no reasoning with a Hater. Some are smarter than others and can keep the Hate swallowed down, but most won't stop until you're dead."

"I know that, but—"

"Do you? Do you really? Because if you did, I think you'd be thinking along the same lines as I am. This place is probably as good as it's going to get, and thinking you'll be able to live anywhere out in the open while there's even one Hater still alive is a mistake."

"You might be wrong."

"I'm not. And don't forget, the rules are you only get to make one mistake these days."

"Aaron was talking about us heading for remote areas eventually."

"And you don't think the other side won't have had the same idea? It's not going to happen, Kara. You need to set your expectations low and keep them there. Thing I've learned from all of this is that people today are still as naïve and unrealistic as they've always been. Don't let yourself get carried away."

"So what's the alternative? Just wave a white flag in the air and wait for them to find us?"

"No, the alternative is we keep our heads down for as long as we can, and we hope and pray the Haters are all gone before we have to put our heads above the parapet again. All the guns and the tanks and whatever else this lot claim to have . . . believe me, in the end, it'll all count for nothing."

She leans back in her seat. Frustrated. Upset.

"I wish you wouldn't be so bloody negative, Matt. Why do you have to be so negative?"

He thinks for a second before making an admission. "Because I care about you. I don't want to see you get hurt."

20

Approaching Bury St. Edmunds

Pinchy drives through the all-consuming evening gloom, navigating from memory. He knows how much he has at stake here, how he's walking the finest of fine lines. If Johannson finds out what he's up to, she'll kill him, but for now, she's distracted thinking about what he told her earlier, and her eyes are off the ball. He also knows that he doesn't have any choice; he has to do this. Getting on the wrong side of Johannson is a frightening prospect, but the alternatives are potentially far worse.

The roads feel endless out here, but they're strewn with wreckage and no longer maintained. There are more obstructions and collisions to avoid with every passing mile. Potholes like craters appear without warning. At times, he has to drive completely off-road. Other times, the road's the only clear route through the floodplains. Occasionally, he loses sight of the tarmac strip in the water altogether and has to crawl forward at half speed.

He always used to think of this country as being small. He could get just about anywhere from where he used to live on the south coast near Brighton. Take the train into London, then take another train anywhere else. Catch a flight. Get on the highway and drive wherever . . . As the miles disappear tonight, his mind drifts back to his former life: the tattoo and piercing shop he'd owned and run, his clients and friends, the laughs they'd had. He remembers a time when skin was a canvas to work on, not something to slash and slice. Turned out to be useful, though, all of that. All the health and safety bullshit he'd had to abide by and the qualifications he'd had to get to be able to split tongues and insert subdermal implants . . . he'd probably have died early on from a nasty wound he'd picked up in a knife fight, but his knowledge of antiseptics and his ability to self-sew his own torn flesh back together saw him through. He glances at himself in the mirror. *You're a mean-looking motherfucker,* he thinks. The new scars have added to the look. His ink and piercings and the gold caps on his teeth were often derided in the old world, but now they're like medals, badges of honor. Everyone else looks the same: gray and shabby, with matted hair and dirt-streaked skin. He's a class apart.

He slams his foot on the brake and brings the car to a juddering halt just centimeters short of the edge of a hole that looks big enough to swallow the Citroën whole.

Need to concentrate. Need to focus. Can't fuck this up.

He drives around the edge of the chasm, then accelerates again. *Am I still going the right way?*

That's the problem with this neck of the woods: everywhere is so far from everywhere else that a single wrong turn can have massive ramifications. It's a relief when the distinctive shape of the sugar beet factory silos at Bury St. Edmunds appear up ahead—long-silenced chimney stacks positioned on the outskirts of what used to be a historic market town. He drives through the open security barriers like they'd told him and pulls up behind the main building.

He kills the engine.

And waits.

And he waits.

Couldn't they have arranged this meeting in a pub? He'd passed a nice-looking place a few miles back. Fuck, what he'd give for a few hours in a pub again. Just one night, that'd be enough. The drink, the noise, the company . . . he always forgets how much he misses the old world until he catches a glimpse of it again. He sinks back in his seat and tries to remember the tastes, the sounds, and the smells. He closes his eyes and wonders if things will ever be like that again.

He sits up with a start when the car door is yanked open. He's dragged out onto the tarmac, but he's quicker than they're expecting, and he immediately has the knife he keeps down the inside of his boot drawn, ready to defend himself. He feels the tip of someone else's blade sticking into his neck, a pinprick threatening to become a scythe.

"You're the best they've got?" a voice says in his ear. "Fuck me."

Pinchy's mad at himself for taking his eye off the ball. He let his guard down. He slumps his shoulders and feigns submission, then elbows his attacker in the gut and reverses positions, shoving him back against the car.

He's quick, but not quick enough.

When he looks back over his shoulder, he sees there are more than ten other fighters surrounding him, all tooled up and ready to smash the shit out of his curiously decorated skull if he makes a wrong move.

"Where's Thacker?" he asks, not letting go of the man he now has in a neck hold.

"Thacker doesn't come to you, pal; you go to Thacker."

"Then take me to him."

"And why would he want to waste his time on an amateur like you?"

"Because I can get him to Johannson."

"You think he needs your help?"

"No, from what I've heard about Thacker, I think he'll take

whatever the fuck he wants, but it's people that leaders need. Best to avoid a civil war if we can, don't you think? You can spend a fucking age trying to find Johannson and get close, or I can bypass all that and take you straight to her."

They tell him nothing and keep him waiting, but Pinchy knows better than to complain. He needs to stay cool and stay strong, to hold his nerve. It's all bravado and posturing, he reckons, and he grips the sides of his seat as the van he's being driven in swerves around another corner. It's been more than an hour now. They must be getting close. It's all mind games, throwing him in the back of this van. They're trying to break him, trying to work out if he's as smart as he says he is.

There are no obvious territorial markers these days; borders are where the hell you want them to be, and they shift with circumstance. Pinchy first heard about Thacker while he was out scouting for Johannson and he came across a dying man. He'd found the poor fucker strung up and left to die, and it had been abundantly clear that this was no random kill. The guy had been left crucified and bleeding out as a warning to others to stay away. He told Pinchy as much with what proved to be his dying breath. Most people would have taken heed, but Pinchy doesn't think like most people. Pinchy's different. He pressed on and tracked down the perpetrators. He worked out where they were based and what they were planning. He joined their ranks and anonymously observed (no mean feat when your face is covered in metal and ink), and it didn't take him long to realize that Thacker's empire is considerably larger than Johannson's. Pinchy immediately knew what he had to do to stay alive and secure his position near the top of the food chain.

It all feels a bit precarious now, though, and when the van

stops without warning and he's thrown forward, he starts to feel dangerously exposed. He cricks his neck from side to side and shakes himself down like a heavyweight boxer waiting in the corner of the ring, ready to come out fighting.

Stay calm.

Stay focused.

Show them they can't push you around.

The back of the van opens, and he climbs out into a well-lit, warehouse-like space. He tries to keep his cool and show them he's as hard as fucking nails, but his legs feel like jelly because he's just stepped out into the middle of a crowd of what feels like hundreds. All he sees is faces, and they're all looking back at him like he's shit on the bottom of their shoes.

A gap opens up between two lines of fighters. Pinchy steels himself and marches up to a single figure standing directly in front of him. He's a mean-looking bastard, hard as nails. Jesus, Thacker is everything Pinchy was led to believe and more besides. Today, Pinchy knows that more than ever, first impressions count. They're eye to eye now. Uncomfortably close. Neither man giving ground.

"I've got information that could be useful to you," Pinchy says. "Looks like you're well organized, but I can get you access to many more people."

"And who says I want more people?"

The reply comes from the opposite end of the warehouse, back by the van. Pinchy spins around, confused, and watches as an average-looking guy steps away from the rest of the crowd. He holds his chin in his hands and looks Pinchy up and down.

"You Thacker?"

"Yes. You must be Mr. Pinch, I presume."

"Yeah."

"Thought as much. I must say, so far I'm not particularly impressed with what I'm seeing. You come in here and start making all kinds of assumptions about what I need and what I don't need, about what a good leader looks like."

"But I—"

"Do yourself a favor, sunshine, and shut your mouth. Don't go digging yourself a hole any deeper than the one you're already standing in. Understand?"

Pinchy's furious. His instinct says, *Fight,* but his brain's saying, *If you show even the slightest sign of hostility, this lot will take you down.* It's hard, almost too hard, but he does what he's told. He bites his lip, then runs the fork of his split tongue over his gold-capped teeth.

Thacker walks up to him and studies him intently. "What's with all this?" he asks, gesturing at his face. "All the metalwork and tattoos? It's all a bit *Mad Max,* don't you think? A bit cliched."

Pinchy puffs his chest out, defiant. "It's from before. I was a body artist. A piercer."

"You put earrings in?" Thacker taunts.

"Mock me all you like, it doesn't bother me. This is who I am. Always has been. I haven't changed."

"Now that's not true, is it? We've all changed. No one's the same as they were before all this began."

"This joker's not worth the risk," the fighter Pinchy originally squared up to says.

"There's no risk, Llewellyn," Thacker replies.

"Do we really need him?"

"Probably not, but having him around will make things easier. You can give us the full spec on Mrs. Johannson's place, can't you, Mr. Pinch?"

"I'll tell you whatever you need to know."

"Good to hear. How many people does she currently have?"

"Around five hundred."

"You can't be more precise?"

"No. They come and go."

Thacker shakes his head and looks past Pinchy to talk to his prizefighter again. "You see, this is why this is going to be so easy. It's like we'd thought: she's completely disorganized. Bit of a brute, by all accounts."

"All the more reason to just walk in there and take the place, don't you think? Show her who's boss."

Another man interjects. He appears from deeper in the crowd. Long-haired, ice-cool, no nerves. "That'd be a mistake."

Llewellyn's not impressed. "Give me a break."

"Let Hinchcliffe speak," Thacker orders.

Hinchcliffe strides forward and puts his arm around Pinchy's shoulder. Pinchy shrugs him off, but Hinchcliffe's unperturbed. "You're right, of course, Llewellyn; there's nothing stopping us marching in there with Mr. Pinch's help and taking over, but if we go there first and introduce ourselves, tell Johannson how the land lies, and *then* turn her over, we'll save ourselves a lot of unnecessary killing. Half the effort, twice the result."

Llewellyn's not impressed. "The world's changed, mate, in case you hadn't noticed."

"Yeah, it has. But I think you've got your focus all wrong, as usual. We're not all savages. Not yet."

Llewellyn and Hinchcliffe look like they're about to come to blows. Thacker positions himself between the two of them, smaller physically but matching them both in stature. He keeps them separated, then turns back to face Pinchy. "What do *you* think?"

"I think he's right," he answers, pointing at Hinchcliffe.

"Why? You wouldn't just be telling us what you think we want to hear, would you? Talk us through your logic."

Pinchy swallows hard. "It makes sense. Go charging into Johannson's base with an army and she'll slam the door in your face. Talk to her, though, and you'll be through that door before she realizes what's going on. I'll get you close. She listens to me."

"Yeah, but you're about to screw her over. She obviously can't trust you, so why should I?" Thacker asks.

"Good question. Look, Thacker, I'll be honest with you . . . I've done my homework, and I've heard about the kind of resources you've got at your disposal. I know you're going to deal with Johannson, and I want to be on the right side when it happens. She's just a nasty bitch, nowhere near your league. From what I've heard, once you've taken over her patch, you'll control most of what's left of the east of the country, and as we reckon everywhere else is dead, that puts you in charge. You'll have a massive foothold and plenty of resources to keep on taking. I swear, I've not seen anyone else in your league. Plus, it'll unsettle the rest of her people, won't it? Make them realize she's not all-powerful."

Thacker paces the room, thinking carefully. "Okay." He looks over at Llewellyn. "You go with him. Make contact with Johannson. See what's what."

"Sure thing."

"I should go," Hinchcliffe says. "No offense, Llewellyn, but you're not much of a diplomat."

"Fuck you," Llewellyn says, and he clears his throat and spits at his rival's feet.

"He has a point," Thacker says.

"Come on, boss," Llewellyn protests.

"No, let's let Mr. Hinchcliffe have this one and see how he gets on. I know how loyal you are, Llewellyn, but Hinchcliffe hasn't had a chance to prove himself yet. You've talked the talk, H; now it's time to show us how good you really are."

"I won't let you down," Hinchcliffe says, grinning broadly, pushing Pinchy back toward the van.

Pinchy digs his heels in. "Wait. There's something else."

Thacker gestures for Hinchcliffe to stop. "Go on."

"Johannson's got a problem."

"Other than me? What's that?"

"There's someone else out there, hiding in the dead lands. She's lost a couple of dozen people to them in the last week alone."

"And you didn't think to tell me about this sooner?"

"I'm telling you now."

"And is that all you've got to say? How are they attacking?"

"They're not. Whoever it is, I don't reckon they're strong enough to take Johannson on. I think they're dug in somewhere, playing the long game."

"Interesting."

"You can make the most of this, Thacker. Johannson's distracted. You can deal with her, then deal with whoever is out there. Kill two birds with one stone."

21

RAF Thornhill

The morning arrives too soon. When he sees Estelle marching purposefully toward him, Matt pretends to still be asleep. She shakes his shoulder with enough force to wake the dead. "Get up, Sleeping Beauty," she says.

"Give me a break, Estelle."

"I don't have time. We're going to start running low on resources here as a result of you lot turning up unexpectedly yesterday. Aaron's going to lead a group to the Cambridge outpost later today. I'd like you to go with him."

"No, thanks."

She's taken aback by his abruptness, frustrated by his response. For once, she's lost for words. Matt feels obliged to fill the silence.

"No offense, but I'm staying here."

Estelle massages her brow, exasperated. Her tone changes. "Look, I don't have time for this, and we don't have the capacity to support hangers-on. You need to pull your weight around here; we all do."

"And I'm happy to do that. I'm not leaving, that's all. If you and your merry crew want to march off into the sunset together, then that's fine, but I'm not going anywhere, and I'm not asking for anything from you. Leave me in the shell of this place once you've gone if you want; I'll sort myself out."

"Can't you see what we're trying to do here?"

"Oh, I can see what you're trying to do, but I don't think it'll work. If you think you're going to be able to survive out there without life being a constant battle, you're wrong. And if you're happy to have that constant battle, if you think you stand any chance against the kind of enemy we're facing, then you're even more off the mark than I'd thought. You don't have a hope in hell."

"But we have to try."

"No, you don't. Seriously, just accept it. Forget your lofty aspirations and find yourselves a quiet corner of the world where no one else can see you and then make the most of the little you have left. Any thoughts you have, Estelle, of making some kind of heroic last stand . . . well, they're just fucking pipe dreams."

Estelle's expression changes. "I'm not going to waste my time here."

"Good."

"Just do me a favor and keep your opinions to yourself. I need to keep these people onside and motivated, and you're not helping."

"I thought your responsibility was to keep them alive?" he says. She pauses. It unnerves him.

"Wait . . . is there something you're not telling me, Estelle? More to the point, is there something you're not telling *them?*"

"I have to give them something to hold on to; otherwise, there's no point. I need them."

"What for? As foot soldiers?"

"I wouldn't go that far, but only the naïvest person would think they're going to be able to avoid all kinds of confrontation from now on. If I'm being completely honest, yes, I think most of them will inevitably be involved in some kind of military action."

"That's not being completely honest; that's being partially

honest. If you were being completely honest, you'd be telling me why you're planning on sending every man, woman, and child to the front line."

"It's not the front line—"

"It's as good as."

"It's a command outpost, and it's our next staging point. You're absolutely right when you say we're facing a constant battle to stay alive. There's only one way that's ever going to change, and that's by us totally eradicating every last Hater."

"Well, that's a war you're never going to win. No one here will survive the kind of fighting you're talking about."

"Says the man who survived a nuclear strike. Remember Einstein's quote?"

"Seriously? You're going to start quoting at me now?"

She ignores him and continues, "'I know not with what weapons World War III will be fought, but World War IV will be fought with sticks and stones.'"

"Come on, Estelle."

"Our enemy may have been reduced to savages, but we haven't. Not yet. I've got enough firepower under my control still to wipe out tens of thousands of them."

"And you think that's the solution?"

"It might be the only solution. If you can give me an alternative, then I'm all ears. We tried reconditioning them, remember? Look how that turned out. They double-bluffed us. They were pulling the strings all along."

"And they probably still are."

"Somewhere, maybe, yes, but not here. Not out in the field. If they still have generals and commanders, they'll be long gone, tucked away in bunkers and hideouts like you were, I expect. No, Matthew, my experience tells me this is a very different scenario we're facing now."

"Your experience? No one has any experience of this."

"Not here, no, but look elsewhere. Cast your mind back. Remember all those wars in Africa and the Middle East, all that religious bullshit that idiots were always scrapping over? The longer those wars continued, the more tribal they became. Order quickly collapsed. Their communications were disrupted or had never been there in the first place. Their societies crumbled, and now ours has, too. The Haters are barbaric, and the strongest, most brutal of them are the ones who've survived so far. They're dumbing down. Replacing thinking with fighting."

"I'm not so sure."

She ignores him. "I believe they also think we're dead and buried. They think they've won, and that means their focus is going to shift to jockeying for position in their new world disorder."

"I think you're massively oversimplifying things."

"And I think you're wrong. I *know* you are. Eventually, we're going to need to take decisive action. We're not going to stay hidden forever. We can turn this around, make the hunters the hunted."

Matt just looks at her. "You're out of your fucking mind. I'm having nothing to do with any of this."

"And ultimately that's your prerogative, but understand this: if you're not prepared to support us, then you get nothing from us. No food, no water, nothing. You can stay here by all means, but you'll be completely on your own. From what I know of you, Matthew, I think that's probably how you want it."

22

Matt finds himself a quiet space away from everyone else to make a den. This used to be the control room of RAF Thornhill. It's a squat, square brick of a building, taller than the rest, perched adjacent to the main hub of the base and overlooking the runway. The windows have been blacked out from the inside with a thick layer of paint-like mud. He scratches a little section clear so he can keep an eye on what's going on out there. It's midafternoon by his reckoning, the sun approaching its peak, but the day is as dull as ever. From outside, the windows look opaque, and that leaves him feeling sufficiently hidden from the rest of the world.

He looks around the shadows of the room. There are desks he can sleep on or under, and more than one exit so he can get out fast if he needs to. The place looks relatively untouched, obviously a little too prominent for the rest of the group's liking. It doesn't bother him, though. He's slept in the shadows of Haters before and survived.

This building's ideal, he thinks. He can imagine himself staying here long after the rest of them have gone. That won't be too long. Estelle seemed keen to ship everyone out. The sooner the better. He's looking forward to being alone again. He could leave the base and try to find somewhere else, but there doesn't seem much point when this entire area will be vacant soon enough.

Matt absentmindedly looks through drawers and cupboards. He finds a couple of coats hanging up and a pair of boots (a half size too small, but still more comfortable than the shoes he's currently wearing). As he's getting dressed, he also finds a pair of binoculars, a rucksack, a lighter, and some waterproof over-trousers. *Very useful*, he thinks at first, but no sooner has he put them on than they're off again. The swooshing sound the stiff, water-resistant material makes as his thighs brush together sounds disproportionately loud. Jesus, even his choice of clothing might affect his survival chances these days. There's no way he'll be able to hide from Haters wearing these pants.

He takes the binoculars over to the window and spots movement near the perimeter fence. He freezes, fearing an imminent enemy attack, but then relaxes because the behaviors he's seeing out there are measured and controlled, not frantic or aggressive. When he adjusts the focus of the field glasses, he sees faces he recognizes among the twenty or so figures outside. There's Tracy Barnish and several other members of the group he arrived here with, and at the front is Aaron Rayner. This must be the party setting out for the Cambridge outpost. If Estelle had had her way, he'd have been out there with them.

23

The CDF Outpost Near Cambridge

It takes them hours to get anywhere near the Cambridge outpost. Although it lies just off one of the main roads into the city, Aaron can't risk taking a direct route. The course they instead follow is necessarily convoluted to minimize the risk of them being tracked by the enemy. It's left unsaid, but the implications are clear to all involved: the twenty-three people currently making their way through open countryside are expendable. Right now, the integrity of the outpost is the only thing that matters. There's far more at stake than these few lives.

After slipping through the border fence at RAF Thornhill, they skirted the edge of the lake, then walked a mile through the forest to where another truck had been secreted in the ruins of a school. From there, a frantic drive east took them to a derelict farmers' market and garden center outside a waterlogged village. There they waited in a dark stockroom for more than two hours until Aaron was certain they'd not been followed. Then the final trek across open countryside began.

Tracy Barnish is terrified. She remembers hearing something about how Matt walked alone for weeks to get back to the city, and she doesn't know how he did it. They've barely been outside for any length of time, and she's struggling to keep calm. They could be attacked at any second. She's replayed countless nightmare scenarios as they've trudged across the land. Tracy's always been wary of Debbie Green, the girl ahead of her in the line. She's highly strung, and Tracy's always been worried that she'll panic and lose control at the least opportune moment. She remembers her screaming when they were attacked at the leisure center, and she imagines the effect that kind of outburst would have out here . . . she pictures Haters homing in on them from miles around, then imagines the noise as they attack, then imagines how that noise would increase if Aaron were to start firing that rifle he's carrying . . . Jesus Christ, everything's so fragile and delicately poised. Catastrophe feels almost inevitable.

And now they've stopped.

They bunch up around Aaron in the corner of a field, up to their ankles in mud at the intersection of two hedgerows. There's a gap, but he pauses before leading them through. "This is us," he whispers. "Do as I do. Follow my footsteps, and not a bloody sound, right?"

Tracy peers through the overgrown hedge. "This is it?"

"What did you expect, neon signs? It's supposed to look like it isn't there, remember."

The CDF outpost is all but invisible. All Tracy can make out from here are a couple of dark mounds in the near distance, but they could be anything—hills, clumps of trees, enemy encampments . . .

They take it in turns to clamber through the hedge, Tracy making sure she's about two-thirds of the way down the line: far enough back so she's not waiting on the other side for too long, but not so far that she's left behind on her own like the final girl in a bad horror movie.

When they're all through and have crossed a wide strip of road, they find themselves at the top of an embankment overlooking an immense construction site and works depot. There are hundreds of vehicles here—most of them connected to the roadworks, it looks like: diggers and shifters and scrapers of all shapes and sizes. In the low light, the lack of detail makes their outlines hard to discern. Their shapes combine to make monsters. Dinosaur-like.

Aaron leads the others down the steep slope, following zigzag tracks that have been trodden into the mud over time. Tracy loses her footing and goes head over heels, falling over and over until she comes to a rough and very sudden stop at the bottom of the embankment, her head thudding against the ground. It hurts like hell, and though she wants to scream out, she manages to keep the pain swallowed down. Debbie gives her a hand and helps her up, but there's not a sound. Not a word passes between them.

They're all down now, but there's someone else coming, following them. There's a collective catch of breath, because there's no doubt from the way this person is moving that it's one of *them*. Aaron pushes his way back through the group, knife held ready. This was a teenage girl once, but now it's a barely human cyclone, all arms and legs and Hate. She can't believe her eyes when she realizes she's stumbled on a group of Unchanged out here in the open, and she throws herself at the pack with only a rock for a weapon. She swings at Debbie, who trips over her own feet trying to get out of the way.

"Come on, love, let's have you," Aaron says quietly, taunting the Hater.

And she obliges.

She flies at Aaron with impossible levels of fury. He catches her arm, twists it around, then stabs her just above her right kidney. The Hater staggers back, only managing three or four steps before her legs buckle and she collapses. The others look on in useless disbelief. "You're gonna have to do better now you're here," Aaron tells them. He stands over the Hater who's still alive, then grabs a handful of her hair, pulls her head back, and slits her throat.

She bleeds out like a slaughtered pig. Aaron gestures for two of the others to carry the corpse, then drags his boots through the puddle of blood he just spilled, mixing it with the mud. Leave no trace.

There's a trench dug around virtually the entire perimeter of the service station outpost, and it's invisible until they're almost on top of it. Aaron leads the group over a narrow pontoon bridge and into the mazelike compound of works vehicles. There's a foul stench here, carried on the wind. "Leave the body here," he whispers to the Hater's impromptu pallbearers. "We'll take care of it later."

In silence, they follow a lackadaisical route up toward the main part of the service station. There are tanks and field guns parked alongside civilian vehicles. A helicopter is sitting in a bubble of space, its rotor blades tied down and weighted. The group soon reaches what looks like a dead end, but it's a misdirection; a pathway that leads to a concealed door. Aaron turns to the others and explains, but he's jumped before he can utter even a single hushed word. Tracy sees the glint of a long, machete-like blade and fears the worst, but before she or any of the others can react, the confrontation is over. Recognition. Friends. All good. The group is hurriedly ushered inside and then locked in the empty storeroom of a retail outlet. *Decontamination*, they're told. *Make sure you're all like us.*

Only Aaron enters the outpost proper. He walks through the shelf-stripped remains of the retail outlet, stepping over and around countless people, and is met by Moira Kay. "What are you doing here?" she asks. "Trouble?"

"No trouble. New arrivals. I need to see Chappell. Got a message for him from Estelle."

"He's next door."

There's a sheltered walkway that connects the main part of the service station to the chain hotel next door. It connects the kitchen of a fast-food joint to a fire door around the back of the hotel reception and is completely hidden from view. Aaron finds Chappell and two other CDF fighters poring over a map they've spread out on a low coffee table.

Chappell looks up. "Aaron. I didn't expect to see you. Everything all right?"

He collapses onto the sofa opposite, exhausted. "Everything's fine. I'm chaperoning. Estelle wants me to stay here now."

"We shipping out from Thornhill?"

"Not yet."

"So what's the story?"

"We're running out of space back at base. Had a load of new arrivals. Around thirty of them. Brought the first twenty with me."

"That's a big number."

"Buried underground until a landslide forced them out of their shelter. We picked them up near the airport."

"And you're sure they're clean?"

"Checked them myself. Pretty unremarkable bunch. Dyed-in-the-wool civvies. There's a GP in the group I brought with me, but other than that, they're just gophers."

Chappell gets up from his seat. "Let me see them."

The group is ushered out of their storeroom holding cell into the main part of the building. It's a sobering experience, nothing like they were expecting. The roughly circular, high-ceilinged hub of the service station is chock-full of people and equipment, with barely any available space. But for most, it's not the people that distracts them, it's their surroundings. Parts of the building have been perfectly preserved, untouched by the CDF. Wide eyes look from one unlit neon sign to the next, remembering tastes, smells, sensations, emotions, and experiences they'd either forgotten or forced themselves to keep bottled up. The bright colors are astonishingly vivid against the shadows and the memory of the muted gray world outside: Costa Coffee . . . all the usual fast-food brands . . . an American diner . . . WHSmith . . . Marks & Spencer . . .

There's an air of positivity among the group, bordering on excitement. They've hidden, meandered, and drifted since the war began, and for the first time, they now feel like they're part of something with a purpose. Aaron shows them up the steps to a mezzanine-level business lounge with views over the land surrounding the outpost. There's no time for pleasantries, and Chappell's abruptness takes them by surprise. "Are any of you useful?"

Exchanged glances. Uncertainty. They stand in a huddle, dumbstruck.

"She's the doctor," Aaron says, pointing at Tracy.

Chappell nods. "Anyone have military experience?"

Nothing.

"Law enforcement?"

Still silence.

He shakes his head. "I'll be blunt, there's no room for hangers-on here. You all need to pull your weight. Your role will be to support my troops. They come first, understand?"

Mumbled acknowledgments.

"You do what you're told, and whatever you're told to do, you do it quietly. There may be a time in a few weeks, months, or years from now when the war will be over and we can be ourselves again; until then, I expect everyone either to fight or to support those of us who'll be putting our necks on the block."

Chappell walks up and down the line.

"At all times, you will remain inside this building unless you have specific orders to the contrary," he continues. "Our troops are billeted in the hotel next door. That area is strictly off-limits to all noncombatants. Do I make myself clear?"

"Perfectly," Tracy says, speaking on behalf of the group. "Look, we're just glad to be alive. We don't want any trouble. We'll do whatever we're asked."

"Whatever you're *told*. You won't be asked."

She nods.

"I'm sure Estelle has given you one of her pep talks, and I'm sure you've seen enough of what's happened out there to realize we're at a crossroads. We are, as far as we are aware, the largest remaining active CDF contingent, possibly the largest remaining *human* contingent in the country. The importance of what we're doing here cannot be overstated. Disobedience will not be tolerated. If you do anything that could be construed as posing a risk to this operation, you will face the consequences. And those consequences, as I'm sure you can imagine, will be stark."

24

RAF Thornhill

Matt has slept well in his new digs. He wakes with a vague sense of optimism—could it be that this place is as good as he dares dream? There's a tattered map of the local area on the wall, and he consults the details by flashlight. Cambridge and Norwich are the nearest cities (that haven't been completely annihilated), and it looks like there are enough small villages and towns scattered around that he should be able to loot from when the time comes and he's left alone here.

But if he's completely honest with himself, being alone isn't his preferred option. He goes down to the infirmary, keen to find Kara. "Decided to rejoin the human race?" she says when she sees him.

"What's left of it."

"You eaten anything?"

"Not yet."

"There was some breakfast going near the assembly hall. You might still make it."

"You coming?"

"Can't."

"Why not?"

"I'm busy."

Matt looks around. Other than passing through on a whistle-stop tour last night, this is the first time he's been here. It's as grim as he'd expected. The smell is overpowering. There's sickness everywhere, spilling out of the beds and onto the floor and along the corridors. There are people who've been injured in battle and others who are clearly suffering from the aftereffects of the bomb and radiation sickness. There are some who are being treated; there are others who are being left to die in as little discomfort as possible.

"You could always help," Kara suggests.

"Maybe later."

"Come on, Matt, prove them wrong."

"Who?"

"Darren and Estelle."

"They need to prove me wrong first. Don't forget I've come across Estelle before. When things turned nasty in the city, she made sure she was long gone. I don't believe a word the woman says."

"Based on what? Based on the fact she got out before the bomb dropped? This place might not have been here if she hadn't."

"It's not that . . ."

"What, then?" She shakes her head, picks up a bucket she's been carrying, and goes to walk on. He stops her, but she pulls away. "What? I'm busy, Matt. I need to get on."

"Come on, Kara. You know as well as I do that this is bullshit. Half these people are never going to get any better."

"Keep your bloody voice down, will you? You're incredible, you really are."

"I'm realistic, that's all."

"You could really make a difference here."

"Don't tell me you're falling for Darren's *new beginnings* bullshit? I'm through helping. I told you, I've done my share."

"I wasn't aware we had quotas."

"I'm the one who got you all to the printing house in the first place, and I'm the one who got you back on your feet when it all went shit-shaped. I've done my bit, and now I just want to be left alone."

"Don't you get it? We don't have any choice; none of us do. We're all in this together. If you'd just—"

Matt snaps, angrier than he has any right to be. "No, it's *you* that doesn't get it. My girlfriend died because I was helping. While I was driving you to safety, she was at home waiting for me. I let Jen down. I killed her."

"That's not true."

"It *is* true."

"Jesus, Matt, tell me you don't actually believe that. What would she say if she could hear you?"

Her words cut deep. He starts to walk away, but turns back to face her. "Look, it's pretty simple. The harder I try, the worse things get. I think it's time to stop trying."

"So you're just going to give up? The guy who fought for so long to get back to his missus is just going to roll over and give up?"

"I didn't fight. It's fighting that caused all of this in the first place."

"Figure of speech. For the record, I think you're being pretty bloody pathetic."

"And I don't care what you think."

"Well, you clearly do, because you wouldn't have come down here looking for me otherwise."

The volume of their voices is filling the infirmary with noise. People are watching with concern, worried that Matt's about to kick off. A sickly looking man scoops up his bedding and tries to get out of the way. He collides with Matt and drops some of his stuff. "Sorry," he mumbles.

"Fuck's sake. Watch where you're going."

They make fleeting eye contact before the ragged man looks down again and continues on his way.

Matt watches the paper-thin figure disappear.

He's confused.

"What's up?" Kara asks.

"Who's he?"

"Don't know. Think he's been here a while. Why?"

"He looks familiar."

Matt's uneasy. He walks a little deeper into the infirmary, looking for the man he just spoke to, trying to place him. He's definitely not from the shelter. Someone from his prewar life, perhaps? No, it's more recent than that. Was he someone from the city-camp? One of the soldiers who interrogated and tormented Matt when he first arrived there? One of his coworkers from the garbage truck or the other cleanup operations he was a part of? A neighbor, or one of the refugees who had camped out in front of his and Jen's house on East Kent Road? Someone he queued up for food alongside? One of the CDF soldiers from the military compound or the convent?

Matt can see him again now, and he remembers.

He stops dead in his tracks, doing everything he can to convince himself he's wrong, that time and pressure have combined to make him imagine something that can't possibly be true. Or can it?

His blood runs cold.

He remembers leading this man up to the convent attic in shackles, then helping chain him up against a bloodstained wall.

He remembers watching him being interrogated by Joseph Mallon.

He remembers following him out through the overcrowded streets of the city-camp with Jayce, tracking him just hours before the place imploded, then exploded, discovering he was part of a Hater cell.

Matt checks himself again. Surely he must be mistaken. What are the odds that this is the same guy? He tells himself it must just be a coincidence—that this miserable shadow of a man must just bear a slight resemblance to the man he remembers . . . the *Hater* he remembers. And if he was one of the enemy, what would he be doing here of all places? Even if he truly had the ability to hold the Hate, why here? Why now?

He's mistaken. He has to be.

"Everything all right here?"

Matt barely grunts at the figure who appears in front of him wearing grubby lab whites.

"Everything's fine, Doc," Kara says. "Matt, this is Giles."

Matt looks the doctor up and down, then tries to look past him again.

Lost him.

The other man's slipped out of view around a corner. Matt starts hunting for him among the sick. What was the fucker's name? David? Andy? It's on the tip of his tongue.

A hand grips his arm and pulls him back. It's the doctor again.

"Is there a problem?"

"I'm fine," Matt says, snatching his arm away.

"You don't seem fine. You seem agitated. Is there something bothering you? Something I can help you with?"

"I said I'm fine!" Matt shouts at him. "Now fuck off and leave me alone."

Kara forces her way between the two of them and puts her hands on his chest. "You need to stop this, Matt."

"I can give you something to help you relax if it'll help," the doctor says.

"I don't need to relax."

"I don't think you understand. I can't have you causing trouble in here."

Matt moves Kara out of the way and continues hunting.

"Where is he?"

"Who?"

"The bloke who was just here."

"You're going to have to give us more to go on than that," Dr. Giles says.

"About my height. Thin. Pale. Sick-looking."

"You've just described half my patients. This is the infirmary. Most people are sick-looking."

"Don't mock me!" Matt yells, blowing up again. "Don't talk to me like I'm a fucking idiot."

"I really need you to calm down," the doctor says, his singsong voice belying a sudden palpable increase in tension. "Slow down and tell me what's wrong."

"There was a guy here a few seconds ago. I need to see him."

"Who?"

Matt looks around again, frantic. Then he spots the face he's been looking for. "Him."

He lunges, but the doctor is one step ahead and pulls Matt back. Matt's incensed, and it takes all the doctor's strength to keep him from attacking. "What the hell are you doing?" he demands.

"You don't understand . . . he's a Hater."

The doctor laughs in his face. "What? Danny? You've got to be kidding."

The mention of his name makes Matt's heart sink and his legs buckle, because now he knows beyond any doubt he's right. Memories quickly come into focus. He remembers Joseph Mallon taunting the Hater . . . torturing him.

"Get help," the doctor manages to say to Kara. Matt's even more agitated now, fighting to free himself from the doctor's grip. He refuses to let Matt go. "You need to relax. Take it easy . . ."

"Are you not listening to me? That man is a fucking Hater!"

The sick and struggling in the infirmary are becoming increasingly nervous. The would-be Hater also looks terrified. He pulls his knees up to his chest and makes himself as small as possible, meek as anything.

The panic is like vomit in Matt's throat. He tries again to squirm free of the doctor's strong grip, but he's not going anywhere. Instead, he rocks his head back, then butts him in the face. The searing pain both of them feel is intense, and they stagger away from each other, Matt with his head spinning and the doctor with blood pouring from his broken nose. Then Matt shakes his head clear and goes for Danny, who cowers, hiding himself behind other equally terrified patients.

Matt raises his fist to strike him, but the punch is never thrown. Darren catches his forearm while Jason wraps his arms around Matt's waist and pulls him back. "Get off me!" Matt screams. "That fucker is one of them! He'll kill all of us!"

Matt feels a sharp stabbing pain above his left shoulder blade. He stops fighting and reaches for his shoulder, feeling like he's been stung by some giant insect. By the time he realizes what the doctor's just done, his legs have buckled. By the time he hits the ground, he's out cold.

"He's a fucking liability," Darren says, standing over Matt, seething. "He's lost it completely."

"I reckon he lost it a long time ago," Jason adds.

"We can't risk this kind of volatility," Estelle says from the doorway. "He's a danger to all of us. This is for his own good."

25

Cambridge

It's like a fucking presidential motorcade rolling into town, Pinchy thinks as he grips the wheel of the Citroën. Thacker's man Hinchcliffe is riding shotgun, followed by a phalanx of several trucks and other vehicles. While not completely over the top, it's a clear show of force and intent. Pinchy glances back in the rearview mirror at the mass of muscles and vehicles he's led into Cambridge. *Now we're really starting to look like something out of Mad Max,* he thinks.

"Nervous?" Hinchcliffe asks.

"Nope."

"You sure? You probably should be."

"I said I'm fine."

"It's just the way you keep checking your mirrors and looking at me out the corner of your eye every few seconds. If I didn't know better, I'd think you were feeling a bit jittery, Mr. Pinch. It's not a weakness, feeling nervous. The weakness is letting it show."

"Which bit of *I'm fine* don't you get?"

"Calm down, Mr. P. Focus on the road."

Patronizing bastard. If it were just the two of them, Pinchy thinks he'd stop the car and kill this fucker right here.

The floods and the battle damage have limited the clear routes in and out of the city to little more than one road east and west. Johannson's people have worked to block exits and other roads as a defense, enabling them to funnel any passing traffic right into the heart of their nest. This convoy arrives there in no time at all, the imposing college building looming up from out of nowhere. The university has dominated the city for hundreds of years, but today it's even more visible on account of the massive amount of destruction that has been wrought on the surrounding area. Johannson's fighters, those who aren't important, respected, or feared enough to live alongside the boss, are scattered around the immediate vicinity. When they hear the noise of the combined engines in the near distance, they emerge from the shadows en masse. To a man, they've felt safe sticking close to Johannson and her generals, but this is something different. Something new. They're used to leaving here to fight, but this is the first time the battle has come to them. There may well be little coordination within Johannson's ranks, but what these people lack in discipline they more than make up for in numbers. They pour out of their shelters flood-like, armed and ready.

"Stop here," Hinchcliffe orders Pinchy, just short of the edge of the crowd.

"But we're still a way out," Pinchy says. "There's no problem. I told you, she listens to me. We should drive right up to the door, make a point."

"I said stop here," Hinchcliffe says again, and the authority in his voice is unquestionable. Pinchy complies. Hinchcliffe turns to face him. "Right, here's what's going to happen. You and I are going to go and have a conversation with Mother Hen. The rest of my people will hold back here. I don't want Mrs. Johannson getting the wrong impression. We want her to think we're working with her, not against her. You got it?"

"I got it."

"Good. Shift yourself."

Hinchcliffe is immediately out of the car. He leaves the door open and raises his hands, showing submission. Pinchy's so nervous he can almost hear his pulse. Mouth dry, heart thumping. He's wishing he'd never started this, but he knows it'll be over soon. Once Thacker's in control here, Pinchy will be set up for life. *You don't get anywhere in this world without taking risks,* he tells himself.

The crowds part as Johannson appears. She strides out of the grand college building with a confidence and swagger that is more than a match for Hinchcliffe's. He stops short with Pinchy close behind, and the crowds swallow them up.

"You must be Mrs. Johannson," Hinchcliffe says, overly sincere, ladling on the bullshit.

"And who the fuck are you?" she demands. She glares at Pinchy. "What the fuck's going on? Where you been?"

Pinchy swallows hard. "Listen, boss . . ."

Hinchcliffe nudges Pinchy and puts a finger on his lips. "Shh . . . Quiet now. There's a good lad." He turns back to Johannson. "My name's Hinchcliffe, but the name you really need to know is Mr. Thacker."

"And who the hell's he?"

"He's my boss. Mr. Thacker would very much like the opportunity to meet with you."

"And I should give a fuck what your boss wants because . . . ?"

Hinchcliffe clears his throat, mock polite. "Mr. Thacker is the commander in chief of what we believe to be the biggest remaining fighting force in the country, several thousand strong."

"So?"

"We think it would be in our collective best interests to meet. I think you'll find you've both got a lot in common. You see, we're recruiting."

Pinchy shifts from foot to foot. He wants to speak up, but the words are stuck in his throat. Johannson glares at him, then glares at Hinchcliffe. "Several thousand? Piss off. Jesus, I'd be surprised if there's that many people left alive. And if he's so damn powerful, why'd he send you clowns?"

"He's a busy man," Hinchcliffe answers.

"And he decided he'd recruit me and my lot to his great cause?" she says, incredulous, gesturing around her.

"Yes, that's right."

"What makes him think we need anybody else?"

"These are times of great change, Johannson. There's little order left in what remains of our country right now. Mr. Thacker is putting that right."

"So he reckons he's top dog, does he?"

"Yes, ma'am."

"Well, he can think again. Fuck off back to wherever you came from and tell him I'm not interested."

"It's not that easy."

"Yes, it is. Fuck off."

Hinchcliffe shakes his head and looks down at his mud-splattered boots. "Mr. Thacker is coming this way whether you like it or not. Your only option is choosing whether you're going to work with us or pick a fight."

"It's true, boss," Pinchy finally pipes up. "You should listen to him."

"What, and you've seen these thousands of fighters, have you?"

"Some of them, yeah."

"So which side of the line are you standing on now, Pinchy?" she asks. "Are you doing me a favor and giving me the heads-up there's a battle brewing, or have you jumped ship and you're here to tell me you think I should roll over?"

Pinchy swallows hard and says words he never wanted to hear himself saying. "I think you're beat. I think you should talk to Thacker. It's that or lose everything."

Johannson looks fucking furious. She fixes Pinchy with a fearsome stare. "You spineless fucker."

"No, Johannson, wait . . . it's not like that. I just think—"

"Shh . . ." Hinchcliffe tells him again, before returning his attention to Johannson. "You really should listen to your man here. He knows what he's talking about. He's seen sense. He made contact with some of our scouts a few days back and immediately saw the potential of you and your people coming into the fold. As I said, Thacker's in the business of creating order from the chaos, and he's inviting you to be a part of it."

"And as I've already said, he can fuck off."

Hinchcliffe massages his temples and looks around at the crowds. If he's at all intimidated by the mass of several hundred fighters jostling for position, he's not letting it show. "Okay," he says, sounding tired now, "let me level with you. Your options here are more limited than you think. It boils down to this: you either play ball with Thacker, or you'll be replaced. It really is that simple."

Johannson is silent for a few overlong seconds, her entire ragged entourage holding its collective breath in anticipation of her inevitable fury. Then she just laughs. A deep, belly-shaking, guttural laugh that echoes through the emptiness of the Cambridge ruins.

She marches up to face Hinchcliffe. He doesn't flinch.

"Don't worry, I'm not going to kill you," she tells him. "What's going to happen now is you're going to go back to this Mr. Thacker of yours, and you're going to tell him to keep away from my territory and keep his filthy hands off my people. If I see you or anyone else I don't recognize sniffing around here, I'll kill the fucking lot of you myself. Understand?"

"Wait, Johannson, please . . ." Pinchy says. "Just think about this . . ."

Hinchliffe has had enough. With a single movement so swift, so violent, so devastating and so completely unexpected that barely anyone realizes what's happening until it's done, he carves a blade through the air and stabs Pinchy through his Adam's apple. Pinchy drops to his knees, clutching his throat and gurgling blood. He looks up at Hinchliffe.

"I told you to shut up, you moron," Hinchliffe says with disdain. "You can keep the knife. I don't need it back."

Pinchy collapses forward. He hits the ground face-first with a thud, shoving the knife in deeper, leaving the tip of the blade jutting out at the nape of his neck.

Johannson is unfazed. Not a flicker of emotion. There are mumbles of dissention in the ranks around her, but she silences all of them with the simplest of gestures. No one argues. Hinchliffe stands his ground also. "You saved me a job with that yellow-bellied bastard," she tells him. "Now get out of here before I order this lot to lynch the fucking lot of you."

"You're letting them go?" a voice asks from behind her. One of her generals or just one of the crowd? She turns around, but the owner of the voice has already slunk back into the masses.

"It's been a pleasure," Hinchliffe says. "Thank you for your time."

"You won't be walking away next time," she warns, but he's not listening. He's already pushing through the crowd on his way back to his convoy.

They disappear in a mass of churned mud spray and fumes.

26

RAF Thornhill

The windowless, cell-like room Matt wakes up in is dark, permanently filled with shadow. It's early morning, he thinks, but which morning? He could have been unconscious for minutes or days. Who knows how long it's been?

The mattress is uncomfortable and sweat-soaked. He's been drifting in and out of consciousness for what feels like forever as the drugs have worked their way through his system. The combination of his reduced body mass and the unscientifically measured slug of chemicals the doctor pumped into his system knocked him out like a sledgehammer. For the longest time, he's been trying to remember where he is and how he got here. He gets so far, then loses track of his thoughts before he's worked it out.

Eventually, he's composed enough to be able to swing his feet off the bed and stand up. He immediately wishes he hadn't, and he leans against the wall as a wave of nausea washes over him. His legs threaten to buckle, and he just about makes it to a basin but can only spit into the bowl, nothing inside to throw up. He steadies himself and tries to wash his face, forgetting it's been weeks since any water flowed through these pipes.

It's only after a few more minutes, once the strength in his muscles has begun to return and he can stand upright without fear of passing out, that he realizes how quiet it is. Utterly, unnaturally silent. It's icy cold, too. He's still at RAF Thornhill, of that much he's reasonably certain, but in which part of the base is he?

Matt resists the temptation to call out, because his time alone since the war began has taught him that's almost always a bad move. Assess the situation in as quiet and unobtrusive a way as possible, then act on whatever you find. But that's a problem today. The absolute lack of noise makes his every movement sound deafeningly loud.

This isn't right. This is very, very wrong. This section of the base feels lifeless and tomb-like. They must have dumped him well away from everyone else near the border fence. Solitary confinement. He thinks he probably asked for it, kicking off like that.

He's halfway down the corridor now, and the sharpness of his drug-dulled mind is gradually beginning to return. The sudden recollection of what happened stops him in his tracks. It's like being drenched with a bucket of ice-cold water, and immediately he's wide awake and alert and afraid. He remembers the paranoia he experienced in the infirmary, seeing that Hater's face again. He edges farther along in the shadows of the mazelike corridors, terrified at what, or *who*, he might be about to find around the next corner.

Wait. He knows where he is. He's reached the mess hall.

Shit.

He's right in the hub of the base after all, and there's no one else here. The main public areas of Thornhill are deserted. The others have packed up and shipped out without him. It looks like it was a sudden exodus; the place has been stripped bare, but no attempt has been made to cover their tracks. He's thinking Estelle and her people are so well prepared that they must surely have had a preplanned evacuation routine, triggered no doubt by the discovery of a Hater in their midst.

But wait . . . they didn't believe him. What changed? He finds the answer when he reaches the infirmary.

It's a bloodbath.

There may only have been a handful of people here at the very end, but the condition their bodies have been left in makes it look like there were many more. There's blood everywhere, and the smell inside the space is worse than he remembers: the stench of sickness, sweat, and spoil now tinged with sickly sweet notes of decay. He bends down and inspects a pool of blood. Dry and tacky on the edges, still wet elsewhere. Half a day old, tops.

He rips the makeshift covers from a window, allowing murky light to dribble in from outside, and tries to piece together what might have happened here. There's Dr. Giles's corpse over there, killed by a single blow to the head. Matt stops in his tracks when he trips over the outstretched legs of the next body. It's Kara. Her face is a frozen snapshot of her final moments. Utter panic. Sheer terror.

Jesus.

He drops to his knees and holds her head in his hands, brushing blood-matted hair from her face.

Should have helped her. Should have done more for her. Shouldn't have let it come to this. See . . . it happened again. Someone got close . . . Someone trusted me . . . and now they're dead.

Matt thinks he's cursed. The people he gets closest to are those who get hurt the most.

Focus. Where's the Hater?

Moving fast, he finds a flashlight wedged under another corpse, which he shines into each of the remaining dead faces in turn. There are eleven bodies in total here, and other than Kara and the doctor, he doesn't recognize any of them. There's no sign of the intruder. Matt knows that despicable bastard had been trained to hold the Hate. He must have been sussing the place out, then fought his way out when his cover was blown. So where would he have gone? Matt thinks he would have gone straight back to whoever it was who sent him here, and he realizes the enemy will likely be on their way here soon. They might be here already.

He doesn't have long.

27

On the Road

Funny how things never work out the way you expect, McCoyne thinks as he half walks, half staggers down the long road he hopes will get him back to the university ruins and the security of the pack. It wasn't long ago he was doing everything he could to put some distance between himself and Johannson and her herd of uncivilized grunts; now all he wants is to be back with them again. There's still some relative safety in numbers, as long as you're fighting for the same side. Knowledge is power, they used to say. They should listen to him when he tells them what he found. Actually, brute force is absolute power now, but a little knowledge will at least give him the slightest edge over the other fight-avoiders. For now, at least.

The floodwater laps against either side of the road here. There's no telling how deep it is, so he keeps to the dotted line in the middle of the tarmac. He's cold, wet, and exposed, but the university is big enough and rambling enough so that he'll be able to find a quiet corner to dry out and get his strength back.

Nothing but the rain and the road and the water in every direction. McCoyne thinks he hears something on the wind, and he looks up and sees a pair of bright headlights racing toward him. He stops and faces off against the rapidly approaching vehicle.

Running's not an option, so he flags them down. He figures he'll dive to one side if the driver tries to take him out (and he wouldn't put it past anyone these days), but instead, the car skids to a halt. It aquaplanes in the standing water and barely stops in time.

Shit.

Of all the cars on all the roads . . . what were the chances of this happening?

It's a red Subaru. Damn. It's bloody Karl Bryce.

McCoyne doesn't bother looking for a way out, because there isn't one. Bryce gets out of the car, then grabs McCoyne by the collar and drops him to the ground. "You ran out on me, you fucker."

"Didn't mean to. I got lost. I went for a piss, and I couldn't find the way back. It was dark . . ."

"Bullshit."

He punches McCoyne in the face, and all McCoyne can do is soak it up. His body is already ruined; another battering isn't going to make any difference. Bryce punches him again, then lifts his fist to strike him a third time.

Knowledge is power.

"Wait. Don't hurt me. I know something you don't."

Bryce stops midswing.

"What?"

McCoyne knows he's going to have to play his trump card early, but he doesn't have any choice. "Unchanged. I found a nest. I can show you."

"Don't believe you," Bryce says, fist pulled back again.

"It's an old army base, something like that. Back down this road. Fuckers are well hidden."

"Keep talking."

"There's loads of them there, all hunkered down and quiet. There was talk they'd gotten another base somewhere 'round here, too. Military. I couldn't find out where it is. Didn't have time."

"You expect me to believe all of this?"

"Why would I lie?"

"Because I was about to kick the shit out of you."

"That's par for the course these days."

Bryce loosens his grip. "Tell me more."

McCoyne sits up and wipes rainwater and dribbles of blood from his face, blows snot from his stinging nose. It gives him a few seconds to think, to work out how to play this.

"No one else knows they're there. You can be the one who tells Johannson, score yourself some points. I know you want to climb the ranks."

He watches Bryce thinking it over.

"I need more than that."

"There's thirty or forty of them at least, maybe more. They're pretty well organized from what I saw. Don't know what weapons they've got or what supplies, though. They stay quiet and right out of sight. Clever fuckers, they are."

Bryce goes for him again, knocking him back to the ground. "What aren't you telling me?"

"What?"

"You must think I'm fucking stupid. How do you know all this? Are you a fucking sympathizer or something?"

"I don't understand . . ."

"Sounds like you had a good look around and really got to know the place. So how did you manage that without killing those bastards?"

"There were too many of them. I killed enough so that I could get away. I couldn't have handled all of them on my own."

"You expect me to believe that?"

McCoyne knows he's already said too much. "I don't expect you to believe anything."

Bryce is struggling to compute.

"So how long were you there? I mean, you walked out on us a few nights back now . . ."

No answer.

"How close did you actually get to them?"

Still nothing.

"Were you just watching from a distance?"

McCoyne shakes his head.

"You were in there with them?" Bryce can't believe where this train of thought is leading him, but there's no other explanation. "Fuck me, you were. You were neck-deep in those fuckers, weren't you?"

His silence says everything.

"You fucker. You *chose* not to kill them."

"Like I said, I killed some," McCoyne mumbles. "Too many to kill all of them."

Bryce is struggling with the implications of what he's hearing. "You can hold the Hate, can't you? Bloody hell . . ."

"I told you, Bryce, there were too many. They'd have killed me if I'd tried anything."

"Cut the crap. Be straight with me if you want to stay alive. Can you hold the Hate?"

"Yes," McCoyne reluctantly admits.

"We're going to go back to Cambridge, get some extra bodies, then you're going to take us to this army base so we can deal with the Unchanged, understand?"

"Okay."

"Then I'm going to kill you. You're a fucking abomination."

McCoyne knows he won't hesitate to carry out his threat. "You don't have to do that, Bryce. I can help you. I can be useful. I can give you an advantage over all the rest of them."

"Yeah, and that's exactly what you're going to do. Because if you put one foot out of line, I'll tell Johannson all about your party tricks. She'll have you strung up in front of the whole damn camp."

28

RAF Thornhill

Matt frantically works his way through the abandoned base, collecting anything of use. Scraps of food, discarded clothing . . . there's nothing much worth taking. It takes longer than he'd like, the last vestiges of Dr. Giles's industrial-strength tranquilizers still working their way through his system. He needs to pull himself together. He has to get out of here.

The last place he checks is the control room where he'd left the rest of his gear. He picks up his binoculars from where he left them and a few other odds and ends, which he crams into a rucksack. He pauses to clear a discreet patch of mud from the obscured main windows.

"Matt?"

Matt spins around, his heart in his mouth, and sees Jason standing behind him.

"What the hell are you still doing here?"

Jason shakes his head, looks on the verge of tears. "Got split up from the others when they left. Didn't want to end up stuck out there on my own, so I came back. I didn't know there was anyone else here. Thought everyone had gone."

"I couldn't leave. Some fucker knocked me out, remember?"

"I know. I'm sorry."

"You didn't believe me."

"I know," he says again. "It just seemed so bloody ridiculous. He said it wasn't true, and we were all thinking he had to be right, because how could a Hater have been in here with us?"

"I recognized him from the city."

"I'm sorry."

"I knew he was different."

"I know that now . . ."

"People have died because you didn't believe me. Kara died. She was my friend."

This time Jason says nothing. He just stands there, numb.

"So what exactly happened?" Matt asks.

"Nothing for a while. The bastard was biding his time. He knew we were watching him, so he waited long enough for us to think he was fine and it was you who'd lost your mind."

"And then?"

"Most of us were asleep when it happened. We heard the screams coming from the infirmary, but by the time we'd gotten there, he'd already gone. Estelle and Darren reckoned he'd gone back to his base or wherever it was he'd come from. They said he'd bring other Haters back here, so they packed up and left. Jesus, Matt, thank fuck I found you. I thought I was going to be here on my own. What are we going to do?"

"When did they go?"

"They've got a few hours' lead on us. We could try to catch them."

Matt returns his attention to the window and rubs at the mud with his sleeve. "Do you know the way to the CDF outpost?"

"I know it's on one of the main roads into Cambridge . . ."

"But you don't actually know the route?"

"No," he admits.

"Great."

"It's a service station on a main road. Can't be too hard to find."

"You think? We'll worry about that later. Right now, we just need to get out of this place."

"Now? Shouldn't we wait until dark?"

"We don't have that luxury," Matt says, and he beckons Jason over to the window he's been looking through. "Look."

They're still a way off and are only visible because of the stillness of everything else, but there's a veritable shitload of Haters approaching. It looks like an army—a mass of frantic movement cutting a swath through the dead lands and closing in on the RAF base at speed. It's a cavalcade of beaten-up vehicles packed with fighters, so many they're hanging off the sides and clinging to tailgates. They don't care if they're seen or heard. They're not here to negotiate. They're not here to rape and pillage. The sole reason these bastards are here is to annihilate the remaining Unchanged.

"We need to get gone," Matt says, stating the obvious.

"But there's nothing here for them. Maybe they'll see that everyone's gone and disappear?"

"You want to take that chance? You're so fucking naïve. They'll turn this place upside down if they think there's the slightest chance even one of us is left alive. We're going. Right now."

"But if we—"

Matt turns on him. "You do exactly what I tell you, understand? You start playing up and I'll leave you for dead. Believe me, it'll be far easier for me to slip away unnoticed if they're busy fighting over your scraps."

29

Approaching RAF Thornhill

Bryce can barely contain himself. This is his opportunity to prove his worth. Now that the tattooed prick Pinchy is out of the picture, there's a chance he can fill the vacant spot at Johannson's side alongside her other generals. He's been waiting for a chance like this. He's going to kill every last Unchanged, then load up their bodies and present them to the boss. She'll realize how useful he could be to her. His giddy excitement makes it hard to stay focused. He salivates at the prospect of killing in huge numbers again, of being spoiled for choice, of hearing their screams and watching them die. It makes him feel nostalgic for those one-sided halcyon days at the beginning of this most beautiful of wars.

They reach the entrance to the base and block the open gates. "You sure this it?" Bryce asks. McCoyne's in the passenger seat of the Subaru, wishing he were anywhere but here.

"Yeah, this is it. I told you, they're hidden right in the center. Well out of sight."

Bryce gets out. The rain is torrential, but nothing can dampen the spirits of this hunting pack. They gather around him, hungry for action. "Get in there and split up," he orders. "Surround them.

Form a perimeter. Block the exits, then start closing in. Don't let a single one of those cunts get out alive."

The men and women surge forward, desperate to hurt and maim. At times like this, they're animals, little trace left of who any of them used to be before the war. Doesn't matter. The old world is dead and gone. As polluted, battered, blood-soaked, and violent as everything now is, long live the new world.

Almost thirty of them pour into the RAF base. Bryce knows the relative isolation of this location was the reason the Unchanged managed to survive here for so long, but now that same disconnection will be their downfall; a bunker is a cell from a different perspective. These people have dug in deep, but all they've managed to do is bury themselves alive.

His pack splits up and forms ragged lines of attack that wrap around the main buildings. Bryce turns back and yells at McCoyne to come forward from his preferred position of avoidance away from the front line. "Best way in?" Bryce asks.

"Take your pick. It's like a maze in there. Doesn't matter as long as all the exits are covered."

The massed Hater ranks are quiet now, the little noise they do make suppressed by the hissing rain. They wait impatiently for Bryce to give the word, desperate to pare Unchanged flesh from bone. Even now, after everything they've been through individually and collectively, this still feels so natural, so right, and so necessary. A year ago, all of this would have seemed impossible: the killing, the bombs, the final war. Yet now it's the memories that are hard to believe. To have restricted themselves with needless order and routine. To have allowed themselves to exist in the pointless monotony of the old world.

These, now, are the moments the Haters live for.

Bryce gives the order, and they attack every entrance at once. They thunder through room after room, hunting for survivors. The musty air stinks of the enemy. To the attackers, it's an all-pervading, cloying, noxious stench that's exciting and repellent in equal measure. They work through each part of each building systematically, leaving no nook or cranny unchecked.

Bryce has reached a large assembly hall near the heart of the base. He kicks through the detritus, but there's nothing and no one here. This place is silent as the grave. Other fighters burst in through different doors. Keller's here. Furious, he corners Bryce. "What the fuck?"

Bryce pushes him away. "Where's McCoyne?"

McCoyne tries to melt away into the chaos, but his way out is blocked by more fighters. Bryce is having none of it. He grabs the sickly man by the throat. "Where the fuck are they?" he spits, having to fight with himself not to squeeze tighter and choke the life out of this useless runt. McCoyne tries to reply, but he can barely breathe, let alone speak.

"I don't know . . ."

"You tipped them off!"

"I didn't, I swear."

"Then what really happened here?"

"Someone recognized me," he admits.

"Bullshit."

"Not bullshit. Don't know how. I'd never seen him before, but he reckoned he came from the same place I did, so it's not impossible."

"You're a liar, McCoyne."

"I didn't know they'd gone. I'd have told you if I did, I swear." He's breathing hard. His voice is weak, and his chest rattles with sickness and fear. "They could only have gone to that other place I was telling you about. Somewhere east. On the road to Cambridge. It makes sense. Remember what Johannson was saying about people disappearing around Cambridge over the last few weeks? It has to be something to do with this lot, doesn't it?"

Bryce thinks for a moment. It makes sense. Fact is, it's all he has to go on right now. Okay, so they might not have found any-one here, but if McCoyne's telling the truth, there might be an even bigger prize waiting for them elsewhere.

He walks deeper into the base and calls the rest of his people together. "Strip it and take anything worth keeping back to the boss," he orders. "Not you," he says to McCoyne, who's already trying to creep away. "You're staying with me."

Matt and Jason are hiding behind the entrance doors many of the fighters just poured through, watching them race past just inches from where they're standing. As soon as the last one's deep enough into the base to be out of sight, the two men go the other way. Matt's furious with himself for dropping his guard. In the short time he's been here, he's become complacent. He didn't work out an escape route after he first arrived here, and he should have, because sooner or later, the shit was always going to hit the fan. He foolishly hoped it would have been later. Just goes to show, when you think things can't get any worse in this fucked-up world, they inevitably do.

They're out in the open now, exposed. Matt carries a wrench he found as a weapon, but he doesn't know how effective it'll be or even if he'll be able to use it. He's scared that his nerves will stop him attacking if he needs to. He knows the Haters have no such qualms. By the time he's thought about it, they've already done it.

Thankfully, the draw of the kill is such that all the Haters have now disappeared inside. "We need to run," Matt says to Jason. "You ready?"

"Run where?" Jason says, answering without answering.

"Over there." He points toward the group of vehicles blocking the main entrance to Thornhill.

"You're kidding, right?"

"Nope."

"You want to steal one of their cars?"

"Yep."

"But what if—"

Jason's question remains unfinished and unanswered, because Matt's already gone. He races across the empty space between the buildings and the gate. He's fucking terrified, because he knows that at the end of this sprint, he'll either be dead or on his way away from here—he can see no other outcomes.

Many of the vehicles still have the keys in the ignition, abandoned at haste. He pushes Jason toward a Ford Transit, telling him to keep out of sight of anyone who might be looking out from the base. Jason watches for signs of movement, peering through the windows of the van back toward the entrance door they'd just escaped through.

Matt walks along the line of cars and other assorted vehicles, deciding which one to take. There are some relatively decent cars here, a fancy-looking Subaru that sticks out a mile, as well as others that are less impressive. He finds a couple of smaller cars at the back of the line—a Ford Focus and a boxy little black Fiat Panda, and he almost laughs out loud at the ridiculousness of these killers turning up for battle in a fucking Fiat Panda.

He stops and thinks.

He's naturally gravitated toward the smaller vehicles, less noticeable. But is that really the best option? What's most important here? Maneuverability? Speed? Power?

"Come on, Matt. What are we doing?" Jason whispers, startling him.

"Trying to make things difficult for them."

"I don't understand. Just pick a car and go."

"One of those trucks," he says, pointing across the way.

"But they're massive."

"I know. And without one of them, they'll be ten seats down or more. They'll struggle to get all their people away."

Matt slides silently into the driver's seat of one of two flatbeds. He pulls the door shut, waits for Jason to get in the other side, then composes himself. Jason's getting agitated.

"What are you waiting for now? Just go!"

"You do realize the second I turn this key, all hell will break loose?"

"Yes! Fucking do it. Now!"

He starts the engine, and it splutters into life, sounding rough as a smoker's cough. It almost dies, and without thinking, Matt revs the motor hard to keep it ticking over, filling the air with belching fumes and far too much noise.

There's a lone fighter left outside. Matt sees him run out from behind a wooden outbuilding, doing up his fly after very obviously taking a piss. When he catches sight of Matt behind the wheel and Jason alongside him, the Hater's insatiable bloodlust is immediately ignited. He runs at the cab of the truck, and Matt knows what he has to do. He puts his foot down and plows into the Hater head-on, sending him flying through the air like a doll. He smacks against the wall of the building he'd just pissed against with a satisfying crunch, then drops to the ground, a heap of broken bones.

The rest of them are coming.

Matt can't hear them or see them yet, but he knows it won't be long. One sniff of him and Jason and the entire pack will be on their tails. He accelerates hard and careers away, almost losing control as the back of the truck fishtails in the standing rainwater. The exhaust is blowing so loud it's as if it's calling back to its owner to come save it. Two of the enemy appear in the doorway, and even though they only get a fleeting glimpse of Matt and Jason, it's more than enough. They know they're Unchanged, and two fighters become four become ten become even more. A trickle, then a flood of blood-starved killers pours out of the base, all of them racing back toward their vehicles.

"What do we do now?" Jason demands, voice full of mounting panic.

"We find the main road, look for signs to Cambridge, then keep driving."

"Then what? All we're gonna do is lead them straight to the outpost. This is a shitty plan, Matt."

"It's not a plan. I've planned fuck-all of this."

Jason keeps babbling, but Matt's not listening. He's trying, and failing, to think rationally because Jason's right: the one thing they can't afford to do is lead the Haters to the CDF. He visualizes the alternative—disappearing into the wilderness—and he remembers the days, weeks, and months he'd spent out there trying to get home to Jen. The grim reality of their situation is sobering, the prospect of wandering directionless terrifying. At least last time, he had something to aim for.

As if the thoughts rattling 'round his head weren't bad enough, Matt glances into the rearview mirror and sees the rest of the Hater convoy pulling out onto the road behind them. Jason picks up on the expression of wide-eyed panic on his face. "Jesus, we're dead. We're fucking dead!"

"You will be if you don't shut up," Matt snaps. "I'll kick you out the door if you're not careful. They'll focus on you and forget about me."

Matt glances across at him and feels the slightest pang of guilt because he knows that right now, if push *literally* comes to shove, he'll do it.

The roads here are straight and long with barely any exits. This truck is practical, not designed for speed, and the chasing pack is gaining fast. "We need to think creatively," he tells Jason, but Jason's too busy watching the crowd of killers behind to respond.

There's a turnoff ahead, the first in a while. Matt shifts down a gear, then accelerates again, hoping to coax a little more speed out of the truck, knowing that every meter might make a difference. He pulls off onto the off-ramp at the last possible moment, almost clipping the curb and losing control, still not sure where he's going or what he's trying to achieve other than staying alive. The chances of them walking away from this feel like they're reducing by the second.

At the end of the off-ramp is a traffic roundabout. "Go the other way," Jason suggests. "Go all the way around, then drive back through them."

"That's not as dumb as it sounds," Matt says, imagining the chaos when the bunched-up vehicles all try turning in the opposite direction at the exact same time. "We might be able to loop back around without them seeing. Sneak around the back of them and go back to Thornhill."

"That's the last place they'd look."

"Exactly."

But all their planning and plotting count for nothing, because they're not even halfway around the roundabout when Matt skids to a halt behind the wreck of a bus lying on its side, blocking the entire width of the road. The remains of some long-forgotten accident or ambush, it's rusted, crumpled, partly burned out, and going nowhere.

"Now we're fucked," Jason says, stating the obvious.

"Not yet," Matt tells him.

Bryce signals for some of the vehicles to keep going to the next junction and for others to block the far side of the road, and then he steers his Subaru down the off-ramp slope. The remains of his pack splits in two, driving both clockwise and counterclockwise around the roundabout, converging on the bus that blocks the road like a dead whale on a beach. The stolen truck is quickly boxed in—no way out—and within seconds, there are Haters crowding around the abandoned vehicle like a pack of hunting dogs.

The driver and his passenger are nowhere to be seen.

"Where the fuck did they go?" Bryce demands. "Fuckers must have made a run for it. Spread out and find them."

The fighters do as they're told without hesitation, because all any of them want is to be the one who does the deed and kills the Unchanged. "They can't have gotten far," a woman with a scar running from the corner of her eye to the curl of her mouth says to Bryce.

"Find them and kill them. They won't get away from us. Fuckers have backed themselves into a corner."

The Haters' assumption that Matt and Jason are currently running for their lives through the forest is way off the mark. They're actually only a couple of meters away, hiding in the luggage space at the back of the crashed bus. The vehicle came to the abrupt end of its final journey in an awkward position with its tail end jammed open, and Matt and Jason have crawled into the gap and hidden. "What now?" Jason whispers, their faces just inches apart.

"We wait. Now shut up before you get us both killed."

Matt wishes he were alone. Everything would be easier without Jason to babysit. He keeps reminding himself that Jen liked him. Christ knows why.

There's much activity outside still. Matt's flat on his belly now in the most awkward and uncomfortable of positions, but he can see the road, and he can see feet.

He's expecting to be there all day and all night, but it's only a short time later when he and Jason unexpectedly catch a break.

Something happens nearby—a noise in the forest, perhaps . . . a tree falling or an animal attacking?—but whatever it is, it's enough. There's a sudden stampede, and all the feet Matt can see start running in the same general direction. He grabs Jason and drags him toward the light. "Move. Now!"

"You're fucking kidding me! I'm not going out there."

"Well, I am," Matt tells him, and he crawls out into the open. Jason follows, not wanting to be left behind, and the two of them crawl along the suddenly empty tarmac, keeping out of sight. "Ready?" Matt asks, and he gets up and runs without waiting for an answer.

There are a handful of Haters still close, but they're staring into the trees to try to see whatever it was that caught the attention of all the others, and with their backs turned, Matt takes the opportunity to go the opposite way. He slips around the front of the bus wreck, Jason on his shoulder, and runs across the roundabout, looking for a way out.

That bloody Fiat Panda.

It's the last car in the world he'd have chosen, but it's their only option. The dumb bastard who was driving has left the door open and the engine running. Matt and Jason jump in and disappear before any of the enemy realize what's happening. They're too busy scrapping and arguing and looking for him in places where he isn't.

"Can't believe we got away with that," Jason says. His heart's hammering, and he's shaking like a leaf.

"We haven't yet."

It's no performance motor, but the little black Fiat is surprisingly responsive. It might just be that it seems quicker because it's a fraction of the weight of the flatbed he was driving previously, but Matt suddenly feels like he can outrun anything. He can't, of course, and although they've opened up the slightest of margins, they're already being followed.

"We should dump the car," Jason says.

"I was thinking the same thing. Fake our deaths."

There's a building up ahead. Looks like it was a gym. Matt slams on the brakes, throwing Jason forward in his seat. "Jesus, Matt, what the hell?"

"Get out and get out of sight."

Jason runs across the narrow gravel parking lot at the side of the building and ducks down behind a stinking trash can. Matt accelerates again and yanks the steering wheel hard over. The Fiat bumps up the curb and then skids across a yellowed grass shoulder, carving deep, furrowed tire marks in the mud. Matt opens his door and dives out, the car still moving at speed. It clips the corner of the gym building, then ricochets into the side of a BMW.

Matt picks himself up, the seconds ticking, and gestures for Jason to get up and help him. "There's a corpse in that Citroën over there," he says. "Get it into the driver's seat of the Fiat."

Jason sees where this is going, and he does as he's ordered. Much of its weight has rotted away. He screws up his face in disgust, trying to ignore the repellent smell and the nauseating, puttylike feel of corrupted flesh between his fingers as he manhandles the cadaver from one car to the other. Matt hunts around for another corpse and finds one that's little more than bones, which he shoves in the seat next to the first. "Have to assume they saw both of us."

At the back of the Fiat, he prizes the fuel cap open and plugs it with rags taken from the Citroën owner's gym bag.

"What do I do now?" Jason asks.

"Get out of sight and stay there."

Matt searches his pockets for his lighter, then sets fire to the parchment-dry cloth. Once he's sure it's caught, he catches up with Jason and pushes him toward the waterlogged wilderness, which stretches out behind the gym. "Just keep moving," he tells him. Jason doesn't need to be told twice.

They've barely made it a hundred meters when the car goes up in flames. "You know they're all going to be heading this way now, don't you?" Jason says.

"Yep. That's what we want."

Matt then changes direction abruptly, putting some distance between them and the road. He turns again but keeps walking, now going back the way they've just come. They drop down when the ragtag convoy of Haters races past on their way toward the fire, then get up and continue on their way. "They're dangerous as hell, but they're so fixated it makes them easy to fool," Matt explains. "They'll find the wreck and assume we're dead, and even if they realize those corpses aren't ours, it won't matter. We'll be long gone."

30

Cambridge

It's dark when Bryce returns to Cambridge. The university is quieter than usual. Only the occasional altercation disturbs the uncharacteristic calm. He almost makes it through to Johannson's private space unchallenged when Myndham appears and blocks his way. "What do you want?"

"I need to see the boss."

"She's resting. Come back tomorrow."

"No, not tomorrow. Now."

"Take a hint and fuck off before I—"

"What's the problem out here?"

It's Johannson. Myndham pussyfoots around the chief, but Bryce isn't having any of it. "Found something, boss," he says, breathless. "You need to hear this."

"And who the fuck are you?"

"My name's Karl Bryce."

She stifles a yawn. "And what have you found?"

"A full-on Unchanged nest."

Johannson's demeanor immediately changes. "Where?"

"Some RAF base about thirty miles away," he says, casually gesturing back over his shoulder.

"And? You killed them?"

He shuffles uncomfortably. "That's the thing . . . they'd already cleared out."

"So you woke me up to tell me you found somewhere the Unchanged used to be? Jesus . . ."

"No, wait . . . I know where they went."

Johannson chews over this news, and for a time, the only noise is the crackle of the brazier fire, which is failing to take the edge off the cold. "Go on."

"They'd not been gone long. Looks like they've moved on to another base. There might be a fair number of them out there. Military, by all accounts."

"How you getting all this information?"

"From a grunt. One of my team. He's a piss-weak nobody who doesn't have the strength to fight. You know the type."

"Yeah, I know the type."

"While we're fighting, he's mooching around, sticking his nose in."

"So what else has he told you?"

"He followed their tracks to their base, managed to kill a few of them, then realized he was in over his head, so he reported back to me. Probably for the best, because if there's as many of them there as he reckons, he wouldn't have stood a chance and we'd be none the wiser."

"Who is he again?"

"Danny McCoyne. You know him?"

She shrugs. "No idea."

"I'm not surprised. He's the kind of person you can forget about while you're still talking to them."

Johannson manages half a smile. Bryce takes that as a sign he's making progress, because half a smile is half a smile more than he's ever seen from the boss lady before.

"So where does he think they are now?"

"Not completely sure. They're clever fuckers, boss. They hide their tracks well. Looks like Pinchy was on to something, though."

"Pinchy? What's that spineless bastard got to do with anything?"

"Your missing fighters . . . he told you whereabouts he thought they were disappearing, didn't he?"

"So?"

"So it's starting to add up. McCoyne says the Unchanged were talking about an outpost on the way into Cambridge, on a main road, he said. If we know where they're hiding, we can cut them off from all approaches, then flush them out. Choke the life out of them."

Johannson gives little away, but Bryce can tell he's piqued her interest.

"There's more," he says.

"Go on."

"If what my source says is right and this is a military outpost, think about the gear they'll have. With this joker Thacker trying to muscle in on your patch, that kind of firepower's only going to help the cause, don't you think?"

"You've got a point."

"I know, and the more I think about it, the more it makes sense. Take out the Unchanged and get hold of their gear, then we'll be ready and waiting and tooled up to the nines when Thacker comes back."

She thinks for a minute, staring into the brazier.

"We'll check it out in the morning," she finally says, after a delay that feels endless. "Give Myndham all the info you've got."

Bryce is wrong-footed. She's walking away.

"Wait . . . no, boss, I want to lead this . . ."

She stops and turns back.

"Why would I want you leading anything?"

"I've brought you information."

"Like I said, all you've done is tell me you found somewhere the Unchanged used to be. Oh, and also that I've got someone here who lets the enemy go without killing them."

"It's not like that . . ."

She's not listening. Myndham steps in and gets in the way of Bryce when he tries to stop her. Johannson keeps walking. "Don't do anything stupid," Myndham tells him. "Listen to the boss. If you want to help, do what you're told and be ready to fight."

31

The CDF Outpost

The exodus from the RAF base took less than an hour, but the journey to the outpost feels like it's taken forever. Following a predefined plan (they'd been ready for this since day one—it was always going to happen), the group split into three teams and walked to separate vehicles left camouflaged in different locations, each between two and four miles away from Thornhill. The nominated drivers then drove frantically across open countryside, each stopping short of the outpost. The groups waited for hours until they were each sure they hadn't been followed, then set out on foot along different predetermined routes. Almost eighty people in total have today joined the hundreds already here.

Estelle Bisseker is up on the observation deck with Chappell and Moira. "You've exposed us, turning up like this," Chappell says.

"You think they had a choice?" Moira snaps at him, equally angry.

"Remember your rank, soldier."

"And with all due respect, remember who we're talking about, sir. I've served under Estelle for years."

"I'm not interested in years; all I care about is the here and now. And I know the two of you have history, but history has no precedent for what we're dealing with today."

"They took every precaution, followed all the protocols."

"You led the best part of a hundred people cross-country. They will have left tracks; it's inevitable."

"You're probably right. And if they find us, we'll deal with them."

"How? We don't know what kind of numbers they'll have."

Estelle has remained quiet so far, but she's in no mood to take this crap. "Listen, Greg, if you don't like it, then you can bugger off. If you can't take the pressure, then relinquish your post and go sit this out with the civvies."

"Come on, Estelle," he says. "We're all on the same side here."

"It was always the plan to move everyone here from Thornhill; we just thought we might have had a little more time before it happened. Now we're here, and we need to focus on the positives."

"There are positives?"

"Yes. We're all in one place now, and we're safe. There are more of us here than we'd expected. We're in a far stronger position than we'd thought we would be."

"What exactly happened back there? Aaron said there was a Hater in the base? Tell me that's not true."

"That's right."

"How?"

"Wily little shit snuck in unannounced. Didn't make a noise. By all accounts, he'd been in the infirmary for some time before we found him out."

"So he could hold the Hate?"

"Yes."

"Why did he wait so long to react?" Moira asks. "I could have understood it if he'd been waiting for reinforcements to arrive, but he was alone, wasn't he?"

"That's right. He only showed himself after he was challenged."

Chappell's confused. "Challenged?"

"One of the new arrivals recognized him."

"Who?"

"Doesn't matter. He's not here now. He was a pain in the backside, always sticking his nose in uninvited."

"Good job he did. Sounds like he saved a lot of lives."

"Possibly. To be honest, I believe the Hater was just looking for a way out of the fighting. It doesn't come so naturally to all of them."

"And he was definitely alone?"

"As far as we're aware."

"But there could have been more of them?"

"Almost certainly."

"And you're sure about your new recruits? They're all clean?"

"Yes. Aaron vouched for them. He tested them before they were allowed anywhere near the base. Look, we've left Thornhill an empty place. There's no indication of how we left or where we were going. There's very little chance they'll find us."

"You think? The Hater that got away, he could have overheard anything while he was with you."

"All the more reason to get things moving here."

"We need to get the new recruits integrated," Moria suggests. "Show them what's what and let them know what's expected of them. See who we've got and what they're capable of."

"I can save you the bother, Moira. They're fit and strong for the most part, but they're not soldiers."

"But you'll still want them to do a soldier's job," Chappell goads.

"You know the score, Greg. I expect everyone to do their duty."

"A couple of minutes ago, you said fighting doesn't come naturally to everyone. Which way is it going to be? There are kids here, Estelle."

"*Everyone* will be expected to contribute. What's the alternative?

Look, I understand your reticence, but we don't have any choice. We have to see this through if we want any chance of ever leading normal lives again."

"Normal lives?" Chappell says, trying not to laugh. "Christ, Estelle, I think we can all kiss the prospect of a normal life good-bye, don't you? Anything resembling normality disappeared the minute the first Hater appeared on the streets and started killing. Look, isn't it about time we started being honest with these people?"

"And tell them I'm going to send them out to war? Look, we all hope it won't come to that. The enemy doesn't know we're here, but thanks to Moira and the others, we have a pretty good idea where they're based and how many there are. With the element of surprise on our side, we'll launch an offensive and wipe them out. With a little luck and a lot of determination and effort, we'll have eradicated what's left of the Haters before a single civilian has to get involved."

"I hope it's as clear-cut as you make it sound."

"It will be," Moira says, agreeing with Estelle. "They're not expecting it. We've enough firepower to wipe them off the map, and as Estelle says, they have no bloody idea what's coming. They strut up and down out there like the planet's theirs for the taking, but it's not. We're taking it back."

"You sound like a pair of fanatics," Chappell says.

"I need you onside, Greg. Lose the attitude."

"Listen, Estelle, you've got my support," Chappell says. "I might not agree with everything you tell me, but you're the boss, and I'll follow your orders."

"Good to hear, because despite what you might think, I have the best interests of this entire group at heart. God help any Haters who get in our way."

"I think God stopped paying attention a long time back."

32

Nowhere

"It'll be light soon."

"I know."

"You said dark was good."

"It is."

"So we need to get under cover, don't we?"

"Just keep moving. Less talking, more walking."

Matt and Jason have walked through the night, finding the main road into Cambridge and following it east. They've been parallel to the wide tarmac strip for hours, moving at a snail's pace, keeping out of sight in the scrub, stopping and hiding whenever they've heard or seen anything that might be the enemy. To Matt, each step has felt like it had when he'd walked alone all those months ago, every minute a painful reminder of all that he's lost. The fact Jason's here and not Jen serves only to rub salt into the wounds. *It's his fault she's dead*, he keeps thinking, and he can't shake that thought. Until now, he's had other people to distract him, but now there's just the two of them. And it doesn't matter what Jason did or didn't do. It's all compounded by the guilt Matt feels when he thinks about Kara.

"We've been walking for ages," Jason says.

"Safest mode of transport these days."

"Think we've passed it?"

"What?"

"The CDF base. Think we've missed it?"

"We haven't. It's about twenty miles from Thornhill, and we're not. Not yet, anyway."

"We're not going to get there before sunup, are we?"

"No, probably not."

"Don't you think we should stop somewhere, then?"

"There isn't anywhere."

"I'm so fucking hungry, Matt. We haven't eaten for hours."

Matt snaps and turns on Jason. "Will you shut up and just keep moving? The last thing I need right now is your bloody noise."

"I'm just saying—"

"Yeah, well, don't. Don't say anything. Right now, nothing you could possibly say is of any interest to me."

He is right, though.

Matt's grudgingly forced to admit that being out here like this will become increasingly dangerous as the light improves. They're both physically and emotionally empty; the kind of slow-build exhaustion that Matt knows through experience will leave them prone to making mistakes. To make matters worse, without knowing exactly where they are in relation to the CDF base, they're walking blind. There could be hours of walking and many miles still ahead of them. A couple of times, Matt's considered trying to get a car started, but he's worried even the creak of a door opening would be loud enough to be heard from a distance. The noise of an engine would surely let every Hater in the immediate vicinity know exactly where he and Jason are, and to drive to the outpost would, as they've already deduced, be the absolute worst thing they could do. He knows they're going to have to finish this journey on foot, and in order to be able to do that, they're going to have to stop and rest first.

They're walking closer to the road again now, but it's another hour or more before they see a building up ahead. The black of night is rapidly disappearing and is now tinged with gray. Daybreak is close. Whatever this place is, it's going to have to do.

Jesus, though, this is better than they'd imagined. For once, it looks like they've caught a break.

They're approaching a fuel station with a chain hotel behind. It's the kind of place Matt would have done everything possible to avoid staying in before the war began, but right now it looks like the Savoy.

"Stay here," he says to Jason, leaving the other man waiting way back in the evaporating gloom while he checks the site out.

Getting inside isn't going to be a problem. The outer reception door has been torn from its hinges and is now sticking out of the unkempt yellowing hedgerow that grows wild around the front of the building. There was a Starbucks here, a separate mismatched building on the other side of the parking lot, but there's no point looking for food there because the place is just a shell. There's not one pane of glass left intact as far as Matt can see, and there are bodies everywhere. Long dead. Skeletons wrapped in rags who died fighting.

The Travelodge looks to have fared slightly better, but not much. Matt's hesitant. There's obviously been a shitload of trouble around here at some point, but when? He knows they can't be too far from Cambridge now. It's likely there are richer pickings a little way farther down the road, but Matt knows he and Jason don't need much: food and water and beds to lie on behind a door they can lock.

He pushes a swinging vestibule door open, then stops in the small, square reception area and listens intently. The hotel is as silent as he'd hoped. The only noise comes from the wind whipping through broken windows, and from a sudden downpour of rain, which clatters against the flat roof. *Looks like you made it just in time, sir,* the receptionist doesn't say. Instead, she remains in her seat staring up at the ceiling, dead mouth hanging open. Her skin has the texture of a dried-up apple. Matt climbs over her desk and into her cubicle. Competing for space with the corpse, he forces a drawer open and helps himself to as many room keys as he can find, filling his pockets. He finds a few other things that may prove useful: some tools, other random keys, a wall-mounted first aid kit. There are plenty more things he leaves untouched. A cash tray full of notes and coins. A computer. A fancy-looking phone and a tablet. There are so many things, he thinks, that used to have value but are now worthless.

Back over onto the customer side of the counter, and he's on his way out to call Jason over when a vending machine tucked behind the entrance piques his interest. He has to look twice, because at first he thinks his eyes must be deceiving him. It's still half-full of food, the sight of which makes him realize just how bloody hungry he actually is.

He starts trying to prize the door open, then remembers the keys he'd just picked up and tries each of them in turn, but none fit. Then he grabs the top of the cabinet and rocks it back and forth, hoping to dislodge an out-of-date chocolate bar or stale packet of potato chips. He has to get it open. This is too valuable a haul to leave. There's enough food in here to keep him and Jason going for days. He kicks the machine in anger, then picks up a fire extinguisher and uses it to try to smash the glass. A spiderweb of splintering cracks spread out from the point of impact, but it doesn't smash. Matt hits the door again, remembering the long-forgotten taste of chocolate . . .

A disheveled Hater woman sprints down the corridor and crashes into reception, the sound of her skittering footsteps hidden by the noise Matt's making.

He looks up just as she hurls herself at him.

The reception area is a tight space, and the closed-in confines make it difficult to move with Matt and the Hater both getting in each other's way and blocking all exits. The woman's in an awful state physically, and that, combined with her excitement and over-keenness to kill, means her initial attack is nowhere near as coordinated as it might otherwise have been. As she lunges at him, Matt tries to crawl under her on his hands and knees. He's almost away when she catches his ankle and pulls him back, dragging him into range again. He kicks and squirms, but even in her awful, wasted state, the danger from the Hater is undiminished. She grabs hold of his collar, then smashes his face against the vending machine glass. He tries to fight back, but he's stunned and full of pain. She thumps his face into the machine again, and he feels himself blacking out, only fear dragging him back from the brick of unconsciousness.

Someone else here.

Jason.

Through flickering eyes, Matt sees him in the doorway. He's aware of a blur of red movement as Jason smashes the fire extinguisher down on the back of the Hater's skull. She collapses on top of Matt, and he pushes himself out from underneath her. He drags himself upright, but before he can make for the exit, the Hater's on her feet again. She lunges, and this time, his only escape route takes him deeper into the building.

Matt doesn't have a damn clue where he's heading now.

It's a long, narrow corridor with rooms on either side. The doors are all shut, and he doesn't dare try any of them because they're likely locked and he'll waste precious seconds—or, just as likely, there will be more Haters ready to join the fray. Instead, he just keeps running, crashing through a fire exit at the end of the hallway and finding himself back outside in the parking lot. Even nature seems to be conspiring against him now, because it's considerably lighter than when he first entered the building. The shadows are evaporating. Nowhere left to hide.

He glances back and he sees the Hater woman barreling along the corridor after him, all arms and legs and rags and wild hair, looking like something out of a nightmare. Matt's legs are heavy, his feet barely coordinated, and there's nothing left in the tank. He breaks right, stumbling around and between the long-stationary vehicle wrecks littering the fuel station forecourt, then climbs onto the hood of a midsize van that's collided with the corner of a car wash and been abandoned. From there, he scrambles up onto the top of the car wash itself, then he keeps climbing, jumping the meter gap onto the flat roof of the small payment kiosk and store. And still he keeps running, because it's that or give up.

He drags himself up onto the canopy that covers the entire forecourt, then runs out of options because it's too high to jump down and the way back is blocked. The Hater woman has followed him all the way. Matt's standing on the farthest edge of the canopy now: a blood-crazed killer in front, and a sheer drop behind.

The briefest of standoffs.

He's barely gotten his breath when the woman races toward him again. He stands his ground, tensed up and ready for impact. At the last possible second, he simply steps out of the way. She just about manages to stop herself from going over, teetering on the brink, but he helps her on her way with a shove to the backside.

Hater or no Hater, the thud and crunch when she hits the deck is sickening. Matt drops to all fours, panting like a dog, and peers over. She's still alive down there, but she won't be for long. She's not going anywhere. Her legs are badly broken, and her right arm is useless and limp, twisted behind her head at an unnatural angle, snapped at the elbow. When she sees him looking down at her, she still tries to move. Matt relaxes. He knows he's safe.

The woman has dropped into the gap between the edge of the forecourt canopy and the Travelodge. Jason's waiting in the hotel doorway. Matt climbs down and walks toward him, but as much as he wants to get out of sight and stay there, he's distracted. He takes an unexpected interest in the Hater woman's suffering, almost a perverse pleasure. Despite the fact her bones are protruding through her flesh in several places, grinding and cutting every time she moves even a fraction, she just can't stop herself reacting. She's driven to want to kill Matt, no matter what the cost. He remains just out of reach, deliberately taunting her, then shuffles farther back when she stretches out her remaining good arm and her fingertips almost touch the toes of his boots. "Fucker," she growls.

"Bitch," he says back, crouching down so she can hear him.

"You won't . . . last long . . ."

"I've done okay so far. Better than you, anyway."

"Won't . . . last . . ."

"Who were you?" Matt asks. He's thinking out loud, not meaning to converse, not wanting to engage. But now he's sown the seed, he's curious. "Who did you used to be before all this?"

"Used to be nothing . . ."

"What, and now you think you're something? Look at you. Christ, is this what we've been reduced to? Is this all that's left? Pretty fucking pathetic, if you ask me."

"Fuck you . . ." she spits, and she exhales hard through gritted teeth, which are speckled with blood. The hatred in her voice is undiminished, but her strength is failing. The life's leaking out of her, crimson blood pooling against the monochrome gray of everything else.

Matt's still crouched. He's no longer afraid and is instead bizarrely curious. "What just happened to you," he says, "is a perfect metaphor for what'll happen to the rest of your kind. You shout, you fight, you attack. You make a lot of noise, then you die.

It's all so pointless. Just look at you . . . bleeding out on your own outside a fuel station in the middle of nowhere. If we hadn't been here to watch, no one would even have noticed. Pathetic."

"You know nothing . . ." she wheezes. Fading fast. Not long left.

"I know a damn sight more than you think."

With her last ounce of energy, she lashes out at him again with her good arm. Matt trips back and falls, smacking hard against the side of a dust-covered Alfa Romeo. He feels a sudden sharp pain in his left shoulder and screams out, voice echoing around the empty buildings, taking forever to fade. There's something sticking into his skin. It's gone in deep. Really deep.

Jason's here now, and from the look on his face, Matt knows this isn't good.

"Shit, mate."

"What is it?"

"Take it easy," Jason tells him, and he takes Matt's arm and carefully pulls him forward. The pain in his back increases. Finally free, Matt shuffles around and sees a jagged shard of metal sticking out from the car's crumpled metal bodywork, and the last three inches of it is vivid red with his blood.

"Fuck," he says, thinking he might be about to pass out. Jason helps him to his feet.

"We need to get inside."

"Fuck," Matt says again, dripping with sweat, struggling to walk, struggling to stay standing.

They step over the Hater corpse. Bitch has died with a smile on her face.

Matt can feel blood running down his back. He stretches his right hand over to touch his left shoulder, and when he brings it back around, it's soaked with red. His legs threaten to buckle, but Jason has his weight and keeps him moving. It's only a few meters, but it feels like a marathon. Eventually, they make it into reception, and Matt leans against the wall, but his legs give way and he collapses. Jason peels off his blood-soaked jacket and shirt, then lowers him down so he's lying on his belly on the muck-covered cord carpet.

"Gonna try to stop the bleeding," he says, but Matt's head is spinning and he can't respond.

What if there are more of them here?

What if more of them are coming?

Am I going to bleed to death?

What if . . . ?

He's gone. Out cold.

33

The Travelodge

When Matt next opens his eyes, he thinks he must be dreaming. Hallucinating. It doesn't feel right to be lying on a bed—an actual, proper, *comfortable* bed—with his head on a pillow. He tries to roll over but stops when he feels the burning pain in his shoulder. He's glued to the sheets with dried blood. To his credit, Jason must have managed to stem the blood loss, but Matt's under no illusions; with the air filled with Christ knows what and every surface covered with a layer of grime so thick you could write your name in it, he knows a wound like this could be the death of him.

"You're still alive, then."

He looks up and sees Jason sitting in a chair opposite, his feet up on a table. There are thin curtains at the window, which let in enough light for him to see his surroundings, and there's an unexpected familiarity that catches him off guard, making him feel both nostalgic and, for the moment, safe. The minimalist decoration. The functional furniture. The cheap artwork hanging on the walls. The TV, remote, jug kettle, and drinks-making facilities. This could be any room in any hotel anywhere in the country.

He tries to lift himself up onto his elbows, but the pain's too much, and he crashes back down.

"My shoulder . . ."

"Really nasty wound, mate. I cleaned it up as best I could. Couldn't face doing stitches, so I superglued it."

"Thanks."

"Water?"

Jason has amassed a decent collection of supplies. He opens a fresh bottle and hands it to Matt, who knocks it back in several large gulps.

"Before you start having a go at me," Jason says, "I've checked every inch of this place, and we're clear. I found the room keys you had in your pocket. A few of the rooms are like this one, haven't been opened since before the fighting started. That woman you pushed off the roof was the only Hater around."

"I'm impressed."

"I managed to get the food out of the vending machine in reception. This lot," he continues, gesturing at a pile of stash, "belonged to our dead friend out there. Proper little hoard she had. Her room stank to high heaven, but all the stuff I brought in here was sealed."

"Where are we?"

"What?"

"In the building? Whereabouts are we?"

"Give me some credit, Matt. We're not in room number one next to reception, if that's what you're worried about. I did think about this. This room is facing the back. There are three locked and empty rooms on one side, two on the other, and four opposite. It's the least conspicuous room from the back of the hotel."

"What about the corpse outside?"

"I left her where she was. Seemed sensible. Looks like she was up on the roof and lost her footing—which I guess she kind of did. I could have moved her, but I thought a trail of blood leading away from here might have been a bit of a giveaway."

"Good. How long have I been out of it?"

"You've been drifting in and out for hours. The Hater had some boxes of pills, so I shoved a few down your throat. Not entirely sure what they were, but you've come around, so they can't have done you any harm. There was some antiseptic in the first aid kit in reception, and the last person to use one of the other rooms left a bottle of antibiotics in the bathroom. I gave you a swig of that, too."

"Thanks."

Jason glares at him. "See. Not quite as fucking useless as you keep telling everyone I am, eh?"

"Sorry."

"I got us safe and patched you up."

"Thanks."

"So I reckon it's about time you got off my case."

"Now's really not the time."

"I know, but you need to hear this. I need you to understand that what happened to Jen wasn't my fault. Believe me, it tears me apart every day thinking about it."

"You could have—"

"No, *you* could have been there for her. I tried, I really did. She wasn't going anywhere without you. I tried to get her to where you'd told us to meet you, but she wouldn't leave. I tried to tell you and get you to go back to the house, but . . ."

"Kara told me."

"Shame about Kara. I could do with having her here. She was the only one who could keep you in check."

"Yeah . . ."

"Look, I don't like being around you as much as you don't like being around me, but that's just how it goes. So let's get some rest, get you sorted, then get to that bloody outpost."

34

The CDF Outpost

There are spotters up in the trees around the base, camouflaged and all but invisible, wrapped tight in the grip of clawlike branches. This is Andrew Ryman's first shift in several days. He'd rather be in the trenches or even guarding the death pit. It's the exposure out here, *up* here, that gets to him. He's watching for enemy movement, but what if *they* spot *him?* He knows he'd be completely alone. He's had nightmares about being stuck up this damn tree with a pack of wild Haters prowling like wolves below, waiting for him to come down. *Can't stay up there forever . . .*

It's hard to stay focused. His mind wanders. He's thinking about the life he used to lead before all of this. Thinking about what his future (if he has one) might hold. Thinking about the cramp in his leg. Thinking about how he's soaked through with foul-tasting rain (again). Thinking about how his face is frozen, and how there's water stinging his eyes, and how he has an itch he wants to scratch but how he doesn't dare move because knowing his luck, the moment he does will be the moment a Hater wanders past and looks up.

He's harnessed to the trunk of the tree, and he pulls the strapping tight. It hurts his belly, but the discomfort's better than the fall. He's lost so much weight over the last few months that a single belt is enough to keep him secure. There's not an ounce of fat on him. The nylon digs into his skin, and he tries to scratch but his fingers are numb with cold. One day, they'll find him dead up here, he thinks. He doubts anyone would notice. He could be up here for weeks before anyone realized he was missing.

His eyes are heavy, and he's just starting to fall asleep when he hears it. The world's so quiet these days that sounds like this are alien and difficult to locate. Thunder? An engine? A distant building collapsing in on itself? It's hard to make anything out through the squall.

And then he sees it.

A single motorbike is tearing along the A14 at a furious speed, its driver skillfully swerving to avoid the floodwater and debris. Andrew fumbles for his binoculars but only manages to catch a fleeting glimpse as the bike races past.

Andrew has to let the chiefs know what he's just seen. All unusual activity has to be reported and recorded, even if it's just a random Hater passing through. He hangs the binoculars around his neck, then fumbles with the clips and carabiners and disentangles himself from the safety harness before shimmying back down to ground level. He drops down into the nearest trench and races through the mazelike network of passages to find Chappell.

Nina Young cruises through the countryside on the kind of bike she always dreamed of owning but never thought she would. It's damn powerful, almost too much, and the thrill of the barely contained engine force she's straddling combines with the openness of the empty world and the prospect of hunting Unchanged to leave her feeling giddy with excitement, struggling to focus. She stops in a rest area several miles farther down the A14, marks her position on the map, then turns the bike around and rides back the way she just came, twice as fast.

Result.

This time when she looks up, the figure in the tree is gone.

Nina knows these roads well, and it's no time at all before she's on the final approach back into the ruins of the university. The bike's nowhere near as quick as email or phones used to be, but it moves at lightning speed in comparison to everything else, and these days it's the fastest way of getting information from point A to point B.

She can't help but feel a swell of pride when she drives up toward Johannson's building and the crowd parts to let her through. Myndham is in the ornate college doorway before she's even dismounted, gesturing for her to follow him inside.

Johannson's waiting deeper in the bowels of the building with her other general. Nina marches up and takes the folded map out of her leathers. She lays it out on a table in front of them. "Well? What did you find?" Johannson demands.

"I did like you said and went straight down the A14." She follows the line of the road with her finger. "Got to this point, and there's a guy up in a tree, some kind of lookout."

"Doesn't prove anything."

"He was Unchanged."

"You're certain?"

"Seventy-eighty percent."

"Go on."

"I carried on, then doubled back. Passed by again a few minutes later, and he'd gone. He was reporting in to someone that he'd seen me, I'm sure of it. As sure as I can be, anyway."

"That's not conclusive," Ullah says, unimpressed.

"You're right, it's not—" Nina starts to say before Johannson interrupts.

"But it's enough. We'd already narrowed it down to a few

squares on the map, and what she's saying puts them right in the middle of that space. This information is good enough for me. That's where they're hiding, it has to be. Well done."

"Thanks, boss," Nina says, smug.

Johannson talks tactics with Ullah and Myndham. Other interested parties hang back and listen in, desperate for any scraps of information that might give them an advantage on the battlefield. Bryce loiters because he knows he needs to stay one step ahead of the rest of the pack. He's determined to show Johannson what he's made of.

"They've got to be dug in deep to have stayed hidden from us for so long, and if they're that well hidden, it'll take them just as long to dig themselves out. Mobilize everyone. Tool them up. We're moving out."

35

The Travelodge

Matt peels himself off the bedding. His wound has leaked again. He lifts himself up onto his elbows and looks behind. The bedclothes are heavily stained with yellow and red. He lies back down, faint and freezing cold, his head pounding. *At least I'm not dead* is the most positive thought he can come up with. He wonders how much blood he lost, what kind of infections he might have picked up from the wound, and not for the first time, it strikes him just how vulnerable everyone is these days. No doctor to ask for advice. No medical supplies to use. No books or websites to consult. Relatively trivial injuries could easily become life-threatening now. It's frustrating. Frightening.

The room is empty. No sign of Jason. A piece of paper has been taped to the back of the chair he was sitting in when Matt was last conscious. With considerable effort, Matt swings his legs around and gets up to read what Jason has written. "Room 17." He wraps a duvet around his shoulders and then, dragging his feet, leaves his room and knocks on the door of number 17. Jason answers quickly, instinctively looking up and down the corridor before he lets Matt in. "Good, you're alive," he says without a hint of sarcasm.

"Thanks again for sorting me out."

"Don't mention it."

"But if you hadn't—"

"No, really, don't mention it. I don't want to hear it. I'd like to think you'd have done the same for me."

Matt looks around the room. Jason's been working hard in here, that much is clear. He appears to have pooled all the supplies in the hotel and is sorting them into some kind of order: food, drink, clothes, bedding. He's a man on a mission this morning.

"Planning something?"

Jason barely looks up. "There's some good stuff here. Can't afford to leave it behind. If we can't find a way of transporting it, then we might have to come back."

"I'm not going anywhere."

"Maybe not today, no, but when we're—"

"I'm not going anywhere," Matt says again. "Not today, not tomorrow. Not for a long time yet, if ever."

"You can't stay here."

"I think you'll find I can. It's relatively secure, hidden from the road by the Starbucks, and you've found us a decent stash of food and water to keep us going for a few weeks."

Jason just looks at him, aghast. "You're kidding, right? You're saying you're going to just abandon all the others?"

"That's exactly what I'm saying. They already abandoned me, remember? Abandoned *us,* actually. I wasn't aware of anyone rushing back to check you were okay."

"Yeah, well, that's because they knew it'd be too dangerous. This is different."

"How? Think about it logically; we're not exactly sure where the outpost is, and even if we were, how are we supposed to get access to it? Do we just go running up to the front door waving a white flag? From a distance, they'll think we're Haters whatever we do. They'd take us out before we got anywhere close."

"Yeah, but—"

"What difference do you think the two of us are going to make?"

Jason shakes his head. "You're a selfish fucker."

"I'm a realist, that's all. And if that means I come across as a miserable prick, then so be it. Sorry about that. At least you've got your own room, neighbor. I'll go back to my place and we'll shut the door on each other. We'll probably get along better that way."

"And this is all the thanks I get?"

"What?" Matt just stands there and stares at him, dumbstruck. Where does he start? What does he want thanks for? "Have you forgotten everything that happened before we got to this place?"

"No, I'm just trying to make the best of a bad situation. I've been through the entire building and got all this stuff together. I found some more antibiotics, too."

"Great. Thanks very much. To be honest, though, I'd trade all of it for a way to make you see sense."

"I am seeing sense. We need the group."

"I'm not arguing with that. Problem is, I don't reckon they need us. We'll struggle to get anywhere near them in one piece, and between the noise we made leaving Thornhill and the noise the others would have made before us, there are probably Haters everywhere out there right now. The countryside will be crawling with them. We struck lucky here, and we need to make the most of that luck, not throw it away."

Matt sits down on the end of Jason's bed and helps himself to some food from a box. Jason looks crestfallen.

"What are you most pissed off about?" Matt asks him. "Being stuck here, or being stuck here with me?"

"Do you really think I'm that shallow? Look, Matt, I get it. You've never liked me. You fought to get back to your house, and when you did, the first thing you saw when you opened the door was me. I used to think about that a lot, about how that must have felt. It wasn't my fault, though. And you're quick enough to crucify me because of what happened to Jen at the end, but that wasn't my fault, either. If I'd told you she wasn't there and you'd gone after her, *everyone* would have died that night, you, me and Jen included."

Matt's emotional. He struggles to keep his feelings hidden and curses himself, worried that Jason will have noticed. He clears his throat. "Doesn't change anything. We're stuck here. We need to make the most of what we've got left, and that's not a lot. Harsh as it is, right now, we need to forget everything and everyone else and focus on keeping ourselves alive."

36

The CDF Outpost

It's late in the day when the attack begins. The conditions are atrocious. Light fading fast.

It's been almost two days since any of the enemy were seen near the outpost, and the soldiers and civilians guarding the place are caught off guard. A spotter catches a glimpse of movement through the gloom and quickly passes word along the line. One soldier tells the next, then the next, and so it continues until the entire length of the trench protecting the eastern flank of the outpost is alive with nervous anticipation. Killing doesn't come naturally to these people, no matter how much is at stake. To the approaching enemy, however, slaughter has become a way of life. It's a necessity. To leave any Unchanged alive would be an unforgiveable sin.

The longer the lookouts are peering out into the overcast early evening, the more concerned they become. Andrew Ryman is in position again, and he can see at least seven figures approaching—no, make that nine—and he's starting to think this might be the big one, the coordinated attack they've longed feared. He scrambles down from his tree-mounted position to report back. He's less concerned with getting the news to the chiefs, more worried about being caught out here and cut off. It's a relief when he finds he's not the only one to have abandoned their post. There's an air of barely contained hysteria inside the outpost. Moira Kay is keeping a tally of numbers. More than twenty Haters have been spotted now. The most they've so far seen in any one attack.

Jesus, but these are particularly vicious bastards, more like wild animals than human beings now. The number of fighters in the trenches has been ramped up, but this feels different from previous incursions. The approaching Haters show absolutely no fear.

Chappell is watching the advance through his binoculars. "They're acting differently."

Estelle just looks at him. "You've really not seen a lot of action, have you? Of course they're acting differently. They know we're here."

"That's impossible."

"Not impossible. It was only ever a matter of time."

The first of them reaches the edge of the trench. When she sees the Unchanged faces looking back up at her, she throws herself down there and attacks. Three CDF fighters lay into her with clubs—wet thud after wet thud like they're tenderizing meat—but her ferocity is such that she kills one soldier and mortally wounds another before she's brought down.

By the time the first Hater has been dealt with, four more have breached this section of trench. Some of the Unchanged fighters have become adept at killing, slitting the Haters' throats and covering their mouths until they've bled out, but these people are the exception. Most of those who are defending the outpost are inexperienced amateurs, and the odds are stacked against them.

Another spotter races back to base. She winds her way along the trenches, jumping corpses and avoiding fights, then scrambling up the muddy bank to the service station building and shoving her way through the crowds. Moira intercepts her. "Problem?"

"One got away," she says, breathless.

Moira panics. "What the fuck?! How did that happen?"

"It's chaos out there, I swear. One of them did an about-face and disappeared. Just turned around and ran. He gave us the slip."

"Shit. Get trackers out there to deal with him. We can't risk any more of those fuckers finding where we are."

There are always several heavily armed CDF fighters ready and waiting in the wings for this kind of eventuality. Caleb Jones and Tony Shepherd are two of the best. They're old hands: both of them long in the tooth, and both having seen action all around the world in their many years of military service. They know each other of old, their paths having crossed on numerous occasions in numerous trouble spots before both of them ended up stationed here at this bullshit service station at the arse end of nowhere. Neither will admit as much to the other, but today, chasing one lone bogie across the Cambridgeshire countryside, feels more daunting than facing any number of religious fanatics or other militants in any of the old-world flashpoints.

They both know how the other operates. There's an unspoken communication between them, which is a bonus because to make any unnecessary noise out here in the wilderness could easily be the end of either or both of them. Shepherd takes the lead initially. He's the tracker, following the trail left by the clumsy Hater who's given them the slip but who foolishly also made no attempt to cover their tracks. Thing is with these bastards, Shepherd thinks, they're so focused on the fight and the kill that they forget about everything else. They've got no chance with Shepherd on their trail. He's a pro. He increases his speed, and soon the would-be killer is in sight, disappearing into a thin copse of spindly trees. Both soldiers know all that matters here is stopping this foul creature before he can get back and alert others of his kind. He knows where the CDF base is now. He has to be dealt with.

Jones allows himself the tiniest of wry smiles. Silly prick has fucked up and run himself into a dead end. The two soldiers follow him down along a narrow, tree-lined track that ends at the entrance to what used to be a farmer's animal shelter: a high-sided, open-ended corrugated metal construction on the outermost edge of a mud-churned field. The Hater's just a kid, swift and lithe. He accelerates and disappears into the building, and Shepherd and Jones split, more than matching his pace and taking one of the building exits each. Shepherd heads for the rear while Jones takes the end through which the Hater just went. He has his silenced pistol drawn, ready to take the monster out with the minimum of fuss. He pauses, steeling himself for the kill, then bursts into the open barn.

And stops. Doesn't fire.

Fuck.

The building's full of people.

They're Haters. All of them. He knows that's true, because several of them are already lynching Shepherd at the other end of the building. They've got him pinned against the wall. One of them is eviscerating him with a wicked-looking blade.

Jones tries to focus and raises his pistol to fire, but it's too little, too late. What good will one shot be when there are more than thirty of them here? His brain is flooded with panicked thoughts, and he turns to try to get back to base, but there are even more of them out here, blocking his way out. He starts to fire, but raising his arm leaves his midriff exposed, and one of the enemy impales him with a sharpened metal railing. The pain is unreal, and for a split second, Jones feels like he's floating, watching all this happening to someone else. He feels the spike going in, then he feels it pushing out the other side, then he feels nothing at all.

Ullah stands over the soldier's corpse. "That's it. We've got the bastards. Get a message back to the boss. Tell here we've located them." He goes to walk away but pauses. "And do something with the bodies. Let those Unchanged fuckers know we're coming. The more nervous they are, the easier they'll be to kill."

37

When the insipid gray sun reluctantly climbs above the horizon next morning, the full implications of what happened last night are revealed. The two corpses have been left in full view of the outpost. One lies in the mud, hacked into pieces, while the other has been impaled and left propped up like a scarecrow.

"We should get out there and recover the bodies," Chappell suggests.

"And what would that achieve, exactly?" Estelle snaps at him.

"It's about respect."

"Respect? We're a bit far gone for worrying about people's feelings, don't you think? Anyone who's made it this far knows what we're up against. The enemy knows exactly where we are now. There's no point pissing around moving corpses off the battlefield."

She's right, of course, but that doesn't make it any easier to swallow. Jones and Shepherd were good men. Experienced men.

"This changes everything," Chappell says.

"It changes *nothing*. If anything, the fact they've found us makes the mission easier."

"You think?"

"I *know*. We're not hiding any longer. We can stop pussyfooting around and start using some of the firepower we've got. Think positive. Stop looking for problems."

Estelle sounds less than impressed with Chappell's attitude. He checks himself, biting his tongue and forcing himself to show his commanding officer the respect her rank deserves.

"What are your orders, ma'am?"

She thinks carefully, though it's not as if she hasn't spent countless hours preparing for this moment. "They've blinked. They've given themselves away. They've played their hand too soon, and they've completely underestimated the weaponry we have at our disposal here. They'll attack us in much larger numbers now, there's no doubt about that. We need to make sure everyone knows what's expected of them and get them ready to fight. We're going to wipe out every last one of those evil bastards once and for all."

Joseph Mallon has done everything he can to avoid the front line, but he senses his already limited options are rapidly reducing. Even when the level of his own personal hate was at its fiercest, in the days and weeks following the slaughter of his family in front of him in their home, fighting back was never something that came naturally. He had to force himself to retaliate, every push and every punch taking ten times more mental effort than physical. That was why he looked for alternative solutions. Maybe, if he was honest with himself, he tried so hard to stop the killing because he couldn't stand the thought of having to get his hands dirty himself.

Right now, he knows that trouble's on the horizon. Closer than it's been for a while. The bodies displayed on the battleground are a clear signal that the inevitable last battles are looming, and the closer they get, the harder he tries to distance himself. He does anything he can to keep himself out of the trenches, volunteering to do the things no one else will do, the shittiest of shitty jobs. This morning, he's at the death pit again, maintaining a 24-7 vermin watch. The food chain's all tied up in knots since the bombs, and there's not so much wildlife left roaming these days—most creatures have been poisoned or eaten, either by other animals or starving humans of one type or another. Joseph's mission here, when he's not dealing with the dead, is to keep the area rodent-free. Mangy dogs, foxes, and rats are attracted to the rotting meat in the pit, and there's always been the worry that increased levels of animal activity might attract even more dangerous predators. Joseph's scared himself stupid before now, imagining a pack of Haters hunting down a pack of rats and somehow ending up here.

This place was a hive of activity when the enemy attacked last night, piles of bodies stacking up. They all look the same when they're dead, and from where he's standing, the lines are starting to blur with the living, too. It's getting harder to differentiate between some of the CDF militia fighters and the Haters. Different shades of killer, that's all, different motives. The CDF say they're killing to end the war, but isn't that what the other side is probably saying, too? It takes Joseph back to the conversations he'd had with those few Haters he'd thought he'd taught to hold the Hate all those months ago. That's the biggest paradox of war, he thinks: everyone knows they're right, and no one will ever admit they're wrong.

Now the sun's up (for what it's worth), the cleanup begins in earnest. Yet more of the dead are carried over and dumped near the pit, and Joseph's glad of the distraction. It helps him ignore the nagging feeling he has that the tenuous normality of the last few weeks is about to come to an end. Going through the motions like this, the same old, same old, prolongs the illusion of safety for a short while longer. Peter Sutton's been sent here again to help. Joseph wishes they'd send someone else.

"Go through that pile of clothes," he tells him when Peter asks what he should do. "Salvage anything that's still got any wear left in it, dump the rest."

Peter dutifully gets to work, though he's not sure any of this stuff is worth keeping. Stripped from corpses, it's stained and soaked and ripped, torn and worn.

There are two male corpses at Joseph's feet, dropped like sacks of potatoes at the edge of the pit. He takes a deep breath and goes to haul the first of them over when the dead man opens his eyes. It's one of the enemy, and the damn monster is somehow still alive! Joseph staggers back with surprise, looking for a weapon, and the Hater manages to flop himself over onto his belly and drag himself along, crawling through the mud. The Hate-fueled strength he still possesses is remarkable. Even though it'll almost certainly be the last thing he ever does, he's still driven to kill at all costs. He snarls and groans with pain and anger. "Kill . . . you . . ." he gasps, struggling to fill his collapsing lungs with air enough to function. The Hater is relentless, like something out of a nightmare. By all rights, he should be dead already, but still he keeps coming.

"Watch yourself, Peter," Joseph says, and he runs over to the back of a van where they've been storing scavenged weapons. He's looking for a decent blade or club, cursing himself for not bringing one outside with him. He finds a carving knife that'll do the trick, but when he stands up again and looks out through the windows in the side of the van, Joseph sees something he can't understand.

Peter's approaching the Hater now, but the monster in the mud isn't reacting. The killer has become calm—too calm—all the fight suddenly gone. Peter drops to his knees and lifts the broken man up in his arms, all his anger and hatred inexplicably neutralized. Peter covers the man's mouth and nose and holds him tight in a headlock until he stops breathing, like he's rocking him to sleep. When the deed is done, he rolls the body down the slope into the mass grave.

Joseph approaches him with the knife gripped tight, still struggling to comprehend what he's just witnessed. It's not what Peter did to the Hater; it's how the Hater reacted toward Peter. Passive. Calm. Accepting. Joseph's paralyzed with fear now because he's tried to unpick the actions and interactions between Haters and Unchanged more than most, and though he does everything he can to try to convince himself he's wrong, in his heart he knows he's right.

Peter must be a Hater.

"It's okay, Joseph, he's dead. I killed him."

Joseph's mouth is dry, his pulse racing. He wants to run, but he can't move, legs like lead. He has a million thoughts racing, but he can barely spit out the first word. "You're . . . you're one of *them* . . ."

Peter almost laughs. "Come on, Joe. Seriously?"

"I saw you. That kid . . . he stopped fighting. He let you hold him. He'd only have done that if . . ."

Peter drops his head. "If what? Go on, say it."

"If you were a Hater."

It sounds impossible, vaguely ridiculous. Peter's expression changes, but it's hard to read. For a split second, he appears poised to make a denial, but then decides there's no point.

"And what would you do if I was? Tell the chiefs? I wouldn't blame you if you did."

"You'll kill us all."

"Believe me, Joseph, I won't."

"Why should *I* believe *you?* You've been lying since you got here. I always knew there was something wrong with you."

"You should believe me because I haven't hurt anyone so far. Not here, at least. I killed that boy just now because it had to be done. He was all but dead already."

"You're a Hater," Joseph says again, still struggling to process everything that's happening.

"Hater, Unchanged . . . I think we need to lose the labels. I thought you'd understand that better than anyone. I knew your name before I got here. I know about the work you were doing with people like me."

"I made a mistake before. I was wrong."

"You weren't. You got it right, but they used you, manipulated you. I know exactly what happened, Joseph. I knew of your reputation from other people who were trying to do the same thing, Simon Penkridge and Selena. I'd been here for a while when you turned up, but I deliberately kept a low profile."

"Why?"

"Because I thought you might expose me. I also figured you were probably the only one who could help me. You'd be the only one who'd listen."

"So why are you here? Are you going to turn on us? Kill us? Are you here like those bastards I tried to help before, back in the city? The ones who brought the whole place crashing down?"

"I wasn't there. Believe me, I know what you were trying to do, Joseph; you were trying to rehabilitate . . . to stop the fighting."

"And look what happened. Hundreds of thousands of people died, and it's my fault. I accelerated the end."

"You really think that? And who said anything about this being the end? We're still alive, aren't we?"

"Barely."

"We can get through this."

Joseph's shaking his head. "This is bullshit. You're just biding your time, waiting for the Haters to find this place. Did you bring them here? Are you the one who brought them here?"

Peter shakes his head. "They're nothing to do with me. Ask yourself, if I'd wanted to bring this place down, wouldn't I have done it already? You're right; I could destroy everything we've built here in minutes. I could go inside that building right now and start a riot that would leave everyone dead. I could finish this war at any moment."

"So why don't you?"

"I told you before, it's not about me. I have family here. My grandson. The lad doesn't know me, but I know him and I want to keep him safe. I want to keep him alive. He's all I've got left."

"The rest of us have got nothing left thanks to your kind."

"You think I don't know that? I'm clinging to the hope that there's still a chance of some of us getting through this and coming out the other side in one piece."

"I lost that hope a long time ago."

"I know. I've known that from the moment I met you."

"You know nothing about me. No one here does. If people here knew what I'd done, they'd string me up. They'd call me a sympathizer. Use me as bait."

"You're too hard on yourself. You were played."

"And I won't let it happen again. Leave me alone, you bastard."

The two men stare at each other. Peter takes off his thick-lensed glasses and wipes the pissing rain from his face. Few people ever come near the death pit. They can't be heard here, can't be seen.

"I'm not going to hurt you, Joe. I'm not going to hurt anyone."

Peter moves toward him, and despite being armed, Joseph starts backing away. "Stay away from me. I'll kill you."

"See what I'm saying? Hater, Unchanged . . . we're all cut from the same cloth."

Joseph lunges at Peter with the knife. Peter sidesteps. "Don't. Please. You and I both know something terrible is coming. Last night's attack was just the beginning, and there's only one way it's going to end. I need to find a way out of this war, and I think you want out, too. We're the same, you and me; we're not fighters. We're just cannon fodder."

But Joseph's not listening. He'd shout and scream for help if he could, but he can't risk the noise. Instead, he turns and runs, dodging in and out of vehicles, slipping and skidding in the mud and grime. He's desperately out of shape, but he sprints like an athlete in his prime because he's sure Peter Sutton's on his shoulder. He pushes through the service station's (non)revolving doors and runs straight into Moira Kay coming the other way.

"What the hell are you doing?"

Joseph can barely breathe, let alone speak. "Hater . . ." he gasps. "There's a Hater here."

Moira's immediately at panic stations. She calls a couple of nearby CDF soldiers over. "Where?" she says to Joseph, though she thinks the location of the Hater will be obvious enough when the damn monster starts killing.

"Outside. It . . . it's one of our people."

She stops and pins him up against the wall, looking at him like he's out of his mind. "What the hell are you talking about?"

"He can hold the Hate. He's been here since the start."

"Who?"

"Peter Sutton."

She bursts out laughing. "Peter Sutton! That drip! He's no Hater."

"He is, I swear."

Aaron Rayner is close enough to overhear. "What's going on?"

"This joker reckons Peter Sutton is a Hater. Have you ever heard anything so fucking ridiculous?"

"It's not ridiculous, Moira," Aaron says. "One of them hiding in the ranks is what undid us at Thornhill, remember?"

"Yes, but Peter Sutton? Seriously?"

"You want to take a chance on this? Since when have they conformed to type?" He turns to face Joseph. "What's your name, mate?"

"Joseph Mallon."

"I've heard Estelle talk about you," Aaron says. He turns back to Moira. "We need to find this Sutton guy and suss him out. And we can't afford to make any noise while we do it. If people get wind of this—whether it's true or not—they'll panic, and we'll lose control of this place before the rest of the Haters get anywhere near."

Moira doesn't argue. She orders half a dozen of her best men to search every inch of the outpost and bring the Hater to her.

But Peter Sutton is long gone.

38

The Travelodge

Matt wakes up slowly from a deep sleep. It's alien—he feels properly rested, and his belly's full. His wounded shoulder hurts marginally less than it did. And he's *free*.

He's not herding other survivors for once, and his current location is so quiet and forgotten that he's starting to believe it might actually be safe to stay here. The food left unclaimed in the vending machine and the dead Hater's stocks indicates there's been little footfall here in recent months. All things considered, he's starting to think this could be the best place to stay shut away and wait for the rest of the world to pass him by. He could sit out the rest of the chaos here. Wait till it all blows over . . .

He feels confident enough to get up and move around, though his energy levels remain desperately low. He rearranges his room, moving all his stuff out of sight into the bathroom and then, with considerable effort, shifting the bed so it's right under the window, highlighting a substantial-looking bloodstain in the middle of the well-worn carpet. From outside looking in, it'll look like the battle's over and the room is bare. Nothing to see here.

Jason hears the shoving and grunting coming from Matt's room and appears in the doorway, concerned. "Everything okay?"

"Getting settled in."

"Waste of time."

"Why?"

"It's time we left."

"Good luck with that."

"Come on, Matt. You can't lock yourself away in here with the others just down the road."

"I can. I have."

"Well, I'm going."

"Like I said, good luck with that. I thought we'd been through this already. The more I think about it, the more I realize what a bad idea leaving here would be. We'll be killed en route or shot at on the way in by Estelle and her merry band."

"Doesn't change anything. I can't stay here. I owe them. *We* owe them."

"We owe them *nothing*. They abandoned us, remember? Left us both for dead in Thornhill."

"It was my fault I got left behind. I already told you."

"Okay, but all I did was try to help them. Fact is, they left us both behind and didn't look back."

"You don't know that."

"I do, and if I'm honest, I don't blame them. I'd have done the same. You and I were expendable. We're *all* individually expendable, come to that. Fuck's sake, Jason, they pumped me full of anesthetic and left me out cold. If I'd come around a couple of hours later, I'd have woken up surrounded by Haters."

"But you didn't."

"No, thank Christ. Look, I'm sorry to be such an arsehole, but it's time to face facts. We need to assume we're on our own. If we cross paths with the others a little further down the line, then great. Until then, all we need to think about is ourselves and our own safety."

"Even if I agreed with you—which I don't—we'd need to find a better place than this."

"You reckon? This shithole is perfect. The burned-out Starbucks and the fuel station are a bonus, because they divert attention from the Travelodge. We're set back far enough from the road here to be invisible to traffic—not that there is any—and we've got plenty of exits. There's just empty fields behind . . ."

"We could still do better."

"Yes, we could, and I've been thinking about that, too. We can rig up a kind of early warning system like they used to in survival horror films—cans on lengths of string, that kind of thing."

"You think about this stuff too much."

"No, *you* don't think about it *enough*. There are bolt-holes and crawl spaces here we can use if we have to, paper-thin walls we can knock through, bath panels we can hide behind . . ."

Matt helps himself to a chocolate bar from Jason's stash and walks around the room, flexing his injured shoulder. He's starting to imagine a future here; a short and unfulfilling future, granted, but a future all the same.

"That giving you trouble?"

"What?"

"Your shoulder," Jason says. "I can smell the wound from here, and you keep wincing. Here, let me take a look."

"Looking won't make any difference," Matt grumbles as he shrugs off several layers, then lifts up his T-shirt. He angles himself around so that he can see his shoulder in the mirror. "Looks a bit inflamed."

"Jesus, that's the understatement of the year," Jason says, and he gently touches Matt's wound. Matt flinches. "It's red hot. That's badly infected, mate."

"I'm not surprised. It'll clear up in a few days. You said you had some more antibiotics, didn't you?"

"Somewhere around here . . . I thought they were—"

Jason's words are abruptly truncated by noise outside. Both men become silent, straining to listen. Whatever's happening out there sounds like it's a considerable distance away, but it's localized, and it's prolonged. And that, they decide, can only mean one thing.

39

Half a Mile from the CDF Outpost

The weaponry available to Johannson's horde is rudimentary, borderline medieval, yet it does the job magnificently. There's little time for deep thought and strategic thinking in the massed Hater ranks, but every last one of them out on the battlefield today appreciates that the effectiveness of any weapon, no matter how basic, can be increased a hundredfold by the intent of the fighter who wields it. Take the cricket bat that woman's swinging, for example; times past, it was just used for leisure and relaxation, but judging from the ingrained bloodstains and the gouges in the wood, it's ended more than its fair share of lives since the war began. The crowbar and claw hammer carried by the sinewy man standing next to her: tools of his trade this time last year, tools of a very different trade today. And the humble automobile: taking the kids to school, driving to work or to the shops, visiting the family at the weekend . . . no longer.

Five drivers rev the engines of their lined-up vehicles impatiently, gripping their steering wheels and staring at their target in the distance like they're waiting for the lights to change at the start of a Formula One race. The quality, design, and speed of these four-wheeled weapons is unimportant. All that matters is the impact they'll have when they hit.

Most people, Hater or Unchanged, might be expected to show a little emotion at a moment like this, a hint of nervousness or even excitement. Not Johannson. She's an imposing, hateful bitch, and she watches her troops with the same stoic scowl as always. Some of these people will die this morning, but that doesn't matter. They'll lose vehicles and weapons—not important. The toxic, ice-cold rain is torrential, but even that doesn't faze her. She's soaked to the skin and shivering with cold, but she ignores any discomfort, it barely even registers, because nothing is more important than what's about to unfold here. Today changes everything. Clarifies everything. It will make indisputable her command over what's left of the human race. She has no idea how many Unchanged are here, but she'll keep fighting until the last one's been killed. Johannson has hundreds of Haters under her command, and a single Hater is worth many Unchanged.

It's time.

The boss hammers her fist against the window of the nearest vehicle, and its driver shoves his foot down and races away at a ferocious speed. He fights to keep control of the Volkswagen at first as he careers over grass and gravel. The other drivers form a loose arrowhead formation behind as they approach the service station, then split when they get close. They've been ordered to attack from different angles.

The Volkswagen driver steers hard left, cutting through a gap in a low fence and now aiming directly at the main building. There's frantic movement up ahead as the Unchanged begin to react to the unexpected raid, and his heart swells with pride at the terror he's causing. He's filled with raw, barely contained emotion the likes of which he hasn't felt in a long time, not since he last killed. Probably not since the night of the bomb, he doesn't think.

He knows this will likely be the last few minutes of his life, yet he keeps driving faster. The word *suicide* doesn't feel appropriate (after all, there's the slightest chance he might not die). His own mortality is insignificant, his survival unimportant. He'll go out fighting, and he's damn sure he's going to take out as many Unchanged as possible with him.

He's approaching ninety miles an hour when he reaches the trench. He plans to jump it, but the width of the channel here is such that he doesn't quite make it. The Volkswagen's nose drops and thuds into the trench wall opposite, wedged hard into the mud and rock. For a couple of numb seconds, the driver's unaware what happened, disoriented. His head smacked against the wheel on impact, and he's concussed. He comes around when the weight of the engine causes the precarious wreck to overbalance and fall forward, ending up nose-first at the bottom of the trench. Awake again now, conscious there are Unchanged all around him, he can't get the door open fast enough. He's ready to fight—*desperate* to fight—but he doesn't get chance. The nearest Unchanged is an armed militiawoman, and she's already realized that the time for keeping quiet here is over. She repeatedly shoots the Hater in the face.

A sniper takes out one of the other drivers from a distance, and the van he was driving comes to a slow and underwhelming stop in the middle of a muddy field, all the venom and fury of the frenzied attack whimpering out to nothing. The three remaining vehicles, however, all reach their intended destinations. Two more suffer the same ignominious fate as the Volkswagen—ending up half in and half out of the trench, driver stranded and unable to fight—but that's okay. It's what the boss ordered. Rile the enemy up. Put them under pressure. Terrify them. By filling parts of the trench with crashed metal, the attackers have already achieved two clear objectives: they've reduced the effectiveness of the Unchanged defenses, and they've sown the seeds of panic. By doing both these things, they've already made the outpost itself considerably easier to attack.

Through a combination of it being relatively light and maneuverable, the driver's skill behind the wheel, and a slight rise just before the trench, the final car jumps the chasm completely. The driver's as surprised as anyone when her front wheels make contact with the ground on the other side. She almost loses the back of the car, but she has just enough forward momentum to keep going. This was never part of the plan, but she intends on taking full advantage.

The first swath of Unchanged troops pour out of the entrance to the hotel alongside the service station. They're running across the parking lot to the trenches when the Hater accelerates again and plows straight into them. The car skids in the wet, then crashes into the main hotel doors and comes to a thudding halt, buckling metal and shattering glass. Many of the soldiers who should have been heading for the front line are wounded. Others, far more than is necessary, immediately about-face and unload, focusing their fury on the Hater invader. The front of her car is wedged into what's left of the doorframe and it's not going anywhere, but she's still trying to reverse so she can take more of them out. The fired-up CDF militia destroy her with Hater-like ferocity.

The last of the first wave of attacking vehicles has been neutralized, but inside the outpost, there's utter pandemonium. Gridlock. Terrified civilians either try to look for shelter or get closer to the front of the building to see what's happening.

Chappell and Estelle are up in the lookout. Their calm is in stark contrast to the civvies down below.

"It's strange, I always thought we'd be the ones to strike first," Estelle says.

"You sound disappointed."

"Not at all. Whoever hits first, the end result will be the same. I've been waiting for this for a long time."

"Do you not think we're underprepared? Moira and I have discussed tactics, but we've not been able to war-game. I'm worried that the longer we've been stuck here, the less battle-ready we've become."

"Grow some balls, Greg. The enemy are dangerous, certainly, but they're just animals. They're no match for us."

"You're right, of course."

"Are there as many of them as we were expecting, do you think?"

"Looks that way, ma'am. Fucking hundreds of them. Pretty much in line with what our scouts told us to expect."

There's a mass of Haters gathered out there in numbers the likes of which haven't been seen in an age. They're advancing like a shifting scab on the landscape. It looks like an army from another age.

"And how long before they reach us?"

"No time at all. An hour if we're lucky."

"Lucky?" she says, looking at him quizzically.

"Figure of speech."

She returns her attention to the hordes outside. "Luck's got nothing to do with it, Greg. It's time to bring out the big guns. Now they know where we are, there's no need to stay quiet."

"Absolutely."

Estelle is smiling. "This is going to be a good day, I can feel it. It'll be hard, and it'll cost us, but it has to be done. We're entering a new and decisive phase, the last battle of the final war. We just need to make sure that when the dust settles, we're the only ones left standing."

Estelle's orders are communicated down the ranks, and the CDF soldiers pour from the outpost exits in massive numbers, spilling out through the gaps between long-unused vehicles like a flash flood, heading for the military hardware that has been tucked away alongside the abandoned construction traffic and civilian vehicles.

The CDF fighters—both those who have been military trained and those who are new to war but who've volunteered to fight on the front line—feel an impossible mix of emotions. After months of waiting, can this really be it? A glance over at the chaos around the front of the hotel where the Hater-driven vehicle just hit is enough to leave no one in any doubt that what's happening here this morning is very real.

The heavy artillery is wheeled out first. Massive machines are woken from their noise-enforced hibernation. A number of self-propelled guns are moved into position along the length of the trenches, with battle-worn Challenger and Warrior tanks also advancing but remaining some distance away from the front line for now. The CDF have a half-dozen howitzers, which are towed out of storage and moved to predefined locations around the front of the hotel and service station. Finally for now, a years-old M270 Multiple Launch Rocket System is driven into a prominent position overlooking the battlefield. The CDF is out of rockets and the weapon hasn't been used in battle for more than a decade (it came from a museum), but the enemy doesn't know that. The launcher is completely useless, but it looks fucking fearsome.

There's been an unlikely silence around here for an age, but now that's been shattered with the ugly noise of war. The roar of individual engines combine to deafening effect, and if there were any of the enemy in the surrounding area who were somehow still oblivious to the presence of the Unchanged, they won't be now.

CDF support crews rush through the vehicle maze to get to their assigned positions, the sudden surge of adrenaline helping them keep their nerves in check. For many people, this feels like a cathartic release after so much nervous inactivity. For the dyed-in-the-wool CDF militia, it's still second nature. For the fresh civilian volunteers, though, this is a new and terrifying experience for which many of them now feel totally unprepared. It's not as if they haven't wanted to learn, but they've had to remain out of sight and utterly silent throughout the entirety of their incarceration at the outpost. In this volatile yet delicately poised environment, spending time familiarizing themselves with the military gear they're about to be using has never been a viable option.

One of the Challenger tanks is manned by a crew of experienced CDF pros. They roll into position a short way back from the trench, directly facing the Hater hordes now charging at them across the churned fields on this side of the outpost. The crew sit and wait with an arrogance that matches that of their enemy, safe in the knowledge that it doesn't matter how many of those bastards are coming, they're not going to get anywhere against this weapon with its impenetrable armor and deadly munitions. There's an ordered chaos inside the tank, but to anyone watching from outside, its movements appear deceptively relaxed, almost balletic. Its turret swings gracefully around, and the main gun is angled slightly skyward. A single shell is fired with a sonorous boom and thud the likes of which haven't been heard since the morning of the bomb. The force of the blast rocks the tank back on its tracks, and before the echoing noise has even begun to fade, the shell hits the oncoming wave of Haters, obliterating scores of them.

Jason and Matt watch from up on the fuel station canopy. They pass Matt's binoculars between them, trying to work out what's happening and, more importantly, where. When the noise of engines is replaced by fighting, and when ominous clouds of dirty gray smoke begin to drift high into the already dirty gray air, they're finally able to begin to orientate themselves.

"Has to be Estelle and the others, doesn't it?" Jason says.

"Has to be."

"They'll be all right. Fuck, listen to that fighting. Guns and bombs and shit. The Haters are probably using sticks and stones."

"You assume. Even if they are, chances are the Haters have an even bigger army, made up of soldiers who don't show fear and who don't mind dying if they think they'll be able to take a few of us out in the process."

"I'm not saying it won't be bloody, I've just got more faith in our people than you have."

"You certainly have."

Matt watches Jason, who's staring at the smoke in the distance like a kid watching a firework display on Bonfire Night. Jason senses he's being watched and puts down the field glasses. "What's the problem?"

"You haven't realized, have you?"

"Realized what?"

"If that is Estelle and the CDF, then we're not where we thought we were."

"I don't understand."

"Come on, Jason, it's not that difficult. We walked east to get here, yes?"

"Yes. So?"

"We came from that direction," he continues, pointing back along the road. "This fighting is the other way."

Jason looks at him blankly. Matt has a folded-up tourist map in the back of his jeans that he'd taken from the Travelodge reception. He opens it out and lays it on the wet canopy.

"Here's the RAF base," he explains, tapping the map, "and here's the hotel where we are." He traces his finger along the road. "And here's where I think the fighting is."

The penny drops. "Shit," Jason says. "We've gone past the outpost. We were following the wrong bloody road."

40

Near Longstanton

When the human race was first torn in two, both Hater and Unchanged alike had to react fast to stay alive. For most Haters, while the impact of the change was fresh and the wounds were still raw, to attack was their defense. As a result, the natural Unchanged presumption was that once they'd started killing, the Haters were unable to stop. For a good number of them, that proved to be the case; their default setting being to fight and to kill. But for many more, the ability to show restraint, to think and *then* to act, gradually returned. And regardless of the ferocity of the Hate that drove them in the first place, for many, the desire for self-preservation has remained their overriding concern. They struggle continually with an emotional conflict: wanting to kill yet not wanting to die. This morning, as the first shots were fired in a battle that both sides know to be pivotal, this internal struggle has tested Johannson's fighters like never before.

She knew this would happen. Counted on it, even. Those who've died on the battlefield so far today are heroes, but those who've turned tail and returned to base aren't cowards; they're fighters who've realized they can't compete with artillery fired at them from a distance by an enemy who is brave only because they're out of range. The fighters now returning are those who realize that in order to be able to do the things they want to do— *need* to do—to the remaining Unchanged, they're going to need to bide their time and choose their battles.

But it doesn't sit well with any of them.

Johannson knows she has to explain this to the battle-starved masses who've just been a part of something they never thought would happen: a Hater army in full retreat from the Unchanged.

The boss holds court in the middle of a vast concreted area where some kind of factory once stood close to the village of Longstanton, about five miles from the battlefield. It's almost an island with nothing but water on two sides of the concrete. This area was well known for its wetlands and nature reserves before the war. Post-bomb, because of the relentless rain, there's now more water here than anything else. The factory ruin is accessible only from a single-lane road that twists and turns through the submerged countryside. Nearby—ten minutes' walk at most— there's a half-sunken housing estate with enough space to billet all the fighters and room to treat the wounded. Those whose injuries can be treated are being patched up. Those who are beyond hope have been left to die. No sense wasting time and resource on anyone who's not going to make it.

The atmosphere is fractious and tense. Johannson is perched on the remains of a wall, flanked by Myndham and Ullah. One of the crowd, a particularly difficult and vociferous bastard called Shenton, mouths off in protests at their tactics. He knows he's risking his neck, but equally he knows his life is already on the line. Everyone's is.

"What the fuck just happened, boss? What kind of tactic is this? Turning and running from the fucking Unchanged."

"We've already been through this," Ullah says, attempting to answer for his chief and trying to sound calmer than he feels. "The intention was never to fully engage this morning."

"Then what was the point?"

"To see what they're capable of. To see what they'd throw at us. And, as it happens, that's quite a fucking lot. Johannson's already explained this . . . we didn't want to turn up and find they've got a fucking tactical nuke. Which, for the record, they might still have."

"So we're supposed to pussyfoot around them, just in case?"

"Look, mate, I know how this feels. We're all sick to our stomachs at the idea of those fuckers still being out there, but what would you rather do? We go in there full-on and find out they've got enough in their armory to wipe us all out, or we wait a couple of days longer and make sure we get it right?"

"So have you seen enough?" Shenton asks.

"I have," Johannson announces, and the volume of her voice silences all others. "They're already bringing out the big guns. They've been waiting for this. I don't think they've got much more than we've already seen."

Shenton's still not convinced. "You reckon? And you think we stand a chance against fucking tanks?"

"Yes."

"Against fucking tanks?" he says again.

Johannson leaps up, grabs Shenton, and slams him back against a pile of rubble. With her face just inches from his, she hisses at him, "Yes."

Shenton holds his hands up in submission, and she lets him go. He scuttles away, leaving her alone center stage.

"You know why we won the war?" she asks the crowd, talking like it's a memory, all done and dusted. When no one volunteers a reply, she answers herself. "People power. Now I know that might sound soft, but just think about it. Think about all the battles you've been involved in and how you managed to stay alive."

She looks around at the countless faces staring back at her, hanging on her every word. At moments like this, in some quarters, her following borders on the devotional.

"I was in this one fight, way back when their extermination camps were operating. Those evil bastards had thousands of our people held in cages, ready to kill, and they were being held there by more fucking military machinery than you've ever seen in your life. Hundreds of tanks and helicopters and jets and guns and whatever.

"Now I was with a group of a couple of hundred, and we were watching all this going on from a distance. We knew we didn't have any option but to go down there and get involved. It looked like suicide, but back then, back when all this started, you, me, and everyone like us knows we'd have done anything to be fighting and killing, no matter what the risks.

"So the charge begins, and hundreds of us are running toward thousands of them, and the combined power we were feeling was just fucking unbelievable. The Unchanged start firing everything they'd got at us, and though our people were dying left, right, and center, they couldn't hit everyone. Too many targets.

"Those of us still standing made it to the death camp and pulled down the fences, and then hundreds became thousands. I remember running at a tank—at a fucking tank, for Christ's sake!—and it was firing right over my head into the crowds, but the fuckers operating it didn't even know I was there. Before I knew it, I was right on top of the damn thing, and then there was twenty of us all over it, and then someone opened the hatch and got inside . . . you see where this is going, don't you? We took control of the tank and turned it against them, and that night we ran riot and killed more of them than you could imagine. We don't need the kind of stuff they've got, because we are the weapons. Those Unchanged back there, they're thinking big, so we go the other way. Small scale. Low-fi. Individual attacks, fucking hundreds of them, same time from all different directions. Confuse the hell out of them, then tear the fucking heart out of their shelter."

She stops speaking for a moment, time enough to let a swell of enthusiastic support build around her. It's deafening. Bouncing off the partially collapsed and partially submerged walls.

"Quiet," she bellows, and silence is restored almost immediately.

"Now you lot might think I've gone soft because of what's happened today. You might think I've lost my nerve. Believe me, I haven't. All I want—all *we* want—is to finish this, and that's exactly what we're going to do. But we need to get it right because we won't get a second chance. So this is what's going to happen. Today was all about testing the water and seeing what they're made of. Tomorrow, we get back out there and we fight again. They'll come at us with their tanks and their rockets and whatever they've got left, and we'll flood them, moving in and around and between them, and we'll take them out. Some of us will die, but that's just how it goes. There are more than enough of us to do this. We'll breach their lines, get into their damn base, and wipe out the whole fucking lot of them."

41

The CDF Outpost

Everything has changed.

Now that the enemy knows exactly where the CDF outpost is, there's no longer any need for the several hundred people here to remain silent. Folks are finally able to move around and do their work with a degree of freedom that would have been unimaginable just a couple of days ago. That's a good thing, because converting this place from a discreet, covert base into a heavily defended fortress was never going to be doable in silence.

Since the first waves of fighting ended, the place has been transformed. The tanks, howitzers, and rocket launchers now have increased prominence, ensuring there are no aspects of the outpost remaining that a Hater can approach without finding themselves staring down the barrel of a big fucking gun. There are snipers on the roof of both the service station and the hotel next door, ensuring that any intruders who somehow manage to breach the initial defenses can be easily picked off. And the trenches, for so long little more than a system of barely discernible black scars zigzagging around the perimeter of the site, are now alive with activity. CDF militia and other volunteers are spaced equidistant along the lines, ready to repel any attack. It's strange—despite the threat level having reached a new high, the number of willing volunteers has increased dramatically. Is it because they think there's an end to the war in sight? Do they believe the odds have tipped in their favor today? Or do the civilians just see this as an opportunity to exact some long-overdue revenge on the bastards who've destroyed their lives? Maybe these people simply feel braver now because they believe the worst that could happen has already happened? The earlier Hater attack was insignificant in comparison to the horror and devastation wrought by the atomic bombs that rained down on the country not so long ago.

As he catches his breath and readies himself to shift another crate of munitions, Darren wonders if the Doomsday Clock is still a thing. If it is, he decides, it's probably stuck at something like a quarter past midnight. He hoists up the crate and turns around and walks straight into Parker, another civvy he's spoken to on a couple of occasions.

"Jesus. Careful, mate. You don't want to drop that lot."

"Sorry," Darren says, and he puts the crate back down and massages his back. "This is all new to me."

"It's new to all of us."

They're in a large, hangar-like building that was clearly part of the construction workers' compound. There's more roadworks material here than war supplies.

"Is this all the ammo we've got?"

"As far as I know," Parker replies. "The plan was always to keep it away from the main buildings. Last thing the chiefs wanted was for this lot to go up and take out what's left of the human race in the process."

"Not a lot, though, is it?"

"I'm no soldier. I couldn't tell you what kind of damage any of this could do."

"I get that. I'm no soldier, either. But in terms of fighting a war, it doesn't look a lot."

"You're right. It isn't," another voice replies.

Both men look around and see Aaron Rayner in the doorway, his stocky shape silhouetted by the gray light outside.

"So what happens if they keep coming?" Darren asks him, sounding nervous.

"I guess we just keep firing at them for as long as we can, then switch back to clubs and fists. Resort to caveman tactics."

"Jesus. Don't fancy my chances in a fistfight with those vicious bastards."

"Then let's hope it doesn't come to that." He takes the crate of ammo from Darren. "I'll take this to the gunners. You two find something useful to do."

"I'll go help Joseph and Dean at the pit," Parker suggests.

"Good shout." Aaron looks at Darren. "You go with him. There's a backlog."

They find Joseph dealing with a huge number of bodies that have been collected from the battlefield after today's fighting. There's no time for niceties this morning. "Help me with that pile over there," he says, gesturing toward an unruly heap of dead flesh, arms and legs sticking out in all directions.

Parker's straight to work, but it's the first time Darren's been over here. He peers into the pit. The sight of rotting dead faces combined with the noxious stench makes him gag. He forces himself to drag a body off the pile. "These are Haters?" he asks.

"Mostly," Joseph says.

"They look different from the ones we saw before we got here. More meat on their bones."

"They're stronger in packs, I guess. Strip them before you dump them. Weapons, clothes, food, anything. If you find stuff worth keeping, pile it up over there."

Joseph wrestles to remove the boots belonging to the cadaver he's currently dealing with, then ties the laces together to keep them as a pair and throws them into a repurposed waste bin.

The next body Darren drags off the pile isn't a Hater. It's an Unchanged woman. Nice girl. He was watching her with a young girl—her daughter, perhaps—yesterday morning. He crouches down and starts checking her pockets, feeling awful for doing so. "Bloody horrible job, this."

"You just have to switch off. Forget they're people," Joseph says, watching him.

"Easier said than done."

"I know. I also probably know what you're thinking right now."

"You do?"

"You're thinking, all this effort, all this killing, and we haven't moved a single step forward. Either that or you're thinking if we can't look after people like this girl, what's the point?"

"It'll be different after the fighting's done, though, won't it?" Darren says. Parker and Joseph just look at him.

"Will it? When exactly do you think that'll be?" Parker asks. "I'm starting to think this is how it's always going to be from now on. As long as there are people with guns in their hands, there's always going to be fighting."

"From what I've just seen, there are hardly any bullets left. What happens then?"

Joseph stops working and stands and stares at him. "Now that, my friend, is the million-dollar question. Between you and me and this pit full of bodes, I don't intend on hanging around to find out."

42

The Travelodge

Matt stirs.

No matter how long he spends here, he doesn't think he'll ever get used to waking up in a proper bed again. He feels guilty, like he's doing something he shouldn't. A soft mattress and a decent pillow are the height of luxury these days.

There are noises coming from elsewhere in the building. He props himself up on his elbow and listens, concerned at first. Whatever—whoever—it is, their movements are controlled and considered, not rushed. If it's Jason, there's no need to panic. If it's a Hater that's just killed Jason and is coming for him next, there's still no point panicking. It won't make any difference. He'll be dead soon anyway.

Matt's dangerous, split-second moment of apathy quickly passes, and he gets up. He almost loses his balance, and when he tries to correct himself, he wrenches his shoulder wound, almost opening it up again. He steadies himself, but his legs almost give way. He feels fucking awful this morning. He's burning up. Tetanus? Sepsis? It could be anything.

Matt inches toward the door and opens it a crack, just enough to see that everything looks as he last saw it. It must have been

Jason he heard, but what's he doing? With far more effort than it should take, Matt shuffles along the corridor to the next room, opens the door, and asks. Jason's answer is disarmingly simple and straightforward. "I'm leaving."

"How many times do we have to have this conversation?"

"It's not a conversation. I'm not discussing anything. I'm leaving for the outpost, and that's all there is to it."

"Fine."

"And that's all you've got to say?"

"You just told me you didn't want a discussion. It obviously won't change anything. You're obviously going to go, and I'm obviously going to tell you you're a complete fucking idiot if you do. It's too dangerous out there."

"The fighting stopped yesterday, remember?"

"The fighting *paused*."

Jason screws up his nose. "Christ, you still stink."

"Swift change of subject."

Jason ignores him. "Seriously, that shoulder's not getting any better. You'll need to get it cleaned up properly."

"I'll ride it out."

"Good luck with that."

"The risk of me dying of blood poisoning or something similar is a heck of a lot less than the risk you'll be taking if you go back out there. The only way the fighting's over is if we've already lost."

"I'll take my chances."

"You'll never make it on your own out there."

"Well, you did."

Jason's words catch him out. He's right.

Soaked with sweat and struggling to stay upright, Matt slumps into a bucket chair in the corner of the room and watches Jason packing his few scavenged belongings into a rucksack.

"Even if I wanted to go, I don't think I could."

"I know. You're better on your own, though, aren't you?"

Matt sighs and shakes his head. "Look, I know I'm probably wasting my breath, but I really think you should reconsider."

Nothing. He tries again.

"I know I've been a bit of a prick to you at times—"

"A *bit* of a prick?"

"—and I'm sorry about that, but you're making a huge mistake. You're risking everything."

"Yeah, Matt, I get that, but what's worse—risking everything or risking nothing? It's always about risk management with you. Fucking accountant. I can't just sit here while our people are struggling. I couldn't live with myself." He hoists his pack up onto his shoulders and walks away, pausing at the open door. "Oh, wait, I'm talking to the wrong bloke, aren't I? Here's me thinking about what I can do to help the others; you're usually thinking about what they can do to help you."

"That's not true."

"You sure?"

"Absolutely."

"Remember all the things you told me about how you survived while you were trying to get back to Jen? About using the noise other people made to keep yourself safe? About using their deaths as camouflage?"

"Yeah, but that was different."

"Really? From where I'm standing, it looks exactly the same. I bet you were rubbing your hands together when all the fighting was going on around the outpost yesterday, because the more noise they were making and the more of them were dying, the better your chances of staying alive."

"You've got this all wrong."

"Don't think so. See you later, Matt."

And with that, he's gone. Matt gets up and staggers after him. "Do you even know where you're going?"

Jason holds up a folded tourist map of the area. "Got it all marked out. Did it while you were asleep."

Still he keeps walking.

"You're making a huge mistake."

"So you keep telling me."

Matt leans against the wall, drenched with sweat, feeling angrier than he expected, feeling completely alone. Feeling like he's let Jason down, then feeling like he's letting the rest of the group down, then feeling like he shouldn't give a shit about any of them, because none of them have ever given a shit about him.

He returns to his own room, shuts the door, and collapses onto the bed. He can't relax. Can't lie still. Nothing feels right.

It's only been a couple of minutes when he hears noises in the distance. Bangs and crashes begin to ring out through the otherwise empty countryside. Distant dull explosions shake the hotel's foundations.

Right on cue, the fighting around the outpost has begun again.

43

Outside the Outpost

When the second Hater onslaught begins, the CDF fighters are ready for them.

It begins as it did yesterday with a number of enemy-driven vehicles racing toward the outpost, this time from several different directions at once. The CDF soldiers are prepared, but there's barely contained panic inside the service station; the non-fighting civilians are more afraid today than when the first unexpected Hater attack was launched. Perhaps it's because they now know what to expect. Perhaps it's because they've again seen firsthand how hard and how vicious those Hater bastards are prepared to fight.

From the first-floor observation deck, Estelle and Chappell marshal the troops. In the absence of radio contact, messages are relayed between the commanders and their fighters by civilian runners who push and shove to get past each other on the steps, such is the number of frantic orders being given. "Get those vehicles stopped at all costs!" Estelle screams. "Don't let any of them through!"

There are six vehicles approaching through the gray mist and hissing rain now. One of them—it was an unremarkable family car before the war—steers an arrogant path straight across the battlefield, its driver apparently unfazed by the relentless volleys of gunfire that are aimed at his vehicle. Tracer fire burns iridescent against the early-morning gloom, numerous shooters all now focusing their fire on this one unassuming car, the farthest advanced. Despite his vicious intent, its driver is killed, and the vehicle grinds to an ignominious slow stop in the middle of nowhere.

But the attention paid to the first vehicle means that, in contrast, others are allowed to make more progress. A mud-splattered ambulance, blue lights flashing like it's responding to an emergency, and another car driving alongside it both get dangerously close to the trenches. The ambulance driver confuses everyone by making an abrupt change in direction, skidding through the mud, then driving parallel with the front of the service station outpost, managing somehow to avoid being caught in any of the cross fire. The other car almost breaches the CDF defenses before a concentrated volley of machine-gun fire reduces it to scrap.

The next two vehicles are flatbed trucks. From Chappell's high vantage point, it's difficult to make out exactly what they're both carrying. The flatbeds themselves are covered over with dark tarpaulins, and his mind starts to race. "What the hell have they got there?" he demands, knowing no one's going to answer.

The flatbeds are immediately forgotten because now there's another complication. A mass of lights burn bright up ahead, and the fog itself seems to part as the final vehicle of this first wave begins its approach.

This thing is fucking huge.

Whoever's behind the wheel of this monstrosity must surely have driven machines like this before the war. The truck looks like it was designed to transport abnormally sized loads, but it's been adapted to suit a different purpose today. Sheets of metal have been welded across the windshield and side windows to protect the driver, narrow slits cut out to enable them to see. Having a limited field of view clearly isn't a problem, because the truck's intended target is obvious; it's heading directly for the service station building. Okay, so the trench that surrounds the base will offer some degree of protection, but the sheer size of the machine now rolling closer makes it a threat. This aspect of the battlefield gently slopes downward, and it seems that even the elevation of the land is beginning to conspire against the CDF this morning.

Estelle is acutely aware of the danger. "Sweet Jesus. We need to stop that thing." She turns around, desperately looking for more runners. When none appear, she leans over the balcony and yells out to anyone who's listening, "Focus all fire on that vehicle! Destroy it before it gets anywhere near us!"

Her orders are cascaded at lightning speed, and almost immediately it seems that every single weapon is directed at the slow-moving beast. Closer and closer it gets, but its speed is increasing if anything. Bullets fail to have any noticeable effect, sparking as they ricochet off the welded sheet metal. A rocket fired through an unprotected side window blows the roof off the cab, but the now driverless truck's velocity is such that its progress continues unimpeded. Its speed increases until a second rocket strike hits the base of the engine compartment, causing the massive machine to buck like a horse, then crash back down on its nose. The tractor unit falls one way, the trailer the other. It's like its neck has been snapped.

The outpost is filled with cheers, but Chappell's not celebrating. "They're playing with us."

"What are you talking about?" Estelle demands.

"That thing was just a distraction, and we bought it," he says. "For Christ's sake, look!"

With attention focused elsewhere, the tarpaulins have been thrown off the back of the two flatbeds, and masses of Hater fighters have emerged. They race forward with predatory speed, but with numerous distracting fires burning brightly nearby and other firefights continuing, their movements are all but hidden in the low light. Keeping track of their numbers becomes infinitely more difficult when they split and splinter, fighters now heading in every direction.

No one's waiting for orders any longer. Civilian or CDF, anyone who has a gun in their hands begins to fire at the enemy. Some take well-considered shots, aiming carefully, but most simply spray bullets in as wide an arc as possible, doing whatever they can to bring an end to the Hater attacks. All thoughts of conserving ammunition are forgotten, because what's the point of holding on to bullets when faced with a large-scale attack like this? If they don't successfully defend the base this morning, everything will be lost.

More Hater fighters appear now, running onto the battlefield on foot. They're coming from all angles, protected by their relative insignificance in the face of the overall carnage.

Estelle knows she's running out of options.

Bryce watches the battle unfold from a distance. He wants nothing more than to be in there fighting, but he's forcing himself to hold back. He grips the wheel of his Subaru, arms locked rigid with tension. It's hard knowing there are Unchanged alive in that place while he's just sitting here watching.

There's a reason, though, and he has to stay focused on that. Danny McCoyne helps him keep control. "You just need to hold back and bide your time, Bryce," he tells him. "We've all been in scraps like this before. They start big, then get smaller. I know it's hard, but if we keep our distance now, it'll be easier when it's time to make our move."

"You sound like a coward making excuses."

McCoyne swallows hard. "I'm not, I swear. I want the same things you do, the same things we all do. I'm just trying not to get myself killed in the process."

Bryce's head is spinning. He's struggling to keep everything in check and under control. He believes his pathetic little non-fighter pet might have a point, but he also knows if Johannson or the others catch wind that he's been sitting out the battle, they'll turn on him quicker than if he were Unchanged.

"I need Johannson to know how useful I can be to her."

"I get that. Like I said, the start of these battles is always the worst part. Let the rest of them take the heat for now, then you go in at the end and take the glory. They're all focused on what's happening right now. You need to focus on what comes next."

He turns and stares straight into McCoyne's hollow face. "You mess with me and you're dead."

"I get that, too."

"Put one foot out of line, do one thing that paints me in a bad light, make one single mistake, and I'll snap you like a fucking twig."

"I won't, I swear."

"I'll haul you in front of Johannson and tell her what you are and what you can do, and she'll have you strung up. Understand?"

"I understand," McCoyne says, and he does. He absolutely does.

44

The Outpost—Several Hours Later

It's less a single battle now, more a collection of countless individual skirmishes, all taking place in the same confined space. Keeping the enemy pushed back feels like trying to plug a dam that's constantly springing new leaks, but the CDF have so far managed to repel the relentless hordes. Aside from their lack of nerves and the sheer fucking animalistic ferocity that every single Hater exhibits, they're proving to be a relatively unsophisticated threat. Their weaponry is limited, and their tactics have so far been easy to predict and counter.

The enemy initially focused on breaching the trenches, but Chappell had already planned for that, deploying armed militia back-to-back along the entire line. The first few Haters to make it over the threshold were immediately killed. A pack of around twenty of them then stormed a part of the trench that had been compromised by one of the crashed vehicles from yesterday, the invaders using the wreck both to help gain access and as cover, but the gunners made short work of them, too. Threat neutralized.

Chappell has overseen the entire operation from the service station mezzanine and has been both fascinated and repulsed by the bizarre, borderline kamikaze Hater behavior he's witnessed. He knows he can use these behaviors to his advantage, and he has a volunteer willing to help. Leslie Wright can't fight, and she can't operate any of the remaining CDF machinery of war, but when he asked for someone to carry out what some would consider a suicide mission, she was the only one to oblige. She used to be a keen long-distance runner, a damn good runner at that, and she's missed the freedom of the open road more than anything since they've been holed up here. Chappell takes her down to the front of the building. She freezes for a moment, the noise and the smell and the proximity of the fighting making her almost change her mind. Almost.

"You sure about this?" he asks.

"Yes."

"And you're fast?"

"Yes."

"Really fucking fast?"

"Yes!"

"Good. Because you're going to need to run faster than you ever have before."

And even though she knows a wrong step or an ill-considered change of direction might end her life, it's a chance she's willing to take. For these few precious minutes of escape, Leslie's ready to risk everything.

Chappell kisses her lightly on the cheek. "Good luck. And thank you."

She stretches her muscles, touches her toes, closes her eyes, takes a deep breath, then runs like hell.

Leslie crosses the trench using a well-defended pontoon bridge. The noise out here is deafening, but she still screams, "Come on, you fuckers!" at them in the vain hope they'll hear. And now she sprints. When they see her, they see an easy target and immediately come for her, but she has speed and surprise on her side, and all they can do is race after her. She heads for gaps in the fighting, running a large and lazy circle, loving being out in the open at last, despite the danger.

She glances back over her shoulder. It's working! She's like a fucked-up Pied Piper with a riled-up mob of killers following her rather than rats. She's been out in the open for less than five minutes, running nearly three-quarters of a mile, when she decides enough is enough and changes direction back toward the crossing point. All she needs to do is put in one last burst of speed, get across the pontoon bridge before they raise it again, then catch her breath, sit back, and watch as the soldiers make short work of the gullible bastards who've followed her.

And it almost works.

With the bridge in sight, a lone attacker comes at her from out of nowhere. She banks hard right to avoid being caught and goes over on her ankle in deep mud. She tries to get up and run again, but the pain's severe, and she already knows she won't make it home. She knew the risks she was taking coming out here, and it was worth it for those snatched minutes of freedom. When Chappell realizes she won't get back, he orders the bridge to be raised and the militia open fire, mowing down more than thirty Haters. He feels enormous guilt watching Leslie die, but her sacrifice is more than compensated for by the slaughter of so many of the enemy. To his surprise, in the time Leslie was out in the open, two other civilians have volunteered to make similar runs themselves.

As the morning has passed and the afternoon has progressed, the balance on the battlefield has clearly shifted in favor of the CDF. More heavy-duty bridges have been laid over the trench. A Challenger tank has just crossed and has taken up position around fifty meters away from the front of the CDF-occupied buildings. With an ocean of space all around it, its crew can take unchallenged potshots whenever the enemy shows signs of trying to encroach again. Even now, when the fighting has been raging for hours and their casualties are mounting, those tireless bastards are refusing to give up. Another Hater-driven truck appears up ahead. The tank's loader inserts a shell into the main gun—kissing it and wishing it well on its journey, praying it hits the mark because they're *really* running low of ammo now—then the gunner takes aim and fires. There are few more satisfying sights these days than a direct hit on a truckful of Haters. When the smoke clears, there's nothing left but a crater and an ugly mass of blackened metal.

Two military utility vehicles now make their first appearance. Looking like heavily armored 4×4s with huge guns mounted on the roof, they burst clear of the outpost and whip around the churned-up battlefield with ten times the agility and speed of any tank. For the drivers, this is starting to feel like sport; chase any lone Haters left out there and mow them down if the gunner doesn't deal with them in time. These vehicles are conspicuous, still painted khaki and beige from when they were last deployed in a desert country on the other side of the world. In most wars, the lack of camouflage would be a problem, but not this one. Today, the crews are proud that their vehicles stand out. After hiding and sheltering in silence for so long, it feels good to be right in the Haters' faces again. Many of the militia wish they'd gone with their instinct and broken ranks like this a long time ago.

It's noticeable now that the noise around the service station outpost is changing; there's more engine noise than gunfire. The tanks and utility vehicles have been ordered to cease fire so the state of play can be assessed. Estelle and Chappell have ventured down to the front line, and it's noted by the rank and file.

She stands on the edge of the trench with her field glasses, watching a final flurry of Haters run for cover in the distance. The only ones who are left are the horrifically injured: the dead and dying. There are CDF militia doing the rounds on foot—finishing them off, then stripping their bodies of anything of value.

It's over.

"We did good," Estelle says to Chappell.

"Yep."

"Is that all the enthusiasm you can muster, Greg? You do realize what we achieved today, don't you? Those creatures exist solely to hunt out and kill people like you and me, and we beat them into submission."

"But they haven't submitted, have they? We'd be stupid to think it's job done."

"True. And we're not stupid. There's still a long way to go."

Chappell sighs. "Today was an expensive day. When you add it all up, it's cost us dear. We lost some good people, and we used up a hell of a lot of ammunition. We don't have huge reserves."

"I know that and you know that, but *they* don't."

"They'll find out if they keep coming back for more."

"Stop being such a bloody pessimist."

"You don't think I'm entitled to be pessimistic?"

"This time yesterday, perhaps, but not now. Not after what we've achieved. We have to make the most of this. Maximize and drive home our advantage. We strike now, take back control, and wipe those bastards out."

"I hope you're right, Estelle."

"You know I am. More importantly, the people inside this base who've been looking up to us to see them through this crisis now also know that we can deliver. They've all seen what we're capable of. We've shown them that the enemy is beatable. Don't you feel a change in the air, Greg? We're on the verge of taking back what's left of our world."

"You can be so fucking pretentious sometimes."

"Mind your mouth. I can always find someone else to do your job if you're not up to it."

"There is no one else, and you know it," he reminds her.

"We need to analyze what happened today," she continues, ignoring his last comment. "We've learned a lot. The Haters have absolutely no military capabilities, that much is clear. They'd have used it by now if they had. They attempted a very visible and very rudimentary attack, and it was a complete failure. You saw them as clearly as I did. Trying to use sticks and stones and knives to fight tanks—there was only ever going to be one outcome."

"I don't think you give them enough credit."

"And I think you give them too much."

"Just don't be so quick to write them off."

"I'm not writing them off, but we will be able to in time. They're falling apart. The longer this goes on, the more basic their behaviors become. They're regressing. They're becoming increasingly unsophisticated and animallike, and we can use that to our advantage."

45

It's pitch-black. Just before three in the morning, the next Hater incursion begins, and this time it's a much smaller-scale affair with a wholly different intent. There's no noise and bluster, none of the arrogance of their previous in-your-face attacks. *Subtlety* and *reserve* aren't words normally associated with Haters hunting Unchanged, but needs must. Their brazen brutality has so far been unsuccessful, and an alternative approach is now called for.

A group of fighters makes its way toward the less heavily defended rear of the outpost. There are guns and tanks and snipers here, too, but they fail to pick up on the six men and women who sneak and crawl across the open space. They split into pairs, each duo lugging containers of fuel behind them. They've spent time watching and have chosen three relatively inconspicuous spots. Once they reach the trench, they empty the barrels out over anything that looks vaguely combustible, then set the fires burning.

It's a distraction, and the Unchanged generals know it. Troops are dispatched to deal with the fires (though the Haters who set them have already slunk away into the darkness again), but the main CDF forces maintain position so as not to leave the front of the outpost vulnerable to attack. It's a simple and straightforward response, and it doesn't work.

With the CDF soldiers split between the small fires to the rear and defending the main hub of the outpost, no one notices another pack of Haters breaching the trench at its most inaccessible point. With attention directed elsewhere, they're free to get in and over the threshold with remarkable ease and speed. They split up and work their way through and around the abandoned construction equipment and those few military machines that have so far remained unused. They're spotted soon enough, but it's a calculated risk because in the poor light, with so many things to hide behind and move around, it's impossible for the Unchanged to know how many of the enemy have broken through. There's a frantic attempt to get a couple of arc lights set up and lit, but they've barely been used since the night of the bombs and it's minutes, not seconds, before the buildings are locked down and the entire area is filled with intense artificial light.

But all that does is illuminate what's coming next.

The Haters are sprinting through CDF territory, causing maximum damage. They set fires, shoving burning rags into the fuel tanks of vehicles. Several of them explode, and they're parked so tight together in parts of the compound that chain reactions cause many more to catch fire. The intention here is not to destroy but to cause alarm, and there's no question that it works. Elements of the civilian population, squashed uncomfortably into the restricted confines of the service station, start to panic because suddenly and without any warning, the battle they've been watching intermittently over the last days from a distance is now being fought on their side of the CDF defenses.

Outside, more Haters throw petrol bombs toward the outpost. Again, these are crude weapons, but their cumulative effect is startling. There are numerous arcs of fire and bursts of flames, and between putting out the fires and dealing with the Haters who've already breached the barriers, there's now absolute chaos in and around the outpost. These people have been living on their nerves since the attacks began, and the proximity of these latest explosions has ratcheted up the fear to another level.

Elsewhere, more troops are dispatched to the trenches. Are these small-scale attacks just a decoy? Estelle and Chappell know they can't afford to let their guard down. Anyone who can use a gun is given one (though there's nowhere near enough ammo to go around), and a new perimeter is established tightly around the hotel and service station buildings. Perched on top, snipers scan the area below and take out anyone they think is an attacking Hater. Trouble is, there's no natural light, and while their infrared sights are quick to show up body heat and movement, all other details are hidden; everyone's body heat looks the same. The snipers can't see faces; they can only try to anticipate intent. The direction someone's moving, the speed at which they're running, if they're attacking or defending . . . these are the only ways left to discern between Hater and Unchanged right now. Each shot carries an unprecedented weight of expectation. *Did I hit my target? Have I just killed one of ours?*

More petrol bombs are thrown through the darkness, dancing gracefully across the sky, then crashing down to earth and causing untold pain. The CDF is so tightly packed in this confined island of space that wherever the firebombs hit, they invariably cause huge amounts of damage. A bottleful of fuel hits a wall and explodes, showering two soldiers with fire. One of them tries to roll along the muddy ground to put out the flames, but there isn't space and all he does he spread the fire. Another lucky firebomb lob hits a small artillery store, and within seconds, the whole damn lot has gone up, sending more militiamen and women running for cover as the munitions explode around them like deadly fireworks.

Yet despite all of this, the CDF is still maintaining control. The snipers finish off those Haters who've trespassed onto their patch, then shift their focus to other figures moving through the periphery. They give their position away when they light their Molotov cocktails and get ready to hurl them at the base. Wising up to the routine, the CDF soldiers manning the howitzers immediately unload before the bombs can be thrown. It's incredibly satisfying watching a Hater burning as a result of the detonation of a petrol bomb they haven't managed to lob in time.

The rust of inertia has worn away since the Hater attacks began, and the troops are now fighting with increasing effectiveness. Another trench is filled with fire, but there are soldiers primed straightaway, immediately dealing with the Haters trying to find a way through. Skilled marksmen and women who feel like they've been brought out of retirement take out the stragglers on the fringes and those who've managed to breach the lines. When a lone Hater makes it almost as far as the entrance to the hotel where the troops have been billeted, he's brought down by a mass of CDF fighters itching to get involved. Right now, looking out over this increasingly chaotic landscape, it's getting harder to keep track of the battle lines.

Not everyone's involved in the fighting. Outside the service station, one of the invaders sneaks quietly through the chaos, sticking to the shadows. He has more control than most. While the Haters can barely stop themselves from fighting, and many of the Unchanged are dragged into the battle because it's that or just capitulate, he moves through the gray fringes between them, going completely unnoticed. He waits for a moment, stepping back out of the way as an Unchanged soldier sprints past, arms loaded up with ammo for the gunners protecting this section of the base.

Coast clear, he continues on his way, down toward a section of the trench that was ablaze just a couple of minutes ago. The fire's out now, everything carbon black. He climbs down, dropping half the distance, then uses a pile of wreckage farther down to climb back up and out the other side. He crawls away on his belly with fighters crisscrossing around him, completely unaware that he's even there. He keeps shuffling forward in stop-start bursts until he's sure he's clear.

He's back at the car at the prearranged point a short time later. He collapses into the passenger seat, weak with effort and covered in grime. "You look like shit, McCoyne," Bryce says.

"Thanks."

The only noise is the rain hammering on the roof of the car and McCoyne's labored breathing. "Well?" Bryce demands, impatient.

"Wait," McCoyne says, clearly struggling.

"I'm done waiting. Talk."

He swallows hard and tries to speak, but his words are lost in a coughing fit so fierce it's like his body's trying to turn itself inside out. Bryce grudgingly hands him a bottle of water, and McCoyne manages to swallow a couple of mouthfuls. He opens the door and spits up a wad of sticky phlegm, then wipes his mouth and leans back in his seat.

"I don't feel so good."

"There's not one little bit of me that gives a shit, McCoyne. Now tell me what you saw in there."

"Not a lot is the honest answer. Most of them were shut away inside, and like I told you, I'm not going to risk getting any closer in case I get recognized again."

"Don't flatter yourself, mate. You're instantly forgettable."

"Apparently not, remember? Anyway, I told you it would work. Going in quiet with a few volunteers was a smart move. They're shitting themselves in there now, total fucking panic stations. They'll be awake all night, waiting for us to hit them again."

"What about gear? What kind of stores are they sitting on?"

"I wasn't in there for long, but I know they're not flush with stuff. I didn't see a lot in the way of supplies. I reckon it'll be easy to starve them out. Block off their escape routes and they're fucked."

"Go on."

"It's like I'm always saying, it's not all about fighting, is it?"

"Not when you're a lazy fucker like you," he goads.

McCoyne shakes his head. "I know how you feel about me, Bryce, but forget that for a sec; it's not the point."

"Then what is?"

"We've been taking heavy losses. *Avoidable* losses. We've just shown what we can do with a few people and a bit of fuel, so why bother exerting all that effort and taking massive risks, when all we need to do is keep the Unchanged locked down? Scare the fuck out of them, then wait until they turn on themselves and destroy everything from the inside out. It worked before in the city, and if it worked there with tens of thousands of people, then a few hundred Unchanged stuck in close confines like that will stand absolutely no fucking chance. Bide your time, Bryce, and start positioning yourself. Go back to Cambridge and find anyone else who's getting tired of Johannson. Start building yourself a fan base, because at some point soon, people are going to realize the boss is running out of ideas."

46

The Travelodge

Matt's sick. Really sick. He feels like death. He's been lying on his sweat-soaked bed for what feels like forever. Fever dreams have swirled around his head: nightmare images of Jen burning, of him being pursued by Haters, of dying alone in this damn hotel . . . It's no way to go out, but right now he can't see any alternatives. His head's pounding, and his throat's on fire. He's burning up.

He knows he must have been asleep, but he's not sure when or how long for. The light levels outside seem to change every time he opens his eyes. Might be a storm. Might be midnight. Matt's not sure he even cares anymore. He's really starting to think he might not make it through another day.

He thinks about everything and nothing while he's lying here. Mostly he remembers the time before the war. It feels so long ago as to be impossible, like his life before all this belonged to someone else. Remember a time when things were so easy that the biggest hurdle to getting through the day was making it through a meeting without being shouted down or submitting a report before the deadline was up? Even in his current less-than-lucid state, he wishes he were back there again, trying to keep his head above water in the corporate world filled with trivialities and in-consequential nothings. And to think, he used to worry about all that vapid, empty stuff like it mattered.

Right now, he needs to find himself a corner of reality to hold on to, an anchor to the here and now, stop himself slipping fur-ther away. He reaches out a heavy-feeling arm and, on the third attempt, picks up what's left of a bottle of water from the side of the bed. He half drinks the dregs, half throws them into his face, but that's good because the tepid water is cold enough to drag him back from the brink momentarily. But the slight shock doesn't last long, and soon he's drifting again. The rain spotting against the glass becomes a clattering storm, and the storm becomes an-other distant battle. In his head, he pictures the outpost he's never actually seen under siege from Haters, and he confuses that with memories of the times he went out hunting for the enemy with Franklin and his crew. He imagines one of the killers seeing him and starting to chase, only for more and more to follow. Before long, in his mind, he's running for his life with a thousand of them on his tail, all of them leaving the outpost and the people there behind just to get a piece of him.

And now he's stuck up in a tree, looking down on hundreds of them looking back at him. And now the tree is the canopy of the fuel station next door, and the Hater who fell and died is calling all the others over to come and get him.

And now he's imagining Jason standing at the end of his bed, shaking him to wake him up from this stupor.

"Matt. Matt, wake up!"

Too real.

"Come on, for fuck's sake. Wake up!"

When Jason punches Matt's arm, the searing agony in his in-jured shoulder leaves him in no doubt this is no hallucination. He sits up, the sickening pain returning him to full consciousness.

"What are you doing back here?"

"We need to hide."

"I'm already hiding. What from?"

"No time to explain. Shift! Now!"

Over the noise of Jason's nervous jabbering, over the sound of the driving rain and swirling wind, Matt's now aware that he can hear something else.

"What is it?"

"Now, Matt!"

Jason drags him off the bed and across the room. Matt stumbles and pulls him back, trying to keep his balance. "What's going on?" he asks as Jason frantically leads him through the hotel to reception. He answers without answering.

"Don't think they saw me. Need to get out of sight. Need to climb. Can you climb?"

"Don't know. My shoulder's pretty bad, and—"

"I'll help you up," Jason says, cutting across him, and before Matt can protest, they're out in the open with Jason pushing him up onto the roof of the van that'll allow them to climb onto the roof of the car wash, then onto the fuel station canopy. Whatever that noise is, it's getting louder, getting closer.

Once they're both up, the two of them lie side by side. "Are you going to tell me what's going on?" Matt asks, whispering. "What have you gone and done? Have you brought them back here with you?"

"I haven't done anything. Just shut up."

Engine noise. Marching boots. Voices shouting.

Matt inches closer to the edge of the canopy and peers down. Can the fighting around the outpost have spread this far so quickly? The road running past the Travelodge begins to fill up with people. CDF? There's no one he recognizes. Haters? These people look strong and well organized, nothing like the feral savages he's seen since leaving the printing house shelter. Whoever and whatever, there are more people down there than he's seen in one place since the night the city-camp fell. It's an endless procession of packed vehicles and personnel.

There are cracks in the colored Perspex that covers the canopy. Since he was last up here, great chunks of plastic have dropped down and shattered near where the dead Hater's body still lies on the tarmac. The metal skeleton of the structure is exposed, and through the crossbeams and welded joints, Matt realizes he can get a better view while keeping out of sight. He slides across, head still pounding, body still shivering. For a moment, he imagines the entire structure giving way beneath him, buckling as he shifts his center of gravity. He pictures the whole damn thing dropping down, handing him on a plate to whoever is down there. It'd be funny were it not so completely fucking terrifying.

A millimeter movement feels like a mile up here. Matt spreads his weight as he watches the activity down at street level. The structure sways slightly and groans somewhat, but it's holding steady, and any noise is inaudible over the combined din of engines and marching feet below. He feels confident enough to whisper to Jason.

"They're traveling the opposite direction from how we got here. East to west. All it's going to take is another burst of fighting near the outpost for this lot to make a cross-country diversion."

"I know. Look at the number of them. Christ, Matt, that'd be the end of Estelle and the CDF."

"Exactly."

They watch more and more vehicles go past—all shapes and sizes, military and civilian, no uniformity—with literally hundreds of men and women on board and alongside. At one point, the burned-out Starbucks and the hotel attract some attention, and for a time the petrol station forecourt below them is swarming with people. Matt's heart sinks when a squad of ten or more disappear into the hotel, then emerge a short time later, their arms loaded up with what's left of his stuff.

It takes the best part of half an hour for this army—because an army is unquestionably what it is—to pass. For a while longer, Matt and Jason stay exactly where they are, not about to risk moving in case they're seen. Eventually, Jason's confident enough to ask the obvious question. "Who the hell are they?"

"No idea. Wait, they didn't see you out there, did they? Jesus, Jason, don't tell me they're looking for you."

"No, I swear. I was trying to cut across the fields to get to the others, but I took a wrong turn. Few wrong turns, actually. I saw that lot coming in and I didn't know what else to do, so I doubled back on myself."

"Hell of a risk. You could have brought them back here."

"Fuck's sake, Matt. It would be great if you could stop worrying about yourself for just one second. Better to have brought them back here than for them to have followed me to the others."

"You're right. Sorry."

"They must be Haters."

"Yeah, the strutting gives it away. Fuckers weren't trying particularly hard to keep a low profile."

"We need to do something, Matt."

"Like what?"

"Like warn Estelle and Darren and the others. I don't know how many people we've just seen, but I doubt there are that many at the outpost. There was only a fraction of that number back at Thornhill. Add to that whoever they're already fighting over there, and their odds will likely be slashed to zero. We have to tell them. We owe it to them. Not to mention the fact those wankers just helped themselves to all your stuff."

Matt rolls over onto his back in the rainwater, looking into the roiling black clouds overhead, the rain spotting at his face. The thought of leaving here fills him with dread, but damn it, he knows Jason's right.

47

The CDF Outpost

The atmosphere inside the service station is nothing like it was. The halfhearted Hater attack in the small hours was successfully repelled, and as of yet, there have been no further incursions. There's a sense of freedom now that these people are no longer hiding, and something else, too . . . Optimism? Hope? Maybe those words are too strong, but there's an undeniable swell of positivity among the soldiers and civilians gathered here. The mood is further lifted by Estelle's saber-rattling. She's currently standing up on the observation platform balcony, preaching to the masses. Given the fact they've been starved of information for longer than they've been here, they're lapping up her every word.

"For a while, we were thinking we were the underdogs," she shouts, uninhibited, her voice echoing off the walls of the cavernous space, "but we were wrong. In the time we've been waiting to strike back, those people out there have regressed to the point where they're little better than animals. They're uncivilized and uncoordinated now. They've lost sight of who they used to be, and they're nothing but mindless brutes.

"It took them months to find this place, and in that time, we consolidated and grew our numbers. We planned and we prospered.

We readied ourselves because we knew this day would come eventually and that, at some point, we'd have to fight."

Joseph, Darren, Parker, and Dean are sitting outside what used to be a branch of WHSmith. "She talks a good talk," Dean says.

"But she's full of shit," Parker whispers back.

"Since the Haters discovered our location, they've launched numerous attacks, and every time they've hit us, we've dealt with them easily and driven them back. They tried a different tactic overnight and, again, we beat them. The mass grave we dug out back is overflowing with corpses. We've slashed their numbers, and yet we've suffered only a handful of casualties ourselves. When this war first began and the CDF was formed, we strategized on the belief that because of their extreme aggression, every individual Hater had the potential to kill many of us. From what I've seen this week, that logic no longer applies. From our position of strength here, with the weaponry we have at our disposal, we now find ourselves with a huge tactical advantage. They've tried to intimidate us, they've tried to break us by force, they've tried stealth attacks, full-on attacks, they've thrown everything they have at us, and *nothing has worked*."

A ripple of spontaneous applause breaks out in part of the building, and the noise quickly spreads. Even the cynics at the back have to admit that this long-overdue collective expression of positive emotion stirs the spirits. A sea of expectant faces look up at Estelle, many of them daring to wonder if they might really have a chance of some kind of future in the battle-scarred remains of this fucked-up world after all.

"They will attack again, that much is certain," she continues, "and when they do, we will be ready for them. We expect that next time they strike, they'll do so in even greater numbers and with far more force than before. Stay strong. There's no need to be afraid. Whether they're in twos and threes or in their hundreds, we will beat them. Whatever they throw at us, we *will* beat them."

"What are you basing this on?" a lone dissenting voice asks. "What information do you have?"

Estelle is unfazed by the interruption, almost encourages it with the enthusiasm of her response. "You're absolutely right to ask. Information these days is limited and hard to come by. Since the first attacks began, we've risked going farther afield. We've also had their bodies and equipment to examine and evaluate."

"And?"

"And their equipment is basic, and they're in generally poor physical condition."

"I'm in poor physical condition!" the ownerless voice shouts back, eliciting a little laughter. It's strange sounding. A little laughter is as much as anyone's heard in an age.

"They're generally weak and malnourished. Many of them bear scars from the bomb. There's evidence of radiation sickness. Some looked so bad it was only the Hate keeping them alive."

"But how many of them are left?"

"As it happens, just a few hours ago, Moira returned from a recce of the wastelands. That's why I wanted to bring everyone together like this. Moira's been able to gather a lot of useful information about our enemy that we didn't know previously."

There's a new noise from the crowd now, a nervous hubbub.

"And there's me thinking this was just a cozy team-building chat," Parker says. "A healthy dose of propaganda to help keep our chins up."

"What, you think it's more than that?" Darren asks, lowering his voice and hoping Parker will do the same.

"Of course it is. Brace yourself, boys. Here comes the sucker punch. She's setting us up for the big one."

Estelle clears her throat. The crowd inside the service station is completely silent, almost too quiet. "As I said, there was another attempt to hit us during the early hours. Unlike the previous attacks, this was a far smaller, lower-scale incursion that was swiftly repelled. We deliberately allowed several of the attackers to get away, and Moira was able to track them. She saw . . . no, wait, it's probably better if I let Moira tell you herself."

There's a brief pause as the two soldiers change places. Moira's no public speaker, but she's seen so much that it's hard to keep the words swallowed down. "Everything Estelle just said is true," she begins. "Our enemy is a pack of low-down, dirty fucking animals."

Cue more cheering.

When the noise drops, she carries on. "There's a village a few miles northeast of here called Longstanton. That's where they are. Don't look like they've been there long, and it don't look like they intend on staying there, either. I was watching them for quite a while, and I reckon there's a hundred and fifty of them left, two hundred tops. Jeez, like Estelle says, they don't look good. They're in bad shape, like they've forgotten how to be people. Most of them are dressed in rags, eating scraps . . . like a frigging concentration camp, it was. We can't write them off completely, though, 'cause there's definitely some kind of order there, an obvious chain of command.

"In terms of gear, they don't have a lot. Plenty of vehicles, not a lot else. We can't assume they're unarmed, but I don't reckon they've got much firepower behind them, if any. Bottom line is, from what I've seen, it looks like there's fewer of them than us now, and they don't have a fraction of the equipment we have."

"Trouble is," Dean whispers to the others around him, "we've only got a fraction of the equipment we had, too."

Estelle thanks Moira and turns back to address her people again. "So the information Moira's given us today has helped Greg Chappell and I to crystallize our thinking."

"Here it comes," Parker warns again.

"The way we see it, we have two options. We can sit here and wait for more drip-fed attacks and take the enemy out piece by piece, or we can take a more proactive approach. I think you're all as tired of fighting as we are, so the sooner we can bring this to an end, the better. I've ordered plans to be drawn up to launch an offensive on Longstanton. We'll hit the enemy hard when they're expecting it least. We're under no illusions—it'll be a hard fight—but my team and I believe the potential rewards far outweigh the risks."

This time, the reaction of the crowd is muted, far more mixed. There's a definite split—the CDF fighters who are trained and armed and ready for battle are vociferous, the civilians and support staff far less so. To her credit, Estelle appears aware.

"Look, before I go any further, I want to say to you all categorically that I'm not asking anyone who isn't prepared to pick up a weapon to fight on the front line—not yet, anyway. I know there are many of you who would struggle with that, and if I'm honest, you're the last people I want out there. What I am saying, though, is that when we launch this offensive, there will inevitably be huge ramifications for all of us."

"Hear that?" Parker says, nudging Darren. "She's not asking us to fight *at the moment.* It'll be different if it all goes tits up."

"*When,*" Joseph corrects him.

"Quit griping," Darren snaps at them both. "She knows what she's talking about. She's seen us all right so far, hasn't she?"

"So far," Parker mutters.

There's another pause as the masses digest Estelle's words. She waits, then elaborates.

"Our brave men and women at the front will need the support of all of us. From the moment our attack begins until the final Hater is killed, our entire focus will be on the battle. Things will be difficult until then—harder than any of us have known so far, perhaps—but this is essential. We've come so far, survived so much . . . all I'm asking is for you all to stand behind our soldiers and support them until the deed is done."

"She's not asking, she's telling," Joseph says, but the increasingly vocal CDF contingent drowns out his dissent.

"We need to activate our contingency plan," Dean whispers to Joseph, concerned by the increase in chest-beating and warmongering.

At the other end of the building, Estelle has the crowd at fever pitch. "One more huge push, that's all it's going to take. One last battle and we'll have removed the Hater scourge from this place forever. Imagine being free to go outside again without fear. Free to talk and debate and argue . . . Free to *live!*"

48

Cambridge

The area around the university is desolate, but the scars of the Hater occupation are visible everywhere: the litter and ruin, the forgotten bodies and burned-out fires, the abandoned buildings with their doors left hanging open, the intentionally blocked roads. Persistent gray rain adds to the gutter lakes that have formed around clogged drains.

There are only a handful of people left around here now. Some move back and forth between the university and the camp at Longstanton, finding more weapons and supplies to transport to the front, replacing vehicles and scavenging spare parts. Others watch from the shadows, hiding. These people are reluctant non-fighters. This is a safe haven for them temporarily, at least until Johannson returns.

Gordon Carter was a museum curator back in the day. The Hate has stripped everything he valued from what's left of his life. He's never been a particularly physical man, and until he was forced to kill his partner when *the change* overtook him, he'd never hit or hurt anyone. That's not to say he didn't feel the same sense of necessity and euphoria when he was killing Unchanged during the early days of the war, but as their numbers quickly dwindled, so did his appetite for conflict. He feels like he used to now; normal Gordon, cultured Gordon, refined Gordon.

He spends most of his time with a group of four others—two men, two women—all of whom are equally ill-equipped for survival in this brutal environment. Marie, Ralph, Jamie, and Helen are like him: weak and afraid, eking out a miserable existence in the shadows, living off the scraps the rest of them discard. He came out here today looking for food, but he's allowed himself to be distracted by the beauty of the interior of this great hall. Much of it has been defaced or destroyed, but so much still remains intact. The paneling, those windows, and that ceiling— oh, that ceiling—are still magnificent, protected for now by their height above everything else. Gordon finds it impossible to believe there could be anything more beautiful than this hall left in this shell of a world today. It's Georgian Gothic, and as he wanders alone through its splendor, he tries to imagine how many kings and queens and other dignitaries have dined here and how many—

"What the fuck are you doing in here, you useless cunt?"

Gordon freezes. Legs turn to lead. He turns around slowly. "Just wondering where everyone was, Mr. Bryce."

"You know where they are. So why aren't you there?"

"I'm not a fighter. You can see that . . ."

"So what are you, then? From where I'm standing, you look like a fucking thief trying to nick food from the chief."

Gordon holds his hands up in surrender. "I've taken nothing. I'm sorry. I swear, I was just trying to—"

Bryce is having none of it. "You lying bastard. Give me one good reason why I shouldn't haul you up in front of Johannson and tell her what I found you doing in her office."

"Please . . . don't do that. I'm ready to fight. I was just looking for something to fight with. Honestly, I—"

Another voice silences his terrified chattering. It's Danny McCoyne. "Bryce, leave it. I think we've got a problem."

Bryce turns around and looks at McCoyne in the doorway. Then he looks past him, but he can't immediately see anything.

"What?"

"Something's not right."

"You're going to have to give me more to go on than that."

"Can't you hear it?"

Gordon seizes his moment and runs deeper into the building. Bryce exits the college hall and stands in the rubbish-strewn square outside, sniffing the air, listening intently. He can hear it now. Engines approaching. Many engines.

"Unchanged?" he asks, his head filling with nightmare images of the enemy's tanks rolling in to obliterate Johannson's stronghold and him being the only one here to defend it.

"Don't think so. Listen again."

"Stop playing games with me, McCoyne. Just tell me what you're thinking."

"What I'm thinking is this is bad news, because whoever that is, they're coming from the east. Unless they've taken a massive detour—and there'd be no point in them doing that—then this isn't to do with the Unchanged. They'd have come from the west."

"Thacker," Bryce surmises.

"Has to be. Thacker's the only one who knows where Johannson's based. Come on, Bryce, we need to get out of here."

"We're going nowhere," Bryce says. "This is exactly where we need to be."

McCoyne thinks Bryce looks unnaturally calm, and that scares him more than anything. He steps back and tucks himself into the shadows of the college building's porch and watches. "You stay there," Bryce warns him. "Don't you fucking move."

The bright lights of the convoy come into view. Christ, from

here the line appears endless. If each vehicle has a full comple-
ment of passengers, then there are hundreds of Haters approaching, maybe as many as a thousand. Bryce swallows hard, hoping
he looks more confident than he feels.

"Seriously, Bryce," McCoyne whines as the first few vehicles
pull up, "this is a really fucking bad idea. I think we should go."

"You're so bloody naïve. Look at the numbers they've got.
Don't you get it? Fuck Johannson; it's these people we need onside. This, my pathetic little friend, is an opportunity for career
progression presenting itself."

Thacker's army stretches back for more than a mile, the mist
and rain obscuring many of the vehicles farther back. Bryce walks
up to the lead 4×4. He's fucking terrified, but he's determined
not to let it show.

A distinctive-looking fighter emerges. Bryce recognizes him
from before. "It's Hinchcliffe, isn't it?"

"Yep. Who the hell are you?"

"Name's Karl Bryce. I was here before when you killed that
prick Pinchy."

"And why are you still loitering around here when everyone
else clearly appears to have fucked off, Karl Bryce?"

Bryce awkwardly shifts his weight from foot to foot.

"Difference of opinion with the boss," he lies.

"How so?"

"Don't agree with her tactics. There's a bunch of Unchanged.
She's taking her time getting rid of them."

"Unchanged? Seriously? Fuck me. You only just found them?"

"Few days back. They're well dug in and heavily armed. Military."

"And they're still breathing?"

"Just."

"But they are still breathing?"

"Yeah. That's what I mean. Johannson's methods are all wrong."

"And I assume you've told her that? That's why you're hiding here on your own while they're all off fighting? You're protesting her tactics?"

"It's not like that."

"What, so you're a coward, then? That's how it looks from where I'm standing."

"I swear, I—"

"To be honest, mate, I'm not interested. Where is your glorious leader?"

"I'll take you."

"Just tell me."

Bryce's heart is racing. His right eye twitches with nerves. Hinchcliffe, by comparison, appears unflappable. His calmness is a hundred times more terrifying than Johannson's aggression. Bryce knows he can't afford to crack now.

"You won't find it. I'll take you."

"You're an insistent little fella."

"My vehicle's just here. Follow me and I'll take you right to her."

"Why should I waste my time with the likes of you?"

"I won't piss you around, Hinchcliffe. I want the same thing you do. I want Johannson gone and the Unchanged dead, and I've got information that could be useful."

"Such as?"

"I know a hell of a lot more about the Unchanged setup than she does."

"And how did you get that kind of info?"

Bryce looks around for McCoyne, who's disappeared. Fucking coward. "I have a source. Bit of a freak, but he does the job."

Hinchcliffe thinks for a second.

"Interesting. Okay, lead the way. Just keep in mind what happened to your friend Mr. Pinch when he annoyed me, though, won't you?"

49

The CDF Outpost

It's like working on a chain gang, but no one's complaining. Despite what's looming on the immediate horizon, grafting like this is strangely cathartic. It helps with the nerves, even for those who aren't sure about Estelle's plans. Whether you think you're able to fight or not, there's no question it makes sense to ensure the CDF army is as well equipped as possible when it goes into battle.

The parking lot and the rest of the immediate area around the service station and hotel has been cleared of debris; the rubbish piled up around the buildings, forming further obstructions and giving the military increased options, recycling on a grand scale. Beyond the trenches, vehicle wrecks are shifted to be used as barricades and forward gun positions. The remaining heavy weaponry available to the CDF is given increased prominence and visibility as a deterrent.

More Hater bodies are cleared from the battlefield and are being burned in a deliberately visible pyre now that it no longer matters, not left to rot down to mulch. Clothing, food, weapons, drugs . . . everything is in short supply these days, and there are more civilians than ever out here stripping the carcasses before they're torched.

Inside the service station, the activity is equally frenetic. There are some people with specialist skills—Tracy Barnish and another GP, several teachers, and trained support workers who look after the few remaining kids—but the bulk of the group are just worker ants, keeping the wheels of the outpost turning by cleaning, repairing, and distributing rations to the fighters.

Parker and Dean were supposed to be helping Darren feed the soldiers preparing for battle. Problem is they've disappeared. Darren's lost them. One minute, they were carrying water from the service station to the hotel; the next, they'd both disappeared. Damn shirkers. Darren's sick of people like them who don't pull their weight.

When he spots Dean through the driving rain, heading in completely the wrong direction toward the mass of vehicles in what used to be the construction workers' compound, Darren chases after him, incensed. Dean's focused on whatever he's doing, and he doesn't realize he's being followed until Darren catches hold of his shoulder and spins him around. "What the hell are you up to?" he demands.

"Calm down, Darren, I just—"

"Calm down? Jesus Christ, don't tell me to calm down. We're on the verge of all-out war here. I catch you making a run for it, and you've got the nerve to tell *me* to calm down?"

Darren realizes Dean's also carrying a decent-sized stash of food in a rucksack slung over one shoulder. "It's not how it looks," Dean says quickly.

"You reckon? I think it's exactly how it looks. You're stealing from the rest of us and covering your own back. Frigging coward. Wait till I tell Estelle about this. She'll have you strung up for—"

"Don't do that, Darren."

"Give me one good reason why I shouldn't."

Joseph Mallon appears from around the side of a massive excavating machine. "Because you'd be making a huge mistake if you did," he says, wiping dripping rainwater from his face. "Same as Estelle is."

"Bullshit."

"It's not. Look, all we're doing is putting measures in place just in case."

"In case what?"

"In case things don't turn out the way she's planning."

Darren pushes past Joseph. Around the corner, right in the middle of this maze of broken machines, is a truck that's already a quarter filled with looted supplies. "You thieving bastards," he says, and he turns to go get help.

Parker has appeared and is blocking his way through.

"I'm not going to let you do this, Darren."

"This is an insurance policy," Joseph explains, standing directly behind him.

"Insurance for who?"

"All of us."

"Bullshit. You're out for yourselves, fuck everyone else. Christ, do you not see how pointless this is?"

"What, the fighting?" Dean goads.

"No, what you're doing. What do you think's going to happen? Are you just going to try sneaking out the back door? The only chance of any of us getting through this is if we're all pulling in the same direction." He pauses and looks again at the relative mountain of supplies they've looted. "Where the hell did you get all that from, anyway?"

"We've been siphoning it off for some time," Parker admits.

"Just you three?"

"A few others."

"Fuck's sake . . . who? How many others?"

"That's not important."

"Of course it's important. We won't stand any chance of winning if half of us are going to run away as soon as the fighting starts up again."

"No one said anything about running away. Like Joseph says, this is a contingency. Aaron Rayner knows we need to—"

"Aaron's in on this?"

"He's aware, yes. Listen, you need to think very carefully before you start stirring things up."

"Are you threatening me?"

"Not yet."

"Not *yet!*"

"You have to understand, this matters too much. We need to keep all our options open."

"This is *bullshit*. You're not getting away with it. I'm going to—"

But Darren's not going to do anything. Not yet, at least. Because his words are interrupted by a now familiar cry that goes up from the CDF soldiers manning the guns and the lookouts along the front line.

"Incoming!"

This time, the enemy's approach is scattershot. The strikes come from so many different directions at once that it's virtually impossible to work out how many of them are attacking.

One of the main gunners adjusts his sights and zeroes in on a pack of Haters racing across the battlefield in a battered old Mercedes Estate. This feels so damn easy now, so natural . . . it's almost like playing a video game. The gunner's energy levels are artificially high, buoyed by adrenaline and the confidence of knowing that the balance has finally tipped in favor of the CDF. The thrill of the kill is astonishing. He's enjoying this so much he reckons he could pass for a Hater himself.

He pulls the lanyard rope, covers his ears, and ducks as the howitzer fires. The shell whistles through the air but misses the Merc and hits the ground just short. The resulting detonation is still savage enough to flip the vehicle onto its roof. Three Hater fighters scramble out of the wreckage and are immediately picked off by CDF snipers from the roof of the hotel.

This is so fucking easy.

A group of attackers bursts out from the cover of a copse of trees. They sprint and stall and zigzag, but it has no effect because they're running straight toward a length of trench lined with armed militia. Their standard-issue SA80 assault rifles are capable of emptying thirty shots from a clip in quick succession, but there's no need for rapid fire here. These soldiers can afford to take their time, choose their targets carefully, and conserve their ammo. When another group of ten or so appears from the same wooded area, one of the CDF militia fires a grenade from the launcher attached to her rifle and takes the whole damn lot out with one shot.

Estelle and Chappell watch from the lookout. There's a quiet confidence about Estelle today. Now that the enemy's numbers have been ascertained and their abilities (or lack thereof) proved, her tactics have been validated. She knows exactly what she needs her troops to do.

"I think it's time, Greg, don't you?"

"You're sure about this?"

"Completely."

She turns away from the battlefield and beckons Moira over. Moira's been waiting for this. She's ready to disseminate the chief's orders to the ranks.

"As we discussed," Estelle says. "Maintain a strong defensive perimeter around the outpost, then send the tanks to Longstanton. I want them on the move within the hour. Wipe them all out. Every last fucking one of them."

"Yes, ma'am."

50

Longstanton

She's no fool. She knows the approaching engine noise and marching footsteps can only mean one of two things: the Unchanged or Thacker. She's on the concrete clearing with her back to him when she hears it. The bulk of Hinchcliffe's convoy has been ordered to hold position a short distance from the village, though there's still quite an entourage here with him, a couple of hundred at least. With the flooded wetlands on two sides, and the road to the clearing blocked by Hinchcliffe's fighters, Johannson's escape routes have been cut off.

"Boss," Bryce says, calling out to Johannson but standing alongside Hinchcliffe. She doesn't react. She has her generals and key lackeys all around her, planning their next move. Bryce clears his throat and tries again, shouting this time. "Boss! Someone here to speak to you."

Johannson finally stops and stands up straight but doesn't immediately turn around. She takes her time and composes herself. When she finally faces Hinchcliffe, she's managed to summon up enough arrogance, swagger, and aggression to match him.

"Thought I told you to fuck off and not come back here."

"You did. Sorry, Mrs. Johannson, I'm just not very good at doing what I'm told."

If Johannson's feeling any nervousness, she isn't letting it show. She knows how this works. She's rehearsed it in her head time and again since Thacker first made his intentions known and sent Hinchcliffe here. Distracted only by the discovery of Unchanged nearby, she's been waiting for this inevitable meeting.

"Lovely to see you again and all that," Hinchcliffe says, "but I think you know how this is going to pan out."

From calm to chaos in a heartbeat, Johannson flies at him, unsheathing a machete from under her heavy outer coat and swinging it at his head.

Hinchcliffe's a step ahead.

He has a riot baton, and as she comes at him, he ducks out of the way, sidesteps, then cracks the baton into her machete-wielding arm with such force that her humerus shatters and she drops the blade, which clatters to the concrete. The pain must be excruciating, but she doesn't let it show. If anything, it just riles her up even more, and she goes for him again, right arm flapping uselessly at her side. Hinchcliffe again anticipates, this time dropping low and thumping the baton into her pelvis, then both kneecaps. Then, just for good measure, he shatters her right fibula. She's left writhing on the ground.

Johannson's generals, massively outnumbered, don't react. Only Myndham, fiercely loyal, shows any sign of retaliation. A glare from Hinchcliffe and all thoughts of resistance are forgotten. "Think very carefully about your next move, my man. By all means, have a go if you think you're hard enough, but do weigh up your options first. Full disclosure—I've brought about nine hundred and forty friends to the party."

No more dissent.

An unnatural hush descends over what remains of Longstanton

now, disturbed only by Johannson's howls of pain and anger. Still writhing on the ground, she reaches out with her remaining good arm and grabs the toe of Hinchcliffe's boot. He takes a step back, then stamps on her face. "Do shut up," he says.

There are gasps and mumbled curses from the crowd. All these people have experienced extreme cruelty, brutality, and barbarism since the onset of the Hate, but nothing like this, and certainly not toward their own. Hinchcliffe takes hate to a new level.

He looks around at the people staring back at him. "And it really is as easy as that," he announces, and he's right. In the space of just a couple of minutes, he's cut short Johannson's previously unchallenged rule and has transferred leadership of her tribe to Thacker.

There's absolute silence now. Deadly anticipation.

"As some of you may remember, I represent a gentleman by the name of Mr. Thacker. He's my boss. As of now, he's your boss, too, and I'm pleased to welcome you to his ever-growing family with open arms. We're in the process of relocating to the east coast, and we'd love for you to come and join us. Now does anyone *not* want to come along?"

Silence.

"Perfect. Now before we all head off into the sunset together, there's the small matter of getting rid of the group of Unchanged I'm told you've found." He looks around for Bryce. "How many of them are there?"

"Between two and three hundred, we think."

"And remind me again, why aren't they dead?"

"Ask her," Bryce says, gesturing dismissively at Johannson. She's on her back looking up into the rain, blood- and mud-splattered, barely alive, groaning through a mouthful of broken teeth.

And yet still she tries to fight. The pain is unimaginable, but it's surpassed by her inhuman levels of anger. Hinchcliffe is losing his patience. He picks up her machete and hands it to Bryce. "Kill her, will you?"

Bryce freezes. It's only for a fraction of a second, but he thinks it's long enough for Hinchcliffe to have picked up on his uncertainty. He immediately drops to the ground and chops the blade down on Johannson's neck. "Sorry, boss," he whispers before getting back up and wiping her blood from his hands.

"Good lad," Hinchcliffe says. "Not the cleanest cut, but it's shut her up, at least." He walks around the clearing, circling the body, looking into the faces of the fighters who, until just now, fought for the dead warrior queen now lying dead on the ground in front of them. "Question to the group," he says. "What exactly is stopping you finishing off those nasty Unchanged fuckers?"

"They've got tanks," someone says, only brave enough to volunteer an answer because their position deep in the crowd gives them a chance of anonymity.

"I've got tanks, too," Hinchcliffe quickly replies, looking in vain for the speaker. "Didn't bring any with me, though. Didn't think I'd need them. Thacker has plenty of tanks. Any other reason?"

Nothing.

Hinchcliffe answers his own question. He turns around to face Bryce again. "If what you're telling me is correct and what I'm seeing is right, I'd say you've struggled because of numbers."

"Yeah."

"So I might have just tipped the balance, given that I brought nearly a thousand folks with me?"

"I'd say so, yes."

"Excellent. What else can you tell me?"

Ullah steps forward and lays out a map. Bryce muscles in, keen to prove he knows more than the rest of them. He jabs his finger at the position of the base on the map, circled in pen. "There. There's a trench around most of the perimeter, and I can show you where their big guns are. From what I can tell, they don't have a lot of ammunition or supplies left. Looks like they've been there since before the bombs. Fuckers must be close to the breaking point."

"Good," Hinchcliffe says, and he picks up the map. He pushes Bryce aside, then gestures for one of his own people to come forward. He hands them the map. "Get the word out—I want a full perimeter put around their location. Block every road and track in a ten-mile radius. Keep back and stay out of sight until I give the order to advance." He looks around for Ullah and Myndham. "You two get out there and let all your people who were loyal to Mrs. Johannson know they're reporting to me now. They fall into line with my troops and my orders, or they'll be killed. Understand?"

Ullah doesn't hesitate. "I understand."

"Excellent."

"So what's the plan?" Bryce asks, desperate to fill the hole in the chain of command left by the death of Johannson.

"Your plan is to do what I tell you," Hinchcliffe tells him. "My plan is to strangle the Unchanged and cut off their air supply. I'm going to put those fuckers in a chokehold and keep tightening my grip until every last one of them is dead."

51

East of the Outpost

Matt and Jason have been walking for hours but have only covered a fraction of the distance they'd hoped. They were both resigned to making slow progress cross-country anyway—it's par for the course—but Matt's struggling badly. His legs are like lead, and he has a raging temperature. It's getting difficult putting one foot in front of the other, let alone doing that in silence with the prospect of having to hide or face the enemy at any moment. He keeps dropping back. Jason waits for him, feeling increasingly nervous every time they slow down. "Come on, Matt, we can do this," he urges. They're midway across an overgrown golf course, the farthest edge of which runs parallel with the A14. They're wishing they'd taken a different route. There are patches of trees here, but also frequent wide swaths of sparse yellow grass that used to be fairways and greens. It's stop-start. Feels like they're having to cover all eighteen holes. They've estimated they could still have about ten miles to go, and that distance feels like forever today.

Matt pauses and wipes the sweat from his brow. Jason keeps going but stops when he realizes Matt's not following. He's leaning against a tree, his face pallid. He slumps, then drops to the ground. Jason rolls him over onto his back.

"I feel like shit," Matt says.

"You look like shit."

Since leaving the Travelodge, his condition has deteriorated markedly. He felt bad when he was there, but the extent of his sickness was masked by the fact he was flat out in bed, not having to move. The exertion is making everything feel worse.

"This isn't good. I think it's blood poisoning, something like that."

"From your shoulder?"

"Guess so. We've been breathing in all kinds of shit since we stuck our heads above ground." He pauses. Winces. "That can't have helped."

"What are your symptoms? What hurts?"

"Everything hurts."

"Describe the pain."

"Why? You a doctor?"

"Don't be difficult."

"Then don't be an idiot. I'm freezing cold, weak as fuck, heart's racing . . ."

"Do you think you can keep going?"

Matt rolls back over and uses the tree to get himself up. Breathless, he announces, "Don't think I have any choice."

He starts walking again.

The sounds of battle give a useful indication of where Matt and Jason are. By no means constant, the frequent noises are enough to confirm they're still headed in the right direction: strained engines, the thunderous boom of heavy artillery being fired, unidentifiable voices screaming orders and instructions to each other, all caught on the wind. Matt's beginning to wonder if there will be anything left of the outpost when they finally get there.

"Wait," Jason says.

"No . . . have to keep moving," Matt insists, breathless. "Need to stay ahead of them."

"No, really, wait," Jason says again, and when Matt looks up, he can tell from the expression on Jason's face that this is more serious than he'd thought. "They're coming."

Another swell of engine noise can be heard like the rumble of a fast-approaching storm. "Fuck," Matt says, and he spits to clear foul-tasting phlegm from his throat.

Up ahead, they can see the first vehicles approaching. Times past, the road would have been obscured by the trees, shielding the golf course, but the temperature, the dampness of the soil, and the toxicity of the air have combined to eat away at the greenery. Branches that would normally have been covered in leaves at this time of year are bare. Previously steadfast roots have lost their grip in the sodden earth, and a number of trees have been brought down by little more than their weight and the wind alone.

There's another road that joins the A14 at an intersection a short way back from their current position. Matt and Jason crouch down behind an uprooted root ball, and Matt points with a trembling hand. "Roadblock. They're sealing off the escape routes."

"Shit. So that's us fucked. We'll never make it to the others in time."

"I can't go any faster," Matt says, wheezing.

"I can see that."

"But we might still do it."

They crawl through the scrub and leaf litter toward the large group of Haters now swarming around this part of the A14. They're blocking the road with vehicles—leaving them end to end and side by side so there's little chance of anyone getting through.

"You sure this is going to work?" Jason whispers.

"Nope. Not even sure I'm going to be able to walk that far."

"You're kidding, right?"

Matt just looks at him, not that either can see the other's face. They're both wearing hoods and scarves now, with only the narrowest of gaps left for their eyes. It's not much of a disguise, but it might buy them a few extra seconds.

"It's like I've always said to you, Jason: watch what everyone else is doing, then do the opposite. The last thing they're expecting is for anyone like you and me to be anywhere near here."

"This is a really fucking bad idea."

"It is, yes, but right now it's the only idea we've got."

They pause, crouched in a muddy ditch with little more than an embankment, a handful of crisscrossing branches, and a few meters of clear space between them and the pack setting up the roadblock. Matt can hardly focus: nerves or sickness? It's impossible to tell anymore.

"Don't think I can do this," Jason whispers, voice muffled by the scarf covering his face.

"No choice. Shut up."

Matt watches as a beaten-up but not particularly old BMW weaves through the partially constructed roadblock. Its exhaust is knackered. It looks in relatively decent shape, but it sounds like a bloody tank. The driver—who's alone—gets out to talk to another man. He leaves the engine running.

Matt elbows Jason in the ribs. "This is us."

Before Jason can react, Matt's already on his feet and is scrambling up the bank. Jason helps him up and pushes him toward the BMW. Their improvised disguises are working for now; they look as shitty as everyone else, and no one's paying them any attention. Matt opens the rear passenger-side door and collapses into the back. Jason goes around the front of the car. He tries to walk and not draw attention to himself, but he loses his nerve and runs. He slams the door shut behind him, and Matt cringes at the noise. "I said try to act natural," he hisses.

"What's natural about this?" Jason screams at him, and he punches the accelerator.

The BMW driver looks around when he hears the distinctive roar of his motor. "What the fuck?"

Whoever's behind the wheel, he can see they're not used to driving a car as powerful as his, because they're struggling to keep control. The back end fishtails all over the road before straightening up and racing away. But the fact his car's been stolen is less of a concern than what he thinks he just saw. Because, just for a fraction of a second, he thought he saw something that filled him with such anger, such vitriol and hate, that he can barely bring himself to spit out the words.

One of the bastards who just took the car was looking out the back window as they drove away. He pulled off his hat and scarve and revealed himself.

"Unchanged!" the Hater screams. "Fucking Unchanged just nicked my fucking car!"

"Are they following?" Jason asks, too afraid to look in the rear-view mirror, too scared to look anywhere but at the road stretching out ahead.

"Yes."

"How many?"

"All of them, it looks like."

"Shit. We're going to lead them straight back to the others. This is exactly what we were trying to avoid."

"Bit late to worry about that now, mate. Keep your foot down. Just get us there safe."

52

The CDF Outpost

There's a sign at the side of the road that reads Services Two Miles, but they can already see where they're heading. The fields around the outpost are swarming with activity. From a distance, it's hard to make out much in the way of specific details, but the position of the outpost itself is made clear by the direction in which the chaos moves: guns and tanks fire out, Haters rush in. Dirty smoke palls in the squally air above the battlefield, guiding the way like the You Are Here marker on a tourist map.

Matt's slumped on the backseat, panting. They've been tearing down the A14 toward this place for several miles now. The outpost doesn't seem to be getting any closer, but the vehicles racing up behind them do.

"Exit coming," Matt tells Jason.

"Is this it? Do I take it?"

"Stupid bloody question, of course you take it!"

Jason yanks the wheel, and the BMW banks hard left. It feels like the car's about to flip, but he manages to keep control. He sees the parking lot and the mass of vehicles and instinctively heads toward it, but realizes too late there's no way through. All tracks and roads have been blocked.

"How do we get in?" Jason screams, sounding frantic. "How do we get them to see us?"

"Good question," Matt mumbles. He wishes he had an answer, but he doesn't. You can plot and plan as much as you like, he thinks, but there's always going to have to be an element of improvisation.

The car bounces up the curb and drives over what's left of a torn-down fence. Jason instinctively ducks and shields his face as a Hater-driven van crosses directly in front of them, only to be taken out by a shell from one of the Unchanged tanks. There's chaos on all sides now. Jason realizes too late that his cut-through has brought them out right in the middle of the battlefield.

"They're going to think we're Haters," Jason says, and Matt thinks he's right. They're just one beaten-up car among many now hurtling toward the base, indistinguishable from all the others.

"We'll have to dump the car, try to get closer on foot."

"Are you fucking crazy? If this lot don't get us, the bloody CDF will. Besides, you can hardly walk. How are you going to run?"

"I'm all ears if you've got a better suggestion."

For the first time, they can see virtually the whole battlefield, the service station and hotel standing defiant in the midst of the carnage. The banks of mud, the battlements made of wreckage, and the regular flashes of flame from the trenches make the place look like something from hundreds of years ago, a medieval fortress under siege.

The pursuing pack have long since given up chasing the BMW, and Jason realizes that driving into the middle of the fighting like this has given them an unexpected sliver of a chance. "I'm gonna take a leaf out of your book, mate!" he shouts to Matt.

"What?"

"We're going to use one of your old tricks—use the fighting as cover."

Jason checks in his mirrors to see what traffic's around, then looks up again and sees he's driving directly at the barrel of a tank's gun. From the way the gun is being lowered, there's little doubt that the next shell it fires will have his name on it. He immediately wrenches the wheel to the right and slides into a gap between two other vehicles that are racing forward at speed to attack, a truck and a sedan. He's out of the way just in the nick of time; the tank fires and the shell hits the space where the BMW just was.

"Hold on!" he shouts to Matt, and he accelerates again until he's almost touching the back of the far slower truck in front. He grips the wheel as the car rattles over deep furrows in the ground. "I'll stick to the back of this truck, try to stay hidden. Sorry it's not a great plan, but it's all I've got."

The nearer they get to the outpost proper, the more Haters there are on foot around them. More vehicles tear across the battlefield, then grind to a sudden halt and unload packs of Hater foot soldiers who sprint forward into the unending madness. A fighter ducks to avoid gunfire, then looks up and makes fleeting eye contact with Jason in the front of the BMW. Despite the brevity of the moment, despite the absolute bloody mayhem consuming everything all around them, despite the fact he's at imminent risk of being shot at from any number of directions, Jason gets the unshakable feeling that he's now the sole focus of that particular Hater's ire.

There are increasing numbers of enemy fighters around here now, using wrecks and moving vehicles for cover as they attempt to breach the CDF defenses, and many more of them are beginning to realize that Matt and Jason are Unchanged. And they're starting to react. Their collective focus shifts. Instead of concentrating on the Unchanged they can't see inside the outpost, a disproportionate number of them now switch their attention to the two Unchanged out here in the chaos alongside them.

The truck Jason's been following is targeted. A howitzer fires, and the truck driver steers to one side to avoid impact. Jason immediately steers the other way, and when Matt looks back, he sees that some twenty Haters on foot have also changed direction and are thundering after the BMW.

Jason and Matt are less than fifty meters from the CDF front line. Matt looks back at the pursuing crowd and wonders if the gunners will see what he's seeing and realize the Haters are hunting Unchanged. Who the hell is he kidding? In the madness out here today, no one—neither Hater nor Unchanged—has the luxury of being able to take stock and consider what they're seeing; they just have to react. The tank commanders and the snipers and whoever else they've got defending the base will just see a pack of Haters coming toward them and will do everything in their power to blow seven shades of shit out of them.

A spray of gunfire rakes the hood of the BMW. "Fuck me," Jason says, checking himself for bullet holes and realizing he's clear. "That was close."

"We could do with a white flag to wave," Matt says, semi-serious.

"No time for that, mate."

Jason's right.

They're approaching the front of the base, and he has to act. He realizes there's only one way he can demonstrate his allegiance to the CDF and hope they'll see him. He yanks up the brake and does a full turn in the mud, just about managing to keep control. "What the hell are you doing?" Matt screams from the back, holding on to his seat.

Jason doesn't answer; he just accelerates into the crowd of Haters now running toward them. They bounce off the hood and windshield like massively engorged flies. Bones crunch under the car's tires.

Jason stops, spins the car around again, and drives directly at those few left standing.

There's no visible reaction from the CDF officers and militia watching the battle from the outpost. Jason's lining up for a third pass when a Hater-piloted Land Rover smashes into the side of the BMW, wiping it out. It skids through the mud, then drops into the section of trench that runs right across the front of the outpost.

For Jason and Matt, all the noise and frantic movement immediately stops. There's nothing now. Space and gravity and muffled quiet. The BMW has landed front-first in the trench, wedged downward, nose in the ground.

Matt's the first to move. "Come on," he says to Jason. "We have to go."

He's aware of armed CDF soldiers swarming toward them from either end of the trench, and he prays they realize who—*what*—he is. He leans forward and shakes Jason, who groans and tries to move. He has a bloody cut across his forehead where his head hit the wheel.

"We need to go," Matt tells him again.

"Can't," Jason says. "I'm stuck."

Matt realizes the steering column has collapsed, crushing Jason's legs.

"Just go," Jason says through gritted teeth. The pain he's in is intense.

"Not without you."

He groans. "Come on, Matt. Don't pick now to turn into a cliché arsehole. I'm not going anywhere. I'll keep them busy. Just get inside and warn the others."

Matt still doesn't move. He and Jason lock eyes in the rearview mirror.

"Go, you annoying bastard!" Jason screams at him. "Fuck's sake! You've been trying to get rid of me since we first met. Now's your chance. Go!"

And this time he does.

Matt kicks the buckled back door open and falls out of the car, then drags himself through the mud and rainwater at the bottom of the trench. He hears Jason shouting to the Haters. "Come on, you fuckers! Come and have me!" Matt looks up and sees the first of them crawling over the exposed rear end of the car, then diving in through the door he left open. He pulls himself forward on his belly, barely enough energy to keep moving, then stops when the first of the CDF soldiers reaches him. They're yelling and priming their weapons, ready to kill him because they think he's one of *them*. He can hardly breathe, but he manages to roll over onto his back and raise his hands in submission. "Don't kill me. Not a Hater. I need to speak to Estelle or Aaron or whoever's left in charge. We're all fucked if you don't let me see them."

53

The mezzanine deck is a focused hive of activity; a council of war. Estelle is poised to launch a decisive forward offensive. Down in the parking lot in front of the two buildings, a column of CDF fighters and gear has formed up. There are jeeps and all-terrain vehicles ready to roll out with gunners manning rear-mounted machine guns. Many more militiamen are on foot, also armed with whatever useful weaponry they've managed to locate: a mix of guns, grenades, batons, and blades. Bookending the attack force are the four remaining CDF tanks. They have limited supplies of shells—the rearmost Challenger only has three left to fire—but that's of little concern. If they were attacking buildings or facing other armored vehicles, it would matter, but today they're going out there to wipe out an army of individuals. The method of their demise doesn't matter—who cares if they're shot, beaten, or crushed beneath caterpillar tracks?

"Everything's in place," Chappell tells Estelle.

"Good."

"And you're completely sure about this?"

"Not questioning me again, are you, Greg?"

"It's just that sending that many troops and that much gear forward is leaving the outpost prone."

"I told you, it's a calculated risk. We still have the rocket launchers and other weapons around the perimeter."

"Some of the larger guns are out of ammo."

"They're still a deterrent. A constant reminder to the enemy that if you get too close to us, there's every chance we'll blow you to kingdom come."

"Of course."

The constant Hater attacks of the last few hours have been repelled with ease, and the longer this fighting goes on, the more confident Estelle is becoming. She turns to speak to Moira, who'll be leading the charge. "Draw them in and wipe them out, got it?"

"Got it, ma'am."

"I don't care if it takes you a whole bloody week to cover the five miles between here and Longstanton. We do whatever we have to do to make sure none of those bastards are left alive at the end of it."

"That's what I'm planning."

"Excellent. I know I don't need to tell you, but this is a pivotal moment. We'll regroup after Longstanton's taken, then keep moving east. There are several military bases along the way where we should be able to rearm and refuel. I know this is going to work."

"I think you're wrong," another voice, an unexpected voice, says from behind her.

Estelle turns around. For a few seconds, there's confusion, but once she manages to see through the layer of grime and she realizes who it is that's standing in front of her, the bewilderment turns to disbelief. "Jesus H. Christ. How the bloody hell do you do it?"

"Who's this?" Chappell demands.

"This is Matthew Dunne. He has an inability to die, by all accounts. Every time I think I've seen the last of him, he turns up again."

"You owe me an apology," Matt says, ignoring him and focusing on *her*.

"Do I?"

He's exhausted, feeling weaker than ever, but the adrenaline and fear keep him upright and talking. Keep him *fighting*. "I tried to help you, and you screwed me over."

"You've got it all wrong, Matthew . . ."

"I told you there was a Hater in the middle of your precious RAF base, and instead of listening to me, you drugged me and dumped me and left me there to die."

"That was never the plan," she says, quickly backpedaling. "Things got out of hand . . ."

"I know. I saw the consequences. It could all have been avoided. Those people didn't need to die."

"This is new territory for all of us. We need to learn lessons, I accept that."

"Give me a break. You sound like a politician."

That seems to rankle Estelle more than it should. "So did you come here specifically to insult or undermine me, or is there another reason for your visit?"

"Yeah, there's a very good reason, actually. I don't want you to make the same mistake again."

"I'm not sure I understand. What mistake?"

"Ignoring me. You need to listen very carefully."

"Go on."

"You're surrounded," he tells her. "There are Haters out there in massive numbers. Hundreds and hundreds of them."

"We know. We've been dealing with them pretty effectively, actually. Did you not see the damage out on the battlefield?"

Matt shakes his head. "This is different. It's another group."

"Then we'll deal with them, too."

"You're still not listening to me, Estelle. There are more of them than you realize. Jason and I were watching from a distance when they rolled up."

"Jason? Is he with you? I wondered what had happened to him."

"He didn't make it," Matt says. "He died trying to get in here with me to warn you."

"People do seem to come off second best when they rely on you for support, don't they?" she says, goading him unnecessarily. "My Mr. Franklin, your lovely girlfriend, and now Jason."

Matt bites his lip. He could react—he *wants* to react—but he doesn't have the strength. Instead, he pauses for a second to compose himself, clears his throat, then tries again.

"Look, Estelle, I understand why none of you wanted to listen to me before, but I'm begging you to listen now. The Haters you've been fighting . . . I think they're just a small faction. While we were out there, a whole bloody army rolled into town."

"And how do you assess the capabilities of this army? What kind of weapons do they have? How do you think they'll fare against my tanks?"

He shakes his head. "No weapons as such, just numbers. Vast numbers."

"How many?" Chappell asks, sounding concerned.

"There's got to be close to a thousand of them. You're massively outnumbered."

"And you're sure they're Haters?"

"Well, they didn't like the look of me and Jason."

"Where did they come from?"

"Somewhere to the east. Can't be more specific than that. They're well organized, though. A class apart from the Neanderthals you're currently scrapping with out there."

"None of this makes any difference," Estelle announces, interrupting the back-and-forth.

"What?" Chappell says. "But, Estelle—"

"You heard me."

"Don't you think we should at least check out what he's saying? If there are as many of them as he claims, then we need to—"

"I said it makes no difference whatsoever. They are savages, and we will continue as planned. My army—a *real* army—is about to leave this place and slaughter each and every one of those foul bastards."

Matt can't believe what he's hearing. "Christ, you're starting to sound like one of them."

"Don't insult me. I'm doing this because I *have* to, not because I want to."

"I think they'd say the same thing. From what I've seen today, going out there all guns blazing would be suicidal."

"And with all due respect, Matthew—which, at this late stage in the game, really isn't much—you've barely seen a fraction of what we've achieved here these last few days. You also have zero military experience. You have no idea what my forces are capable of."

"What, that lot out in the parking lot?"

"Don't give me a reason to throw you out there for the Haters to finish off."

"Why not? That's what you're planning to do to your people, isn't it? Please just think about this, Estelle. I hear what you're saying, but I don't think you fully appreciate what they're capable of. You're all only seeing little bits of the puzzle from here, and you're playing with your people's lives."

"These people are assets. They knew what they were signing up for."

"They signed up for this? I thought we were all just here by default."

"It's only my soldiers who'll be going out there to fight."

"Leaving this place defenseless."

"It's a necessary means to an end."

"Whose end?"

"Stop it, you infuriating little man. All that's important here is the total eradication of the enemy."

"Whose aim also happens to be the total eradication of us."

"Exactly. We don't have any choice. We need to fulfill our objective at all costs because if we don't, we're dead."

Matt's exasperated. There's no point arguing. He looks around at the other faces up here. Chappell is staring at him.

"So how come you're still alive?"

"What?"

"You heard me. If it's all kicking off out there, how come you made it back here safe?"

"It's what I do. I just have the knack, I guess."

Chappell sounds concerned. "Tell us exactly what you saw."

"I've already told you. Haters. Hundreds and hundreds of them. And they're stronger and much better organized and equipped than any I've seen since before the bomb."

"And are they capable of thinking tactically? Some of the ones we've been dealing with these last few days have been borderline suicidal."

"Well, by virtue of the fact they're in the biggest fucking pack I've seen, I'd guess their leaders are doing something right. Listen, most Haters I've come across out there aren't stupid. They're going to go with the safest option, same as we would. Same as most people here *have*. I think you have to assume they're more than capable of organizing themselves properly and fighting back."

"I'm not convinced."

"What?"

Chappell addresses Estelle but points accusingly at Matt. "I've never met this bloke before. Never heard anyone talk about him, either."

"To be honest, I've done my best to forget about him," Estelle says. "He's a bad penny who keeps turning up. A lucky little bastard."

"That's what concerns me. You said he'd got an inability to die and that people come off second best when they're around him. Now he's telling you he managed to sneak past this massive Hater army. Does none of this strike you as a little strange? Convenient?"

"You think I'm one of *them?*" Matt says, incredulous.

Chappell ignores him, talking directly to Estelle now. "When did you first come across him?"

"Back in the city. He followed Franklin through the crowds after an incident."

"He tracked one of your best men?"

"Franklin spotted him, but yes."

"Then what?"

"He went out in the field with Franklin to round up Haters in no-man's-land. He almost bought it a couple of times, by all accounts."

"But again, he made it back safe?"

"Yes."

"And before he turned up at Thornhill?"

"I'd forgotten about him until then, to be honest. If I'd been a gambling woman, I'd have put money on him being right under the nuke when it exploded, cuddled up in the arms of the love of his life."

Matt flinches at the mention of Jen but doesn't react. To show any aggression now would be the worst thing he could do.

"So he escaped the bomb, got out of Thornhill alive, and now he's made it here in one piece? How do we know he's not one of those freaks who can hold the Hate?"

"He's not," another voice says. Matt looks around and sees Aaron Rayner standing at the top of the steps leading up to the observation deck.

"Vouch for him, can you?" Chappell asks.

"I can, as it happens," Aaron says, and Matt slumps against the wall with relief.

"How?"

"The group he turned up at Thornhill with—they would never have gotten there if it weren't for him. We found them holed up in a leisure center after you'd sent us scavenging around the airport, Estelle, and we tested the lot of them to make sure they were like us. It was your man here who was holding them all together. He's no Hater; he's just good at what he does. Whatever that is."

"We don't have time for this," Moira warns. She's remained focused on the battlefield where the fighting continues to intensify in response to the CDF activity out front.

Estelle considers her options. "You're right. We've got bigger fish to fry. I'll be watching you, though, Matthew Dunne. One step out of line and you're history."

Matt can't help himself. "To be honest, Estelle, if you go through with this, there's every chance we'll all be history. I'm going to ask you one last time, please reconsider."

She ignores him and turns to face Moira and Chappell. "What he's told us changes nothing. If there are more of the enemy around here, that means there are more of them for us to kill. Moira, get out there and give 'em hell."

"We should listen to Matt, Estelle," Aaron says. "He knows what he's talking about."

Estelle's having none of it. "He clearly knows how to look after himself, but looking after everyone else is my responsibility. We're going to go out there now and take back everything those Hater bastards have stolen from us."

54

The interior of the cavernous service station is filled with noise from outside, adding to the disorientation and fear of the remaining civilians. Matt's found Tracy Barnish, as close to a friendly face as he expected to see. She's been given access to more medical supplies than she's used to. "It's to patch up the troops," she tells him, looking over her shoulder. "Don't let them see me wasting this stuff on you."

"Wasting it?" Matt says, indignant. "Am I in that bad a state?"

Her silence says plenty. Matt's sitting in front of her with his shirt hitched up so she can get to his wound. He glances back and sees her face is screwed up. "This is really bad," she says. "There's a lot of poison in there. I'll give you something to take the edge off the pain and get your temperature down. I'll try to have a proper look at it later. That's if there is a later."

She sounds less than convinced. As if to underline her point, one of the tanks outside fires, and she steadies herself as the ground shakes. The tumultuous din inside the building mounts as the CDF advance continues.

"This might hurt," Tracy tells him.

"It already does."

He winces as she straps him up, and he stares down at the ground, tracing the lines between the floor tiles with his eyes in a vain attempt to distract himself from the pain and from what's happening outside. A pair of soldier's boots appear just in front of him, and he looks up. It's Aaron.

"You finished with him?" he asks Tracy.

"Good as," she answers, rolling Matt's shirt back down.

"Good. Come with me, Matt."

"Where to?"

"Never mind that. Just move."

Matt follows the soldier out through the side exit between the service station and the hotel. They pause in the narrow gap between the two buildings, which offers a clear and uninterrupted view of the violence unfolding as the huge CDF offensive gets under way.

"Shouldn't you be out there?" Matt asks.

"Probably."

"Then why aren't you?"

"Hedging my bets."

Another shell is fired from the gun of one of the Challengers, then a barrage of rockets is launched from several of the defensive positions around the perimeter of the outpost. Matt walks forward to get a better view and to try to gauge the scale of what's happening out there now. There are Haters up ahead, but they're being easily held back at present. "It won't last," Matt says, scanning the horizon for any sign of the Hater forces he and Jason saw advancing. "Kill them and more will come and take their place."

"I don't doubt you. One way or another, the balance is going to shift. Will they run out of bodies, or will we run out of ammunition?"

"They're not going to run out of bodies. Not from what I've seen."

Aaron just grunts.

Another rocket screams overhead at a ferocious speed, temporarily filling the air with dry heat. It strikes its distant target and obliterates more of the enemy. But when the dust and smoke clears, it's like it's had no effect whatsoever. More Haters have already filled the hole that was blown in the ranks, taking the place of those who've been killed, marching over what's left of their bodies.

"Come on," Aaron says, pulling Matt toward the back of the buildings. Matt's reluctant. The chaos on the battlefield is a strangely compelling sight.

"Settles the nerves when you can actually see what's going on."

"You think?"

"I do, as it happens."

"You can stand there and gawp later. Right now, I need you to come with me."

Matt doesn't want to go anywhere with anyone. "Not until you tell me the real reason why you're not fighting."

"You said it yourself. Because we're not going to win."

Aaron's honest admission takes him by surprise. The soldier picks up speed and leads him through to the sprawling parking lot compound out back. He stops suddenly, and Matt walks into the back of him. Aaron points out into the distance. There are swarms of people moving through the fields on this side of the outpost. Vehicles are beginning to clog the approach roads.

"I told you," Matt says.

"I didn't doubt you."

They descend into the maze of vehicles. There are people moving down here, too, and Matt panics and backs up, worried they're invaders, that the perimeter of the outpost has been breached. And then he recognizes one of them. "Fuck me. Is that Joseph Mallon?"

"You know him?"

"Christ, yes."

When they get down into the parking lot, Joseph doesn't seem as surprised as Matt. There's little time for pleasantries and catchups. "Aaron said you were here," he says. "He said you've seen what's happening out there. You going to help us get out of trouble, Matt?"

Matt's heart sinks. "What?"

"After what I heard you saying to Estelle, I figured you'd want out," Aaron says.

"No, no . . . not me. I'm done. Don't you understand? There is no way out."

"You don't really believe that, do you?"

"Yes. And I keep telling people, I'm through with running and hiding. There's no point. I'm sick and I'm tired, and I only came back here to give you the heads-up. I'll tell you everything I know, but I'm not going anywhere."

"If you didn't care, you never would have come back," Joseph says. "Your mouth's saying one thing, I reckon your heart and your head's telling you something else."

"I see you've lost none of your ability for talking bollocks."

"I'm sure I deserve that, but please listen to me."

"I listened to you before, remember? Look where that got us all."

"I was wrong."

"Too damn right you were."

"My actions contributed to the deaths of thousands. Maybe hundreds of thousands."

"Yeah, but I was never bothered about the hundreds of thousands. I was only ever interested in one of them. When she died, I died."

"Go easy on the cliché, Matthew. We've both made mistakes and done things we regret, I'm sure, but we need to forget about that now."

"I don't know if I can." Matt sighs. "Look, I don't know if

news has reached this part of Estelle's little empire yet, but we're fucked."

"We get it. Thing is, you might be finished, but not everyone feels the same way," Aaron tells him. "There are innocent people here who deserve more."

"I don't dispute that, but your boss has signed all our death warrants. I don't think anything any of us does will make any difference now."

"We need to try," Aaron says. "We can't just give up. We need to at least try to get people away from here. You're an old hand at it, so I'm told."

Déjà vu. Matt rolls his eyes and looks up into the swirling cloud overhead. "Now you're definitely talking to the wrong man."

"Aaron's right," Joseph says. "I felt the same way as you, Matthew, but we can't just give up. I wanted to, Christ knows I wanted to, but I realize now there's a chance I can make amends for the damage I've caused. Estelle seems intent on leading us into oblivion. We're just looking for a back door to get us out of here."

"Getting out is one thing. Getting out and staying alive is another matter entirely. Trust me, it's worse than you think out there. This whole area is swarming with them, and—"

"If we stay here, we're all dead," Aaron says, cutting across him angrily.

"Do you seriously think there's an alternative? If you leave here, you might last a few hours or days longer, but they'll find you and kill you in the end. I'm sorry, I can't help you. No one can."

55

The CDF is gaining ground. Moira leads the charge, and it feels so fucking good to be out here fighting at last. All the apprehension of the days, weeks, and months leading up to this moment immediately dissipated the second she set foot on the battlefield. The men and women of the CDF know that this could be it, that the end of the war might finally be in touching distance. There will always be enemy stragglers to mop up, of course, but with the majority of them dead, things will soon feel very different. She visualizes her endgame: eradicate these Haters, find somewhere to restock and refuel, then hunt more of them out and do it all again. Lock, load, fire, repeat. Obliterate the enemy, then regroup, rebuild, and start living again.

Even Estelle's out here, buzzing now she's out on the front line. She's riding on the back of a six-wheeled Wolfhound: a heavy-armored tactical support vehicle. She usurps the gunner from his position and sprays bullets into the swarming crowds of Haters with undeniable glee. The rest of the vehicle's crew use clubs and axes to batter and bludgeon any of the enemy who avoid the gunfire and are foolish enough to get too close.

Some of the CDF militia look like they're out-hating the

Haters, such is their enthusiasm for violence. Others appear completely fucking terrified, gripped by a nervous inertia now there's no longer any separation between them and the enemy. Yet soon even the most reticent fighter is forced into action as the two armies collide. It's testament to how unorthodox this far-reaching war is that in the months since the rise of the Hate that split the human race in two, this is perhaps the first traditional battle to have been fought between the opposing sides. For months, the uneven balance of power has seesawed between the *Changed* and Unchanged. Initially, the Haters were isolated and unsure, but as their numbers rapidly grew, so did their collective confidence until they'd assumed control and the Unchanged became the hunted minority. Then, at the height of the fighting, the bombs fell and killed tens of thousands: the great leveler. It forced an unexpected and fragile equilibrium, and for a time, every individual survivor was as vulnerable as the next irrespective of their allegiance.

Both sides regrouped after the nuclear blasts, and now they face each other as equals. The Unchanged have the structure and weaponry the Haters never had, while the Haters compensate with a level of individual aggression that very few Unchanged could ever hope to match. The difference is perfectly captured in a snapshot that plays out ahead of Estelle's Wolfhound. Six bloodthirsty Haters have two CDF militiamen cornered, but before the Haters can do what they're instinctively driven to do and kill, a tank rolls in and obliterates the whole fucking lot of them.

The CDF offensive is moving forward with more speed and less resistance than expected. A wide swath of empty land, churned with mud and littered with bodies, has opened up between the outpost and the forward fighters, leaving the outpost as exposed as Chappell feared.

He's alone on the mezzanine now, watching the fighting. A lone CDF soldier pounds up the stairs. "We need to strengthen the defenses, sir," he says.

"Strengthen them with what? Anyone who can fight is already out there. There's only the gunners left."

"There are plenty of people here still. We can use them in the trenches."

"They're civilians. They'd be fucking useless."

"Be better than nothing, sir."

Chappell walks across the mezzanine and looks down over the crowds of civilians. Does he have any choice? He turns back to face the soldier. "Okay, do it. Volunteers first."

"With respect, anyone who's going to volunteer is already out there."

Chappell shakes his head sadly. "Then take whoever you need."

"Yes, sir."

Alone on the mezzanine now, he does up his jacket and checks the pistol he's carried for weeks but never used. He knows it's time for him to go out there, too. Steeling himself for the inevitable, he turns back to the window and watches as an armored Bulldog troop carrier cuts a swath through the carnage, its caterpillar tracks carving a graceful arc between other, less maneuverable CDF military vehicles. The grubby khaki machine motors forward, belching exhaust fumes, then straightens up and heads straight for a crowd of Hater fighters coming the other way. There must be forty or fifty of them bunched up in a pack, arrogantly dismissive of the CDF's relative armed might. Rocks and lumps of masonry are hurled at the Bulldog, but they don't even dent its armor, barely scratch the paintwork. Its driver keeps it moving forward at speed, plowing into the pack and forcing the enemy to scatter or die. Many dive for cover, then immediately pick themselves up and come back at the Bulldog, which slows, then stops as the driver changes direction to mop up those who are left. Some of the closest surviving fighters clamber up the front and sides of the powerful vehicle, only for the top hatches to burst open and for several of the CDF crew to emerge and start firing their SA80s into the throng. Many Haters are immediately killed, but others use the bodies of the fallen as cover. One manages to scale the back of the Bulldog unnoticed. She attacks the soldier shooting from the rear hatch, coming up behind him and grabbing his rifle from over his shoulders. He refuses to let go, and they grapple for the weapon, wrestling with each other until the CDF soldier in the front hatch shoots both of them dead. He then spins around and unloads on two more Haters trying to pull the Bulldog's driver from her seat.

It takes less than a minute for the Bulldog's crew to be completely overcome. Now under Hater control, it's driven directly into another CDF vehicle, crippling both of them.

Bullets and bombs, beaten by brute force.

"It's a fucking bloodbath," Chappell says to himself.

"And this is just the start of it."

He looks around and sees Matt standing just behind him.

"Estelle's out there if you've come up here to try to argue your point again."

"I haven't. There's no point. You should have realized that by now."

"I have. It's the rest of them that need persuading."

The conversation is interrupted by sounds of more trouble downstairs as militiamen try to herd civilians toward the trenches. "But we're not soldiers," someone argues.

"We're all soldiers now, pal."

The group—there are maybe twenty of them—is pushed and shoved out toward the battlefield. Those who are given any weapons at all are handed basic, rudimentary weapons before being sent down into the trenches to defend the outpost. One man tries to climb back out, only for a CDF soldier to threaten him with the butt of his rifle. He tries again to escape and this time gets a boot in the face for his troubles.

"If I didn't think we were screwed before, I do now," Matt admits, and Chappell's silence infers his agreement.

"What else can we do?"

"Your chief has boxed everyone into a corner. I tried to warn her."

"Estelle's always too busy talking to listen. I always thought—"

He stops talking abruptly, distracted by something he sees outside, an unexpected reaction. Until now, there's always been a degree of visible cohesion in the CDF ranks, but it's like a switch has just been flicked—everyone for themselves. The soldiers who have been advancing alongside the tanks and heavy artillery start to split and double back. Then the rocket launchers that have any rockets left to fire erupt into life, and missiles begin racing through the cold, wet air, spears of white light streaking over the fighting in the muddy fields surrounding the base before hitting previously unseen targets on the border in several directions at once. More missiles are fired, a tumult of destruction, and in the rapidly reducing gaps between the wild detonations, both Matt and Chappell can now see what's caused the sudden panic in the CDF ranks: there are hundreds upon hundreds upon hundreds of Haters now pouring onto the battlefield, converging on the outpost from every conceivable angle.

"Sweet Jesus," Chappell says, struggling to take in the enormity of what he's witnessing. The enemy advance is like a flood, an unstoppable wave.

"I tried to warn you," Matt says pointlessly. "You wouldn't bloody listen."

"*She* wouldn't listen," he snaps, pointing deep into the madness to where Estelle is still fighting on the back of her Wolfhound support vehicle.

Estelle gestures wildly, screaming orders at those soldiers still in shouting distance, struggling to compete with the unprecedented CDF bombardment of the Hater hordes.

It's all pointless, though she'll never admit it.

Whatever she does now, she's lost.

There are only two tanks left with any shells now, but there are too many targets. Individual soldiers try standing their ground and firing into the masses, but their impact is negligible. When they focus on shooting one Hater, by default they inevitably ignore many more who show them no mercy. Even the brief, few seconds' pause to change an empty clip is enough time for Haters to attack and kill. The CDF out in the combat zone is catastrophically outnumbered, and the rapid Hater advance continues largely unchallenged. There's no finesse to the way they fight, no tactics or control, just an unstoppable flood of sheer Hate coming from all sides. The attacking wave has become a tsunami. Multiple tsunamis.

A sustained burst of machine-gun fire temporarily stems the flow of attackers surging toward Estelle's Wolfhound. It's Moira Kay. She's fighting like a Terminator, bringing down Hater after Hater, cutting through the heart of them with her SA80. The Wolfhound is surrounded, too many bodies clustering around it for the crew to be able to drive forward in any direction. Moira unloads her weapon again, then runs through the channel she's just carved through the crowd. She hauls herself up onto the back of the vehicle and grabs Estelle, who spins round, Glock pistol drawn and ready to fire.

"Order a withdrawal, Estelle. We can't win this."

"We have to," Estelle says, and she pushes Moira out of the way, then shoots dead a Hater who'd almost made it up onto her vehicle.

"There are too many of them!" she yells, voice hoarse as she struggles to make herself heard over the cacophony of noise.

Estelle fires several more shots. More and more Haters are converging on the Wolfhound. Moira sidesteps and drenches a section of the crowd with another round of automatic gunfire.

"They'll kill us all, Estelle."

Estelle pulls Moira close, faces just millimeters apart. "You're a soldier. Keep fighting."

"But, Estelle—"

"Don't question orders! Fight on!"

Moira looks into her commanding officer's face. Fear? Delusion? Sheer fucking terror? She's not sure what she sees in Estelle's eyes, but it's clear she has no intention of giving up the fight.

Moira swings the butt of her weapon into the face of an attacker who grabs at her ankle, then fires off several shots and takes two more out. The dead drop down into the clambering crowds below, and Moira jumps down after them. She keeps her finger on the trigger, killing herself a path away from the stranded Wolfhound.

Estelle's oblivious to the scale of the ever-growing battle. She reloads her Glock and fires into as many hate-filled faces as she can, but even if she had ten times the number of bullets, it still wouldn't be enough. The Wolfhound is surrounded by a crowd twenty or thirty deep for the most part, their numbers increasing as more of the CDF is overcome. When the bullets finally run dry, the attackers advance with renewed enthusiasm. Estelle is tackled and dropped to the ground. She's buried under bodies, hopelessly outnumbered.

Now watching from outside the outpost, Chappell finally loses sight of his commanding officer. When the Haters swarming over the Wolfhound lose interest and start looking for other Unchanged to kill, he knows for certain that she's dead.

"That puts me in charge. I'd order a retreat, but I doubt anyone would make it back."

The last remaining armed tank fires another shell, the force of the blast jerking it back on its caterpillar tracks. Knowing it'll take time to reload, Haters immediately begin to climb over it like maggots feasting on rotten meat. The driver tries to shake them off, and the gunner moves the gun turret and barrel wildly from side to side, but it has no effect. In desperation, either because the crew is going to try to clear the attackers from the top of the vehicle or because they're going to make a break for it, the loader's hatch at the rear pops open. The first soldier does not even get his head and shoulders free before he's hauled out and killed. His rifle is yanked from his hands and used to kill the remaining crew.

Whether it's down to beginner's luck or some previous military experience, the Haters who've taken control of the Challenger tank manage to load, aim, and fire its remaining arsenal of shells, destroying two more tanks. The turret turns a graceful one-eighty, and the final shell is fired directly at the outpost itself. Matt and Chappell run for cover, then throw themselves to the ground as the hotel next door is hit.

Chappell picks himself up, pushing past scores of panicking civilians now swarming back the other way. He stares at the bloodbath in front of him in disbelief. Countless people are dead, and the front of the hotel has been decimated. There's broken glass, crumbled concrete, and body parts everywhere. When the whistling in his ears starts to fade, Chappell realizes that even though he can still hear gunfire, it sounds more random now, less controlled, far more sporadic. The noise washes and fades. There are brief pauses . . . silences, almost. "Is that it?"

"Nope," Matt says. "Not even close. That's objective one complete, I think. Estelle's precious CDF is finished."

"It hardly took them any time."

"You're right, and I reckon it'll take them half that time again to finish the rest of us off."

There are great swarms of Haters sprinting toward the outpost now, almost completely unopposed. Hundreds that look like thousands running as one, closing in and choking the very life out of the faltering Unchanged resistance. It's a stampede. Matt thinks it'd be impressive if it were not so completely fucking terrifying.

The civvies still down in the trenches start climbing out and running for cover, and the snipers and other gunners have all deserted their posts.

Chappell gestures at a nearby howitzer, its barrel pointing down at the ground, dejected-looking. "Going to see if I can't take a few more of them out," he says.

"You're wasting your time."

He shrugs. "Probably."

The shell-damaged hotel begins to collapse in on itself, filling the air with unimaginable noise and suffocating clouds of grit and dust. The crowds of retreating civilians are forced back toward the service station, but the main entrance is already gridlocked, no way through. The foyer is packed solid with backed-up people trying to get through the revolving door.

Matt knows there's no way through. He can barely stay standing, but the combination of the drugs the doctor gave him and the fear of being torn apart by the advancing pack of killers is enough to keep him moving. Crowds of people come at him from all angles as they herd toward the building behind him, seeking refuge. He's pushed and shoved, inadvertently fighting against the flow. One man collides with him head-on, and the two of them grasp each other instinctively, desperate to stay upright.

It's Darren.

It takes both of them a second to recognize the other.

"Help me, Matt."

"Nothing I can do. Nothing any of us can do."

And Darren pushes himself away without another word. Staggering zombielike toward the outpost entrance.

Matt stumbles on, half walking, half falling down the side of the service station building, holding on to the wall to keep himself upright. Everywhere he looks, he sees more and more Haters advancing from all directions, encircling the outpost and severing every escape route, cutting the base off from the rest of the world. Part of him wants to look for somewhere quiet to hide, to take advantage of all this suffering and disappear like he always does, but this time he knows there's no point. Dr. Tracy was economical with her words earlier, but he doesn't think he has long. If the Haters don't get him, the sickness will.

So this is how it ends.

But not for everyone.

Jesus Christ, these people don't know when to give up.

Joseph, Aaron, and a couple of other men are still at it, leading civilians out from an exit at the back of the main building and loading them into trucks. Joseph looks up and sees Matt approaching. "We're leaving," he says.

"I doubt that very much, mate."

"Well, we can't just give up."

"I don't think you have any choice."

Matt looks into the back of the nearest truck, and a crowd of pallid faces stare back at him. All the kids. People from the RAF base and others he remembers from the printing house before that. The kind of people whose suffering he used to hide behind to stay alive. The kind of people he's sacrificed on far too many occasions to keep himself safe. He looks for Jason, then remembers he's gone. Christ, even he managed a vaguely heroic death. In comparison, Matt feels himself coming to a miserable, inglorious end. Jen would be so disappointed . . .

Sick. Injured. Exhausted. Finished.

"You going somewhere?" Aaron asks, spotting Matt, who's hardly able to support his own weight. He's breathing heavily, leaning against the side of a helicopter that's never going to fly again.

"Not going anywhere. No one is."

"Help us?"

"We've already been through this. It's too late."

"It's not. I can help," another voice says, taking everyone by surprise. Matt turns around and finds himself looking at a tall, wiry, bespectacled, blood-soaked strip of a man.

"And who the hell are you?"

"My name's Peter Sutton, and I—"

Joseph pushes himself between Matt and Peter, brandishing a wicked-looking knife. "He's one of them! He's a Hater!"

"Joseph, please . . ."

Aaron gets to him first. Peter puts his hands up in submission, but he's on the ground with Aaron on top of him before he can react. Aaron holds the tip of a blade against Peter's throat.

"Hater scum."

"Wait," Peter says, desperate, "please. I've never hurt any of you, and I never will. I know how to hold the Hate."

Matt edges forward, struggling to stay standing. "Don't listen to this bullshit. Kill him. Joseph used to breed freaks like this, but they can't be tamed. You can't control them. They talk the talk when it suits, but when their backs are against the wall, they'll kill you without hesitation. I know. I've seen it happen again and again."

"I'm different," Peter says, tears streaming down his face now. "I swear. My grandson's in the truck. I'm not going to do anything that puts him or any of you in danger."

"Last one of his kind I was stupid enough to trust turned on me when I needed her most."

"I don't want to fight. That's why I hid here with you for so long. If I was going to kill anyone, I'd have done it already."

"Why should I believe you?" Aaron asks, tightening his grip on Peter's throat and pricking the skin under his chin with the knife.

"Because you're outnumbered and surrounded. You've barely got any time left. You don't stand a chance without me. Do you think I'd have come back if I didn't want to help? I could have waited until it was all over."

For the briefest of moments, the conversation stalls, and all any of them can hear is the noise of the rapidly advancing enemy tightening their grip on the outpost. All eyes are on Aaron and the Hater.

"Finish him," Matt urges.

But he doesn't.

Peter's face is filled with fear, waiting for the pain that doesn't come. Aaron stabs the knife into the ground next to his head instead and gets up.

"What the hell are you doing?" Matt demands, too weak to do anything himself. "Get rid of him. Deal with him."

"No," Aaron says. "We can use him."

The Hater is lying curled up in a ball now, sobbing.

"What? This piece of shit?"

"Yes, him. I believe him."

"Then you're deluded—"

"He's right—why would he have come back? Why would he not be fighting?"

"Because he doesn't want to die? You really believe that?"

"Right now, I don't have anything else to believe. Half a chance is better than no chance at all."

"It's on your head," Matt says, and he goes to walk away, but Aaron stops him.

"Don't, please. There's still a way we can do this."

56

There must be more than a hundred Haters for every single Unchanged left alive now. Chappell keeps firing into the endless crowds for as long as he can. He knows it won't make any difference, but this is all he has left. He takes a small crumb of comfort from the fact that his seems to be the only weapon still firing. Could these be the last bullets fired by human hands?

In the distance, the CDF advance has been permanently halted. From his slightly elevated position, Chappell is aware of an eerie lack of movement out there now. Dirty smoke belches upward from ruined, useless fighting machines. There are bodies everywhere. A handful of Haters move from corpse to corpse, finishing off those unfortunate CDF soldiers who are somehow still breathing, but the majority of enemy fighters are now advancing toward the outpost, forming part of the storm surge of Hate that's rolling toward what's left of the human race.

Chappell shoots again, hitting one man in the leg who drops to the ground and is immediately trampled by a horde of his kill-hungry brethren.

He shoots another square in the chest and takes a perverse pleasure in watching him being blown off his feet and back into the crowd, knocking several more of them out like pins at the end of a bowling alley.

The next one he kills is nearer; close enough for Chappell to see the hate writ large across her face and close enough for him to take her out with a satisfyingly clean head shot.

The next are nearer still. More and more and more of them. Too many. He's overcome, but Chappell fires shot after shot until the gun clicks empty. And now there isn't even room to swing and aim. They're on him, all over him. Grabbing his clothes and tearing his skin. He kicks out and swings his fists, yelling out in rage, but his dogged resistance lasts only seconds longer before being brought to a brutal end.

Near the rear of the bottleneck of people still trying to get clear of the fighting and into the service station, Darren tries to worm his way through the tightly packed bodies, terrified he's going to be the last to get inside. He's pushing and pulling the people around him, shoving them out of the way, but then stops momentarily when he becomes aware of a sudden change. Other people have noticed it, too. Now that the last guns have stopped firing, an eerie calm has descended. It feels like a vacuum. Darren looks around and wishes he hadn't, because all he can see now is so many Haters that they're individually indistinguishable, their movements agitated and excited and almost too fast like an over-cranked film. It feels like the whole damn lot of them are coming directly for him alone.

The permanently open doors allow more and more people inside, but there's nowhere for any of them to go. The revolving door is still revolving, but only just. It judders around inch by inch, moving at a hopelessly slow speed because of the people packed into this enclosed, overfull space. No one gives a shit about anyone else any longer. It's every man, woman, and child for themselves.

Darren tries to dig his way through the crowd, shoving people out of the way that he's previously helped, concerned only with putting maximum distance between himself and the approaching Haters.

"What do we do, Darren?" someone asks when they recognize him, but he doesn't answer. He just shrugs them off.

All that bullshit he used to spout about this group being the future of the human race . . . about how they'd be here after everyone else had gone, after all the fighting was over . . . they're just empty words. Hollow promises made to keep other people in line and to keep himself safe.

Another woman throws her arms around him, sobbing. "Help me, Darren. Please . . ." Darren pushes her away, fighting harder and harder to wade through the bodies and get to safety. He makes it as far as the glass-fronted foyer, but no one's going any farther. The revolving door is now stuck: filled with people, arms and legs trapped, preventing it from moving.

Darren can't go forward, and the people behind are stopping him from going back. He's trapped.

The fastest Haters make short work of the slowest civilian survivors. They grab the outliers by whatever they can get a hold of—belts, collars, hair—then separate them from the crowd and kill them with knives, clubs, spears, bludgeons, fists, boots . . . whatever is available.

Darren feels the pressure lift as more of the crowds behind him are hauled away and slaughtered. *The more of them there are for the Haters to kill*, he thinks, *the better my chances of getting away*. He pushes forward again, but he can feel the enemy on his back, can see their reflections in the glass, and he knows he's next. He tries again to worm his way deeper in, literally throwing other people out of the way until he reaches the non-revolving door.

There's a narrow gap, maybe half as wide as he needs it to be, but it's the only option he has, and he squeezes his head and one arm and shoulder through and tries to use his bulk to lever the door around.

It's stuck tight, and so is Darren.

He kicks and thrashes, but he's not going anywhere. He looks back and sees there are very few of his people left alive, but plenty of the enemy still fighting. One Hater grabs his legs and pulls him back out into the foyer, then another drops down onto his chest and thumps a stubby blade into his heart.

Moira Kay is somehow still alive. She can hardly believe it herself. She has an advantage over the enemy, though, in that she knows this area backward. There's not a single square inch of the outpost that's unknown to her.

The longer she's spent out on the battlefield, the more like a Hater she's become. She's covered from head to toe in blood and mud. Her rifle long lost, she's carrying a nail-skewered baseball bat she snatched from the grip of a Hater she killed in the midst of the carnage, and she swings it wildly at anything that's still moving. With the vast majority of enemy fighters concentrating on the madness at the front of the service station and partially demolished hotel, she's able to disappear the other way. She drops into one of the trenches, wincing with pain and nursing a stab wound, then deals with a few more rogue attackers before heading for the rear of the building. Exhausted, she hauls herself out of the trench, then disappears into the maze of abandoned vehicles.

She turns a corner, then stops. There's a crowd of people ahead, and she doesn't have enough energy left to run again.

"Moira? That you?"

Thank Christ for that. It's Aaron.

"What the hell are you doing out here?" she asks, breathless.

"Getting this lot away," he says, and he steps back to reveal a truck filled with desperate-looking refugees.

"I'll help," she tells him without hesitation.

57

They don't have long. The hordes are closing in fast. "You know where you're going?" Aaron asks Matt, handing him a set of keys.

"Driving away from here, that's all I know. To be honest, I think that's all I want to know."

"Just follow Moira for as long as you can."

"I will."

Joseph reaches out and shakes Matt's hand. "Thank you for doing this."

"Well, it went so well when I tried something similar last time," Matt says, managing the briefest wry smile.

"This is different."

"Yeah, I know."

He looks at the keys in his hand and for a second is almost overcome by the enormity of what he's agreed to do. His body feels broken, shutting down fast. Everything comes down to this. This is all he has left.

"Ready?" Aaron asks. "Leave it any longer and those fuckers will be riding shotgun."

"I'm ready."

Aaron bangs his hand against the door of Moira's truck, and she acknowledges him with an immediate thumbs-up.

Matt gets into his truck and starts the engine. There's an unexpected wave of familiarity as the vehicle rattles and rumbles into life—a flashback to the night of the bomb—followed by an equally strong and almost overwhelming feeling of despair. No going back now. Nowhere left to go back to. This place is another dead end among many, and he knows that everywhere else will be the same, no matter where they end up today.

But although there's nothing left to look forward to, when he glances in his mirror, he's suddenly keen to get moving. It's happening just as he'd thought it would. He could have written the script. The service station is falling with almost dismissive speed. The enemy is crawling over every inch of the building like locusts, stripping flesh from the bones of the place. He knows the only people who have any chance of making it out of here alive are those who've reached the trucks.

Moira pulls away, and Matt follows. Aaron brings up the rear in a third vehicle, a short and tight-packed convoy. The chaos elsewhere around the fallen outpost is such that they initially go unnoticed. A few Hater stragglers see the vehicles and sprint down to intercept them, but Moira accelerates, mowing them down with satisfaction. Once she's clear, she puts her foot down and crosses the trenches, clattering over the nearest pontoon bridge. She steers up onto the road, then drives the wrong way around the traffic roundabout before swinging down onto the A14 and heading east.

McCoyne hammers on the window of Bryce's car. "I see them!"

"What?"

"I told you they'd try something. There's a group of them try-ing to get away, sneaking out the back door. Three trucks. They'll hit the roadblocks, but they look big enough to get through. Make a move now and you'll catch them. Hinchcliffe will know you're worth keeping onside if you can catch three truckloads of Unchanged his army missed."

Bryce doesn't need convincing. "Good work. Get in."

"But you don't need me. I should stay here and—" McCoyne protests.

"Get in!"

58

The Road Heading East

The road ahead is blocked across its entire width. Moira knows what she has to do. There simply is no other option. All that matters now is getting these trucks as far from the carnage as they can. The massed Haters, on an adrenaline-fueled high after an easy victory, start hurling missiles. A brick bounces off the windshield, then another smashes through, leaving the glass a spiderwebbed mess. Moira punches it clear so she can see, then locks her arms and braces for impact.

Foot down. Eyes screwed shut.

The collision between the truck and the roadblock is hard and unforgiving. Moira feels the front wheels bounce up, then crash back down. She's through, but several of her tires are blown, and she loses control on the landing. The cab overbalances, and all she can think about are those civilians relying on her to help them get away. Still hanging on to the wheel, she throws her weight right over to the opposite side of the cab in a vain attempt to re-gain control and keep moving. For a moment, it feels like it might work, but the truck has sustained catastrophic damage, and she knows it's hopeless.

Her frantic escape is over almost as quickly as it began. The massive vehicle skids along the road on its wheel rims before finally stopping, black smoke spewing from the exhaust. Aaron had given Moira a handgun, which she grabs without thinking because she knows it's only going to be seconds before the inevitable attack.

There are so many of them that they block out the light. Some rip out what's left of the shattered windshield, others yank at the doors to get them open. Their numbers are such that they block their own way through, giving Moria an unexpected few seconds to think. She looks around at their crazed, hate-filled faces, knowing that all any of them wants right now is to kill her. She thinks about the instantaneous yet fleeting pleasure that ending her life will bring them, about the repellent euphoria the one who does the deed will inevitably feel. She manages to shoot a couple of them, but they're immediately replaced by others, and she knows there will always be more.

It sickens her to think that her death will bring so much ravenous excitement, but that's just how it is. "Sorry to spoil your party," she says, and she shoves the pistol into her mouth and fires, denying them the pleasure.

Without looking back, Matt powers through the gaping hole in the Hater blockade left by Moira's truck, then steers hard around the end of the beached wreck and accelerates away, clear. Aaron follows close behind, tucked in tight.

"Shit," Matt says as he glances in the rearview mirror. A red Subaru swerves out onto the road behind both of them and begins to accelerate. Matt has a quarter tank of fuel remaining, not even a hundred miles. All he can do is keep driving until he runs out of gas or the Haters give up. He knows which will happen first.

Aaron flashes his headlamps, and Matt appreciates the fleeting attempt at communication. He's nervous as hell being out in front. It's the fear of what's coming, he tells himself, combined with the inevitability of everything. He starts talking out loud, trying both to distract and to motivate himself. "You can do this, mate. Estelle was right; you're a slippery bastard. You should have died ten times over by now."

There are more Hater-driven vehicles teeming all over the road behind the two trucks now, too many to count. Some, like the Subaru, are much quicker than his own cumbersome, heavy-duty vehicle. He's struggling with the steering. Aaron, on the other hand, seems to be having little problem. He has a definite speed advantage, with the nose of his truck now almost touching the tail of Matt's.

Just get as far as I can.

If he focuses ahead and not behind, being alone in the cab with nothing but empty road in front, he starts to feel like the last man on earth again. He remembers standing on the beach on Skek and thinking the same thing months ago on the morning normality died and this nightmare began. Christ, that feels like a lifetime ago now. Several lifetimes.

"Pretty good that you made it this far," he says, congratulating himself, and he wonders how much farther he can go.

Another quick look in his mirrors and he sees that the road behind is a mass of movement and headlights now. Aaron swerves and drifts, deliberately blocking as many of them as he can. Matt thinks this would look amazing filmed from above, like those big police chases they used to show on TV back in the day. It's like a scene from the climax of a movie. He knows how it's going to end. There's only one direction this is going. It's the end of the line.

Aaron's protecting Matt's truck as best he can, and Aaron scores a minor victory when a jeep from the chasing pack gets too close and he side shunts it into the central crash barrier. The jeep bounces off the carefully engineered metal strip, out of control, arcs around, and takes out another three vehicles. Tangled together, they hold up some of the pursuing pack for a few precious seconds.

The driver of the red Subaru spots a gap and accelerates through. Compared to the rest of the wrecks making up this haphazard procession of vehicles, his is a performance vehicle, and he leaves the bulk of them in the dust. Aaron tries to shut the door on him, swinging his truck out toward the central barrier again and blocking the way through, but the truck's not as responsive as he'd hoped, and he oversteers, almost losing control. It's only a slight wobble, but it's enough to massively affect his speed. The engine groans with effort, and Aaron has to change down a gear to keep moving.

The truck has become unexpectedly exposed. The driver of a Transit puts her foot down and rams the back of the truck, shunting Aaron wildly off course. He corrects himself quick, but not before the Subaru has whipped up the inside. Its driver swings out right in front of the truck, then brakes. The unexpected speed change takes Aaron by surprise, and he slams his foot on the brake without thinking. The Transit, a 4×4, and a rust-colored sedan all plow into him, and he loses control.

The cab of the truck smashes into the central barrier and comes to a sudden, wrenching halt. The trailer slides out behind it, blocking all but the inside lane, leaving only a narrow strip of tarmac clear for the pursuing pack to get through.

Aaron is out of his seat and out of the cab in a heartbeat. He jumps the median and sprints along the opposite road, but he doesn't get far. A motorbike rider drives through a gap in the barrier, accelerates hard, then lances him with a crudely forged spear.

Just one truck remaining now, with the red Subaru leading the charge.

"Careful. He'll run us off the road," McCoyne says, gesturing at the vehicle up ahead.

"He won't risk it. He'll just keep going if I don't do something."

"He'll have to stop eventually."

"Yeah, but what if we stop first? Hinchliffe will be pissed if let them get away. These are the last Unchanged."

"So you need to take control of the situation. Force him to go where you want him to. Deny him the open road. Send him somewhere where he doesn't have any options."

The Subaru accelerates again, then pulls up alongside the truck and holds steady. Matt looks down and can't believe his eyes when he sees it's that same scrawny fucker in the passenger seat he's come across before. The one who killed Kara and the others and led the Haters to Thornhill. The one he'd helped Joseph Mallon to torture back in the city-camp. One of the group who was responsible for starting the chain reaction that caused his hometown to be reduced to a pile of toxic ash. He's aware it's a tenuous connection, but Matt directly links this one particular bastard to Jen's death. Now he's the one filled with hate. It helps him stay focused. *Strangely fitting that it should come to this,* he thinks.

But what the hell are these fanatics planning? He can't work out their tactics—if they even have any. Their actions seem as uncoordinated and haphazard as ever. It angers him to think that so much of the human race has been destroyed, so much that was good in the world has been lost, and that these dregs are all that remains. These base, unsophisticated fuckers. For a moment, he's consumed by rage himself, forgetting everything he's been sent out here to do, all the people he's pledged to try to protect.

His hands grip the wheel tightly.

He's ready to swerve into the Subaru and wipe these bastards off the road. But before he can do it, the Subaru driver accelerates again, then stops at an angle, blocking most of the road.

What the fuck?

Matt's forced to react at speed. He sees an unexpected opportunity and swings the truck down an off-ramp he spots at the last possible moment. He swerves around a cluttered traffic roundabout, driving through the gaps between wrecks, then accelerates out onto another road that loops back under the first.

He quickly realizes he's driving straight into the heart of the dead city of Cambridge.

59

Cambridge

The road stretches out ahead of the truck, but with every passing meter, Matt's less confident of the split-second decision he's just made. He realizes he's been played. At some point between the beginning of the war and the height of the fighting, there was an attempted exodus from here, and one side of the road he's now motoring along is lined with an endless procession of motionless vehicles facing out of town—a failed evacuation. At points, the forgotten traffic has spilled over onto this side of the tarmac, causing Matt to have to slow and steer carefully around, and at other times, rainwater has pooled in huge, stagnant lakes, blurring the lines and making it all but impossible to follow the road. Matt knows he's made a wrong move—his last move, perhaps—but for now, all he can do is keep driving. There isn't room to stop and turn around. There isn't time to try. Every meter might make a difference.

After being out in the open, the suburbs of Cambridge feel like an enclosed, claustrophobic place. The dark, empty homes and offices on either side seem to close in like the walls of a prison cell. There are turns he could take, but what would be the point? The truck is a cumbersome, unrefined vehicle, and if it's a struggle to get down a major route like this, what hope would he have trying to navigate the twisting side streets?

Apart from the truck, there's no other movement or noise out here right now. It feels deceptively calm. If he ignores the chaos down at ground level and focuses up, the world looks almost like it used to, and for a few brief seconds, he allows himself to remember. The routine. The pressures. The mundanity and pointlessness of the day-to-day. Then he thinks about the triviality: hours wasted in front of the TV with Jen, going out and getting drunk, lying in bed until lunchtime on a Sunday and making love together because they had nothing else to do and, even if they did, what better way to while away the hours? Despite everything, he smiles to himself. These memories are all he has left now.

The wing of the truck clips the door of a weather-bleached Skoda that's been left open, blocking the way. The sudden noise and impact drags Matt back into reality, and he remembers the importance of what he's doing and forces himself to focus. Another wreck is straddling both lanes now, and another and another. He lifts himself up in his seat and sees that the clear section of the road ahead is narrowing noticeably, but he has no choice but to keep going.

The tired engine roar of the truck is amplified here, echoing off the buildings on either side, but Matt's becoming aware of another noise now. Another engine. Different pitch and tone, but unquestionably moving in the same direction as he is. The space he's driving through now is continuing to reduce, but he allows himself a momentary glance in the side mirrors.

It's the red Subaru again. And behind it, more Hater-driven vehicles. There might only be a fraction of the number that originally followed him and the others away from the CDF base, but that doesn't matter because he's still hugely outnumbered.

Matt steers around the rubble of a battle-damaged building and out into a bubble of relatively clear space, and just for a second, he thinks there might still be a way through up ahead. The road curves, but any hope he had disappears in an instant. Until now, the unfinished exodus has been largely confined to one side of the road, but here the mass of cars abandoned trying to exit the city of Cambridge has blocked both sides of the road.

This is it. Time's up. There's no way through and no way back.

It looks as if a scrapyard has been dropped into this part of the city from a great height. Matt slams his foot down on the brake, virtually standing on the pedal, desperately trying to bring the truck to a controlled halt before he hits the sprawling mass of metal. His speed is such that he doesn't make it, and the truck thuds nose-first into the endless sea of wreckage.

Finished.

Nowhere left to go.

He looks around and realizes that he's come to rest among the ruins of the university. How tragic, he thinks, that a place that was a pinnacle of learning and achievement has been reduced to this. It's symbolic of the deterioration of the world as a whole.

Matt wants to keep going. He wants to run, wants to get out and clamber over the mountain of twisted metal and get away, but he knows he won't make it this time. Yet even though what's coming is inevitable, he can't just sit still and wait for them to kill him. His body is spent, filled with poison, but he still can't stop. With the same determination that keeps the Haters killing, Matt wants to keep living. The red Subaru stops directly behind the truck, preventing any escape, and other vehicles block the road farther back.

He gets out and makes a halfhearted attempt to scale the closest of the countless wrecked cars. His legs are heavy, and he can't see any way through, but he drags himself up onto the roof of a Mini, then half jumps, half falls across the gap, onto his truck. With considerable effort, he hauls himself up onto the roof.

He walks to the end of the truck and looks down. There's just one Hater directly below him, yanking at the padlock that secures the roller door to get to what's inside. Dumb fucker smashes his fists in frustration when it refuses to budge. Matt sees other fighters approaching on foot now. Hundreds of them, it looks like.

He takes the key to the padlock from his pocket and dangles it above the Hater's head, waving it way out of reach and taunting the whole fucking lot of them. "Looking for this?" he shouts, laughing at their rage.

When the truck rocks slightly, Matt realizes he's not alone up here. He turns around and finds himself face-to-face with the Hater he recognized from before.

"You'll burn yourselves out in the end, you know that?" he wheezes, but Danny McCoyne's not listening. He steps forward and snatches the padlock key from Matt's hand, then pushes him over the side of the truck.

Matt drops onto a pile of metal and rubble. A metal rod has skewered his gut, and another sharp spike has lanced his right thigh. He tries to get up, but he can't move. He feels blood pooling under his back. Warm. Strangely comforting.

"Give me that fucking key, McCoyne!" Bryce yells, gesturing wildly. He catches it and opens the padlock with hands that tremble with excitement at the prospect of finally killing the very last of the Unchanged. The lock clicks, and he looks over his shoulder, grinning wildly at the expectant hordes gathered right behind him.

He throws the door open and then staggers back, confused.

"What the hell . . . ?"

The truck's empty.

Lying on the ground, paralyzed and racked with pain, Matt starts to laugh. The expression on the Hater's face is the most perfect thing he's seen since this damn war began. It's also the very last thing he sees. Another Hater permanently silences Matt with a boot to the side of the head.

A pissed off–looking fighter shoves Bryce angrily in the chest, smashing him into the truck. Bryce vents his frustration on McCoyne. He grabs his collar and pins him against the side of the empty vehicle. "You useless cunt," he spits in his face, shouting to make himself heard over the noise of the dissipating crowd and the engines of the rapidly disappearing convoy.

"How was I supposed to know? I don't have fucking x-ray vision, Bryce."

"They could be anywhere by now. Fucking miles away." He jabs a finger into McCoyne's face. "You're going to help me find them."

McCoyne pushes him away. "I'm not. I'm done. I quit."

"You think you have any choice? You can hold the Hate and you give me an advantage. And with a new boss in town, that matters. Remember this: I'm the only one who knows what you can do, and I've got you over a barrel. You play ball, and I'll make sure you're looked after. You fuck me over, I'll hand you over to Hinchcliffe myself and tell him you're a sympathizer. I'll tell him you helped them get away, that you tipped them off, and he'll kill you in a fucking heartbeat. Whatever happens, *I win*. Stay in line and do as I tell you, and there's still a chance you won't lose."

"Don't you get it? I don't have anything left to lose. It's all gone already."

"Melodramatic prick." He gestures over his shoulder as the last of the other vehicles reverses and leaves. "Want me to call that lot back and have them deal with you right now?"

"Do what you like. I just told you, I quit. I don't care anymore. Go fuck yourself."

Bryce is livid, but before he can react, McCoyne snatches a knife from his belt, lunges forward, and thumps it hard into the other man's gut. Bryce staggers back, looking down at the blood spreading across his chest. McCoyne snatches the knife back and stabs him again. And again to be sure. And again. Then one more time just because he feels like it.

Blood spills down onto the tarmac.

"I'm nothing special. Just one of the crowd," McCoyne says, standing over Bryce, who's dropped to his knees now, clutching his eviscerated belly. "No one needs to know what I can do."

And he waits until he's sure the other man's dead before getting behind the wheel of his Subaru and following the rest of the pack back to the fallen CDF outpost.

60

The Outpost

It's nightfall before the Haters have finished here. Under orders from Hinchcliffe, the outpost has been broken down and stripped of everything of value. Now the remains of Thacker's army, their numbers swollen by the survivors of Johannson's brutal regime, are ready to begin the journey back to their leader's stronghold in the town of Lowestoft on the east coast. There's a seemingly endless queue of vehicles snaking away from the silent, skeletal buildings, the only lights in an otherwise completely dark landscape. Diggers and JCBs drive alongside civilian vehicles as well as the remaining CDF military machines. So what if they're all out of ammo? Hinchcliffe doesn't care, and neither will Thacker.

The last vehicle in the line has a sun-bleached image of a long-dead woman's flawless face on its side. The last trip this truck made was to deliver something inconsequential to somewhere that didn't matter before the war: shipping tons of makeup and beauty supplies from the manufacturer's warehouse to a distribution center. Frozen and unblinking, the woman's face on the side of the vehicle gives nothing away, no indication of the cargo being carried today.

The drive to Lowestoft takes the best part of two hours tonight through icy, pouring rain. When they're close—somewhere between ten and fifteen miles away, the driver at the back estimates—he kills his lights, slows down, and drops away. He waits until the rest of the pack has disappeared around a gentle curve in the road.

The Hater behind the wheel waits a while longer until he's sure the others are long gone. He's glad to have finally put some distance between him and the rest of the pack. He helped strip the outpost and played his part in collecting up and burning the Unchanged bodies, but it was all just for show. Peter Sutton is a Hater. He knows he's like the others, but he also knows he's nothing like them, too.

He guarded the keys to this particular truck with his life and made sure he was the one who ended up behind the wheel. Before he secured the roller door, he told Joseph about a place he knows not far from Lowestoft. He remembered a friend telling him about it before the war began: a decommissioned nuclear bunker near a farm. The world aboveground remains filled with Hate. For now, staying buried is their only option.

To Hinchcliffe and his cronies, Peter's a rank-and-file killer; just another member of the pack, just another driver in the line. To the remaining Unchanged he's carrying in the back of this truck, though, he's everything.

Their last and only hope.

About the Author

David Moody

From the UK, DAVID MOODY first self-published *Hater* on the internet in 2006, and without an agent, succeeded in selling the film rights for the novel to Mark Johnson (producer, The Chronicles of Narnia film series) and Guillermo del Toro (director, *Hellboy, Pan's Labyrinth*). With the publication of a new series of Hater stories, Moody is poised to further his reputation as a writer of suspense-laced SF/horror, and "farther out" genre books of all description.